Praise for Lisa Walker

'A dark and twisty s
ambition that will ke

'This quirky and un
Spain's
Allie Reynolds

'A gripping and twisty whodunit where suspicion, guilt, and murder collide on Spain's most sacred road'
Donna M Cameron

'Pacy, twisty and layered revenge tale'
Joanna Barnard

'Authentic and enriched by hard-won psychological insights'
The Sydney Morning Herald

'Engaging, action-packed, fast-paced'
Books and Publishing

'Strong, authentic female characters. A ripper read'
The Big Issue

'Multifaceted, fresh and entertaining'
The Adelaide Advertiser

'Clever sleuthing, lively characters, vibrant setting and snappy pace'
Sisters in Crime

'Spiced with quirky humour'
The Herald Sun

LISA WALKER is the author of seven adult and young adult novels, published in Australia by HarperCollins, Penguin Random House, and Wakefield Press. Two were also published by Harper360 in the US and UK, and one has been optioned for film. Her recent young adult cosy crime novel was shortlisted for the Australian Davitt Awards in two categories.

She has also been published in *The Guardian*, the *Big Issue* and the *Sydney Morning Herald*, and has had a radio play produced on ABC Radio National. A dual citizen of Australia and the UK, she lives in Northern New South Wales, Australia and has a PhD in creative writing.

THE PACT

LISA WALKER

ONE PLACE. MANY STORIES

HQ
An imprint of HarperCollins*Publishers* Ltd
1 London Bridge Street
London SE1 9GF

www.harpercollins.co.uk

HarperCollins*Publishers*
Macken House, 39/40 Mayor Street Upper
Dublin 1, D01 C9W8, Ireland

This edition 2026

1
First published in Great Britain by HQ,
an imprint of HarperCollins*Publishers* Ltd 2026

PB ISBN: 9780008772475
TPB ISBN: 9780008772505

Set in Sabon LT Std at HarperCollins*Publishers* India

Printed and bound in the UK using 100% Renewable
Electricity at CPI Group (UK) Ltd

This book contains FSC™ certified paper and other controlled
sources to ensure responsible forest management.

For more information visit: www.harpercollins.co.uk/green

For my fellow peregrinos, John, Simon and Tim.

I'm sure you will agree I have exercised great restraint. But patience has its limits, and we've reached them, you and I. Now, the moment of reckoning has arrived. I can feel it humming in me – a blend of nerves and something sweeter. Anticipation.

With one tap on my keyboard, I will draw you to me. You will be exactly where I want you for thirty days. Thirty days to relish your escalating trepidation and dread. How delicious.

Let the journey commence!

Chapter 1

Revenge Plot

I spot my first pilgrim as I step from the train in Bayonne.

'Are you doing the Camino?' The small, rounded woman approaches, the price tag still dangling off her backpack, a camera bouncing against her chest. She beams a one-hundred-watt smile. Her accent is distinctly American. Unlike the other pilgrims on the platform, she wears a full face of makeup, including a slash of crimson lipstick.

'Yes, that's right.' The cacophony of background chatter batters my ears. I can't believe I've joined a group activity; it's not my thing at all. Will I become known on the trail as the lovely English girl? Or, more likely, as the not-so-lovely one.

'That's the platform for the train to Saint Jean Pied de Port, where the walk begins.' The woman points, and I grudgingly fall into step beside her.

The journey here was a marathon – a train from London to Paris, then another train south. I'm tired and bedraggled with layers of grime clinging to me, but here I am. As Lula used to say, a writer with ambitions will sacrifice anything for art.

A ticket stub dances over the platform in the breeze as announcements blare in crackling French. Pilgrims stand out amidst the crowd. Backpacks. Walking boots. Muscular calves. Like me, most have walking poles strapped to their packs. The scent of sweat and determination hangs in the air.

A tall man with scraggly blond hair walks past and my breath catches. *No, it's not him.* Of course it's not. This pilgrimage was a last-minute decision and I'm one day late. He would have been here yesterday. If at all. I gnaw my lip. What if I've come all this way for nothing?

'Looking for someone?' asks the woman.

'Yes. An old . . . friend.' I hadn't realised there'd be so many pilgrims; he could be hard to track down.

'Oh, you have a walking companion?'

My pulse twitches. 'Yes.' But he doesn't know it yet.

'That's lovely. I'm on my own, but I'm sure I'll make lots of friends on the way. There are no strangers here, just friends we haven't met yet, right?' She beams.

I murmur noncommittally. I'm not into instant friendship.

'I'm Ree.'

I can hardly refuse to reply. 'I'm Tess.'

'I have to do a tinkle, so bye for now,' says Ree.

A tinkle?

Wiggling her scarlet-painted nails, the woman heads for the restroom, and I board the train. Hopefully I won't run into her again. Dropping into a seat, I pull out my phone, put on my glasses and refresh my messages, but there's nothing new. I let out a breath, trying to ease the jitters. The message will come, it has to.

My eyes fall on the invitation, which is still there in my emails. I read it again.

To: All Ravensthorpe Alumni
Subject: Remembering Lula

Ravensthorpians!
Three years have passed since our dear Lula's departure. In her memory, I extend to you an invitation for a commemorative pilgrimage. The Camino de Santiago de Compostela held great significance to Lula. Thus, it appears only fitting to honour her in such a manner.
May I also convey to you the creative possibilities of such a journey. As Lula would say, we must feed our writerly souls at every opportunity. How better to unleash inspiration than to walk with others who understand the commitment and dedication required in this path we have chosen?
In keeping with the pilgrim way, no RSVPs shall be taken. Instead, let those who wish to pay tribute to Lula's spirit convene at Saint Jean railway station at the hour of ten in the morn on the sixth of April.
Salutations, Iris.

Iris, one of the Ravensthorpe tutors, has a flamboyant signature style. *To all Ravensthorpe alumni.* Am I even an alumna? I was there for less than a year.

As the train lurches forward, my eyes drop to the backpack at my feet, catching on the rectangular shape of my e-reader. Lula's Camino memoir calls to me in a ghostly whisper. *I'll be with you every step of the way, pilgrim.* A sour taste fills my mouth.

Dusk falls as I arrive in Saint Jean and my reflection glows in the window – glasses glinting and hair writhing in Medusa-like coils. I pat it down as I step off the train, pulling on my puffer jacket to ward off the chill. It's cold for April. My nose twitches at the unfamiliar scent of mountain air. It's been a long time since I've left London.

A nearby pilgrim consults his guidebook. 'Up this way,' he directs his companion.

As they walk away, I eye the scallop shells dangling from their backpacks.

Lula's voice echoes in my head. *In the old days, pilgrims collected a scallop shell from the sea to show they'd completed the pilgrimage.*

My skin prickles. It's as if she's beside me on the platform, her breath warm on my ear.

I haven't booked accommodation, and I've got no idea what to expect but, hoisting my backpack, I follow the gang through narrow, cobbled streets and up a hill. Pink-stoned shops nestle beside whitewashed, terraced houses and window boxes burst with vibrant spring flowers. I'm not here for European charm though. It's time to restart my stalled life. To fulfil my pledge to Mum.

Church bells echo through the streets as, panting, I come to a halt outside a door with a sandwich board – *one bed left.* Fate has selected my lodgings.

*

6

We gather around a circular wooden table for a communal dinner, the aroma of garlic and vegetables filling the room.

'We will throw a ball around the table to introduce ourselves,' says our host, a jovial, balding Basque man with a resonant voice.

I'm not a fan of ball sports. I'd refuse, but it's too early to launch the not-so-lovely English girl.

'Tell us all why you're on this journey.' He raises a tennis ball in the air.

The American woman I met at the train station – Ree? – catches the ball. 'My Camino is about seizing the day.' Her voice quivers as she tucks her shining black bob behind her ears. 'My best friend died a few years ago, and I realised I was only existing, not living.' She lobs the ball towards a middle-aged Dutch man.

'My Camino is about learning to live my own life, not the one others choose for me.'

And so it goes on. Most give the impression they've planned this adventure for years. It's the climax of their lives. Almost all begin with the phrase, *My Camino*.

My Camino is about recovering from grief. My Camino is about self-discovery. My Camino is about freeing myself from damaging obsessions.

There's a special language that comes with this walk. They've all been reading the same books, watching the same movies. They're embarking on a mythical quest.

The ball flies my way. I catch it. It was either that or get knocked out. I don't want to ruin the vibe, so I invent a cover story on the spot. 'My Camino is about turning things around. I'm doing it because I drink too much, I'm in a rut, and I've got no idea what to do with my life.' There may be a smidgen of truth buried in that fluff.

Murmurs of encouragement encircle me, a symphony of empathy. These people are so nice, I almost feel bad for lying.

*

As the group disperses, I sidle over to interrogate our host, the warden, beside the crackling fire. The scent of burning wood hangs heavy in the air.

'It was moving, what you said about your Camino.' His voice is warm.

'Oh. Thanks.' The story has claimed me now. For the rest of the Camino, I'll be the plucky little trooper who's trying to turn her life around. It paints a gallant picture.

The fire casts a glow on the warden's face. 'People do this for all sorts of reasons.'

I take a breath. 'You haven't run into an English guy called Ethan, have you? Blondish hair. My age. Looks a bit like Kurt Cobain? Could have started yesterday?' *Bit of a tosser*, I don't say.

He shakes his head. 'There are so many pilgrims.'

'Mm. So, where do most people get to on their first day?'

'Most go all the way to Roncesvalles, but some climb up to Orisson, on the hilltop first. It is beautiful there.' His eyes sparkle. 'A good way to start your pilgrimage.'

Hilltop. Sounds like an Ethan thing to do. 'So, after Orisson, they go on to Roncesvalles?'

'Yes.'

If I can get to Roncesvalles tomorrow, perhaps I'll catch him, and the other Ravensthorpians, there. 'Is there a bus?'

His brow furrows. 'To Roncesvalles? No one has ever asked me that before. Everyone walks. There is a bus that shuttles luggage. Maybe they take passengers?'

I have no intention of walking. The first day is the hardest. All the blogs say so. It makes sense to avoid it. 'Well, big day tomorrow, better hit the hay.'

In the bunkroom, a rancid odour of garlic and sweaty socks assaults me. I haven't slept in a dormitory since a year nine school camp in Portsmouth. Can I hack it? Suppose I'll have to.

I'm sharing a room with five people. On one side is the American woman, a Japanese girl, who's making paper cranes in her bed, and a South African man. At the table he'd given each of us a slip of paper printed with a prayer.

I'd handed mine back. 'I'm not religious.' He'd looked offended, so I'd relented. 'Okay, what the hell, give me a couple.'

On the other side is an Italian man with curly, dark hair and a girl from Poland.

Flopping onto my bunk, I pull out my phone and Google the bus to Roncesvalles. There's one per day, leaving at nine-thirty a.m.

I check my messages – *still nothing* – then survey the room. Everyone's asleep now. The South African man is snoring, the raspy rhythm invading the silence. I close my eyes. His snores reach a wheezing crescendo. I'm never going to sleep. But it's okay, I don't have a tough day tomorrow. I'm catching the bus.

My eyes fly open, heart pounding. Tomorrow, if my deductions are correct, I'll come face to face with Ethan. After three years, our paths are converging again.

*

Clang! I jolt awake. The cleaner stands over me with a broom, her metal bucket beside her.

Nine-thirty says my phone. Panic rises in my chest. *Damn.* I've missed the bus.

The cleaner gestures at the empty beds around me. 'You are supposed to leave by eight.'

'Pardon.' As she sweeps around me in a pointed way, I scan the trip notes for today on my phone. *Twenty-seven kilometres. 1,300 metre height gain.* Way too much. But what choice do I have? Taking a breath of stale, sweaty air, I reach for my backpack.

Soon, I'm enjoying café au lait and croissants in an empty café. All the other pilgrims must be half-way to Roncesvalles. Finishing my coffee, I pull out my e-reader. Okay, Lula, how do I start this?

I'm outside the pilgrim office when it opens, she says, smugly. *Inside, I pick up a booklet to prove I'm a pilgrim. Now I can stay in the hostels. By eight a.m., I'm on the trail.*

I check the time. Ten-thirty.

Do better, Tess.

You're dead, Lula. You can't tell me what to do

10

anymore. Jaw clenched, I pay the bill, which reminds me of my dire financial situation. I push it from my mind. *La, la, la, the universe will provide*. This hippie thinking is out of character. The Camino must be working its magic already.

The man at the pilgrim office speaks a little English. He gives me a cardboard booklet. 'Get it stamped when you stay in an *albergue*. Then you can get your certificate at the end. The Compostela.'

The Compostela is a get-out-of-purgatory-free pass, murmurs Lula's supercilious ghost. *It lets you skip the queue into heaven.*

I shake my head to dislodge her from my mind.

The man's forehead crinkles. 'Are you all right?'

'Oh. Yes, all good.' *Keep it together, Tess.*

The man hands me a scallop shell. 'To tie on your pack.'

A hefty visitor's book lies on the desk. Signing it, I flick back through, scanning the names. My skin tingles as I see it. His scrawl is instantly recognisable. *Ethan Hill.* I let out a breath. *He's here.* I check the date. He's one day ahead. If he stopped in Orisson, we will intersect today.

So, who else from Ravensthorpe has turned up for this jaunt? My eyes snag on another name. *Theo.* I swallow. This complicates things. I've psyched myself up to deal with Ethan, but . . . *Okay.* I suck in a breath. *Ethan and Theo. Deal with it.*

I flick my eyes up and down the page, but it doesn't look like any other Ravensthorpians signed the book. Heaviness fills me. *Why?* Was I hoping to see Jaz's name?

I'm about to close the book when the hairs lift on my

arms. *Lula Thornton.* The name is written in neat capitals. Is this someone's idea of a joke?

Wouldn't miss this for the world, says Lula's voice in my head.

With clammy hands, I slam the book shut.

'There is a scale if you want to weigh your pack.' The man points. *Eight kilos is suggested maximum,* says a sign.

I lift my pack onto the hook.

The man whistles as the dial on the scale whizzes past eight, all the way to thirteen, the metal hook creaking under the weight.

I attempt to sling my bag over my shoulder in a nonchalant way. *Thirteen kilos?* That's not so much. My stagger spoils the effect. 'Better hit it.'

'Can I ask why you are doing the Camino? I like to make a note.'

Before I can put a lid on it, my not-so-lovely English girl breaks free. I flash him a smile. 'Revenge.'

Chapter 2

Fish out of Water

Three and a half years ago

'Just be yourself. They'll love you.'

Mum's words echoed in my head as I battled the morning rush hour out of Deptford, the scent of exhaust fumes in my nostrils. I gnawed at my fingernails as I drove. Despite Mum's pep talk this morning, I was jittery as hell.

As usual, cars, buses, and trucks fought for supremacy on a road built for horses and carts. Ravensthorpe was in the countryside south of London, so I had a long drive ahead and Mum's little Hyundai wasn't built for speed.

*

'Ravensthorpe is the best university-level creative writing programme in the UK,' Mum had said. 'Their alumni feature in the bestseller lists and awards every year. So, whatever they do there, it works.'

The school had an eccentric reputation. It only taught creative writing, taking in fifty students each year for a three-year live-in degree. Its alarming fifty per cent failure rate meant less than a hundred students were in residence at any time. It wasn't cheap, but Mum had saved up for precisely this purpose.

'When you finish school, you're going to Ravensthorpe,' she'd said, for as long as I remembered. Her confidence never faltered. Writing was Mum's secret passion. She'd had a short story published once and had started a novel but hadn't got far. As a teenager, she'd dreamed of going to Ravensthorpe, but my arrival when she was seventeen put paid to that.

'You were a beautiful mistake,' she said, but I still felt guilty. Life as a single mother didn't allow time for creative expression. And so, she transferred her dreams to me.

My father was never on the scene. 'We're better off without him,' Mum said. While Mum was resigned to being a hairdresser, she had high hopes for me. 'Read widely, that's the key. I named you after *Tess of the D'Urbervilles*, so you have fiction running through your veins.' She adored her tragic heroines.

As soon as I learnt to read, Mum fed me an eclectic mixture of novels. Agatha Christie stalked Jane Austen. Salman Rushdie shadowed James Patterson. I'd never learnt to discriminate between highbrow and lowbrow. It was all equally transporting, the pages welcoming me into their worlds.

Non-fiction didn't have a place in our house. 'Fiction is more truthful than fact,' Mum often said.

*

After three hours, I drove through a village with thatch-roof cottages. Turning up a narrow, winding lane, I came to a colourful mosaic on a wall. My pulse skipped a beat as I read the letters, picked out in shards of glass. *Ravensthorpe, established 1965.* Ravensthorpe's creation was a mythical story. Founded by radical author and activist Terence Styles, it aimed to embody the avant-garde sixties. From what I'd read, the flower power legacy lingered on.

I drove through the open gate, and there it was. A rambling three-storey brick building covered in ivy and surrounded by meadows of flowers. Coloured flags fluttered outside the front door and a duck-filled pond glinted in the sun. At the meadow's end, a grey stone tower, the remains of an old church, rose above a dense copse of trees.

Mum should have been here, but she had to work. 'Give me a call when you get there,' she'd said.

Pulling up in the driveway, I pressed her number.

She answered. 'What's it like?'

'It's beautiful,' I whispered. 'Like Manderley.' I was in an intense Daphne du Maurier phase. But as I gazed at the building, my throat tightened. 'I don't belong here though, Mum. I bet the other students didn't go to a state school.'

'Don't be ridiculous, sweetheart. They'll be lucky to have you. You're a special girl, Tess. This is what we've been working towards. Remember, brilliance . . .'

'. . . will rise to the surface.' I completed her favourite saying, a bittersweet taste on my tongue. What if there was no brilliance within me to rise? I had to go through with this though, I couldn't let her down. And I wanted it too. I wanted it so much it made my chest ache. Hanging up, I uncoiled my legs from the car, wiping my sweaty hands on my jeans. They would see straight through me. I wasn't the cutting-edge young creative I'd pretended to be.

The application had required a writing sample, and an essay on why I wanted to attend. I'd sent an excerpt from a novel I'd worked on for years. For the essay, I'd waxed lyrical about how Ravensthorpe would stimulate my creativity. Unexpectedly – to me, though not to Mum – it worked. A letter appeared, inviting me down for an interview. *Places in the programme aren't awarded on academic results, it is all about 'fit'*, it said. 'Fit' wasn't defined, but online forums hinted at a strange and demanding interview process.

Clenching my hands, I walked along a mossy stone pathway towards the building. *How do I act as if I belong?* A brass bell hung beside a wooden door, which was carved with a Celtic tree of life. My eyes traced its intricate branches. Mum had a necklace with a tree of life on it. *It's a symbol of rebirth*, she'd told me. The buzzing of bees reached me as I touched the warm wood with my finger. *Can I be reborn here?*

Putting my hand to the bell pull, I jangled it, only then noticing the electric buzzer beneath. Should I push that too? Would it be too much? As I hesitated, wracked with indecision, the door creaked, and opened.

A suntanned woman with a mop of messy shoulder-length brown hair, and sharp hazel eyes appeared. She wore a moth-eaten jumper, tattered wool trousers, and dark green wellies. Was she the gardener? She had the muscular, lean body of someone who did physical work.

She smiled, displaying white teeth. 'You must be Tess. I'm Lula.'

Of course. Lula Thornton. Head of creative writing and Ravensthorpe star. Author of many acclaimed novels and a bestselling memoir, *Undone.* I'd seen her photo on the website, but she hadn't been so dishevelled there.

I swallowed. 'Hello.' She was younger than I'd expected, late thirties, I guessed. 'I've just finished reading *Undone.*'

Lula raised her eyebrows.

'It was . . .' Why hadn't I prepared for this? 'Amazing.'

She smiled, but I'd got off to a bad start. *Amazing.* I sounded like someone with a limited vocabulary.

The book was about Lula's breakdown while walking the Camino pilgrimage in Spain. What fantastic material. My problem was I had nothing to write about. I intended to rectify that.

In the corridor behind Lula hung a poster-sized photo of a group of young people. My ghostly reflection hovered over them in the glass. An artwork. *Me and Them*, you could call it. Or, *Odd One Out.* Me: a beanpole with glinting glasses in supermarket-bought jeans and button-up shirt. Them: tight vintage dresses, berets, and multiple tattoos.

I'll change, I wanted to tell Lula. Give me a chance and I'll become like them.

'Let's have a look around the grounds.' Lula strode off down the path, gravel crunching under her wellies. An appley scent drifted back to me from her hair.

I am a cutting-edge young creative, I said to myself as I negotiated the uneven paving stones. *I am someone to watch.*

Lula explained Ravensthorpe's philosophy as we walked. 'We give students the freedom to determine their own learning pathway . . . We minimise technology as it inhibits creativity.' She pulled a red lollipop from her pocket and inserted it in her mouth. 'Trying to give up smoking.'

The sun was warm, and I started to relax. Superstitiously, I placed my feet in the outline left by her boots in the dirt. The air smelt of fresh-cut grass, lavender, and possibility. My heart tightened with yearning. Imagine, spending three years here.

'What would you say is the cultural value of your writing, Tess?' Lula asked abruptly as we paused at the pond where the water rippled in the faintest breeze.

I gulped. This was it. The strange and demanding test. My mind whirred. I had no idea how to answer. I wasn't even sure I understood the question. 'I don't think . . . that's up to me to determine. All I can do is write the best stories I can and let them speak for themselves.' I barely resisted the urge to add *ma'am*.

'Good answer.'

Despite her low-key appearance, she was intimidating.

'And what does vulnerability mean to you in your writing?' she asked as we inspected the vegetable garden.

'Being honest about my feelings and experiences, even if it makes me uncomfortable,' I blurted. 'That's what lets readers connect.'

Pulling out a wizened carrot, she offered it to me.

Was this part of the test? I brushed off the dirt and crunched it in my teeth just in case. 'It's very sweet.'

She opened the door to the accommodation block, a renovated red-brick barn. Inside, it was airy, with exposed beams and wide windows.

'And what are you willing to sacrifice for writing success?' She pulled open a bedroom door. Her eyes gleamed gold in the sunlight as they met mine, the lollipop stick dangling from her now-crimson mouth.

Hairs rose on my arms as if an icy wind had filled the room. I felt it. This was the most important question. The one that counted. Gazing into the light-stippled space of an empty bedroom, I imagined myself there. I'd be a different kind of Tess. One who belonged. *Sacrifice.* I went with my instincts. 'Everything.'

Her eyes didn't leave mine; she was waiting.

'My time. My energy. My ego.'

She turned away. It wasn't enough.

'My life.'

Lula turned back, her eyes wrinkling at the corners. 'I think you're going to be a good fit here, Tess.' She threw out her arms. 'Welcome to this special place.'

A thousand-watt beam split my face. At last, my real life would begin.

*

At first, Ravensthorpe seemed a utopia. A place where everyone did as they pleased, and the free-wheeling sixties' spirit reigned. Spending the day sunbathing nude – yes, nude! – beside the pond, was as acceptable as attending tutorials. To be honest, the nudity wasn't for me. I rarely ventured into the sun-dappled water, but when I did, I wore my faded one-piece swimsuit.

Usually, I huddled in the shade with a book, watching the bacchanalia of young bodies roast in the sun. They flopped on top of each other like puppies and splashed in the pond, their laughter filling the air. I longed to join them, to belong, but an invisible wall stopped me in the same way it had at school.

My schoolmates had found my preoccupation with books and writing peculiar. Here though, surely, I would find kindred spirits?

There was one girl who stood out from the pond crew. She was there to swim, not lounge around. Every afternoon after class, she dived into the pond, entering with barely a ripple. She'd stroke vigorously up and down through the golden-brown water for half an hour or more. Eventually she'd emerge with her short, blonde hair slicked flat against her head. Goggle marks circled her eyes.

My own swimming hadn't progressed since primary school lessons. The classes, which took place in the steaming chlorine of an indoor pool, hadn't given me a taste for more. I found her impressive.

There was a bunch of students who never seemed to go to classes. They were always at the pond or roaming around the grounds throwing acorns at each other. Why were they here, paying all this money, if not to work? I suspected they came from vastly different backgrounds to me.

The Ravensthorpe students had a particular style. They didn't all look the same, far from it. Each had created a unique identity. Nerdy hipster. Punk. Retro aristocrat. It was a costume. A performance. My T-shirts and denims wouldn't do, I needed a new persona to brand me as an exciting young talent.

In my first fiction writing workshop, Iris, a renowned poet with purple hair and tattoos winding down her arms, explained the format. 'You will take it in turns to read your work. Those whose work is up for discussion must remain silent while it is critiqued. Your words stand without explanation, as they do for a reader.'

My gut clenched, and I pushed my glasses up my nose as the scent of musty books tickled my nostrils. Would I be exposed as an imposter?

The first few tutorials did nothing to dispel my apprehension. The other students spoke with BBC vowels, but their work was gritty. It was experimental, with titles like *Absence* and *Post-post-modern*. They flung words together in curious combinations. Daisies cowered. Shoppers gambolled. They wrote whole pages with only one sentence. And they all knew the right words to critique it.

At the second workshop, Tabitha, a golden-skinned girl with abundant dark hair, read her piece. *Anti-anti-consumerism* was about a girl on a shopping spree. Her protagonist hacked off her limbs, one by one, because they looked ugly in the changing-room mirror.

My jaw dropped. Why couldn't I write like that?

The critique began. 'Transgressive.' 'Intersectional.' 'Deconstructive.' Praise flowed like the River Thames.

I'd open my mouth to interject, then close it as discussion moved on to esoteric realms where I could not follow. I didn't have the background to enter at any level. I'd been the star of my A-level English class, but none of us talked like this.

The night before I was 'up' in tutorial, I barely slept. My piece wasn't like the others. It was realistic. It had relationships. Action. No limbs were maimed. No flowers cowered. It was all wrong, but it was all I had. Also, this was a fiction workshop, and my story was only masquerading as such.

'Okay, Tess, let's hear from you,' Iris said.

My voice emerged in a croak. 'This is a story about the relationship between a daughter and her eccentric mother. It's called *The Birthday Party*.' I'd based the story on my eighth birthday party. Mum was a health nut and despite my pleadings, she'd refused to adjust her standards for my party. I coughed and read from my laptop.

'The year Lily turned eight, she begged for a birthday party. Finally, her mum agreed, and Lily invited five of her classmates. There wouldn't have been space for more than that in their cramped flat.

'Dressed in her favourite yellow kaftan, Lily's mum circulated with an air of bohemian charm, but her cheese ball and carrot slices were met with polite refusals. Chatter filled the air as the girls awaited the main course. But the guests barely touched her mum's spicy curry, and snickers greeted Lily's favourite dessert – baked bananas.

'At the door, her mum handed out treat bags – brown paper bags they'd decorated together. The girls' faces lit up. At last, Lily thought, we've done it right. But as her guests tore the bags open, their faces fell. Inside lurked, not the anticipated rainbow lollies, but dull-brown sultanas and

unsalted nuts. The bitter taste of disappointment lingered as Lily's door closed behind them.

'The next day, at school, Lily kicked a classmate who called her mother a weirdo. Unrepentant, she was suspended for a week . . .'

This too, was drawn from life. Mum was into kickboxing, and it had rubbed off on me. My story concluded with Lily's dawning realisation that her goddess-like mother might not be infallible. It was a coming-of-age story of sorts.

After I stuttered my way to the end, there was silence, and a few side-eye glances. Tabitha smirked.

'Thoughts?' prompted Iris.

'It's a little cliché,' said Tabitha. 'That mother–daughter trope has been done to death.'

Trope. That word popped up a lot at Ravensthorpe. I knew what it meant but I'd never used it. It was a rare day when someone didn't point out how a reluctant hero or a villain dressed in black was an overused trope. I'd begun to suspect my writing was one hackneyed trope after another.

'Is this, uh, commercial fiction?' This came from Theo, who I often saw backflipping into the pond. He was athletic; muscular and olive-skinned, like someone more at home playing football than writing. A tattoo of a wolf snarled from his shoulder.

It was a rhetorical question, as I wasn't allowed to answer, but my cheeks burned so hot my glasses fogged up. Commercial fiction was synonymous with bad writing around here. I sank lower and lower in my seat as the critique continued.

'The vocabulary is very plain, isn't it?'

'The prose is a bit workmanlike.'

'Maybe try second-person point of view to give it more edge?'

That night in my room, I opened a warm bottle of wine, which I'd bought at the village store. I needed to ease the tightness in my chest. To dampen the blaze that spread though my body when I thought of the workshop.

My writing was terrible, and I didn't fit in. I had no brilliance to rise to the surface.

Chapter 3

First Contact

Now

Yellow arrows point the way out of town. As my boots tap on the cobbles, the visitor book floats in my mind. *Theo. Ethan.* I swallow. *Lula.* Who the hell wrote that? And why?

The terrain is not too tough at first and my mind is free to roam. I remember what the pilgrims said last night. *I'm taking control of my life. I am the captain of my destiny.* Their words don't seem as trite now. In a twisted way, I'm here for transformation too. I check my messages, but still no luck. *It will come.*

The hill gets steeper. I go up, up, up, down, up, up, up, down, and so on. My training regime of a stroll to the shops hasn't prepared me for this. After an hour, my legs are burning. After a couple more, I'm in serious pain. If Ethan wasn't somewhere ahead, I'd give up. But giving up is not an option. I'm doing this for Mum.

What have I got myself into? Thirty days of walking, ten hours a day. *Three hundred gruelling hours of walking.* I may not survive it.

I pause in a beech forest to eat the baguette I bought at the café. It could be beautiful here, but a damp mist encircles me and it's all very *Wuthering Heights*. My mind drifts to Jaz and her favourite Heathcliff quote.

Be with me always – take any form – drive me mad! Only do not leave me in this abyss, where I cannot find you.

The baguette lodges in my throat and I cough. I haven't seen Jaz since Lula's funeral, three years ago, and we didn't talk then. I've Googled her obsessively but found nothing. Why? She was an incredible writer. But, out of our group, Ethan is the only one who's been published.

Ethan's debut novel lurks on my e-reader too. *Darker Matters* was a smash hit, spending almost a year on the *New York Times* bestseller list. *A tour de force. Better than Sebastian Hill in his heyday,* the reviews said. Ethan's father, Sebastian Hill, is literary royalty. He's won the Booker once and been shortlisted twice. I haven't judged Ethan's book for myself. It's been eighteen months since it came out, and I still can't face it. I will, I'm building up to it. There will be plenty of time to read on the trail. And also, I'm hoping it will be the spark I need to find my own lost writing voice again.

The path becomes muckier and more treacherous as I climb higher. I tumble several times and am hoisted up by sturdier pilgrims. They offer a robust *Buen Camino* before vanishing up the hill. A pox on them and their sinewy calves. How can they say *Buen Camino* with such

26

conviction on the first day? Have they attended pilgrim training school?

'Buen Camino,' I attempt as the next pilgrim passes me.

He strides on without acknowledging me, his legs going like pistons.

Did I say it wrong?

The trail shows no mercy. I'm surprised not to find pilgrim corpses lining the way. They must be forged of stronger stuff than me. Several lifetimes later I summit the hilltop, coated in mud and teetering on the point of collapse. Only the need to find Ethan has propelled my quivering legs onwards and upwards.

Slumping onto a rock monument surrounded by patchy snow, I tug on my woolly hat. My damp clothes cling to me as I realise that, somehow, I've brought everything except a raincoat. Here I am then. *Roncesvalles Pass*. The border of Spain and France. I've never walked over a border before, but I'm too drained for excitement.

Lula's silky voice whispers in my ear. *On the Roncesvalles Pass, a vulture soars above, and Spain bathes in a golden light below.*

I strain to imagine it, but dense, wet fog encloses me.

Here died the tragic Roland, hero of the epic poem 'Song of Roland'. Ambushed on Roncesvalles Pass, he refused to call for help until it was too late.

'What a dreary spot for a fight.' My voice replays in my head. I sound like Eeyore.

I force myself to stand and, as I do, my eyes fall on a scribble of white chalk. On the face of the monument, written in capital letters, are the words: *What do you fear?*

27

My breath hitches as I remember Lula, her hand scrawling those very words on a whiteboard.

A sound emerges from the mist – the scrape of a boot on rock. Heart thudding, I peer around me. 'Lula?' My voice emerges in a whisper.

It's quiet – too quiet. The only sound is the wind rustling through the trees like a warning. My eyes snap back to the chalked words. The writing is fresh, untouched by the damp. I need to go. Now.

As I stumble down the hill, exhaustion ambushes me. I march onward in a stupor, trying to outrun the looming darkness. And the disquieting sense I'm being stalked by a ghost.

*

Night descends, and I trudge through half-melted snow as a light emerges in the distance. A stone wall appears, with a door. I hobble through into the foyer of an ancient building. Warmth and the scent of old wood enclose me. *Salvation.*

The woman behind the counter points at my boots, so I take them off. She hands me a piece of paper which requires me to answer questions. I can't be bothered finding my glasses, so I tick boxes randomly. I'm desperate to lie down.

She takes my form. 'You have a horse?'

'Oh, no. I'm walking.'

She changes the form. 'You are doing this for religious reasons?'

I don't have the energy to consider this question, so I nod. Whatever.

'The pilgrim service is at six p.m.'

'Okay.' I hope they don't round up all the religious types as I have no intention of going. I pay for a bed, plus dinner and breakfast, and she stamps my credentials.

Staggering upstairs, I collapse onto my bunk. For an ancient monastery, the building's well fitted out. The bunks are separated into pods of four. It's a nice surprise; I was expecting something more spartan. Sleeping bags on the other beds indicate I have pod-mates. There's no sign of Ethan, or any other Ravensthorpians. I bite my lip. What if this is a wild goose chase and I never find them?

It's some time until dinner, so after a catnap I drag myself off the bunk. On creaky legs, I head for the shower, hoping it might revive me. Undressing, I stand in the cubicle, anticipating a refreshing torrent as I push the button. The water's hot, but after about ten seconds it stops. *No way.* Showers are my happy place. I know water's precious and all that, but in the state I'm in I need it.

After several pushes I discover if I lean my back on the button, the shower keeps flowing. As the water cascades over me, I gaze at the tattoo on my hip. *She burned too bright for this world.* I got this quote to remind me of Mum, though she wouldn't have approved of the tattoo. The worst part about leaving Ravensthorpe had been torching Mum's dreams. I'd spent her savings and got nothing for it.

Embarrassingly, on the drunken night I acquired the tattoo, I mistook it for a quote from *Wuthering Heights.* Now, it stands as a memorial to poor scholarship. You can't believe everything you read on the internet. *Who knew?*

I lapse into a trance as the water wraps me in its embrace. 'Sweet Caroline' erupts unprompted from my mouth. Like Mum, I always channel Neil Diamond in the shower. As I reach the climax, a banging noise pierces my reverie. Someone's knocking on the door. How rude. 'Hang on, hang on,' I yell. 'Won't be too much longer.'

'You've been in there long enough.'

I freeze. The voice is English and instantly recognisable. *Ethan.* Unbelievable. Of all the ways to run into him. I remove my back from the button and the water stops. Panic flutters beneath my ribs. I'd hoped to meet Ethan under more auspicious circumstances. Will he go away if I wait, and I can engineer a more favourable meet-cute later?

There's another sharp knock at the door. 'Are you coming out?'

I pick up my towel. I can't cower in the shower cubicle forever. *Or can I?*

Ethan knocks again.

No, I can't. Okay, here goes, may as well get it over with. Rubbing myself down, I pull on my leggings and T-shirt, arrange my face into a startled expression, take a deep breath, and. . . *Ta-da.*

Ethan glares at me as I emerge from the shower. He blinks.

I gulp. Up close, the familiarity of his face is shocking. His jaw is stubbled, and his dirty-blond hair is pushed behind his ears. A gold earring glints in one ear. His hair's a little shorter, but otherwise he's just the same.

A girl saunters past us into the vacant shower, hips

swaying, musky perfume wafting behind her. She's wearing skimpy black underpants, a matching bra, and a silver cross on a chain around her neck. I'm clearly overdressed.

Ethan's ice-blue eyes don't even register her presence, they're locked on mine. Should I be flattered? But then he says the first words he's spoken to me since I left Ravensthorpe three years ago. 'What the hell are *you* doing here?'

My pulse stutters as his words reverberate in my ears. 'I'm . . . walking the Camino.'

'Iris sent you the invitation?' He sounds incredulous.

'Yes. Guess I'm an alumna.' I feign a lightness I don't feel. 'Of all the gin joints, in all the towns, in all the world, hey?'

Ethan's jaw tightens.

The tsunami of false confidence that has carried me all the way from London to Spain retreats, leaving me beached and breathless.

'I don't know why you're here.' His voice is a savage hiss. 'But I don't suppose we'll see much of each other anyway. I'm aiming for at least thirty kilometres a day.'

I swallow. 'Me too.' If that's what he's doing.

He snorts, as well he might. I've never walked thirty kilometres in my life. A man emerges from a shower, a towel draped around his neck, and Ethan pushes past me into the cubicle.

I stare after him, rooted to the spot. I knew this wasn't going to be easy, but the tension between us left me reeling. The room tilts, off-kilter. As I touch the wall to steady myself, my legs go slack beneath me.

No. This isn't just stress. It's deeper than that. Darker. Familiar. *Not now.*

Fuzziness creeps through me. The fluorescent lights glow and dim like they're breathing.

Oh, God. It's happening again.

And just like that, I'm not here anymore. I'm back.

Back on the Ravensthorpe tower.

*

'Are you okay?' A guy with a towel around his waist peers into my eyes, his brow furrowed.

I blink, my vision clearing. I'm next to the showers, my legs trembling, my breath coming in ragged gasps. 'Yes. Thanks.' My voice emerges as a croak. I stumble to my bed, clothes clinging to my damp skin, hair dripping down my back.

Flopped on my bunk, I take deep breaths, attempting to calm myself. I should be used to this by now, but I'm not. These flashbacks leave me shattered each time.

*

My first flashback hit the night before Lula's funeral. I was at the Tube station, bone-tired after a dinner shift at *Alfredo's*, the restaurant where I'd started waitressing. I'd only left Ravensthorpe a week ago, so I wasn't used to it yet. The work, the frantic rhythm of life in London. When the fuzziness filled my head, I mistook it for exhaustion.

But then my vision warped. The tunnel walls rippled like a viscous, treacly wave. An eerie golden light pulsed from the abyss that had swallowed the last train.

A cold sweat broke out on my forehead. And yet, beneath the rising panic, a cool part of my brain recognised this. I'd felt it before. *Where?*

The memory pounced. On the night Lula died.

And, in a flash, I was back there. On Ravensthorpe tower.

The scent of burning wax in my nostrils. Huddled in the dark, in the howling winter wind. Tiny snowflakes kissing my nose. Jaz, Ethan and Theo, half-glimpsed shadows, their murmurs mingling with the wind. And Lula of course.

Always Lula.

Despite the cold, warmth enveloped me. There we all were, the dream team, together at Ravensthorpe, poised on the brink of possibilities. I could rewrite history. Make the right choices this time.

A harsh gust ruffled Lula's messy hair, and her lips curved upwards. As if one of us had cracked a joke. It wouldn't have been that though. Lula was amused by other things. Setting us all against each other mainly. Orchestrating discord.

'Some writers talk about the core wound,' Lula's honied voice filled the air. 'The buried splinter that worms its way out. You can run, but you can't hide, Tess.'

Her words stabbed my chest like an icy finger. The vision dissolved.

You can run, but you can't hide? Lula would never use a cliché like that.

The walls ceased their undulations. The glow from the tunnel dimmed. The world went sharp again. I was alone in the Tube station.

Lula dead. Ravensthorpe lost.

*

After that first time in the underground, the flashbacks reoccurred, each episode bringing the same bone-chilling dread. They struck months apart, or days. I learnt to recognise the triggers: exhaustion, anxiety, and changes in light, like that first time in the tunnel.

Researching my symptoms, I found a name for my condition. Hallucinogen-persisting perception disorder. HPPD. It wasn't uncommon among those who used psychedelics. Even once, like me. There was no known cure, but with luck, it would decrease in time.

Think of it as a lucid dream, one website said. *You can control the action.* I liked that; it helped me manage the fear. I was awake, but I was dreaming, that's all. I hadn't mastered control of the flashbacks yet though.

The prelude to Lula's death played out in the same ghastly detail each time.

Chapter 4

The Chosen Many

Then

'Lula's only into memoir.'

'She hates anything too commercial.'

'She doesn't even read the submissions. She just picks the people she likes.'

Lula's writing masterclass was the holy grail at Ravensthorpe. A shimmering aura settled on the students accepted into it. They were the ones with potential. Out of fifty first year students, she only took twelve.

Despite the long odds, I slaved away on my submission every chance I got. It was a rework of the birthday party story I'd read out in Iris's class. The mother–daughter trope might have been overused, but it was the best I had. I'd taken careful notes of everything Iris said in class and planned to implement her advice in reworking my piece. If I was going to make a success of this, I had to get better.

I usually wrote in my favourite space at Ravensthorpe, the old library, a grand room lined with towering bookcases, the highest reached by a stepladder. Sitting on the creased leather chairs with my laptop on the polished table in front of me, I felt I'd entered a hallowed space.

One library shelf was devoted entirely to Lula's books, including translations into various languages. She'd published ten books so far, after her first bestseller when she was twenty, and I was working my way through her canon. My current read was *Lil*, a novel about a schoolgirl who becomes dangerously obsessed with a female artist. Lula inhabited her characters on a deep emotional level few writers could rival. It was riveting, how she got inside the head of the neurotic teenager, Lil. Lula had won The Women's Prize for that one, five years ago.

Against one of the library's walls stood an old wooden cabinet with slim drawers. On pulling them out, I'd discovered printed sheafs of writing left by former Ravensthorpe students. I'd spent hours poring through them, thrilling at the sight of now-famous authors' names. Once they were nobodies like me, and in time, if I worked hard enough, I would be like them.

Opening my notebook, I read through my notes from Iris's class. *Write what you know.* I was already doing that. Tick. *Use unusual word combinations, evocative descriptions, and inventive metaphors.* I looked at my story. *Workmanlike.* My classmates' critique had stung, but was there some truth in it? My prose got the job done, but it lacked flair. I could do better.

I went through my story, finding opportunities to improve it.

Eighth birthday? Boring. Delete. *Eighth orbit around the sun?* Better.

Dessert? Dreary. Delete. *Indulgent finale.* Improved.

Lily's mother circulated in her yellow kaftan? Yawn. Delete. *Her mother's yellow kaftan was a sunbeam in the labyrinth of their modest abode.* Awesome.

By the time I submitted my story to Lula, no one could have called it workmanlike.

A throng of students clustered around the corkboard outside Lula's office on the morning the masterclass selections were to be announced. Her office was on the third floor, accessed by two spiral staircases. I'd never been there before. Outside her door stood a bookcase displaying the published works of former students. I pulled one out, a Costa Award winner. *I owe it all to you, Lula,* read the inscription.

A pang pierced my chest. Lula was the key to my destiny, but would she see my potential? The chances were slim.

On the dot of nine, a staff member elbowed her way through and pinned a piece of paper to the corkboard. I hung back, sheepish. What were my odds? Only as the other students dispersed, did I approach. Pushing my glasses up my nose, I scrutinised the printed list. My breath hitched and I blinked in disbelief. Had I misread it? No. There it was, near the bottom. *Tess Brody.* Jumping up and down, I hugged myself tightly, holding in my racing heart.

'I can visualise your name on a book cover already,'

Mum said, when I called to tell her. 'It's twice the size of the title and embossed in gold.'

This burning ambition, a book bearing my name, was the only future Mum had ever imagined for me. The only future I'd ever imagined for myself. No alternative scenario existed.

*

Fervent rumours swirled in the week leading up to Lula's first masterclass. The main takeaway being that it was vital – vital! – to impress.

In the canteen one day, a third-year student named Richie filled me in. A fellow loner, he seemed to recognise my outsider status. I was only a first-year though, and unlike Richie, I still had time to find my tribe. Over Richie's shoulder, I eyed the pack of girls at the next table. Their ragged outfits would have signalled 'street kid' if not for their artfully tousled hair. You needed money to pull off that look. If I tried it, I'd only look shabby.

Richie wiped Bolognese sauce from his chin. 'Every year, one student becomes "The Chosen One".' He punctuated the phrase with air quotes. 'And then . . . Lula introduces them to her New York agent.' He paused, waiting for my reaction.

Sensing it was expected, I gasped.

He picked up on my lack of genuine awe. 'You heard of Ellery Eppis from Eppis Lawson Literary?'

I shook my head.

'The Kingmaker?'

'Nope.'

He rolled his eyes. 'Ellery mentors The Chosen One while they're at Ravensthorpe. When they're ready, Eppis Lawson pitches their manuscript to the big five publishers.'

This time my gasp was real. Now I got it. This was a shortcut to publishing success.

'You know Casey Palipana?'

I nodded. Casey was last year's hot young thing. Her book *Chocolate Bird* was a Richard and Judy pick and topped the bestseller list.

'She was The Chosen One three years ago.'

'How does she choose?'

'Lula will tell you to form a critique group,' Richie said. 'You have to do that yourself; she doesn't create the groups. But it's crucial to get in a group with the right people.'

'Why?'

He snorted. 'Lula will choose one of the groups to participate in a winter retreat. And one person from that group will become The Chosen One.'

I frowned.

'It's weird, right? But that's the way she operates. She's a sadist, I suppose, but she gets results. The thing is, if you want to be The Chosen One, you have to strategise. I know what you're thinking.' He wagged his soft, white finger at me. 'You're thinking you want to be in a group with a bunch of good writers?'

I nodded.

'Well . . .' Richie forked at a towering pile of spaghetti. 'Yes and no. What you want is to be in a group where you are the best.'

'But—'

He held up his hand. 'You need to be the best of a bunch of writers who are good enough to be chosen for the retreat.' He chewed slowly. 'It's a delicate balance. You watch. People will start sizing you up.' He grinned, exposing a tomato sliver wedged in his tooth. 'Let the games begin.'

*

I arrived at Lula's class five minutes early, expecting to have my choice of seats. Inside, a ring of chairs surrounded a long, wooden table. Only two were vacant.

Dropping into one, I gazed out at the pond through the leadlight windows. It was one of those rare English autumns marked by endless sunny days. Today, the sky was a startling periwinkle blue. *Periwinkles symbolise new beginnings,* Mum had said. She never mentioned how criminals used to wear periwinkles on their heads on their way to the gallows. I'd found that out for myself.

We waited in silence, stealing furtive glances at each other, sizing up the competition. A couple of students scribbled in notebooks. They were under the spell of a potent and demanding muse, or so they'd like us to think.

Theo and Tabitha peered at a phone screen and snickered.

'What a stinker of a review,' said Theo.

I hadn't expected to see him here. So, despite his rugger boy appearance, he could obviously write. I assumed he was talking about Lula. Her latest book had just come out – a novel inspired by Celtic mythology. *She needs this one to be a success*, I'd overheard a self-important third-year pronounce in the corridor.

'I've heard her sales are tank—' Tabitha stopped abruptly as the door banged.

We all straightened as Lula sauntered in. Ragged jeans. Long-sleeved plaid shirt. Thick brown hair which smelt of apples but looked like she'd just crawled out of bed. On her feet she wore her trademark dark green wellies. They were a strange affectation for someone who made her living at a keyboard, not on a tractor, but she carried them off with aplomb. So much so, that a number of students had copied her style. The red lollipops had become a popular accessory too.

Ignoring the vacant chair, Lula paced up and down, a red lollipop dangling from her hand. 'Congratulations. You are here because you can string a few words together.' She came to a halt, her eyes flickering around the room. 'But don't get complacent.' She continued to pace. 'First things first. I don't care about you; I care about the work. So, I won't be pandering to personalities. I am not your mother, or your friend, or your favourite teacher from school. I am here to drag the best possible writing out of you, so don't waste my time. Understood?'

We all nodded.

'You'll begin sharing your writing in the next session.'

My stomach tightened at the thought of the impending humiliation.

'But first, I want to pose you some questions to consider as you write.'

Is there a meaning to life? If so, what is it? she wrote on the whiteboard. Turning, she surveyed the room.

An uneasy silence fell. Was she expecting an answer?

Lula's gaze roamed around the table. I looked down at my notebook as her golden eyes met mine. There were twelve of us in the class. Apart from Lula though, it appeared no one knew why we were here.

'Yes.'

All heads swivelled to the speaker – a girl with short blonde hair, wearing a tight red vest and flared jeans.

'And it means whatever we want it to mean.' Her voice was clear and self-assured. 'In my case, it's art. Specifically, writing.'

It was the swimmer, the girl I'd seen doing laps across the pond. She had a fine-featured angular face and slate-grey eyes. Her skin was pale and free of makeup. She didn't need any, she was striking.

Lula smiled. 'Well done. And you are?'

'Jaz.'

Lula continued posing questions, and Jaz had an answer for each one.

Should your writing be used to influence political or religious views?

'Possibly. Good writing is disruptive, it questions the status quo.'

Why does the world need your writing?

'Because I have a unique view on what it means to be human.'

I gazed at her in awe. Would she be The Chosen One?

Lula put her hands on her hips. 'Your first task is to

write a piece that attempts to answer, or at least pose, an important question. Because, if we aren't tackling big questions, people, what is the point? This isn't an Instagram post you're writing here. You have the last ten minutes of class to outline your ideas.'

A big question. An important question. My mind went blank. I scribbled random musings in my notebook. *What makes food spicy? Why does fish smell?* I chewed on my pen. *What is the nature of consciousness?* I added before closing my notebook.

We all headed for the door.

'Cool T-shirt.'

I halted. It was the blonde girl. Jaz. Was she talking to me?

I hadn't upgraded my image; the right persona hadn't arrived. I was wearing a faded grey T-shirt with a picture of Kate Bush on the front. It was from her 2014 London concert, which Mum had attended.

'Thanks. I love her music,' I said.

'Me too. She popped up on my Spotify last year. And wow.'

A smile blossomed on my face. Apart from Mum, I'd never encountered another Kate Bush fan.

'How great is *The Kick Inside*?' she said.

'Ground-breaking.'

'Has anyone ever told you that you look like her?'

'Kate Bush? No.' I glanced down at the singer's wild hair on my T-shirt, liking the comparison.

'You're taller though.' She smiled. 'Want to go get a cup of tea?'

43

'Sure.' Even if she was intimidating, it seemed silly to say no. I hadn't made any friends yet.

In the warm, wood-lined common room, we threw ourselves onto a tattered couch with a mug of peppermint tea.

'Did you always want to come to Ravensthorpe?' Jaz asked.

I laughed. 'Yes, from the moment I was conceived.'

She raised one eyebrow.

'Mum wanted to come here, but, well, I arrived instead, so . . . I'm carrying the torch for her.'

Jaz sighed. 'I wish my parents were like that. They think I pretend to like writing to spite them. They wanted me to study Classics at Cambridge.' She rolled her eyes. 'The only reason they're paying the fees is because I didn't get in anywhere else. Grades don't count here.'

I stared at her. But she was brilliant. 'What happened?' As soon as the words left my mouth, I wanted to recall them. I sounded so judgemental. What did grades matter if you were a writer?

Jaz rolled her eyes. 'Issues. Boring stuff. It was a stupid uptight school.' She pulled out her phone and tapped at it. A song came on – 'Wuthering Heights' by Kate Bush. 'I can't listen to this song without dancing.'

'Me neither.'

Her grey eyes met mine. Placing our steaming mugs on the table, we got to our feet. As we twisted and twirled around each other, I felt a premonition.

Jaz and I would be the best of friends.

Chapter 5

Buddy Love

Now

Ethan is wearing a moth-eaten jumper – a loose, red, woollen affair which must have once belonged to an obese old man. The sleeves are rolled up, but it still slides over his hands. He doesn't look like a ground-breaking young author. Although, Lula used to wear jumpers like that, so perhaps he does.

He glares at me as I jostle past a pilgrim clump to claim a chair next to him at dinner. I return a faux-innocent smile, though I am far from relaxed. It's so strange being around him again after all this time. We lean away from each other, as if there's a force field between us. Where once we were magnetically attracted, now we are repelled. My spine prickles as I move my gaze to Ethan's right. *Theo*. He's even more muscular and sporty looking than he used to be. The tattooed snout of a wolf protrudes from his bicep-hugging black T-shirt.

Theo's mouth lifts at one side. 'Surprised to, uh, see you here.'

I force out a carefree laugh. 'Crazy, huh? Turns out I'm a Ravensthorpe alumna. Who knew?' Dragging my eyes away, I scan the table, but there's no one I recognise.

Theo's eyes lock on mine. 'Jaz is here too.'

'Jaz?' My breath catches, and my eyes dart around the table again.

'She started with us yesterday,' says Ethan. 'Don't know where she's got to.'

Theo and Ethan exchange a glance.

'She's, like, a little whacky?' says Theo.

'Whacky how?' Jaz never used to be whacky. A little manic at times, but not whacky.

Theo's mouth twitches. 'You'll see.'

Mysterious. 'So, where's everyone else?'

'We're it,' says Ethan. 'Plus Jaz.'

'But Iris must have sent the invitation to hundreds of Ravensthorpe alumni.'

'Guess we're the only ones who felt the urge to commemorate Lula,' says Theo.

I swig from my wine glass to loosen the knot in my chest. We do have more reason than most to remember her. 'Where's Iris?'

Ethan shrugs. 'She hasn't showed up yet either.'

'What? That's so weird, considering she organised it. Have you tried to contact her?'

'No. Too hard. We've left our phones behind,' says Ethan.

'You what?'

Theo flicks his dark hair off his face. 'You know what

Lula said, right? The only way to do the Camino is to be offline.'

'Well, keep up the good work.' I have no intention of disconnecting; I'm waiting for a vitally important message.

The jug of red wine on the table is refilled as the meal progresses. I top up my glass a few times. My body is in shock from the walking, and it eases the pain. Not to mention the intense social awkwardness. I'd never imagined it would just be us four here. 'Maybe the others will turn up soon?'

Ethan shrugs. 'Maybe.'

Everyone around the table volunteers the story of why they're on the Camino. Everyone except Ethan, Theo, and me.

'So, what made you decide to do the Camino, dear?' Ree, the American woman, asks Ethan, enthusiastically. Despite the arduous day, she is fresh and well groomed with a full face of makeup. Maybe she caught the bus.

Ethan pushes away the dry fruitcake we've been given for dessert. He picks up his glass of water and takes a drink.

Ree's smile is dimming by the time he replies. 'Our tutor . . .' he gestures at Theo and me, 'died in an accident three years ago. We're walking the Camino in her memory.'

She murmurs sympathetically.

'She was a Catholic. Of sorts. She wrote a book about the Camino. At the funeral, her priest . . .' Ethan takes another sip of water. 'Her priest told me I should do the Camino.' His cheeks pinken. 'To help move on.'

Again, she offers encouraging words.

Ethan shrugs. 'He said I should try to find faith. It would

47

help me. I thought it was bollocks at the time, but I'm in a rut right now. And it was as good a plan as any. So here I am, waiting for a miracle to convert me.' He sounds sceptical.

I narrow my eyes. Ethan's story sounds about as likely as mine.

'Who went to the pilgrim mass this evening?' Ethan asks.

A few people nod.

'It was moving,' says Ree. 'It made me feel I was truly a pilgrim.'

'I didn't understand the service.' The origami-making Japanese woman twists her fingers. 'But I felt it.'

'I felt nothing. Maybe I need to try harder.' Ethan's voice is flat.

Ree fixes her dark eyes on him and touches his arm. 'You must open yourself to divine intervention.'

Ethan drops his glass to the table. 'Yes. Well, I've got nothing better to do, I suppose.' He turns to me. 'How about you? Why are you here on the Camino? Apart from remembering Lula of course.' His voice is dubious.

I play for sympathy. 'I'm doing it because I'm unemployed, and out of ideas. I want to turn my life around.' I pause. 'Also, I'm writing an article. About my transformation.' This addition to my cover story has one benefit. It's at least partly true.

Ethan's gaze pierces me. 'Who are you writing for?'

'I'm writing on spec. Maybe you can help me out with some contacts?'

Ethan snorts and doesn't deign to reply.

The restaurant staff push us outside as soon as we finish. There's snow on the ground and the air's icy, but I'm warm

48

from the wine. I totter across the courtyard, up the stairs and collapse into bed. Being horizontal has never felt so good. A chorus of breathing fills the room as I dissolve into sleep.

Sometime in the night, I wake with a raging thirst and bursting bladder. A sonata of snores echoes up and down the hallway. I stumble to the toilet and back, using my phone to light the way. Plastic bags rustle as I get back to bed. People are getting up. I check the time. *Five a.m.* What's wrong with them? *It's frigging dark, people.* Sinking to my bunk, I pull the sleeping bag over me.

A muffled noise comes from the bunk above me. Ethan's bunk. It's a sniff. Or a cough. Or . . . a sob?

Whatever. I'm not about to start feeling sorry for him now.

*

'*Buenos Dias.*' The warden flicks the switch so light floods the room. The dormitory is empty. It's a repeat of yesterday.

As I crawl out of my sleeping bag, my body screams. I need a day off, but I've got to keep up with Ethan. At sloth-like speed, I pack up my gear, which has somehow expanded since yesterday.

Backpack loaded, I make my way across the cobblestone courtyard to the restaurant. I'd paid for breakfast, but it seems to be shut. Peering through the window, I spot the barista. I mimic drinking a cup of coffee, but he shakes his head, pointing at the clock on the wall. I'm too late. There's no alternative but to plod on.

49

Luckily, it's only about forty-five minutes' walk to a café where the scent of fresh coffee greets me. Here, I use my few Spanish words to order coffee and potato tortillas. When I finish, I buy another espresso, to delay the inevitable. As I set forth, the coffee's dark taste lingers on my tongue.

The trail is less steep than yesterday. With a full belly and caffeine in my veins, I'm cheerful despite my aching legs. I can do this.

The clopping of hooves, accompanied by a tuneless whistle, interrupts my thoughts. I turn. It's Theo who, bizarrely, is leading a donkey. I must have overtaken him somewhere. He's wearing a red cap, turned backwards on his head and the same muscle-clinging T-shirt as last night. He stops whistling as he reaches me.

I clench my hands, our last encounter flashing through my head. I can't avoid him though; we're going to be on this trail together for a month. I should try to make conversation. I eye the donkey. That's a safe topic. 'You came prepared.'

'Yeah, I, uh, read this book about a guy who walked the Camino with a donkey, and it seemed a cool idea.' If he finds my presence unsettling, he doesn't show it. 'This is Dapple, I bought her in Saint Jean.'

'Are you a *Don Quixote* fan?'

He frowns. 'I didn't choose the name; it came with the donkey.'

'Dapple is the donkey Don Quixote's offsider, Sancho Panza, rides.'

He nods vaguely, as if he might, or might not, have heard of *Don Quixote*. I think Theo just pretends to be a bit thick for reasons of his own.

'So, it's a boy donkey?' In the story, Dapple was a male. *He shall pace ye with the best ambler that ever went on four legs.*

His face is blank. 'No. A girl.'

'Oh.' I stroke Dapple's nose, and she blows hot air onto my hand. I've never noticed before what sweet faces donkeys have. 'She's beautiful.'

Theo's brow wrinkles. 'Mm. She's got a mind of her own.' This sounds not completely positive.

I gaze at the panniers hanging off the donkey's back. 'It must be nice not to carry your things.' Why didn't I buy a donkey?

'Mm. That part is way easier.' Again, there's a note of doubt.

A strained silence falls. 'What are you up to these days?' I ask. 'Been writing?'

For some reason his cheeks flush a warm pink. 'Yes. Uh, this and that. I've had a few publications. Pretty niche. Nothing you'd have heard of. I'm working in communications. Copywriting at an ad agency.' He gazes out at the sun-dappled forest.

My leg twitches with an urge to kick him, to shake up his macho mask.

He flicks his hair out of his eyes. 'Well, *Buen Camino*, I guess. Might see you round.' He walks on, whistling, Dapple picking her way behind him.

My guts churn as I stare after him. Of all the people I'd rather not spend a month with. This had better be worth it.

After a few hours, I stop for a lunch of *bocadillo*. This is less exotic than it sounds – a dry crusty bread roll with

51

salty salami inside. It takes a lot of chewing. My lunch stop stretches out. The sun's shining and it's pleasant to sit here watching pilgrims go by. They're a motley crew. Some look like they dash up mountains before breakfast. Others, like me, are limping and haggard already, sweat slicking their brows. How many will make it to the end?

A girl appears in the distance, backlit by the sun. She's dragging her feet as if each step is torture, her backpack straining on her shoulders. There's something poking up over her head. A wooden cross? *Strange*. I eye the cross as she comes closer. It isn't full-sized, you couldn't nail a person to it. It's more hobbit-sized.

As the girl approaches, the sunlight shifts. *Her face*. A jolt runs through me. Her nose is sunburnt, and her blonde hair pokes out from beneath a green cap. She is still angelic-looking though, fine-featured, and fair-skinned.

'Jaz?' My voice barely makes it out.

Jaz's face pinkens. Leaning forward under the weight of her cross, she raises one hand. 'Hi, Tess.' Her tone is casual, like this was inevitable. The others must have told her I'm here.

I stare. The pulse thumps in my neck, as I remember how she ignored me at Lula's funeral.

Her mouth twitches. 'Sorry, can't stop.' She gestures towards her cross and keeps walking, her gaze fixed ahead.

I swallow the hard lump in my throat. I've imagined seeing Jaz again so many times, but never like this. It's been three years, and now it feels like we don't know each other at all.

And what's up with her cross? Who carries a cross across

Spain? Then again, who in their right mind even walks across Spain?

So, Ethan is in search of a miracle. Jaz is carrying a cross. Theo has a donkey.

In a flash, I get it. It's Ravensthorpe all over again. Why be an average hiker when you can go one better? They've acquired a new Camino persona. A story for the trail. Of course they have.

And here I am, the unbranded boring outsider again.

Chapter 6

Meet-Cute

Then

'Rock chicks?'

I dragged my eyes away from the squirrel cavorting in the oak tree above. 'We don't like heavy metal.'

Jaz sighed. 'We don't, do we?'

Jaz and I were lying on the grass at Ravensthorpe, watching the other students wander by. I crunched on a carrot from the veggie patch. The veggie garden was haphazardly tended by a roster of students, producing abundant carrots and potatoes, but little else.

Our discussion regarding a Ravensthorpe persona was ongoing. Jaz agreed we needed an upgrade. We had to attract the right people to our critique group, and for that we needed branding. So far, we had considered and rejected goth, punk, and now rock chick.

'Dark academia?'

'Taken.' Jaz pointed at two girls in plaid skirts and black coats.

'Balletcore?'

'Too late.'

A couple of girls wafted past in leotards and floaty skirts with ballet slippers.

'We need something that expresses our aesthetic,' Jaz said.

'What is our aesthetic? Wellies?' I suggested, as a cluster of Lula lookalikes in knee-high wellies and plaid shirts strolled past sucking lollipops.

Jaz laughed.

'I've got it. "Wuthering Heights".'

Jaz raised her eyebrows. 'Ooh, I'm liking that.'

I tapped at my phone. 'Did you know there's an annual "Wuthering Heights" Day, where people dress up as Kate Bush and dance to the song?'

'No way.'

'This is last year's Edinburgh event.' I showed her a video of a group in flowing red dancing to 'Wuthering Heights'.

'Oh,' Jaz breathed. 'Perfect.' She flung out her arms. '*Be with me always – take any form – drive me mad! Only do not leave me in this abyss, where I cannot find you.*' She paused. 'Heathcliff was an arse, but he had great lines.'

'Let's do it.' We jumped to our feet. It was charity shop time.

Bishopsgate village was half an hour's walk from Ravensthorpe, down a quiet laneway. The locals regarded Ravensthorpe students with suspicion. They were used to our arty ways, but that didn't mean they liked them. This amused the Ravensthorpe gang, and they played up their eccentricities for effect. When in the village, they acted as if they'd stepped out of an Oscar Wilde play or *Brideshead Revisited*. It was all *Oh, pass me the teddy bear* and *I can resist everything except temptation*. This sat uneasily with me. They were poking fun at people who weren't like them. What would they say if they saw our flat in Deptford?

Jaz and I spent a wild afternoon in the charity shop. I've never laughed so much. In the end, we walked out in flowing dresses and straw hats with a bag of outfits in each hand. Our look wasn't true to the period, but it didn't matter. We had a vibe. And it was ours alone.

And so, we made our mark at Ravensthorpe. We were the *Wuthering Heights* girls.

'*Whatever our souls are made of, his and mine are the same,*' I'd say if I passed Jaz in the corridor.

'*Why did you betray your own heart?*' she would reply.

We were pretentious, but we didn't care. Everyone at Ravensthorpe was pretentious.

Every day was golden that autumn – sunny, warm and suspended in a soft-focus haze. Or so it seems, looking back.

The Ravensthorpe grounds were full of woodland glades, and meadows which swallowed you whole the moment you lay down. Jaz and I spent hours stretched out, gazing up at the sky, making up stories. Clouds morphed into mythical beasts, squirrels leapt like acrobats. The whole world felt lightly enchanted.

One stupid, perfect night, tipsy from Prosecco, we swam

naked in the pond at midnight and fell asleep on its grassy banks. In the morning, we woke, shivering, to the honks of angry geese.

Jaz sat up; grass tangled in her hair. 'Do you think we'll be friends when we're old and grey?'

'*I could as soon forget you as my existence!*' I proclaimed, channelling Heathcliff.

We didn't only lounge around; we worked hard too. In the third week of her masterclass, Lula told us to write a story about forgiveness.

'How do you ask for forgiveness?' I asked Jaz.

She was lying on her stomach on the lawn and, like me, had a red lollipop dangling from her mouth. We had succumbed to the craze. Removing her lollipop, Jaz licked her crimson-stained lips. 'Depends. Major, or minor offence?'

'Let's say major.'

'The way I see it, forgiveness is a process. If you've injured someone, you owe them. Sometimes an apology isn't enough. You have to make amends and show you won't reoffend.' Jaz paused to suck on her lollipop. 'There's no requirement for someone you've injured to forgive you.' She met my eyes, and her voice dropped. 'Some acts are unforgivable.' Her words hung in the air.

It was soon after that I met Ethan.

*

I'd first noticed Ethan at one of the weekly general meetings. 'Ravensthorpe runs on a democratic basis,' Lula had

57

emphasised during the first-year induction. 'Everyone's vote is equal. The teaching staff is just a voice, like any other.' This was one of Ravensthorpe's core principles, as set out by its founder.

Students took turns to chair the meetings, which were held in a cavernous room filled with cushions and beanbags. On one of these beanbags, next to Theo the muscular back-flipper, lounged an intriguing boy. As we debated the length of evening quiet hours, I watched him from the corner of my eye.

Tall, with shoulder-length dirty-blond hair, he wore a tweed jacket over a T-shirt. Sunglasses perched on his blue cap. He wasn't traditionally handsome, but that was beside the point. He had an intangible quality – magnetism.

I saw Ethan around the place a lot after that, but we never spoke. He was always surrounded by a posse: Theo, Tabitha and a bunch of others. They hung on his words. Every time he went past, my heart beat faster. Sadly, there was no sign my intense attraction was reciprocated.

When I spotted him across the table in Lula's masterclass, my pulse leapt. I'd heard the gossip about him by then. He was from writing aristocracy; his father had won the Booker. Ethan was tipped as the 'writer most likely' to be The Chosen One this year. Rumour had it Lula was a regular guest at the Hill family home in Highgate. I squirmed to imagine Ethan's reaction to my writing. I'd worked hard on it, but I suspected it still wasn't up to scratch.

The day it was my turn to read, I knocked back a glass of wine beforehand to give me courage. I didn't have high expectations of praise, but there was one low bar I wanted to get over. Students often cried during their critiques in Lula's class. I didn't want that to be me.

My reading passed in a wine-tinted blur, exacerbated by fogged-up glasses, due to the heat in my cheeks. It was the birthday party story again, but the new version, the one with flair.

Anticipation crescendoed for the pièce de résistance: Lily's mother's legendary fiery curry and the luscious finale of baked bananas . . .

This time, the reaction from the group was more positive. *Interesting vocabulary choices. Cool turn of phrase there.*

'I liked the metaphor of the sunbeam in the labyrinth,' said Ethan.

I glowed.

But Lula frowned. 'I disagree. You sound like you've got a thesaurus stuck in your throat. This story about Lily's mother . . . Is it really about your own mother?'

I swallowed. 'Yes.'

Her eyes bored into me. 'Do you love her?'

'Yes. Of course.'

'Hm.' Lula looked sceptical. 'Well, write it like you hate her, and see what happens then. Class dismissed.'

My cheeks burned, though as far as Lula's critiques went it was relatively gentle. And I had achieved my goal. No tears.

Ethan smiled at me as we left the classroom. My eyes lingered on him as he strolled down the corridor with his posse.

'*Remind my heart to beat*,' Jaz murmured, quoting *Wuthering Heights*. 'You haven't got a crush on Ethan

Hill, have you?' Her tone was light, but I sensed her keen interest.

I shook my head, dragging my eyes away from him. *Ethan and me?* The idea was preposterous, he could have anyone he wanted.

*

I ran into Ethan soon after that at an eighties-themed gig in the village. I couldn't resist the theme, though I had to go by myself. Jaz was up next for Lula's workshop and was frantically polishing her piece. I figured I'd have a bop for an hour, then head back to work on my writing.

I stepped inside the village hall, and there he was. Leaning against the wall with his hands in his pockets. My stomach flipped. What was Ethan doing here? Wasn't this too corny for him? And where was his ever-present posse?

It was fancy dress, so I'd come as Kate Bush of course, in a flowing chiffon dress – it was a warm evening. Ethan wore a flannelette shirt over baggy faded jeans – a grungy rock god. He raised his hand as I paused at the door.

I glanced over my shoulder, but there was no one behind me. Was he waving at me?

'I haven't seen anyone here from Ravensthorpe yet,' he yelled over the music. 'Want to hang out?'

'Sure.' My voice emerged as a squeak.

He eyed my outfit. 'Stevie Nicks?'

I shook my head. 'Kate Bush. And you're Kurt Cobain?'

'Got it in one.'

'But wasn't he more of a nineties artist?'

'Oops.' Ethan put his finger to his lips. 'Don't tell anyone.'

I raised my eyebrows. 'Your secret is safe with me.'

'Anyway, check him out.' Ethan pointed towards the stage.

The DJ was wearing a tight white suit, and a blue and red lightning bolt zigzagged across his face. His red hair was spiked up with gel.

I looked back at Ethan. 'So?'

'Ziggy Stardust was early seventies. David Bowie was into three-piece suits in the eighties.'

'Well, I guess eighties-adjacent is absolutely fine then.'

Ethan and I danced together for most of the night. I was baffled, but ecstatic at this startling turn of events. The DJ may have mixed up his decades, but he kept the dance hits coming. It was sweaty out there on the dance floor. Bodies shoved us here and there, but deft manoeuvring on my part ensured we stayed next to each other. I wasn't much of a dancer, but it didn't matter. There was only enough space to jig around on the spot.

Then, somehow, right near the end, the crowd swirled, and I lost him. As the music finished, I stumbled out onto the street. There he was, leaning against a lamppost with a girl. A Siouxsie Sioux lookalike in leather pants, teased-back hair and kohl-rimmed eyes. *Tabitha*. She had her arms around his waist.

My chest tightened. *Of course*. Tabitha, my workshop nemesis, had the clothes, attitude, and polish I associated with money. Of course he'd end up with her. But as I turned to go, something happened. Looking back, it felt predestined, as if a puppet master had plucked invisible strings.

A faint whining noise drew my eyes to the road. A furry creature crouched on the cobblestones. A car was coming. I couldn't see it squashed so I sprinted out, scooping it up. The car roared past, barely missing me, music blaring, the teenagers inside yelling indecipherable curses as I ran, heart racing, to the kerb.

Ethan and Tabitha stared. Stepping towards me, Ethan put out his hands. Gasping for breath, I deposited the puppy, a bundle of black and white, into them. He stroked its head with one finger.

'Um, Ethan, I'm going now,' said Tabitha.

'Bye.' He held the puppy up to eye level. 'I now christen you, Zebra.' He turned to me. 'Can I keep him?'

I scanned the emptying street as my breath settled. 'Don't think he's got anywhere else to be.'

We strolled back to Ravensthorpe together, along the shadowy lane, chatting. I was surprised how comfortable it felt. Ethan was different without his posse, quieter and more serious. It was as if we were old friends, picking up on an ongoing conversation. Naturally, we talked about Ravensthorpe.

'I love the freedom to express myself,' Ethan said.

I nodded, though I wasn't sure if I'd found the right 'me' to express yet. As we walked through Ravensthorpe's stone gates, I plucked up my courage. 'My friend and I are forming a critique group. Are you interested?'

Ethan laughed. 'You haven't read my writing.'

'I heard your reading in class. It sounded pretty good.'

'Thanks.' He seemed genuinely pleased. 'I didn't realise I was auditioning.'

'Well, guess what?' I pointed at him. 'It was a highly competitive audition, but you passed the first round with flying colours.'

He agreed to get together and talk about it tomorrow. I knew Jaz would be keen to rope him in. He was the great Sebastian Hill's son after all. I didn't care so much about that part, I just wanted to spend more time with him.

Richie's advice came back to me. *What you want is to be in a group where you are the best.* I dismissed this. I'd never be The Chosen One. But with Ethan in our group, at least we'd have a fighting chance of making it on to Lula's winter retreat.

'You haven't got a friend who'd like to join, have you?' I asked.

'I might.'

When we reached my accommodation block, he leant over and kissed my cheek. My body tingled as the scent of cigarette smoke wafted up my nostrils. On him, it smelt good.

'See you tomorrow, Kate Bush.'

'Not if I see you first, Kurt Cobain.'

He walked across to the main building, the puppy held to his chest. When he opened the main door, the spilling light made a halo of his messy, blond hair.

Excitement fizzed through my veins. I was on the verge of something big.

Chapter 7

Science Fiction

Now

Dapple the donkey is munching grass outside a concrete building. She lifts her head as I approach, swivelling her furry ears towards me.

I tap robotically with my improvised wooden walking poles as I advance through the falling darkness. 'Intruder alert, intruder alert. Alien with large ears.'

This afternoon, when I'd reached for my fancy new collapsible walking poles, they weren't on the side of my pack. An image flashed into my mind – my poles leaning against the wall in Roncesvalles. There was no way I was going back. Climbing over the stone wall beside the trail, I found two branches. *Perfect*. Who needed poncy shop poles?

'Exterminate, exterminate.' I pole in time with my steps as I approach the *albergue*, dropping the robot act as I go inside. Larrasoaña hostel is not as atmospheric as the one in

Roncesvalles. Metal bunks rest cheek by jowl inside a vast, and almost empty, space. My breath snags as I see them.

Ethan, Theo and Jaz are lying on their bunks looking glum. Ethan has his eyes closed. Jaz has her cross on the pillow beside her. *Weird*.

Groaning with relief, I remove my backpack, perch on a bunk, and slap on a bright face. 'I'm starving. What's the deal with food here?'

Theo swivels his head towards me. 'There's no food. That's why we're all lying here. We're, uh, conserving our strength.'

'There's only one café, and the owner's on holiday,' says Jaz.

My chest aches as her eyes flicker away from mine. What made me think we might be able to pick up our friendship? 'What about drink? There must be somewhere to drink?'

'Don't you think we'd be drinking?' says Theo.

'But that's ridiculous. Lula said it's a historic pilgrim town. Doesn't that mean they feed pilgrims?'

'We've read her book too,' says Theo. 'That's why we're here, obvs.'

'She's pranked us.' Ethan's voice is morose.

'I'd go on,' says Theo, 'but it's a long way to the next town and I'm, like, weak from lack of food.'

I lie down on my bunk and gloom fills the room. Theo whistles tunelessly. I check my messages, but still nothing. My stomach gurgles. 'Maybe Lula's giving us a test.' My words drop into a well of silence, broken only by Theo's droning whistle.

Darkness falls outside. Despite my hunger, I doze off for a while.

'What kind of test?' Ethan's words wake me.

It takes a moment to tune in. Turning my head, I meet his eyes. 'Perhaps she led us here for a reason?' I'm just trying to start a conversation. My revenge plan won't work if I can't gain his trust. 'It's a spiritual challenge. We have to stick together and come through.'

Ethan gives me a blank look. 'Were you always such a Pollyanna, or is this new?'

'I'm just trying to stay positive.' Sitting up, I open my backpack. 'I have a small bottle of gin I can contribute to the cause.' I place it on the table in the corner. 'And . . .' I dig around in my pack. *What's that?* My fingers touch a plastic bag, and I pull it out. Inside the bag are four lollipops. Four *red* lollipops. Where did they come from? I didn't buy lollipops.

My pulse skitters as an image fills my head. *Lula and her crimson-stained lips.* 'Did one of you put these in my bag?' My voice comes out croaky.

They glance at the lollipops, shaking their heads.

'Groupie,' Theo mutters.

It's what we used to call the Lula lookalikes. I hesitate, then place the lollipops on the table next to the gin. They're individually wrapped, so no one's tampered with them. Why am I even thinking that? Most likely another pilgrim put them in the wrong backpack in Roncesvalles. An easy mistake with so many backpacks around. That must be it.

'Yay, my fave.' Jaz adds two oat bars to the table. 'I was planning on gnawing these in private, but I'm keen for a lollipop so . . .'

Theo fishes around in his backpack and drops a plastic-wrapped package on the table. 'Cheese bread.'

Ethan gazes at the bunk above him. 'I've got nothing. Not a thing. Unless you want Ibuprofen?'

I'm surprised he doesn't have something stronger. Guess he didn't want to bring his stash over the border. 'You can still join our feast.'

'Oh, no, that's not fair,' says Ethan. 'Don't worry about me. I'll meditate on the spiritual benefits of fasting. I might have an epiphany.'

'Your contribution can be non-edible,' I say. 'Hey, aren't you that bestselling author Ethan Hill? Why don't you read to us?'

Ethan glares at me.

'Yeah, why not. Read from your work-in-progress,' says Theo. 'It'll be like old times. You, uh, do have a work-in-progress, don't you?'

Ethan's jaw clenches. 'Of course I do.'

Theo shrugs theatrically. 'Just asking.' He picks up the gin. 'Chin chin.' Taking a sip, he passes it on.

My feet are throbbing, so I take a large gulp to dull the pain. 'Here's tae ye. I've got a bit of Scottish in me somewhere.'

Ethan raises the bottle. 'Cheers.' He takes a decent swig.

Jaz passes the gin on without drinking. She was never much of a drinker. But neither was I until Ravensthorpe.

The oat bars arrive, followed by the cheese bread. It's all delicious. There must be some Camino magic in the air as one small bottle of gin and a few snacks are enough to get the party rolling.

'Best oat bar I've ever eaten,' says Theo.

By the time we're sucking on our lollipops, I'm bizarrely full. *Loaves and fishes.* 'Storytime,' I say.

Ethan groans, a lollipop stick poking out of his red-stained lips.

'Yay, storytime,' says Jaz.

'Do I have to?'

'Come on, mate, sing for your supper,' says Theo. 'How lucky are we? A private reading from Ethan Hill.'

Ethan scowls at Theo as he perches on the side of his bunk. Pulling his lollipop stick out of his mouth, he takes a puff on a vape. The scent of tobacco used to cling to him at Ravensthorpe. What does he smell of now?

His vape smoke wafts towards me. *Strawberry*. I preferred the tobacco.

A faint moon glow appears through the windows. Outside, Dapple brays, her harsh hee-haw adding a Wild West ambience.

Ethan gazes out the window. 'This is weird, huh? Us all being here together.'

'So strange no one else turned up,' says Theo.

'Especially Iris,' I say. 'Considering she organised it.'

'Maybe we'll see her tomorrow,' says Jaz.

'It's almost like a miracle.' Theo's voice is mischievous. 'The fab four together again.'

Ethan snorts. 'Okay, this story I'm working on. It's about religion. Seems an appropriate time to air it.' Pulling out his notebook, Ethan gazes at each of us in turn. It's his celebrity author technique, but it's not working. He's nervous. '*Is God simply a metaphor?*' he reads. '*Or is there truly an omnipotent presence out there?*' He glances towards the moonlight. '*Bearing witness to our thoughts and utterances?*'

He goes on, but I lose track for a while. It's been a long day, and what with the gin and the food . . .

'*Are we to worship the likes of Thor, Zeus or Aphrodite? Or the curious Vanuatu cargo cult?*' Ethan waves his vape.

I catch snatches here and there as I tune in and out. What is this? A monologue?

'*We used to gaze upon the night sky, marvelling at the falling stars, wondering if each one was a soul released from its mortal coil . . .*'

It's not exactly a page-turner. As Ethan reads on, Theo and Jaz nod off to sleep. My eyelids droop too.

Ethan stops and meets my gaze. It's like there's only the two of us here in the room, with the past an invisible third. He runs his hands through his hair. 'So? Do you have a critique?'

'Very . . .' I struggle for the right word. 'Spiritual.'

Ethan grimaces, lies down, and closes his eyes.

Was he hoping for a more enthusiastic response? Listening to him has reminded me; I need to read his book. It's background research for my plan; I can't put it off any longer. Turning on my e-reader, I put on my glasses and open *Darker Matters*. Hopefully all the critics were wrong and it's awful. That will cheer me up no end. Curling up in bed, I take a breath, touch the first page, and – *damn it* – I'm immediately entranced.

This writing is unlike anything he shared at Ravensthorpe. Had he been hiding it? It's confident, original and cerebral.

He's hit the sweet spot between commercial and literary. It's an Oprah's Book Club kind of book, and I say that with the greatest respect.

Ethan's protagonist is a groovy physics lecturer at a university. '*The theory of relativity posits that time itself is an illusion,*' she tells her first-year students. '*Past, present and future co-exist in a single moment. Everything that will happen, has already happened.*'

It's embarrassing to admit, but I've never been sure what the theory of relativity is all about. Physics hasn't played a big part in my life. You'd expect it to be a dry topic, but Ethan has the golden touch. As I read, my brain explodes. For a few minutes at least, I understand the true nature of time. It's both enlightening and thrilling. Jealousy constricts my chest; no wonder it was a bestseller.

The physicist holds up a CD to an auditorium. '*Imagine the entirety of time is contained within this disc, but, like a needle on a record, we can only access the track we are currently playing.*'

My hands tighten around the e-reader, as a tickle of unrest niggles at my brain.

'*Such a notion is both exhilarating and terrifying, for it suggests our fate is already predetermined . . .*'

The words sound familiar. But I've never read this book before. I re-read the page. It makes my fingers tingle. Why?

Chapter 8

Space Opera

Jaz is basking in a meadow beside the path, with her trousers pulled up to her knees and her cross lying beside her.

I wave.

Her hand twitches in return.

Despite this cool welcome, I walk over and sink to the grass beside her. I can't pretend we were never friends. I'm not even sure why we're not anymore. Whose fault was it? Mine? There's a tangle of confusion and hurt between us I'll never unpick.

An awkward silence falls, so I work on my flower garland to keep busy. I've been stringing pink and yellow flowers together as I walk, and I'm nearly done.

Jaz gets to her feet.

'Fun night last night, huh?' I'm trying to make her stay.

Jaz gives a tense smile. 'I didn't like Ethan's writing.'

'Me neither, it was deadly, wasn't it? Which part did you

particularly hate?' I adopt Lula's mellifluous tones. 'Do you have any actionable suggestions?'

This attempt at humour falls flat. 'All of it. I'm, um, a believer now.'

'That's . . .' My mind goes blank. 'Cool.' Talk about the girl least likely. The cross isn't just a pose, it goes deeper. I place the completed garland on top of my curls. *Voilà* – my Camino persona is activated. 'I'm leaning towards paganism, myself.'

I'm trying to get under her skin, to find a hint of the Jaz I used to know. At Ravensthorpe, when religion was raised, she said you may as well believe in a spaghetti monster in space. Did Lula's death change her?

I gesture around at the fields of flowers, the ancient castle on the hill. 'According to Lula's book, this was a pagan path before it was the Camino.'

Jaz narrows her eyes, the cross a dark silhouette over her head.

I can't hold back anymore. 'What's up with the cross?'

'It's complicated.'

Her tone doesn't encourage me to delve deeper.

She walks off with a terse goodbye but stops a few paces away and turns back. 'Thanks for the lollipop.'

I stare at her. The words seem loaded. Was it Jaz who put the lollipops in my bag? If so, why? 'You're welcome. Happy memories, huh?'

Her mouth tightens and she walks away.

I let out a long breath as I slump back among the butter-coloured flowers. It reminds me of lying around at Ravensthorpe with Jaz.

Do you think we'll be friends when we're old and grey?

The memory makes my chest hurt. Didn't Einstein say some moments feel like a lifetime? My mind returns to Ethan's book and my flash of understanding about relativity. In another space-time dimension, are Jaz and I still lying on the grass talking about friendship? It's a nice thought. My odd feeling about Ethan's book seems silly now. It was a bestseller. I could have heard those words anywhere.

The sun is making my head spin. I gaze at the sky. It's a blue I've never seen in England. A duck-egg colour, with wisps of clouds. I hear Jaz's voice.

I can see a cloud-elephant.

That's not an elephant, it's a tiger.

And there's an emu.

More of a flamingo.

The thumping in my chest feels like the Earth's heart beating. Sitting up, I adjust my garland, and yawn. It's only another eight kilometres or so to Pamplona. According to Lula, it's among the most beautiful cities on the way. They must be going there.

I struggle to my feet trying to ignore my aching muscles, slide on my John Lennon sunglasses and insert my earbuds. My temples pulsate with the beginning of a headache. Above me, the clouds form the shape of a wolf. My chest tightens.

It looks like the tattoo on Theo's shoulder.

*

I'm shattered by the time I get to Pamplona. My pack seems full of lead and the concrete trail into the city bruises my feet. Still, as I sight the medieval walls, a thrill runs

73

through me. This city has welcomed footsore pilgrims for centuries. It's mind-blowing.

Yellow arrows lead me through narrow streets to an ancient stone-walled deconsecrated church – the *albergue*. Inside, I lie on my bunk, still wearing my garland. The bunks are built into the church naves and above me a transparent ceiling forms the second level bunkroom floor. It's cool and, despite the chatter of pilgrims, calming. These walls hold the memory of endless years of prayers and songs.

After fruitlessly checking my messages for about the hundredth time today, I close my eyes, and imagine pilgrims singing.

*

The fire crackles, and a mug of liquorice tea warms my hands.

Ravensthorpe is cosy and familiar. The tattered couches, the deep-red velvet curtains.

Theo turns the music up. As a choral chant fills the air, an icy dread seizes me.

*

I wake with chanting in my ears. My muscles are clenched, ready to run, and it takes a while to shake off the unsettling dream. What happened that night at Ravensthorpe? I wish I could piece it all together.

My flower wreath falls off as I sit up. I'll go out and buy something for dinner.

In the lobby, I run into Theo, who's coming in. 'What's up with your face?' he says.

I scratch at my forehead. It's itchy. Pulling out my phone, I inspect the flaming red spots on my forehead. 'I made a flower wreath.'

Theo narrows his eyes. 'What sort of flowers?'

'I used those yellow ones from the field and the pink ones from the bushes beside the track.'

'That'll be it. Hasn't anyone ever told you about oleander?'

I shake my head.

'Look it up. It's deadly.'

I touch my forehead. 'If you eat it, you mean?'

'Yeah. They use it for suicide in Asia. You probably won't, like, die from wearing it on your head.'

Probably. How reassuring. 'You know a lot about plants, huh?'

For some reason, Theo's cheeks redden. 'Not that much.' Flicking his hair, he walks away.

Outside, the air is fresh. I zip up my jacket. Cobbled streets lead past colourful terraced houses. I emerge into a plaza lined with gaudy tulip-filled flowerbeds, and spot Ethan, sitting at an outdoor table in his floppy red jumper. He's writing in his notebook and has a bottle of beer in front of him.

I head towards him. If we don't start talking soon, I'll have come here for nothing.

He looks up as I approach. '*Buen Camino*.' His voice is wary.

'*Buen Camino* to you. Mind if I join you?'

He flicks his hand towards an empty chair. It's not a warm welcome, but I lower myself into it.

A waiter approaches.

'*Un otro vaso por favor*,' says Ethan.

'You speak Spanish?'

Ethan shrugs. 'Enough to ask for another glass.'

A new glass comes. I take this as an invitation and pour beer into it. 'Cheers.'

Ethan raises his glass.

'I'm glad we're not here for the running of the bulls,' I say, to break the silence. 'I've seen videos of bulls chasing people down the streets. It looks scary. Although, if they did it in a humane way it might be exciting, I guess.'

Ethan is silent.

I chatter on. 'I'm not against the idea of running with animals.' Dapple's soft brown eyes appear in my mind. 'I'd quite like to run with a donkey.' I scratch at my forehead.

His eyes follow my hand. 'What happened to your face?'

'I used oleander flowers in a wreath. Theo tells me they're poisonous. Rookie mistake.' Silence falls. I try not to scratch.

'Why are you here?' His eyes meet mine. 'It's so bizarre.'

My gut clenches. 'Iris invited me. And I told you, I want to turn my life—'

Ethan's mouth curls. 'You been in therapy?'

'Kind of.'

He taps the rim of his glass with his finger. 'Do what you want. Keep up if you can.'

My hackles rise. 'I'm fitter than I look.' This is a lie. I have no idea if I can keep up with him. Another silence falls. 'So, how's your quest for belief going?'

Ethan lets out a breath. 'How do you think?'

'Bit of a stretch, isn't it? For you.' Like Jaz, Ethan never showed any interest in religion at Ravensthorpe.

His shoulders twitch. 'It's an interesting test. Can I have an experience which leads to finding faith?'

'So, it's not just about Lula?'

Ethan flinches and drains his glass. 'I'm not going to talk about Lula. Not with you.'

I let it go. There's nothing to gain by getting Ethan offside. Not yet. 'Okay. How's the writing going?'

He rolls his eyes. 'You heard me last night. It was shit, wasn't it?'

Ethan always was self-critical, but this time he's right. I nod.

'I haven't written a decent word since *Darker Matters*. That's why I'm here. Partly, anyway.'

'You're researching a story?'

'Research. Inspiration. A reset.' He shrugs. 'You know what Lula said.'

'Good writers go to extraordinary lengths for their story?'

He nods, and we drink in silence for some time. I remember something I read about his father. 'Were you brought up religious?'

He grimaces. 'Yep.'

I file the information away. 'So, were you a believer? As a child?'

'I believed what I was told to believe. Then, gradually, I didn't. When I was ten, I refused to go to church.'

'How did that go down?'

'Badly.'

I can imagine his famous father would be a tough taskmaster. 'So, how are you planning to push this search for faith along?'

He sighs. 'The plan is, to go to all the pilgrim masses along the way. Hope for a miracle. And try to put my cynicism on hold.' He pauses. 'I'm not going so well with that. To be honest, I might not go the distance.'

I grit my teeth. He can't give up; I need him to finish. 'What the mind can perceive and believe, it can achieve.'

Ethan snorts. 'I saw that graffiti too.' Draining his glass, he gets to his feet and meets my eyes. 'Don't try to keep up with me. The past is the past. Let's leave it there.'

Heat floods my chest, and I bite back a retort. I only wish I could.

*

The walk out of Pamplona is torture. I've taped my blisters, but they stab like knives. I check my messages as I walk. *Nothing*. I hope this isn't all a waste of time.

The path winds past fields of green crops and an earth-coloured church, and heads towards a blue-tinted hilltop with spinning wind turbines. *Don Quixote country*. As I climb, wrought-iron outlines of pilgrims emerge, marching beneath the turbines. One rides a donkey; others are on horses, and several on foot.

On the hilltop, I perch on a rock, pulling out my lunchtime *boccadillo* and Ethan's novel. As I read on, something strikes me. His student characters, two girls and two boys . . . They're familiar. Has he based them on us? They're different enough that no one except us would recognise them, but there are definite similarities. Well, I suppose every writer draws from what they know. I read on.

'*We hate boredom because it gives us time to contemplate the pain of existence,*' says the physicist. '*Our whole life is a quest to avoid thinking about the fact we die.*'

Boredom. Didn't Lula and I talk about that once?

After lunch, angry dark clouds build on the horizon as I stride down the hill. I quicken my pace. Can I get to Mañeru before the storm hits?

'*Buen Camino.*' The words come out of nowhere.

My heart bounding, I spin around.

The speaker, a young woman with blazing red hair, slows her pace to walk beside me.

'*Buen Cam—*' My greeting falters and my mouth dries up. I stare at her, my mind racing. It can't be her. But it is.

I haven't seen her since Lula's funeral.

Chapter 9

Anonymous

So, the full cast are now on their way, each carrying their own secrets, hopes and obsessions. Will they make it to Santiago? Who knows? Their journey's just begun, and already they're undone. Is that a poem I hear? Why not?

> *As the curtains ease apart once more,*
> *Let's give these damned players a hand of applause.*
> *Take your places, for Act Two is nigh,*
> *And I'll make these puppets fly.*

Not bad, is it? A little raw maybe, but it's just between you and me, isn't it?

Your friend,
Anonymous

Chapter 10

Body Swap

Then

My reflection stared at me from a limousine window. Black shirt. Black felt hat. Knee-length black puffer jacket. I looked like a tall, skinny mob wife.

A well-swept footpath led past manicured gardens to the old stone church where Lula's funeral was being held. Chelsea was like a different country to Deptford. Shiny cars, drivers at the wheel, lined the street. Guess I was the only one who gave my chauffeur the day off.

I was almost at the church when I saw it. Down a side-lane, a red vintage sports car gleamed in the winter sun. I scanned the road. No one would see me. Adrenaline surged through my veins. Without knowing it, I'd been waiting for this moment.

Pulling my keys from my pocket, I strode towards the sports car, Doc Martens tapping on the pavement. My vision narrowed. There was just me and the car. I touched the tip of my key to the shiny paint. Gritted my teeth against the high-pitched shriek of metal on metal. Dragged it from one end to the other.

Panting, I pulled my gin from my pocket, took a sip, and surveyed my work. *Not quite there.* Grabbing the aerial, I snapped it off too. *Perfect.* As I straightened, smoothing my skirt, I saw the homeless woman. My pulse skipped a beat. She crouched on the ground, her eyes wide. I'd been so intent on the car, I hadn't noticed her.

She was all rugged up. Ragged beanie pulled low, scarf around her chin and tatty grey jacket buttoned high. Green eyes and a white nose were the only body parts on display.

Scrabbling in my pocket, I found a tenner and thrust it at her.

She looked startled but took the note. A sheen of sweat gleamed on her forehead, despite the cold.

'Are you okay?' I asked.

After a moment, she nodded.

'Right.' I eyed the car. I wasn't too worried. It was unlikely she'd report me to the police. 'I don't make a habit of this. It's a special occasion.'

She didn't speak, just stared at me with those sea-green eyes. It was unsettling.

'You don't need anything? I can get you a coffee?'

She shook her head.

'Okay.' I was now fashionably late, so I raised my hand at her and strode back towards the main road.

An organ was playing as I walked to the church door. Churches and I were strangers to each other. I sort of got it. The robes, the singing, the stained-glass windows. It was only the actual God thing I had trouble with.

My stomach tightened as I scanned the crowd. Velvet jumpsuits. Full-length black dresses. Hats with veils. Black feather boas. The Ravensthorpe gang. I'd got the dress code wrong. I pulled my hat lower to hide my face.

The organ stopped as a white-robed priest came to the pulpit. Mourners rose to their feet. The usher gave me a quick once-over. Frowning, he waved me forward with a gloved hand. 'Back row,' he muttered, handing me an order of ceremony.

Dropping onto a bench, I took in my surroundings. My eyes came to rest on a pew near the front. Beneath a wide-brimmed black hat was a head of short blonde hair. *Jaz*. The air puffed out of me.

As if she sensed my gaze on her, she turned, her lovely face framed by the hat. Her eyes widened, and she nudged the broad-shouldered guy in a black suit beside her. He swung around, his shiny hair flopping over his face. *Theo*. He rolled his eyes at her, and they turned back to the front.

A woman edged in beside me. Cheeks burning, I glanced at her. She was young, and pale-faced, with close-cropped flaming red hair. Her black trouser suit was cheap and ill-fitting. Not one of the Ravensthorpe gang.

As my eyes flickered from her trouser suit back to her red hair, my heart contracted. I recognised her. She was one of the police officers who'd come to Ravensthorpe. The older man had asked all the questions, so I hadn't taken much notice of her. What was she doing here?

Were they still investigating? I edged along the pew away from her.

More Latin followed and some singing. Everyone except me seemed to know the words. Digging out my glasses, I tried to follow along in the hymnal. *'The darkness deepens, Lord . . .'*

We stood and sat, stood, and sat. I followed along, one step behind, like the new kid in kickboxing class. Mum had dragged me along a few times. It was exhausting. *Kickboxing is both brutal and beautiful*, she'd said. *And you never know when you might need it.* I hadn't continued with the classes, but Mum and I sparred at home now and then.

'We will now hear from one of Lula's students at Ravensthorpe, Ethan Hill,' said the grey-haired priest.

My chest tightened. I knew he'd be here, but still.

Ethan stood up in the front row and walked to the pulpit. His dirty-blond hair brushed the shoulders of his buttoned-up jacket. As he clenched his jaw, his gold earring sparked in the light.

'Lula left us too soon. She had so much still to give.' He went on in the same vein for some time.

A few stifled sobs came from the pews. My own eyes were dry. I guess I wasn't entirely devastated.

'A talented writer, and a generous teacher . . .'

Did Lula's publicist write this speech? Ethan's words washed over me, but I examined his face.

Recognising when people were holding back was a good skill for a wannabe journo. Over the last week or so, I'd recalibrated my career goal. All I'd ever wanted was to be an author. Now though, even the thought of it brought bile to my mouth. I wouldn't be going back to Ravensthorpe.

Ethan sounded like a politician. He was hiding something. But we all were, weren't we?

'Lula's life was short,' Ethan concluded, 'but she spent it doing what she loved. And at least we have her work to remember her by.'

Oh, please. As he stepped down, he stumbled, righting himself with a hand on the pulpit. That explained his lifeless speech. He'd hit up the benzos to get through the funeral. Should have guessed.

My eyes fixed on the candle-ringed coffin, and a sense of loss tugged in my chest. I pictured Lula's face in the tutorial room. Her languid smile as she delivered a shattering critique of my work. Lula was an elemental force; it was hard to believe a coffin could contain her. Like a vampire, she'd need a rock in her mouth to stop her returning.

The priest came back to the pulpit. His sadness seemed genuine. Everyone stood and sang 'Amazing Grace'.

'I once was lost, but now I'm found.' A tuneful voice rose next to me.

I risked a quick glance at the singing policewoman. She was barely older than me.

After the song, the priest swung incense over the coffin and sprinkled water on it. Frankincense filled my nostrils as his words drifted over me. One phrase lodged in my mind. *Life is changed, not ended.* I could see why you'd want to believe that.

Sinking in my seat, I buried my face in the Order of Service as the mourners filed from the church. I breathed easier as the policewoman edged from the pew.

From the corner of my eye, I caught a glimpse of blonde hair. I froze. Jaz had nailed the *Wuthering Heights* funeral look in a flowing black midi dress. I raised the Order of Service higher. *Lula Thornton will be cremated in a private ceremony,* it said at the bottom. Weren't Catholics usually buried? When the aisle was empty, I got to my feet.

Outside, Ethan, Theo and Jaz were talking to the priest. They looked suitably distraught. I sidled forward, among the crowd, keeping out of their line of vision.

The priest put a hand on Ethan's arm. 'You've read Lula's book? A pilgrimage helped her. It might help you too.'

'A pilgrimage?' Ethan sounded as if he'd suggested a striptease. 'I'd rather gnaw off my right hand.'

'Think about it.'

Ethan shrugged off the priest's hand. 'I will . . . Father.' The last word was dragged from his throat. He turned, strode up the street, and disappeared into the side lane.

A moment later, a muffled exclamation burst from the laneway. 'Oh, for fuck's sake.'

I kept a straight face. Time to make a quick exit. A double-decker bus was coming up the road. Heart thumping, I ran for it. Inside, I climbed the stairs and dropped into the front seat.

As my bus roared past the church, the breath snagged in my throat.

The young policewoman was gazing straight at me, her red hair a bonfire in the winter sun.

Her image replayed in my head as we drove on. Grey

coat buttoned up to the neck. Beanie and scarf in her hand. *Green eyes. White nose.* Ice spread down my spine as we swung around a corner. She was the homeless woman. Except she wasn't.

She was an avenging angel.

Chapter 11

Rags to Riches

Now

The policewoman's white T-shirt is dust-smeared, and her short hair sticks up from a forehead so pale it's almost translucent. She shows no sign of recognising me, but the air between us crackles with tension.

Those sea-green eyes on me as I'd gone by in the bus. For weeks afterwards I'd expected a knock on the door. But it hadn't come. Sweat trickles from my armpits. She knows who I am. She must. Why else is she here?

I take a deep breath, trying to control the panic that flutters in my chest. Should I confront her? Find out what she's doing here? But . . . what if this is a strange coincidence, and she doesn't know who I am? In which case, it would be better to lie low.

Playing for time, I ask the usual pilgrim questions.

In a soft Irish accent, she tells me she started from Saint Jean the day after me.

'You must have put in some big days.'

'I don't stop. If I stop, I seize up.' She sips from her hydration pack.

It's like we're playing a high-stakes game of chess. Is she following me? Or us? If so, it must be connected to Lula. Does she know what we did? No, I won't admit I recognise her; it might lead in undesirable directions. Maybe this will all blow over.

Instead, we talk about the *albergues* we've been in, and where we're going next. When I stop for a drink at a fountain, she waves and keeps going. 'Can't stop. Don't want to seize up. *Buen Camino.*'

My heart thumps, as her long legs propel her along the trail. Should I tell the others she's here? Or keep this to myself until I find out what she's up to? Knowledge is power. Can I turn this to my advantage? It's so strange it's just the four of us here from Ravensthorpe. And now the policewoman. Could she really be here by coincidence? Or . . . did Iris invite her too?

Pulling out my phone, I re-read Iris's email, then type in a quick message. *Hi Iris, Ethan, Theo, Jaz and I are on the Camino, heading for Mañeru tonight, hope you can join us soon, cheers Tess.* I press send and immediately get back an autoreply.

Greetings! Iris is on a soul-nourishing journey in the serene offline world. Fear not, your missive has been received. Iris will return your communication once she returns, rejuvenated, to the digital symphony.

With tranquil wishes,
Iris's sanctuary guardian.

Hm. Well that makes sense, I guess. Iris is probably here on the *Camino*, and we'll run into her soon. But did she only send the invitation to the four of us? *And the policewoman?* My pulse flutters. It's so weird she's here. But she didn't seem to recognise me. And it's not like I can back out. I'm committed. Mum's voice sounds in my head. *The only way out is through.*

As I perch on the edge of a time-weathered stone bridge, fat drops of rain splatter around me. Clouds roll in. Thunder rumbles and the air cools, as if a fridge has opened.

The hairs lift on my arms as my vision swims, the edges blurring. Below me, the dull-brown river undulates like a snake. Rain drops glitter like fireworks, exploding in bright bursts. The thunder rolls through me, vibrating my body.

Beira, the Celtic queen of winter, carries a hammer to control the storms, whispers Lula.

Then she's gone, the brief flashback snapped shut.

My stomach twists. *Beira, the Celtic queen of winter.* It's a memory from the Ravensthorpe tower. A new one, half-formed. I close my eyes, willing my brain to produce more, to tell me what happened. But rain patters on my head, and no more memories come.

Pulling on the plastic poncho I bought in Pamplona, I struggle to my feet. Five kilometres to go.

Two pilgrims in matching silver ponchos overtake me, looking like characters from *Star Wars*. Probably I do too. My poles tap the ground – a four-legged robot.

As I reach Mañeru, a dense cluster of houses, it's pelting

and my poncho is letting in rain. I'm focused on getting to the hostel. Getting dry, getting warm. A sign in the distance says *albergue*, but as I head towards it, I spot an alcove with a vending machine. It's sheltered in there and I can't resist the siren call of a hot drink.

Getting a coffee from the machine, I wrap my hands around the paper cup. As I drink it Theo and Dapple the donkey pass by, both heads bent against the rain. I call out, 'Hello', but he barely acknowledges me. In fact, he speeds up.

Putting my paper cup in the bin, I head out into the rain and soon reach the hostel. Inside, it's cosy and warm. I'm taking off my poncho when the warden rushes up.

'No, no. *Completo*.'

I stare at him. 'You're full?'

Behind him, Theo is taking off his boots. He doesn't even look guilty.

The warden gestures towards him. 'Last one.'

Damn. If I hadn't had that coffee. I want to throw a tantrum. My whole body's aching and now I've stopped, I'm shivering. Is Ethan here too? I scan the boots lined up in the foyer, but they all look the same. Thunder rumbles and the rain intensifies outside. I consult the track notes. The next town's three K, and I've already walked twenty-nine. I've never walked thirty-two kilometres in my life, but there's no point in crying. Pulling my poncho on, I head out.

Lightning flashes and thunder rolls across the hills as I plod through olive trees and vineyards towards a hill.

I jump at a loud crack as lighting forks down, striking a nearby rise. Lula's icy voice fills my head.

I am Beira. I cause thunder and storms.

I shiver, splashing through a puddle, poling with my heavy sticks, trying to outrun the storm. And Lula's voice. My leggings are soaked and rain seeps through my neckline. My poles stick in the mud at every step. My backpack gets heavier, and my boots rub my heels. Two pilgrims with feet encased in plastic bags walk past, the bags dragging in the mud. They look ridiculous, but what do I know?

At last, I reach the town, follow the yellow arrows through maze-like streets, and stumble into the *albergue*. Breathless, I tell the warden, a plump middle-aged woman in black, I've come all the way from Pamplona.

Unimpressed, she stamps my card and gestures towards the bunkroom. 'Jesus meditation is at eight p.m.'

Will I offend her if I say I'm not interested?

The bunkroom smells like twenty wet dogs are in residence. All the bottom bunks are claimed. There aren't many comforts on the Camino, so the convenience of not climbing up and down takes on significance. Late arrivals draw the short straw.

There's no sign of Ethan. He must be at the other *albergue*. We've fallen out of sync. What if I never see him again? I spy a wooden cross on a top bunk. *Jaz*. Is she taking a break from the others?

I'm collapsed on my bunk when the Australians arrive, their loud voices preceding them. There are about ten of them, and they overwhelm the bunkroom with their chatter and above-average size. It's time to get dinner.

I run through the rain to the store, where a glum shopkeeper drags himself away from the football on television. The rain washes over the church as I devour my empanadas under its overhanging roof. They're delicious, filled with spicy meat and beans.

All is quiet when I get back. The Jesus meditation, whatever that is, must be in progress. I expect Jaz is there. Sitting on the lone couch next to the window, I stretch out my legs. A stabbing pain runs up my calves, and I close my eyes. I've never felt so tired in my life. This had better be worth it.

'Tess.'

I jerk upright. Jaz is in front of me.

'Did you walk all the way here?' Her face is suspicious.

I rub my face. 'Of course. Pretty easy day. Thought you might have gone on further.' Should I tell her about the policewoman? No, that's my secret for now. 'Been to the Jesus meditation?'

'Yes.' Her voice is guarded.

'How was it?' I can't get used to the idea of Jaz as a believer, but I suppose Lula's death changed us all.

'The warden read out texts from the Bible and we contemplated them. The Australians had a lot to say.' Her voice is dry, she sounds more like the Jaz I knew. Running her hands through her hair, she sighs, and heads towards her bunk.

Climbing the ladder into my bunk, I slide my phone under the pillow. I'm trying to sleep when an argument erupts outside the window. It's the Australians. I only catch the odd word, *Jeremiah*, *transubstantiation*. There appears to be a religious difference of opinion. The argument fades and the group begin to sing 'Amazing Grace'. I put my earplugs in, but there's no getting away from it.

My phone goes *ting* and I pull it out. My heart leaps at the sender's name. I can hardly bear to look. It's her – Camryn Li, the editor of my favourite magazine, *Artemis*. Clenching my teeth, I tap on the message, my eyes squinting over the first sentence. My glasses are down on the ground, in my pack.

Dear Tess, we loved your pitch here at Artemis!

I bite my tongue. Don't let the next word be 'but' . . . I enlarge the text.

A contract is attached for your feature titled 'Moving on from Lula: Ethan Hill Seeks a Miracle on the Camino.' Hard deadline four weeks from now. Please confirm you can deliver on time; the advance must be repaid if your feature is late.

I re-read it, excitement rushing through my blood. *Yes, yes, yes.* Is this really happening? Tapping on the attachment, I check the bottom line – four hundred pounds. Two hundred now, and the same on delivery. Not bad. There won't be much left once I get my credit card out of debt, but this isn't about money. My eyes slide down to the final paragraph.

The core of this story is Lula Thornton's death. As this has been widely covered already, you will need to bring a fresh perspective. In particular, we will need Ethan's reflections on this, three years on. As you are no doubt aware, it is unusual for us to contract an untested writer, but I am sure your insider perspective will bring an exciting new angle to this story.

I stare at Camryn's message. I've got a contract with *Artemis*! I pull at my hair, my elation dying. But what if I can't find Ethan? What if he won't talk to me about Lula? What if he finds out I'm writing about him?

How do I find the dirt I need to make him pay for what happened to Mum?

Chapter 12

Mother-Daughter

Then

Last night's pizza box was still on the kitchen table. Stuffing a slice of Meat Lovers in my mouth, I gazed out the window at the dingy off-licence. An ambulance raced past, siren wailing. I'd only left Ravensthorpe a few months ago, but already it seemed a fantasy.

I slipped a gin miniature into the pocket of my puffer jacket. I'd hidden my stash behind the pile of books on the shelf. It was the one place Mum would never look.

She hadn't read a single book since I'd left Ravensthorpe. 'What's the point?' she'd said last night, her eyes glued to the TV. 'Novels are useless. They just remind me of what you're never going to be now.' Her voice was dull. It had been that way ever since I'd told her I wasn't going back to Ravensthorpe. All the life had drained out of her.

Mum was usually so exuberant. She dressed in colourful kaftans she bought at the market. When she went to work, she teased her dark mane into 80s-style hairdos and wore bright blue eyeshadow. She cooked exotic foods and did kickboxing and read at least three novels a week. So, to see her now . . . It was as if a butterfly had lost interest in flying.

I zipped up my puffer jacket over my waitressing uniform. 'Going to work, Mum,' I yelled towards her bedroom. I was on the lunch shift at *Alfredo's*.

She didn't reply.

The restaurant was hectic, and I was exhausted by the time I finished my shift. I didn't want to go home though. It was a Saturday, so Mum would be there after working the morning in the salon. She'd start up again. How I needed to go back to Ravensthorpe. How her dreams had been shattered. I felt bad enough as it was. I knew what it meant to her. Her own dreams, destroyed by my birth, had been transferred to me. And now I'd trashed them.

I wandered aimlessly through Farringdon, then down towards the Thames. Passing a Waterstones bookshop, I gazed in the window. Casey Palipana's book *Chocolate Bird* was there, stacked into a pyramid with a poster behind quoting Margaret Atwood – *a stunning feminist tale*.

My chest ached. That could have been me, but now it never would be. My muse had perished when I fled Ravensthorpe. I'd tried, but there was no reviving her. The thought of writing made my stomach churn. At the river, I sat on a bench overlooking the muddy water. Pulling up my hood, I sipped my gin as happy tourists wandered by. Only as night fell, did I head back home.

The smell hit me as soon as I walked in. *Alcohol*. My throat tightened. Mum was in front of the TV, sipping one

97

of my gin bottles. The others lay in a row beside her. Empty. Her hair was greasy, though she'd worked today, and she was wearing her grey tracksuit.

I'd never seen Mum drink before. She was a health nut. Hence the lack of lollies at my birthday party. 'Sobriety and kickboxing are the key to a healthy life,' she always said. 'I lived a crazy, self-destructive existence when I was young and stupid,' she'd told me when I was thirteen. 'I was an addict, and I ended up on the street because of it. But I haven't touched drink or drugs since you were born, Tess.'

Mum's eyes were red and unfocused. 'Found your stash. That's all books are good for, is it?' She tipped the last drop of gin into her mouth. 'I don't understand. Why did you leave Ravensthorpe? You had it all in front of you. All that opportunity and inspiration.'

I gritted my teeth. 'I told you. I couldn't get on with the other students. I didn't fit in.' I hadn't told her the details. It would break her heart.

'But it's what you're meant to do. You've worked so hard this year. You're a writer, Tess. You can't turn your back on that. I know what it's like, not to follow your passion, it eats away at you. It's a gnawing pain that never goes away.'

Guilt bit at my stomach. It was the first time Mum had acknowledged the true cost of birthing me, the way it had thwarted her dreams. But now, I felt a brief flare of doubt. Writing a novel was her dream, but was it still mine?

Standing up, she met my eyes. 'I've been saving my whole life for you to go to Ravensthorpe. You'll be famous one

98

day. A book with your name on it.' She touched my arm. 'Isn't that what you want?'

A weight settled on my shoulders. 'Of course I want that. But I can't have it.' I clenched my fists. 'I can't go back there. You don't know what it's like.'

Mum blinked. 'What happened there, love? Why won't you tell me?'

I couldn't. I just couldn't.

'Was it a boy?'

I shook my head, although it was partly that.

'Who's this boy you've been seeing? You've never told me.'

My stomach clenched. 'No one. It's over.' I hadn't told Mum about Ethan. She'd have crowed about it to her family. And she'd have wanted me to leverage the relationship, to get an introduction to Sebastian Hill. I didn't need the pressure. And given what happened I'd been right not to tell her. My mind flashed back to Ethan, to that night at Ravensthorpe, and what he'd done. My fingernails bit into my palms. And from that one crime of his, disaster had flowed.

'What's it all been for, then? This is my life, Tess.' Mum took my hands. 'Making you a success is my life, love.'

A wave of heat flooded my body, and I pulled my hands away. 'Your life? What about my life? Have you got any idea what it's like trying to live out your stupid fantasy? Do you know how hard it is to get published? To become an author? It was never what I wanted.' This wasn't true. I had wanted it. I'd wanted it more than anything. But I wanted to hurt her, so she'd leave me alone.

Mum's face paled. 'You don't mean that.'

'I do. You need to stop trying to live through me. I'm not a literary genius and I never will be.'

Our argument went on and on. All my hurt and rage bubbled over. I said things I didn't mean. Her ambitions for me were a trap. I needed to gnaw my way out even if I lost a limb in the process. 'It's over. I'm never writing again. Ever. I'm going out,' I yelled, stomping towards the door.

'Don't go, Tess,' she called after me, but I slammed the door behind me.

I headed down the road to the local pub. It was rammed of course, and I ran into people I knew from school. They'd never been friends, but my time at Ravensthorpe had cast a shimmer of coolness over me. They were all: *Where you been, Tess? We've missed you here in Deptford.*

There was a band playing, and it turned into a big night. I knew Mum would be trying to call me, but in my rush to escape, I'd left my phone behind. I'd go back and talk to her later. Make up. Tell her I was sorry. I just needed a break from thinking about Ravensthorpe. I didn't even hear the sirens go past the pub.

After the pub closed, I stumbled home. I'd expected Mum to be up, waiting for me, but she wasn't. Her bedroom door was open, but she wasn't there either. My stomach knotted. Where was she?

My phone was beside her lounge chair. It had about ten voice messages on it but before I could listen to them, someone knocked at the door. A chill spread down my spine as I saw the police officers' sombre faces. I held on to the door, swaying. Their words reached me in fits and starts. '. . . hit by a car.' A ringing noise filled my ears. '. . . crossing the road.'

The policewoman clutched my arm as my legs turned to jelly. *Had she been coming to look for me?*

'Not the driver's fault . . . rushed out.' Her voice was gentle.

One more word pierced the ringing in my ears.

'. . . dead.'

*

I wore a brightly coloured kaftan at Mum's funeral. That's the only thing I remember. Oh yes, and Kate Bush's 'Wuthering Heights' played over the speaker as her coffin went through the curtain.

It was so quiet in the flat without her laughter and chatter. Her workmates brought casseroles that lay uneaten in the fridge. I took the pills I'd been given and slept, waking only to cram takeaway pizza into my mouth.

I didn't understand it. Mum was upset, and she'd been drinking. She wasn't used to it. But it wasn't like her to be so careless. To rush across the road.

I returned to work after ten days. I needed the money, but I couldn't summon the necessary good cheer. There were complaints – who wants to be served by a crying waitress? After a couple of shifts, Alfredo took me aside.

'I am so sorry for your loss, Tess, but . . .' He gave a tired smile. 'Do you think you might find it easier to work in the kitchen for now?'

And so, I was demoted to dishwasher. Alfredo was right,

it was easier. No one cared if I sobbed into the sink while I washed the pots and pans. In a way, the job saved me. It got me out of the flat, where Mum's absence hit hardest. It was mindless work, but the physicality of it took me out of myself. It didn't matter if I hadn't slept, or if I was drunk, which I frequently was, I could scrub pots on autopilot. I asked Alfredo for more shifts. He saw how much I needed it, so he agreed.

The nights were the worst. Despite the racket from the street, the flat had a peculiar quietness. All the noise was sucked into the void of Mum's absence.

Every morning, I expected to find her there. Every morning, the warmth drained from me. She was gone. I'd pick up her yellow kaftan and hold it to my face, inhaling the scent of the patchouli oil she used to dab on her wrists.

One morning though, my head felt clearer when I woke. And when I pressed her kaftan to my face, I felt her there. It wasn't just her scent; it was more than that.

Revenge is a dish best served cold, said her voice in my head.

I sat up in bed. She was right. Ethan had ruined my life. Because of him, if indirectly, Mum had died. In a world where Ethan hadn't done what he did, I would still be at Ravensthorpe. Mum would still be alive. Everything would be perfect.

Are you going to let him carry on with his life as if nothing happened?

Chapter 13

Gothic Mystery

Now

The Australian group are singing 'Morning has Broken'. Odd choice at this time of night, but I suppose it's morning in Australia.

Clenching my phone, I re-read Camryn's message. She's waiting for my reply. This article is what I wanted. What I need. It's a gift. So why, now, do I feel this tremor of doubt?

Sitting up in my bunk, I stare down at Jaz's body under her sleeping bag. I'd like to talk to her about it. But I can't trust her, she'd probably tell Ethan. Maybe fresh air will help to clear my mind. Crawling down from my bunk, I walk through the lobby and open the outside door.

I can hear the singing, but I can't see the Australians. They must be around the corner. Lightning flickers in the distance and a sharp ozone smell hangs in the air. My fingers tingle.

I am Beira, I cause thunder and storms.

'Hello there.' A woman's voice emerges from the dark.

I yelp. *Lula?* My eyes adjust, and my stomach twists. Lula's ghost might have been preferable.

The policewoman is sitting on a bench against the stone wall, her red hair glowing in the dim streetlight. A small black notebook rests on her lap and she's holding a pen.

I take a deep breath, trying to slow my galloping heart. What the hell is she doing here? Is she taking notes about us? She has to be following us.

'Sorry if I scared you.' She flips her notebook shut, a practised one-handed motion.

Taking a step towards her, I drop onto the bench, keeping a safe distance between us. There's no point in trying to avoid her.

All conquering Lord, whom sinners adore, drifts towards us from the darkness.

I glance at the notebook in her hand. It's palm-sized, and spiral bound. Like the one she wrote in when she interviewed me at Ravensthorpe. I grit my teeth. Is it the same notebook? Does it have our interviews in it? I don't know how to act around her. What would someone who was innocent do?

A glow of lightning lights up the church tower opposite us. 'I've heard lightning is good for spiritual experiences,' she says in her lovely sing-song voice.

What? My mind skips to Lula again. *I am Beira.* There's an odd atmosphere in the air. The night, the singing. It does feel strangely . . . *Spiritual.* Whatever that means.

Drive Satan before thee, sing the Australians.

Her face turns towards me, and her green eyes meet mine. 'So, we meet again, Tess who keys cars on special occasions.'

I tighten my hands on the bench. 'I only did that once.' My voice comes out croaky and weak. I don't sound convincing.

Cast down the blasphemer . . .

'What brings you to the Camino?' It's a standard pilgrim question, but the way she says it sounds loaded.

I gaze at her, my pulse fluttering as I cycle through possible answers. *To get revenge. To find out what happened that night. To try to move on.* I choose the most innocuous reason. 'I'm writing an article.'

'What about?'

That Satan may feel . . .

Their taste in hymns is terrible. I hesitate. 'It's confidential.'

Lightning flickers and her face glows, moonlike. 'I'm good at keeping secrets. You know that.'

I think of the laneway. Her eyes on me as I scratched Ethan's car. She never reported me. Her presence is unsettling, but there's something about her that demands confession. It's like she's a deep well and my secrets will sink to the bottom. Do they learn that in the police? I need to give her something.

'I've been commissioned to write a feature. About Ethan. And how he's trying to find inspiration on the Camino to write his second book.' It's not the whole truth, but it will do.

Her hands tighten around her notebook, and she waits.

I feel compelled to fill the silence. 'I haven't told him though.'

She still doesn't speak.

I feel judged, though I shouldn't. He totally has it coming. 'Is that, um, illegal?'

'Not my area of expertise. He's a celebrity, isn't he? That changes things. Does he still have a right to privacy?' She pauses. 'It's not black and white. You'll have to work out the shades of grey for yourself.'

My brow wrinkles. *Not helpful.* Why am I even talking to her? She is not my ally. Most likely, she is the exact opposite. And Camryn is waiting for my reply. I stand to go, but then I hesitate. I need to find out why she's here. 'I don't remember your name. Or should I call you officer?'

'You can call me Nola. I'm not in the police anymore.'

This sounds like good news, but it's probably not. 'So, you're here in a . . .?'

'Private capacity.' Her voice has an edge.

What does that mean? Is she a private investigator? I glance at her notebook, wanting to snatch it off her. What does she have on us? I open and shut my mouth, then blurt it out. 'Are you following us?'

The Australians move on to the next hymn. *How great thou art . . .*

Nola's eyebrows flicker, but then her mouth twitches into a smile. 'No, I'm just walking the Camino. Like you.'

'Right.' *Like me.* What does that mean? 'Okay, well, *Buen Camino.*'

'See you down the trail.'

Not if I see her first. Sweat trickles down my back as I leave. I don't believe a word she says. Right now, though, the article is my top priority.

Back inside, I climb up to my bunk. *You'll have to work out the shades of grey for yourself.* Thanks, Nola.

It's Ethan's fault you had to leave Ravensthorpe, says Mum in my head. *You'd be a published author by now if you hadn't. I'll be so proud to see your writing in Artemis. It's not a novel, but it's a start. And he deserves it.*

She's right. What am I thinking? Of course I'm going to write the article. Taking a deep breath, I reply to Camryn's message. *Thank you! I'll deliver my feature by the due date.*

As the message disappears with a swoosh, a surge of exhilaration fires through me.

After three years of plotting and planning, the first stage of my revenge plan is finally in motion.

Chapter 14

Gothic Adventure

Then

As the months after Mum's death ticked over, I wondered if I would ever find the perfect revenge for Ethan's crime.

The Count of Monte Cristo waited twenty-four years to nail his tormentor, Mum's voice said in my head as I sat on the Tube on the way to work. *So, there's no hurry. We've got time to figure out the best plan of attack.*

We'd been so close, the two of us. People you love don't disappear. I knew she wasn't there, but the revenge plan made me feel like she was. In the flat. On the Tube. In the restaurant. And death had only focused her ambitions for me.

With Mum's help, I pondered and planned. My first ideas were pitiful.

'Should I send him scary letters demanding money? Or sign him up for scam email accounts?' I asked Mum's photo, which stood on my bedside table. Taken on her thirtieth birthday, seven years ago, she wore a full-length buttercup-yellow kaftan. The same kaftan which now swirled around my legs.

No, *The Count of Monte Cristo wouldn't have been satisfied with that,* said Mum. *You must become a huge success then snub him in public at a literary festival. Or buy a house next to his and ruin his life with wild parties.*

Death had made Mum impractical. I supposed that was only natural. 'There have to be some good revenge ideas in books,' I said.

Oh, yes, there are always good ideas in books.

On the Tube to and from work, I brushed up on the classics. Later, at home, pacing up and down in Mum's yellow kaftan, I discussed my findings. '*Great Expectations:* Make Ethan fall in love with a girl who will break his heart?'

Difficult.

'*Wuthering Heights:* Marry Ethan's brother and make his life a misery?'

Does he have a brother?

'I don't think so.' I gazed out the window as a police car roared past, siren wailing. 'What about *The Iliad*? I could gather an army and lay siege to Ethan's house?'

Mum gave a raucous chuckle. A shared vision always raises your spirits. *What about popular fiction?* Gone Girl: *Frame Ethan for murder?* And Then There Were None: *Invite Ethan to a remote island and kill him?* Girl with a Dragon Tattoo: *Tie Ethan down and tattoo his crime on his chest?*

'All tempting,' I said.

Bringing Ethan down is only one part of the revenge though. You need to become a successful writer too.

'I'm trying.' In the eighteen months since I'd fled Ravensthorpe, I'd queried over a hundred media outlets offering to work for free. This was the only strategy I'd come up with to kick-start my career. Writing fiction made my guts roil, but journalism sounded manageable. Exciting, even. So far though, my strategy wasn't working.

You'll be a waitress forever if you don't shake things up, said Mum.

The next day, something hideous happened. Something that blew my pathetic revenge fantasies out of the water. Ethan's debut novel came out and immediately rocketed straight to the top of the bestseller list. He hadn't even graduated from Ravensthorpe yet, but suddenly he was everywhere. On talk shows. On the side of buses. On posters in the Tube. Overnight, he became that rare beast – a literary celebrity. Every time I saw his face, or his book, nausea flushed through me. I tore down his book posters if there was no one around, turned off the TV when he came on, but it wasn't enough.

I was shopping in Tesco when it came to a head. The only route to the checkout was past a towering pile of his books topped with a poster of his face. He was wearing a black jumper and a seductive half-smile, like a cross between Brett Easton Ellis and Kurt Cobain. The queue was slow, and his blue eyes followed me the whole way. Gloating. Bile rose in my mouth. I drove my trolley into the book pile, sending it flying, and abandoning my shopping, fled Tesco with muttered apologies.

At home, I read through my revenge list. It was time for action. My eyes snagged on Agatha Christie's *And Then There Were None*. 'I know,' I said to Mum's photo. 'I'll dig up dirt on Ethan, and . . .' No, I wouldn't invite him to a remote island and kill him. A flush of elation raced through me. 'I'll write a tell-all article which will rocket me to journalistic fame and destroy his career.'

Fabulous idea, darling. Two birds. One stone.

The ironic part about this plan was that I already had plenty of dirt on Ethan. But that dirt would stick to me too. I needed something new.

*

Despite my fabulous idea, my revenge plan ticked over slowly. Another year of waitressing went by – I was back out the front serving customers, now my tears were under control. In my spare time, I staked out Ethan's house in Camden. I watched him go into Waitrose and come out with bottles of wine. I set a Google alert on my phone to track any mentions of his name in the press. And I created a fake identity to follow him on his socials. It was all useless.

Then I got that bizarre email from Iris inviting me to walk the Camino. It shook me up. Had it really been three years since Lula died? The others would have graduated from Ravensthorpe by now, and here I was, still waitressing while Ethan got away scot-free. I ignored the email though – why would I want to spend a month hiking with a bunch of random Ravensthorpians?

But then something strange happened. The day after

Iris's email, I followed Ethan as he caught the Tube to Chelsea and walked to the church where Lula's funeral had been held. I lurked in the laneway nearby, the one where I'd keyed his car. He was in there for ages.

The next week, he went again, and I noticed the sign outside the church advertising confession. So that's what he was up to. My spine prickled. What was he confessing? It was lucky for him priests were sworn to secrecy.

The week after, he'd just walked from the church back to the Tube when a bomb dropped on his socials. The words jumped out at me from my phone as I waited at the bus stop.

It's been over a year now since Darker Matters *came out, and as you know, I've been struggling with my second novel. I'm taking an inspiration break and going offline for a month. See you on the other side.*

Pushing my glasses onto my head, I rubbed my eyes. *Inspiration break. A month.* My fingers tingled. The timing of his post suggested it was connected to his church visit. The priest's words at the funeral came back to me. *A pilgrimage helped her. It might help you too.* Was he going to accept Iris's invitation? Walk the Camino in memory of Lula? If so, it would make a fantastic article. And what an opportunity to find some excellent dirt.

It was now two days until the Ravensthorpe pilgrimage started, and the walk took a month. It made sense. Spain was a long way to go on a hunch though. I needed more.

Next day, when I took up my position at the bus stop opposite Ethan's house, the curtains were drawn. It had a sleepy air. A tousle-haired newspaper boy cycled past.

'Hey, was the paper order for this house cancelled?' I called out. It was worth a shot. Maybe he got *The Paris Review* or *The New York Review of Books*.

The newspaper boy brought his bike to a wary standstill. Taking ten pounds out of my purse, I held it up.

The boy eyed the money. 'I can find out, back at the newsagent. But I'd want more than ten.' I pulled out another five, but he shook his head. 'Twenty.'

'Jesus. Inflation's been shocking since Brexit, hasn't it? Okay, here's my phone number.' I passed him a scrap of paper and the money.

'You're not going to rob it, are you?'

'You've got my name and number if I do.'

'Okay.' He tucked the bill in his jeans pocket. 'I get back there in about an hour.'

I sat at the bus stop, keeping watch on the house until my phone rang.

'Deliveries are cancelled for a month,' said the boy.

'Thanks. You're worth more money.' I hung up, gazing out at the street. It was looking good, but I needed more. *The priest.*

I got to the church in time for confession. *First time for everything.* Inside, it was quiet, and my footsteps echoed as I headed for the wooden confessional on the side. There was no one waiting. What did the priest do in there while he waited for a sinner to come along? Read a book? Write his sermons?

I'd seen enough movies to know the drill, so I slid into the vacant booth and, kneeling on the bench, put my face to the grill. I was a B-grade actor in a budget drama. The

113

absurdity appealed. 'Bless me, Father, for I have sinned. It has been a year since my last confession.'

'The Lord be in your heart and upon your lips . . .' The deep voice I recognised from the funeral echoed around the confessional. 'Amen.'

Silence fell. I wasn't sure what to do.

'Go ahead.'

My mind turned to Ravensthorpe. To Ethan. 'I have committed the sin of anger and resentment.'

'Do you repent?'

Not at all. 'Yes.'

'Is there anything else?'

I was under-prepared. An empty Mars Bar wrapper crackled in my pocket. 'I have also committed the sin of gluttony.' When I thought about it, hardly a day went by. 'Also impure thoughts, jealousy, and blasphemy.'

'Anything else?' The priest sounded unfazed, but weary.

'Drunkenness, lying, swearing.' A blue glow emerged through the grill. Was he checking his phone? I mentally checked through the seven deadly sins. 'Pride and sloth,' I added. 'That's all.' I had more sins, but I wasn't going to confess them.

The priest said a prayer concluding with, 'The Lord has put away all your sins.'

'Thank you.'

'Say an act of contrition and three Hail Marys.'

Was that all? I'd have sinned some more if I'd known forgiveness was so easy. 'I'll do that, but I'd like to do more. That's a lot of sinning when you put it all together, isn't it? Maybe I should do a pilgrimage to repent?'

'A pilgrimage could be helpful.'

'What pilgrimage do you recommend?'

'This isn't a travel agency.'

That was a bit unpriestly. I peered through the grille. Was he taking the piss? 'No helpful tips for a sinner like me?'

He sighed. 'The Camino, in Spain. It will take you one month. Plenty of time to repent.'

'Do you often recommend the Camino?'

'No, but as it happens, you're the second person I've encouraged to go there lately. I should get a commission. If there's nothing else?'

That was confirmation enough for me. 'Thank you, Father.'

'*Buen Camino, peregrina*,' he said as I left. 'Happy travels, pilgrim.'

Leaving the confessional, I walked out into the cemetery next to the church. Lula was cremated, but Catholic ashes were never scattered, that would smack of paganism. They must be interred. It wasn't hard to find the right spot – three years after her death, the memorial had fresh flowers. I walked over and surveyed the offerings. My eyes skipped over the notes from adoring fans and landed on a photograph. It was the photo from the Order of Service at Lula's funeral, but its colours were bright so it must have been new.

Lula was leaning against the main door at Ravensthorpe, wearing blue jeans and wellies. She was laughing into the camera like she'd been told the funniest joke in the world. I picked the photo up and turned it over. Someone had written in black pen on the back. *Life is changed, not ended. RIP, Anonymous.*

Interesting. Was *Anonymous* Ethan? He wouldn't want to leave his name, being a celebrity and all. Someone would probably souvenir it.

I caught the bus, my mind whirling. The Camino. I wouldn't get a better story.

At home, I had a shower and paced around the kitchen in Mum's kaftan. 'I can't believe it, this is perfect. *Perfect.* I'll pitch a feature about Ethan to *Artemis.* It's my favourite magazine. It would be a blast to write for them.'

I'm so proud of you, said Mum.

'It has to be inspirational, funny, or gut-wrenching. That's their thing.' I pulled at my hair. 'But inspirational isn't my style, and funny might not be achievable.'

Gut-wrenching, then?

'Yes. That, I can do. But it won't be just the readers whose guts I'll be wrenching. It will be Ethan's too.'

That's a good start, said Mum.

'What?'

Would writing an article be enough for The Count of Monte Cristo?

Chapter 15

Spy Versus Spy

Now

IF YOU WRONG US, SHALL WE NOT REVENGE?

The neat, black words are penned on the wrapper of a lollipop, which is poking up from between the strings of my walking boot. My breath catches as I recognise the quote. Shakespeare, *The Merchant of Venice*. I scan the boot room, but it's empty.

I lean closer. The writing looks the same as Lula's name in the visitor book back in Saint Jean. And now I think of it, the chalk words on the Roncesvalles Pass. *What do you fear?* My heart pounds. *Nola and her black notebook.* Is it her? Is she trying to unsettle me? Shake out a confession? Pulling the lollipop out, I throw it in the bin. She'll have to do better than that.

Sitting down, I pull on my boots, then reach for my poles. 'What the hell?' They were right next to my boots,

but they've vanished. My stomach clenches. *Pole thief.*
Lollipop messenger. Are they the same person? I scan the
boot room again, but no, the poles aren't there. What kind
of ratbag steals makeshift walking poles? I'll find that thief
and I'll teach them a lesson.

Or . . . if it turns out to be Nola, maybe I'll just find some
new poles.

As I set off, birds chirp from the bushes in a harmonious
way, and my tension dissipates. I have a contract to write
a feature. *Me, a feature writer!* I'm a successful journalist
with an advance on the way. More importantly, after three
years of licking my Ravensthorpe wounds, I'm fighting
back.

This cheerfulness lasts for an hour. Then my feet ache
and the pack pulls at my back. I won't have a feature if
I can't find Ethan. And if I do find him, I still won't have
a feature if he won't talk about Lula. *A fresh perspective*,
Camryn said. By the time I arrive in Lorca, six K later, I'm
grumpy and ravenous.

As I approach the café, I spot Jaz and her wooden cross
at a table outside. I come to a standstill. Propped on the
wall beside her are my poles. *Jaz is the dirty rotten pole
thief.* My mind whirls. Is she the lollipop messenger too?
Jaz looks up as, clenching my fists, I stride towards her,
ready for a showdown. I'm even looking forward to this.
A fight might clear the air. Crack that icy wall between us.

'Nice poles.' I point to them.

Jaz eyes the poles doubtfully. 'I found them at the last
albergue. They're a bit crooked.'

I put my hands on my hips. 'Why did you take them then?'

She frowns. 'I thought I'd try them out.' Realisation passes over her face in a red tide. 'Oh, no. Are they yours?'

'Duh.'

'Sorry. I thought I was last to leave the *albergue*.' Her face turns redder.

I glare at her. 'Did you leave something in my boot when you took my poles?'

She frowns. 'No. Why?'

'Never mind.' I lower my arms. Either she's not the lollipop messenger, or she's a good actor. What a pathetic fight. It didn't even touch the sides of my frustration about the way she's been blanking me.

Jaz gestures at an empty chair. 'There aren't any free tables inside.'

Dropping into the chair, I eye my poles. 'They are crooked, aren't they? You can keep them.'

'No, no, they're yours, I couldn't.'

The sun hits the table, and I enjoy its warmth on my legs. The waiter comes past, so I order a tortilla and coffee. I eye the cross, which rests on the wall beside my poles. 'You stole my poles, so you owe me. What's up with the cross?'

Jaz blushes. 'I'm . . . repenting.'

I stare at her. 'Repenting?'

'For what we did.'

I don't need to ask what she means.

Jaz sighs. 'I've been seeing that priest a bit. Lula's priest.' She catches my eye. 'Don't worry, I haven't told him what happened. But I read an article about a man who carried a cross around the world for fifty years after he killed

119

someone in a car accident. When Ethan said he was doing the Camino, it seemed like a sign.'

'Right.' My brow wrinkles.

'Besides, it will make a good story.'

That sounds more like the real reason. Like Ethan, Jaz is here for the story. 'So, you three have kept in touch, huh?'

'Not really. Things were never the same after . . .' She pauses. 'But when Ethan decided to do the pilgrimage, he asked me and Theo if we wanted to get the gang back togeth—' Jaz stops abruptly, her face turning pink. I was in the gang, but he hadn't invited me.

I let it pass. 'It's weird there's only us four here.' *And the policewoman.*

Jaz lifts her shoulders. 'Maybe everyone else was busy?'

'Or we were the only ones invited?'

Jaz frowns. 'But Iris sent the invitation to all the alumni.'

Iris, who is on a *soul-nourishing offline journey.* 'Supposedly.'

Jaz's brow wrinkles. 'What? You don't think she did?'

I lift my shoulders. 'It's just strange, that's all.' My mind returns to Nola, and the lollipop. *If you wrong us, shall we not revenge?* It's on the tip of my tongue to tell Jaz about Nola, but I don't. I'm not part of the gang; I have no reason to trust her. And once they know we're being followed anything could happen. I might end up in the firing line, like I was at Ravensthorpe.

'You still writing?' I ask Jaz.

'Trying. Nothing published. I'm hoping Ethan will give me an intro to his agent.'

'Have you asked?'

'Not yet. On the train, he was complaining about how now he's famous, people are always after him for stuff like that.' Jaz pauses. 'Ethan's a bit of an arse sometimes.'

'Maybe it's gone to his head. Didn't Stephen Fry post something amazing about his book?'

Jaz rolls her eyes. 'And Reese Witherspoon.'

'Who's his agent, anyway? Is it Ellery Eppis?' *Ellery Eppis*. The name is burnt into my memory. Ellery, past mentor to The Chosen Ones, is an enigmatic figure. The only way to approach the agency is through a personal introduction. The website has no contact details and little information, apart from a stellar list of clients.

'No. He's with Christie King. Apparently, she's very simpatico, as they say in America.'

'Nice for some.' My eyes move to the cross. 'Can I pick it up?'

Jaz nods.

I lift it. 'Whoa. It's heavier than my backpack. You'd better take the poles; you need them more than me.'

Jaz shakes her head. 'No, I'll manage.' She stands. 'Better get going. See you on the trail. *Buen Camino*.' She lifts her cross onto her shoulder, raises her hand, and walks on.

Is she whacky? Or heroic? I can't decide. She could still be the lollipop messenger, but at least we've started talking.

I've been keeping an eye out for Nola, but she hasn't shown up. I'll find out more about her. Pulling out my phone, I Google *Nola police* but nothing comes up. I try *Nola private investigator*, but that's also a dead end.

What's her surname? She must have introduced herself at Ravensthorpe. I ponder, but nothing comes to me. I'll ask next time I see her.

As I haul myself to my feet, my back spasms. I was getting used to the aching legs, but this is a whole new level of pain. Which part of my body will pack it in next?

As I hobble through undulating farmland, the spasm in my back morphs into stabbing. Pilgrims pass me with breezy *Buen Caminos*. A lycra-clad cyclist almost runs me off the track, but not without a *Buen Camino. Buen Camino, Buen Camino.*

I attach a sign to my pack saying I am a silent pilgrim, says Lula. *It stops the incessant* Buen Caminos.

Sounds like a plan.

Some hours later, I run into Jaz, leaning on a stone wall on the outskirts of a sprawling town and reading a paperback version of Lula's Camino memoir. '*Buen Camino.*'

'*Buen Camino.*'

I slump next to her. 'How far to Villamayor?' That's where Lula stayed, so most likely it's their destination.

Jaz studies her printed track notes. 'About eight kilometres.'

Two hours. Two hours of nursing my spasming back along the path. 'Is that where you guys are headed?'

'That's the plan.' Jaz flicks through Lula's book. 'Here's something to look forward to.'

I sigh. 'The only thing I'm looking forward to is lying down.'

'There's a wine fountain down the road.'

'Right,' I snort.

'No, really.' She reads from Lula's book. '*It's a monastery tradition, to give wine to pilgrims.*'

'What a great tradition.'

Jaz reads. '*I imagine wine spraying into the air, falling in ruby-red drops. I'll swim in it, spouting wine out of my mouth like an aging cupid.*' She meets my eyes. 'I can see Lula doing that, can't you?'

'Absolutely.' I haul myself up. 'Let's do it. It's a dream come true.'

Jaz and I walk through the town, then downhill towards vineyards. I keep up with her, breathing through the pain. Stone buildings appear in the distance. 'Is that it?'

She glances at me. 'You're psyched, huh?'

'Sure. What's not to love about a wine fountain?' We climb towards the buildings. And there it is. Not a gushing fountain, but two silver taps with a gate around them. The door, thankfully, is open. I try the taps. A slow trickle of red flows from one. 'Look, one's water and one's wine.'

'*Wine must only be drunk in moderation on site,*' says Jaz, reading from the sign beside the taps.

I snort, take out my hydration pack and hold it under the tap. 'I need this to get me to Villamayor.' I take a sip. It's not bad. I drink more.

'Wave at the camera.' Jaz points to a wall-mounted camera above the tap.

I wave gaily, taking another sip of wine as I do.

'It's a live webcam.'

I lower my wine-filled hydration pack out of sight. What if the wine fountain owners are checking up on me? Or, even worse, Camryn Li? *I'll be in touch soon to check on your progress*, she'd said. She obviously takes a hands-on approach. But no, she's a busy woman, she has better things to do than lurk around on webcams.

As we leave, Jaz gestures towards a pointed hill in the distance. 'That's Villamayor. See you there.'

The hill is so far away it's no bigger than a pimple. 'Is there anywhere before—' But she's gone.

My phone buzzes and I pull it out. It's a text from an unknown number.

Enjoying the wine?
Your friend,
Anonymous.

My heart jolts. I'm alone, but I feel watched. My eyes rise to the webcam. Someone's watching me. Someone who knows my number. It's not Camryn, I've got her number saved in my phone. I step away from the webcam's line of sight. My phone buzzes again.

How was the beer at the plaza in Pamplona?

Who saw me drinking beer with Ethan in Pamplona? The others don't have their phones, so that rules them out. Unless they're lying. Sweat trickles down my neck as I gaze along the track. Jaz has vanished.

Who are you? I reply.

My phone buzzes. *Someone who knows what you did.*

Chapter 16

Friends to Lovers

Then

Jaz and I were sipping peppermint tea on the couch in the Ravensthorpe common room when Ethan appeared, the day after the eighties gig. He had the puppy tucked against his chest and was dressed in faded black from head to toe.

My fingers tingled with the urge to touch him.

Beside me, Jaz straightened, flicking her eyes between me and Ethan. I bit my lip. Was this a bad idea inviting Ethan to join our critique group? Jaz hadn't been as pleased as I'd expected when I told her.

'Ethan Hill?' She mock-swooned, clutching her chest, and quoted Heathcliff. '*Remind my heart to beat.*'

She'd clearly known I was lying when I denied having a crush on him.

A boy hovered behind Ethan, and he waved him forwards. 'This is my friend, Theo.' It was the backflipping, wolf-tattoo guy, looking paler than usual. 'He had a big night, so go easy on him.'

They were an odd pair. Ethan, the quintessential arty author, and Theo, who seemed hypermasculine, an outdoorsy, team sports kind of guy. But he'd made it into Lula's masterclass, so there had to be more to him.

Theo and Ethan flopped onto two lounge chairs opposite us. We drank tea and chatted about books we liked. As Richie said, forming a critique group was an important decision. We all read short excerpts from our work. It went swimmingly, until our last reader, Theo, opened his notebook.

I couldn't get a grasp of his story, his characters spent most of their time arguing about words. And for some reason he read in an American accent.

'Matthew rises to his feet. "I'm doin' it, irregardless," he spits out.

'"Irregardless ain't no word," I snap back.

'He flips open the Webster's. "Hellfire, it's in here," he says with a sneer.'

I gazed at Theo when he finished, searching for a comment that would display my excellent critiquing skills. 'That's, um . . .' It was terrible, but it didn't matter. I wanted Ethan in our group. And if that meant taking Theo, it was a price I was prepared to pay. 'Very meta,' I said at last.

Theo tilted his head.

He wanted more? 'I mean, the way you reflect on the act of writing, while writing, it's . . . ironic.'

Theo smiled. 'I'm glad you picked up on that.'

Touching Jaz's leg, I blinked twice, our pre-arranged

signal. She gave me a blank look, paused for several long moments, then blinked back.

'So, what do you reckon?' I asked. 'You want to form a critique group with us?'

'Sure,' Ethan said. 'Let's do it.' If they'd had a signal, I'd missed it. His eyes met mine and heat spread from my head to my toes.

'So, we, uh, need a name for our group, right?' said Theo.

'How about The Booker Prize Winners?' Jaz's tone was arch.

Ethan's cheeks coloured. 'No way.' It was clear he didn't want to be reminded of his famous father.

I cast around for ideas. I wanted to impress him, make sure he didn't regret joining our group. In our last class, Lula had talked about the importance of writing from the core wound. She'd written the words on the board in capital letters.

THE CORE WOUND.

'It's a hidden splinter inside you that wriggles its way out,' she'd said. 'Your core wound is going to make its presence felt in your writing at some stage.'

It had felt ominous, the way she'd said it. As if we were all one step away from being felled by a repressed trauma.

'Forget all that stuff Iris goes on about.' Lula had grinned. 'Don't tell her I said that. *Word choices. Metaphors. Flowery writing*. That's window dressing. I care about story. You need to write with your heart, not your head.

Don't intellectualise, tap your deep emotions.' Her eyes had met mine as she said this.

Lula had also scoffed at Iris's directive to *write what you know*. 'You're too young, and not that interesting. Use your emotional truth, then make it up from there.'

Emotional truth. My mind flashed to what she'd said about my birthday party story. *Write it as if you hate her.*

Now, I cleared my throat. 'How about The Core Wounds?'

'Yeah. Good one.' Ethan adopted Lula's mellifluous tones. 'The dark heart of you will feed your writing.'

We all laughed, and I glowed inside.

'Cool.' Theo held up his hand. 'Here's to The Core Wounds.'

We all slapped it. 'To The Core Wounds.'

'May we mine our hidden splinters for gold,' said Jaz.

'Hey, it's my twentieth birthday tomorrow. You two should come along to my party,' Ethan said. 'It's down at the old barn, so we won't disturb the nerds.' The last weekly general meeting had decreed ten-thirty was quiet time in the main building.

The next night Jaz and I rocked up to the barn, a decrepit stone building on the grounds' outskirts, next to the ruined tower. The tower was an object of fascination to me. I'd been told it was the remains of an old Templar church, which added to its attraction. I'd developed a fleeting interest in Templars after watching the *Da Vinci Code*. I'd even visited Temple Church in London, which features in the movie, and seen the effigies of thirteenth-century Templar knights.

The tower at Ravensthorpe was kept locked. It was said to be unsafe, and possibly haunted. This gave it the irresistible allure of forbidden fruit. Jaz and I had often discussed how to get inside. As yet though, our plans had come to nothing.

I'd spent over an hour deciding what to wear. In the end, I'd gone with a flowing red dress, matched with a fake rose in my hair and red lipstick.

'Kate Bush singing "Wuthering Heights"?' Jaz asked when I came out of my room.

I nodded, and we sang a couple of lines from the song, twirling and collapsing into giggles at the end.

Inside the barn, hordes of overexcited partygoers milled around, yelling over the music. Some, I didn't recognise. They must have been from the village.

Ethan was looking very 1960s Carnaby Street in an orange vinyl jacket and tight yellow flares. Sparking with energy, he danced in the middle of the barn, accepting birthday hugs and kisses. The whole room revolved around him.

I came to a standstill. What was I thinking? This was Ethan Hill. Why would he be interested in me? But he waved us over to dance with him.

Jaz wormed her way into the centre, dancing sinuously with her hands held high. I bobbed around on the edge, feeling out of place. Jaz met my eyes and beckoned to me, but then, a warm hand grasped mine. My pulse leapt. It was Ethan.

He stuck to my side after that. We danced and drank the gin-laced punch, and chatted on the sagging couch, eating salt and vinegar crisps. He pulled a plastic bag from his pocket and shook a couple of colourful pills onto his hand.

'Want one?' He held his hand towards me.

I shook my head. I was wary of drugs; I'd heeded Mum's warning. Sure, I drank, everyone drank at Ravensthorpe. But drink and drugs were a bad combination.

Ethan threw a pill into his mouth, washing it down with a mouthful of punch. It didn't affect him much. He just became more relaxed, more smiley. I guessed he was used to it.

The more we talked, the more I liked him. It was surprising. There were two Ethans, it seemed – the extroverted public one, and the quieter private one, who I was getting now. Our background was so different, and yet we were on the same wavelength. And it didn't hurt he was devastatingly attractive.

'I worry I'll freak out once I get into the real world. This is kind of a utopia here, isn't it?' He gestured out at the barn, at the hordes of dancers.

Utopia was overstating it, but I nodded. Ravensthorpe was its own little world. A beautiful fantasy.

Somehow, we started telling primary school war stories.

'I was a total outcast in primary school,' he said. 'Everyone hated me.'

I stared at him. 'Hard to imagine.'

'It was a nightmare. I was this chubby, geeky kid who liked to read my poems out loud in class.' He laughed. 'I didn't know it wasn't cool.' He paused. 'I can't believe I just told you that. I never talk about it.'

'I'm glad you did.' I felt the story explained him, though I wasn't sure how at the time. It exposed a secret part of him, and it made me like him more. Was that what he'd seen in me? Someone who didn't fit in? Was his easy popularity all an act?

'Felicitations, birthday boy.'

Lula. I hadn't expected her here, at a student bash. She wore a loose flannelette shirt over a white T-shirt and looked not much older than the students. Her appearance created a ripple. Lula's new book might have been panned, but in the Ravensthorpe world she was a celebrity. The students watched her, while pretending not to.

Ethan stood up, and they gave each other a one-armed hug.

I couldn't imagine being on hugging terms with Lula.

'How's your old dad?' asked Lula.

Ethan's jaw tightened. 'Grouchy as ever.'

'Give him my best.' Lula gave Ethan a pat on the back and made her way towards the punch bowl.

A soft body nudged my feet. Zebra had been sleeping in a blanket-lined box under the couch, but now he'd staggered to his feet.

Picking the puppy up, Ethan planted a kiss on his furry face. 'If it wasn't for Tess, you'd be a pile of squashed fur now, wouldn't you, Zeb?'

Jaz was dancing with Lula now. She flashed her eyebrows at me over Lula's shoulder. *Wow*. I never would have had the guts to dance with Lula. I swallowed. They were so close together . . . It made me uncomfortable, but this was university, not school. And here at Ravensthorpe, the free-love sixties vibe still ruled. We were artists, after all. Different rules applied.

'Lula's charismatic, isn't she?' Ethan must have noticed my eyes on her.

I nodded. Lula compelled attention without trying.

'Sorry I'm not as fascinating.' Ethan nudged me with his shoulder.

I turned to him. Was he fishing for compliments? 'But you are.' It was more than true. I wanted him. I craved his touch. My heart raced as Ethan leant towards me. *Was he . . .? Were we . . .?*

His lips touched mine.

I closed my eyes, lost in the feeling. It was the best kiss I'd ever had. Though, to be honest, that wasn't saying much. My previous sexual history was dull and better forgotten. I wrapped my arms around him, feeling his body beneath his shirt. Not muscular, but strong. His fingers were soft on my cheek and his hair brushed my face.

It wasn't quite true to say I was lost in the feeling. Part of me floated above. *Look at me, Tess Brody kissing Sebastian Hill's son.* Now I was only two degrees separated from literary fame.

When I opened my eyes afterwards, my cheeks hot, Lula was gazing at me intently, speculation on her face, and Jaz had vanished.

Chapter 17

Ghost Story

Now

'Isn't this pilgrimage great?' Ree, the American woman, calls as I stumble into dinner.

'Yes, terrific.' I scan the room for Nola's red hair, but she's not here.

'If God had wanted us to stay in one place, he would have given us roots, right?' Ree

looks so fresh, her dark bob sleek, her lipstick freshly applied. She must be catching the bus.

With difficulty, I summon the lovely English girl. 'Absolutely.'

Ethan, Jaz and Theo are on the other side of the *albergue*'s dining room. It's atmospheric here, with stone walls and exposed beams, but it could be a dungeon for all I care. Head thumping, I shuffle towards them, trying to ignore the pain in my back.

'You look tired, Tess,' says Ethan.

I slump into a chair, suppressing a whimper. 'No, I'm fine. Pretty easy day.'

His mouth twitches. 'It was, wasn't it?'

There's a prayer before we eat, but it's worth it as the food is fresh and tasty. There's wine of course, but after my excessive intake at the wine fountain, I go easy. Is now a good time to raise the topic of Lula? I'm still screwing up my courage when Ethan leans forward.

'Did you see the old castle up on the hill? I'm heading up after dinner. You can get the key from the bar. Want to come?'

I stare at him. After the day we've had, he now wants to climb up to the castle?

He gazes back at me with a mock-innocent expression.

I grit my teeth. He's throwing down the gauntlet. This is so bloody typical of Ethan.

'I'm keen,' says Jaz.

'Count me out,' says Theo. 'I've seen castles before.'

*

The door to the abandoned castle is ajar as I finally hobble towards it. There's no sign of Jaz and Ethan; they've left me for dead. Cool shadows envelop me as I step into an antechamber, still puffing from the climb.

As I limp, footsore, along a narrow stone corridor, there's a bang behind me. Heart thumping, I turn. The door is closed now. Was that the wind? It wasn't windy a moment ago. Did someone close it? What if I can't get out? Only Ethan has the key, and the stone walls are so solid, no one would hear me if I yelled.

134

Walking back, I pull at the door. It doesn't budge. My stomach clenches as my mind darts to the text I received at the wine fountain. *Someone who knows what you did.* Has someone locked me in? Where are Ethan and Jaz? Have they left me here?

Taking a deep breath, I yank at the door, over and over. At last, with a creak, it opens. I breathe out, my muscles loosening as I peer outside. There's no one around. The air is dead calm now, but it must have been a gust of wind.

My eyes drop to the ground and unease roils in my stomach. In the soft dirt is a footprint. It's fresh, I haven't walked over it. There are two other sets of footprints beside it that look like Ethan's and Jaz's. So, this is someone else.

My mind flashes to the imprint of Lula's green wellies on the mud at Ravensthorpe. They had a distinctive tread – not the usual tyre-track, but circles made from studs. Like these ones. My skin prickles.

Did Nola sneak up and slam the door? Did she send the texts at the wine fountain too? Or was it Theo? I only have his word for it that he doesn't have a phone. And I wouldn't put it past him. He was keen to stay behind. I let out a breath. I'm probably overthinking this. It was the wind.

Turning away, I follow the shadowy stone corridor. I breathe easier as I emerge into a courtyard where Ethan and Jaz are perched on a wall. They're silent and relations seem tense. What have I missed?

Trying to ignore the pain in my back, I crawl up to join them. It's quite a view. To the west, a yellowish trail unfurls

135

like a ribbon, up and down hills, over flats, on and on into the distance. *The Camino*. My eyes trace its curves until it skirts beneath snow-capped mountains and vanishes over the horizon. There's a long, long way to go.

Until this moment, I hadn't registered what I'd signed up for. This is, what, day five? And I'm already a physical wreck. 'How far have we got left to go?' I hope I don't sound as desperate as I feel.

'About six hundred and fifty kilometres. Give or take.' Ethan puffs on a vape, looking out at the trail.

Six hundred and fifty kilometres. It doesn't sound like a distance humans are meant to walk. I imagine myself plodding along the rest of it, my whole body screaming with pain. It's not possible. I may as well give up now.

But what about revenge? cries Mum. *Would The Count of Monte Cristo give up now?*

I sigh. No, he most certainly would not.

Ethan's gold earring glints in the light. 'So, why are you carrying that cross around?' he asks Jaz. 'Religious reasons?'

'Nah. Not really.' She wraps her arms around her legs and her mouth twitches. 'Like I said, it'll make a good story. If I can ever get it published.' She glares at Ethan.

Ah. This explains the tense atmosphere. Did Ethan refuse to introduce her to his agent?

Jaz gestures towards the setting sun, her face golden in the light. 'Isn't that kind of magical though?'

The sun is sinking below the horizon now, its last rays lighting the Camino's path. It does look mystically inviting, a yellow-brick road.

'A blob of hot plasma disappearing over the horizon of

136

the third rock from the sun doesn't mean there's a God,' says Ethan.

Jaz presses her lips together and keeps her gaze fixed on the sun.

*

In the morning, I stumble downstairs from the bunkroom and head for the long wooden table where Jaz is having breakfast. As I try to sit, my back spasms and I sink to the bench with a yelp.

'Are you okay?' Jaz asks.

'No. I'm falling apart. It's that pack, it's done me in.' I swallow. 'I'm going to have to . . .'

Jaz stares at me.

'Pull the pin.'

Not good enough, Tess, says Lula. *You must let the Camino be your teacher.*

Shut up, Lula. Go haunt someone else. My body feels made of lead. What made me think I could do this?

'Would a donkey help?' Theo is at the next table; he was so quiet I hadn't noticed him. He gestures towards the window. Outside, Dapple is tethered to a tree, eating grass. 'You can borrow her for a while. Just to, uh, help you out?'

Why is he being so nice?

Theo eyes me. 'She's a good donkey.'

Dapple's head comes up and she meets my eyes. Her furry ears swivel in an endearing way. I remember her hot breath on my hand and her soft hair when I patted her. It's silly, but I felt a rapport.

A donkey. I won't have the pack on my back. And it's romantic – an animal companion. Didn't Jesus have a donkey? That's a whole lot of pilgrim cred right there. It's the perfect solution. So why do I feel so suspicious? Still, what choice do I have? 'Yes. I'd love to borrow your donkey. Thanks.'

Theo's face brightens. 'No prob.'

'My rellies in Ireland have donkeys,' Jaz says. 'Apparently they're good at sensing danger.'

I eye her. 'Hopefully I won't need that function.'

Ethan comes down the stairs and pauses at the door, pack on his back. He meets my eyes. 'See you at Los Arcos?'

Yes. It's the first time he's acknowledged we're in this together. My castle ascent was a test. I've shown him he can't shake me off. And with the donkey, I'll be unstoppable. I raise my hand, stifle a wince, and salute. 'Los Arcos.'

My excitement at becoming a donkey pilgrim soon wears off.

'Dapple,' Theo explains after breakfast, 'works to, like, union rules? Lunchtime is at least two hours. She won't carry you, only your bag. It fits in the panniers. She has to be well fed and housed and allowed to, uh, socialise with other donkeys. Also, you have to brush her coat and pick out her hooves every day. There's stuff for that in the panniers.' After delivering this news, Theo vanishes with a spring in his step.

With Dapple by my side, I arrive at Los Arcos a few hours after the others. It takes another hour to find a spot for her to spend the night, brush her coat, and pick the mud out her hooves. It's been helpful to have my pack carried, but I'm still in agony from my blisters and aching calves.

'Where's Theo?' I ask Ethan and Jaz at the *albergue*.

'Missing in action,' says Ethan.

A revelation hits. He's vanished so I can't return his donkey.

Chapter 18

Circle of Friends

Then

When the leaves on the oak trees drifted to the ground, Ethan and I moved our assignations from the forest to the bedroom. I floated through each day on a body-tingling sexed-up wave. I burned at his touch, but was this love? How could I separate my true feelings from the satisfaction of being Ethan Hill's girl?

My social status at Ravensthorpe soared. I even had my own posse. Jaz was still my best friend, but it wasn't just the two of us anymore. We hung out in a gang. At first, I felt bad about this, we'd been such a tight twosome, but she assured me she was fine with it.

'Why wouldn't I be?' She smiled brightly. 'I'm in with the in crowd. What's not to like?'

Ethan and I were an odd couple – our backgrounds were so different – but we worked. We enjoyed hanging out together – touring the countryside in his beloved vintage sports car, reading novels, scribbling in our notebooks, reading to each other from our work as we sat side by side in bed, laptops in front of us.

Ethan was writing an Ian McEwan-esque novel about a Scottish hermit obsessed with eradicating a crayfish which had invaded the lochs:

'As he disentangles himself from the knotted sheets, the sun sinks into the hills. Dropping his feet to the cold stone floor, he casts a glance at the map affixed to the wall. The scarlet pins have multiplied, creeping northward, a testament to the adversary's prowess.' He looked up from his laptop, his messy hair falling away from his face. 'Is it all right?'

He was always self-critical about his writing, which was strange, considering his background and talent.

'Brilliant.' I squeezed his hand. *How did I get this lucky?* Maybe, like Mum said, I really was special.

'No one ever criticises my writing,' said Ethan. 'Because of my father, I guess. But I can trust you to tell the truth, can't I?'

'Of course. When your writing is terrible, I won't hold back.'

He smiled. 'Good. That's what I like about you. You're authentic.'

I met his gaze. *Authentic.* Was that just another way of saying working class?

'And also . . .' His eyes flickered over my nightwear – an enormous T-shirt with Mickey Mouse on the front. 'I find Disney characters sexy as hell.'

My heart fluttered as he put his laptop aside and leant towards me for a kiss.

I was working hard too, but not on my birthday party story. *Write it like you hate her,* Lula had said, but how could I do that? I'd started a Margaret Atwood-inspired dystopian feminist thriller, instead.

Jaz appeared to have no interest in any Ravensthorpe guys. Or girls, for that matter. I'd quizzed her about Lula, after Ethan's party.

'I noticed you two dancing together.' I flashed my eyebrows. 'Anything happen there?'

'Tess!' She laughed, her cheeks pinkening. 'That would be totally inappropriate.'

'What about Theo?' He was good-looking, with the golden skin and dark eyes he'd inherited from his Italian mother. And they had swimming in common.

Jaz snorted. '*If he loved with all the powers of his puny being, he couldn't love as much in eighty years as I could in a day.*'

It was the ultimate *Wuthering Heights* put down.

*

'I'm not sure if I want to write, or have written,' I said as we lounged around in the common room drinking whiskey sours.

Our critique group had started a new project. *Drink like a writer*, we called it. We had made our way through F. Scott Fitzgerald (gin rickeys) Truman Capote (screwdrivers) and Jack Kerouac (margaritas).

Today, we were channelling Dorothy Parker. Jaz's choice. I was looking forward to Oscar Wilde's tipple of absinthe, myself. It was getting colder now, and the fire crackled in the fireplace.

'What's the difference?' asked Theo.

'It's not always enjoyable, but the end product will be worth it,' I said.

'Is it ever enjoyable?' said Ethan. 'I've never thought about doing anything else though. I suppose it's in my DNA.'

'Yeah, yeah, we all know about your fabulous writing DNA, mate,' said Theo.

Ethan's cheeks flushed. He and Theo were good friends, but they had a competitive edge.

All groups form their own dynamics. You sink into roles which can be hard to extricate yourself from later. In our group, Jaz and Ethan had become the designated brains, while Theo and I were the lightweights. When Jaz and Ethan fell into debates about science, politics or law, Theo and I rolled our eyes and teased them.

'We're the clowns, they're the sages,' I said.

Theo grinned, apparently accepting this classification with good grace. 'Go the clowns. Boo the sages.'

And yes, there were occasions when the possibility of another combination of lovers hovered in the air. But we knew it would never happen.

'When I write, everything fades away.' Jaz sipped her whiskey sour. 'It's the only time I feel at peace.'

For me this was only partly true. Writing could be like diving into a still, clear pool, or grappling with an angry, tentacled monster.

We took it in turns to read from our work. Jaz was

143

writing a novel about a girl who was obsessed with her teacher.

'*She gazed at him as he wrote on the whiteboard, imagining the classroom gone. The two of them, in a night club. Her hard plastic chair now a leather-topped bar stool; the ticking wall clock drowned by a thudding disco beat. Sweeping back her glossy hair, she accepted a cocktail from the livery-clad waiter as he leant towards her, his breath hot in her ear . . .*'

From there, things took a dark turn, as her protagonist's fantasy world leached into reality. Jaz had said she had issues at school. Did her story draw from her life? All writing did, of course, it was just a matter of degree.

'Hey, did you see Lula's new short story in *Granta*?' Theo's voice had a mischievous edge. 'It's a bit whacky.' His eyes flicked to me as he held out his phone.

Ethan, Jaz and I leant our heads together. The story was about a birthday party gone wrong and was strangely familiar. Written in Lula's signature style, it was an emotional deep dive. Bile rose in my throat as I read it. In the end, the protagonist, a gawky, socially awkward, working-class girl, kissed a popular upper-class boy. Afterwards, she smugly congratulated herself. She had it made.

'Funny story.' Ethan's attempt at lightness fell flat.

An awkward silence filled the room.

I handed Theo's phone back, my cheeks burning. I remembered Lula's eyes on me as I kissed Ethan at his birthday party. And the party in her story was so much like my own. There was even a cheese ball.

It was obviously me.

'Well, cheers.' Theo lifted his drink, and the conversation moved on.

I drained my whiskey sour, but it tasted like vinegar. Lula was a celebrated, award-winning writer. She didn't need to steal ideas from her students. Had I only imagined the similarities?

*

By November, frost crunched under my feet as I walked from my bedroom to the main building. The pond steamed as sun hit it and disconcerted ducks huddled on the edge.

The buzz in the corridors was all about which group would be chosen for Lula's winter retreat. We'd put in an application, with samples of our work.

We hadn't discussed the retreat much in our group. We didn't want to think about what would happen if we were chosen. How we'd be pitted against each other in a writerly version of *The Hunger Games*. Had Lula designed this whole process for her own amusement? Or, it occurred to me, as fodder for her writing.

My nineteenth birthday came around.

'Party time for my best girl,' Ethan said.

I didn't like being the centre of attention, but I went along with it. It was an excuse to let our hair down. Not that we needed one. Ethan liked to party, and I'd learnt to match him drink for drink. Despite his encouragement, I hadn't said yes to his packets of pills though.

'Are you ever going to cut loose?' he asked me the last time I turned him down.

'I don't need drugs to cut loose.'

He looked into my eyes. 'But I want you in the same headspace as me. We'll be able to connect at a deeper level.'

I laughed it off, distracting him with a kiss, but these arguments made me feel like a bore. I hadn't told Ethan about Mum, or my fear of addiction. In Ethan's world, risk-taking came without consequences. I'd seen what happened to kids at school who got into drugs though, and it didn't involve luxury rehab facilities. In my world, there was no soft lining.

A crowd showed up at the barn on the night of my party. I had no idea who half of them were. We'd styled it as a 1920s writers salon. Jaz and I found elbow-length gloves in the charity shop and the guys wore bow ties and slicked their hair back, Gatsby style. It wasn't exactly Gertrude Stein's salon in Paris, but a few students read poems or flash fiction.

After the readings, I wandered outside, drink in hand, to cool down. We'd lit the pot-belly stove in the barn, and it was practically tropical.

Lula joined me beside the barn. I'd got used to her turning up at student events, but to me she'd always be the intimidating tutor. Not to mention I now felt she was taking notes on everything I did.

'Nice dress.' She raised her glass.

I blushed. She'd never said anything personal to me before. I was grateful though. I was wearing a tight, blue velvet dress from the charity shop. It had a zip all the way down the front. When I'd looked in the mirror before I left, it was clinging in all the wrong places. I didn't have anything else suitable though, so I wore it anyway.

Lula wasn't in any hurry to mingle. We stood together, looking out at the forest, clouds of mist emerging from our mouths into the frigid air. An owl hooted as we traded witticisms, and I imagined telling Mum about it later. *Too wit, too woo. Look at you. Tess Brody chatting to a famous author.* Lula was so friendly I decided I'd misjudged her story. It was fiction, after all. Silence fell for a few moments.

'I see you, Tess.' Mist drifted from Lula's mouth.

My pulse jumped. 'What?'

'You and I are the same. You want success so much it hurts.' Her mouth twitched up on one side. 'Watch out, it's worse than heroin. Once you've tasted it, you'll do anything for another hit.'

I stared at her, unable to reply. Was she talking about herself, or me?

'That's why I chose you for my masterclass, you're hungry. But you're not trying.'

My stomach knotted. 'I am, I—'

She held up her hand. 'That birthday party story . . .' Her eyes met mine. 'There's something you're not saying. And until you do, your writing will be boring and weak.'

The breath rushed out of me. I felt like she'd hit me.

'We'd better circulate.' She winked. 'Don't want people talking about us.'

As we walked back inside the barn together, I almost ran into Jaz. Her cheeks flushed as her eyes flicked between me and Lula, and she turned sharply away.

Chapter 19

Betrayal

Now

The priest recites the service in Spanish. There's the usual standing and sitting. Some singing. The Australians join in with gusto.

The San Juan de Ortega church is cavernous, designed for hordes I expect they rarely see these days. I'm only here because Lula's book said they serve garlic soup afterwards. I'm starving.

When the pilgrims line up to take the wafers, Ethan joins the queue, kneels and accepts the wafer on his tongue. Is he allowed to do that? He's not a believer. Jaz and I are the only ones who abstain. It's odd, I'd have thought she'd be up there like a rat up a drainpipe.

Afterwards, the priest hangs a silver cross on a leather string around each of our necks. A souvenir. I'm next to Ethan as we go out the door. 'What happened to the garlic soup? It's the only reason I'm here.'

He gestures towards the monastery. 'Turns out it's on over there.'

'So, I sat through that mass for nothing?'

'I'm sure it did you good.' Ethan pauses. 'It's weird, but I'm finding it addictive. It helps not understanding Spanish, I can just imagine it's all terribly meaningful.'

Inside the monastery, we join Theo, who reappeared this afternoon, at a wooden table. The pungent garlicky aroma of soup fills the high-ceilinged room.

I finger my new cross. 'Why didn't you eat the wafer?' I ask Jaz.

She toys with her spoon. 'I can't.'

Ethan glances her way. 'You're not supposed to take communion if you're not in a state of grace, right?'

Jaz's face colours. 'I'll take it in Santiago. Once I've atoned.'

'Atoned?' says Theo. 'For what?'

'What do you think?' Jaz hisses.

My temples thump and the words burst from my mouth. 'Are we going to keep pretending it never happened?'

They stare at me, their eyes widening as my words reverberate like shock waves. It's as if I've smashed a glass on the floor.

I take a deep breath. 'I think about it all the time. About what we did.'

'I don't,' says Theo. 'I mean, it's not like we killed her.'

'Well,' says Ethan. 'Rather depends on your point of view, doesn't it?'

Theo snorts. 'You've got to admit, she was a jerk, the way she set us all against each other. That winter retreat . . .' He shakes his head.

I meet Theo's eyes. 'So, why are you here?'

He lifts his shoulders. 'Thought it would be cool to hang out with the old Core Wounds gang. Wasn't expecting you to show up, still, the more the merrier, I guess. Especially since no one else could make it.' He eyes me. 'So, uh, why are you really here?'

Heat rushes to my cheeks as I search for an answer that won't blow my cover. 'It's just . . . What happened at Ravensthorpe. I feel like we need to come to terms with it.'

Theo throws up his hands. 'We've all moved on.'

This is clearly untrue, but no one contradicts him.

We eat in an uneasy silence.

'Tomorrow's the last day before the *meseta*,' says Ethan eventually.

My stomach quivers. The *meseta* has become the main topic of pilgrim conversation lately.

It's a raised, flat, treeless plain, says Lula. *A wilderness of endless crop fields.*

'Pilgrims go crazy there, right?' Theo pushes his floppy hair off his forehead. 'It's an old Roman road, and it's hard and straight for one hundred and sixty kilometres. I've heard some people cry and refuse to go on.'

I gulp.

'Lula says it's the most spiritual part. It will make or break you,' says Jaz.

Theo snorts. 'Some people can't hack it. They catch a bus across the plain.'

I widen my eyes, as if catching a bus has never crossed my mind.

'The *meseta* is the place for miracles,' says Jaz.

'Yeah, I saw that graffiti too,' says Theo.

The *meseta* sounds like a performance review – one I'll almost certainly fail.

*

'God, were there two elephants fighting in there last night?' says a voice behind me as Dapple and I trudge through a stony olive grove.

The cool misty morning has turned to drizzle, and Dapple's head droops with displeasure. I've been doing my best to bond with her – long lunch breaks, frequent brushing and hoof-picking – but right now, she is unimpressed.

Jaz appears. 'Can you believe that snorer? I thought someone was operating an angle grinder next to my head.'

Dapple nudges Jaz with her nose and gazes dolefully at the rain.

'Oh, you poor darling. Donkeys hate rain. Here, I've got a spare poncho.' Jaz digs around in her backpack and produces a lightweight bit of yellow plastic. We arrange it over Dapple, tucking it into her harness and panniers.

Dapple eyes me dourly, as if to say *how did I get stuck with you?*

'Tess?' says Jaz as we walk on, rain trickling down our faces.

'Mm?'

'I'm sorry about what happened at Ravensthorpe. Between you and me, I mean.' Her cheeks pinken.

My stomach twists as I meet her gaze. I've wanted this so

151

much, for her to acknowledge what she did, but she's been acting so weird and cold, and now it feels like too little, too late. 'It was a long time ago.'

'I called you afterwards, so many times, but you never replied. I figured you were too angry to talk to me.'

'What?' I stop and stare at her. 'But it was you. I texted you. You never replied to my messages.'

Jaz's eyes widen. 'I texted you too, but it didn't go through. I thought you'd blocked my number.'

Those days after Ravensthorpe. . . I'd been so distraught, so desperate to talk to Jaz. Especially after Mum died. Had I got things mixed up?

Jaz meets my eyes. 'Maybe we got confused?'

I try to put the pieces together. How had that happened?

'Anyway, I'm sorry, I should have stood up for you at that meeting after Lula died. I wanted to tell you that later, after Lula's funeral. But you never came back. And I couldn't reach you.'

That meeting. It would have meant so much to have just one person on my side. Taking a deep breath, I let it go. 'It's okay.'

We walk on together in silence, serenaded by a chorus of unspoken words.

Jaz turns back to me. 'The phone . . . It's so strange we didn't get each other's messages. Do you think someone could have tampered with my phone, so I didn't get your calls?'

'What? Who would do that?'

'I don't know.' Jaz's brow wrinkles as we walk on.

Now, though, I can't let the idea go. She messaged me, I

messaged her, but somehow . . . 'Did you ever see anyone touching your phone?'

Jaz comes to a standstill. 'Now you say that . . . I did see Ethan pick it up once.'

My heart skips a beat. 'When?'

'Not long after you left.' Her eyes meet mine. 'He said he thought it was his, we've got the same model. So, I didn't think anything of it. But . . .'

I wait, an uneasy feeling in my stomach.

'There was something off about him, he looked nervous, like I'd caught him out.'

I stare at her. 'You think Ethan blocked my number in your phone?'

She grimaces. 'It would explain why I never got your messages.'

I frown. 'But why would he do that?'

Jaz meets my eyes. 'Maybe he didn't want us to get together and talk about what happened. What he did to you.'

My skin prickles. It makes a weird kind of sense.

'If I had my phone here, we might be able to figure it out, but . . .' Jaz lifts her shoulders.

We gaze at each other.

'I should have believed you back then.' Jaz touches my arm. 'I'm so sorry.' She seems about to say something else, but then she raises her hand. 'See you soon.' She strides away.

The rain patters on my head and the pulse thumps in my neck. *Ethan*. Jaz was the best friend I ever had. And we could have been friends all this time. Did Ethan deliberately ruin our friendship? Fists clenched around my poles, I follow Jaz up the trail.

If Ethan did that, he more than deserves what he has coming.

Chapter 20

Secret Identity

Ethan, Theo and Jaz are sheltering beneath a bridge outside Burgos. They are deep in conversation but fall silent as they see me.

Have I interrupted something? My chest tightens. Are Jaz and I friends again, or not? I don't meet Ethan's gaze. Did he block my number so I couldn't call Jaz?

Rain pattering on our heads, we wind our way through the narrow, cobbled streets, emerging into a plaza with Burgos Cathedral above us.

'Woah.' I look up, blinking away raindrops. The cathedral is strikingly gothic, all pointy spires and curlicues.

'Didn't stint on the spires, did they?' says Ethan.

'Reminds of me of that *Hunchback of Notre Dame* movie,' says Theo.

'Oh, yeah,' Jaz says. 'How cool was that epic fight scene on the roof?'

'You can go up on the roof of Santiago Cathedral,' says Ethan. 'We should do that.'

Santiago feels so far away it's hardly worth talking about.

A group of umbrella-carrying tourists approach. A ripple passes through them as they spot us, and they aim their cameras in our direction.

Ethan glares at them, his poncho hood pulled over his dripping hair. 'Look, darling, real pilgrims.'

'I've never been a tourist attraction before,' I say.

'It's not you, it's Dapple,' he says.

Dapple, it's true, looks very cute in her yellow raincoat. She enjoys the attention, lifting her head and pricking her ears.

The tourists come closer, following their cameras.

Ethan puts out his hand, palm upwards. 'Five Euros a picture. Ten with the donkey.' They lower their cameras and back away.

As we climb the stairs towards the *albergue*, I fall behind. Dapple is slow on stairs. The others are out of sight when my phone buzzes. The hairs lift on the back of my neck as I pull it out. It's the same number that texted me at the wine fountain. I've saved it in my phone as *Anonymous*. I shield my screen from the rain with my hand, my mouth turning dry as I read.

The cathedral's towering spires,
A grandeur they admire.
But they're oblivious to me,
And the darkness I inspire.

As I stare at the words, my phone buzzes again.

Do you like my poem? Not bad for a quick effort, is it?
xx Anonymous.

Jaw clenched, I scan the square. The last time Anonymous texted me I was under the webcam at the wine fountain . . . Is there a webcam here too? *Camino webcams*, I type into my phone. It appears there are over ten webcams along the Camino, and yes, there's one next to Burgos Cathedral. I inspect the surrounding buildings but can't find it. I raise a middle finger to my anonymous messenger anyway.

Who's doing this? If they're trying to freak me out, it's working. The creepiest thing is, they could be anywhere. In front of a computer screen in another country. Or – I gaze towards the stairs where the others have vanished – close by. I picture the three of them huddled under the bridge. Is it one of them?

*

The *albergue* is spacious and modern, with a lift to its four floors. The warden tells me there's a stable for Dapple a few streets away. I settle her in and return, draping my wet clothes over the heater next to the others.

'Any of you guys write poetry?' I ask, casually, as we head down in the lift to the kitchen.

They shake their heads.

'Fat chance,' says Theo.

'Wouldn't know where to begin,' says Jaz. 'Why? Do you?'

157

'No. Just wondered.' Something occurs to me. 'Iris is a poet, isn't she?'

'Yeah, she's pretty good,' says Ethan.

I wouldn't call my watcher's poem good, but it was written quickly, so points for that. Iris is allegedly in a *serene offline world*. But who knows?

'Wonder what happened to her,' says Theo.

'I know, so weird,' says Jaz. 'She could still turn up I guess.'

Again, I think of them under the bridge, and I don't mention Iris's autoreply.

'So, the *meseta* tomorrow,' Theo says in an ominous voice. 'Everyone's going to go *loco*, huh?'

'As long as it's not us.' I'm feeling strong, my blisters have healed, and Dapple and I are getting along fine. Well, mostly fine. Apart from my anonymous stalker poet, there's no reason at all why things shouldn't go to plan.

*

I wake in the dark feeling uneasy. Jaz is asleep on the opposite bunk. I crane my neck. The top bunk is empty. Ethan isn't there. Half an hour later, he still isn't there. What the hell is he up to? I need to keep tabs on him if I want to write this story.

Padding down the row of bunks, I catch the lift to the ground floor. The lounge room is empty. It's midnight and pilgrims go to bed early. Did Ethan go out? I try the front door, but it's locked. So, Ethan's locked out until morning. What's he up to out there? I'm awake now, so I head for the kitchen. A cup of tea might help calm me down.

My pulse leaps as I walk through the kitchen door. A woman is standing near the kettle with her back to me. *Short red hair. Long legs in black hiking trousers. Nola.* My mind flashes to the poem. This can't be a coincidence. I'm backing away when she turns.

'Cup of tea?' She's holding two cups in her hands.

The hairs prickle on my arms. 'How did you know I was coming?'

She lifts her shoulders. 'Saw you go past a minute ago.'

Her notebook presses against the pocket of her hiking trousers. Is it full of sinister poetry?

Jaw clenched, I hold out my hand for the tea. I have to get more out of her this time. Find out why she's here. Pulling up two stools, we sit side by side at the breakfast bar that runs along the window. Our reflections hover, ghostlike, against the cathedral's dark peaks.

I turn to face her. 'Why did you leave the police?'

'Oh.' Nola sips her tea. 'Jump right in there, huh?'

'I didn't think small talk was your thing.'

'You're right. It's not.' She pauses. 'PTSD.'

I stare at her, my mind ticking over. *Post-traumatic stress.* Was that anything to do with Lula? 'What happened?'

'There was an incident. It didn't end well.' She presses her lips together. 'I thought walking the Camino might help, so here I am.'

I open my mouth for a follow-up question, but she puts up her hand.

'Don't want to talk about it.'

I change tack. 'I've forgotten your last name.'

She meets my eyes in the window. 'Have you now? I

159

did such a good job of introducing myself at Ravensthorpe too.'

My heart races at the mention of Ravensthorpe.

'Does PC Kelly ring any bells? So, what are you up to, Tess? Roaming around at night again?' She lifts her eyebrows. 'Guilty conscience?'

My spine tingles, but I ignore her dig, waving my arm towards the door. 'Ethan's out. If he doesn't come back . . .'

'You won't be able to write your article?'

'No.' What's he up to out there?

Nola meets my eyes. 'That's not the only thing keeping you awake though, is it?'

I swallow, and don't reply, turning back to the glass to gaze at her pale reflection. She must be the sinister poet. 'Do you write poetry?'

'Of course.' She gives a half-smile. 'Have you ever met an Irish person who doesn't? We were the first poets in Europe and all.' Draining her tea, she pushes her stool back and slides her long legs to the floor. 'I'm going to get some sleep. See you down the track.'

'Wait.' My hands clench my mug. 'You didn't answer my question last time. Are you following us?'

Nola meets my eyes. 'Oh, come on, Tess. I've already told you why I'm here.' She walks away.

I still think she's following us. I twist my hair around my fingers as her reflection vanishes into the darkness. Pulling out my phone, I Google *Nola Kelly* combined with *police* and *private investigator*. Strangely, there's still nothing. What am I going to do about her? Should I tell the others?

I picture them gazing at me from under the bridge. They

were talking about me. I'm sure of it. No. Once they all know about Nola, I'll lose my advantage. I need to figure out her angle first.

*

The night passes restlessly. I'm unsettled after talking to Nola, but right now she's not my main concern. I stare at the bunk above me. What if Ethan's bailed? How will I write my article then?

Rustling plastic bags signal morning. Running downstairs, I pace up and down next to the front door until the warden arrives to unlock it. Pulling the heavy wooden door, I step out. Relief washes through me. Ethan is curled up on the paving under an overhang. Rain patters on the cobblestones beside him. He's sleeping, though I don't know how he can, on bare stone.

Early-rising pilgrims stream out the door. I've never been awake for this mass exodus before.

Ethan groans as they march past him, opens his eyes, and sits up, his hair a tangled mess. His eyes are glazed, and his cheeks pale. He looks spaced out. 'What?' He meets my gaze.

I lift my shoulders. 'Just wondered where you'd got to.'

Neither Ethan nor I are in a fit state for walking, but the *albergue* evicts us at eight-thirty. Theo and Jaz have already left. The rain eases as we make our way through the narrow streets. On the outskirts of Burgos, we run into roadworks, and tramp through mud, past noisy bulldozers. In my sleep-deprived state, it's torture. Ethan must feel worse than me, but he appears stoic.

161

I pull my boot out of a sticky patch of mud. 'Guess the old pilgrims didn't have to put up with roadworks.'

Ethan gazes at me wordlessly.

'Just roaming bandits and the plague. They had it easy, ay?'

Ethan sighs. Clearly, he'd rather be anywhere else than here.

I should shut up. Today is only about survival. My legs ache as we head towards a high, green plateau. 'Is that the *meseta*?'

Ethan gazes at the plateau.

'Doesn't look so bad. But that's what people say in movies before things turn to shit.'

Ethan rolls his eyes. I want to ask him what he got up to last night, but I suspect it won't get me anywhere.

We climb onto the plateau and stop in a village for lunch. Ethan has a coffee and vapes. I have a *boccadillo* and my now-habitual glass of wine. It helps me through the day.

Ethan eyes the wine as I sip it.

'What?'

He nods at my glass. 'Alcohol is a drug too, you know.'

I clench my jaw. He's not bringing up our old Ravensthorpe argument, is he? 'What did you take last night, anyway?'

'None of your business.' He drains his coffee, stands, and strides through fields of wheat into the distance.

Dapple, who's grazing nearby, gives me a *don't even think about it* look. Donkey lunch rules are not negotiable. My wine's half-drunk, but I push it away. I don't have a problem with drink, and Ethan certainly can't talk, but still.

My eyelids droop.

*

I wake with a start, my heart pounding. *The tower, the snow, the wind. You can run, but you can't hide.* It was just a dream, but it had the vivid quality of a flashback. If only I could remember what happened after that.

'Let's go, Dapple.'

Dapple raises her head from the grass, and we set forth at a snail's pace.

A man carrying only a bulging plastic shopping bag in each hand overtakes. We give each other the old *Buen Camino* as he strides by. Is he planning to carry those bags right across the Camino?

The track rolls on and on. There are pilgrims in the distance, but Dapple and I are alone. As I tramp through monotonous fields of wheat, my mind wanders. A memory comes to me – Jaz and I swimming in the Ravensthorpe pond at midnight. Falling asleep and waking to the honk of geese. *Jaz's hair on the grass. The smell of damp earth.*

Dapple snorts a spray of mucus onto my neck, pulling me back to the present. It must be the walking that's stirring up these memories. I haven't thought about that day for ages.

My nails bite into my palms as I gaze out at the wheat fields. Would Jaz and I have been friends all these years if someone hadn't blocked our calls? Was it Ethan?

*

In the heat of the afternoon, I flop onto a bench beside the trail. Staring out at the fields, I picture the Ravensthorpe tower. *You can run but you can't hide.* Are the memories I have during the flashbacks real or imagined? The Lula of my visions uses platitudes in a way she never did in life. Does that mean it's all invented? Does my mind create a false memory along with the rippling walls?

I don't know exactly what happened the night Lula died. I need to sort it all out in my head. If I can't figure things out, here on the Camino, I never will. I'm here for revenge, and to restart my life, but my Ravensthorpe memories are like a thicket of brambles in my path. Happiness lies somewhere beyond their thorny embrace.

As Dapple breathes down my neck, a new idea strikes me. The best way to process my thoughts is to write. What if I work my way up to it? To the night it happened. If I write a Ravensthorpe memoir, will I untangle the truth along the way? It might help me to make a start on my article too.

Taking a deep breath, I pull my laptop out of Dapple's pannier. A nervous patter fills my chest.

Am I ready to confront my past?

Chapter 21

Haunted House

Then

'Let's get on with it.' Flames flickered on Lula's thick, brown hair.

Three critique groups huddled in the common room, everyone avoiding each other's eyes.

Ethan was beside me, his white-knuckled hand on my leg. He had the Hill name to live up to, after all. *Imagine*, the shame of not being chosen. Theo and Jaz kept their eyes on Lula. I felt numb, it was best not to expect too much.

Clearing her throat, Lula pulled a scrap of paper from her pocket. This was theatrical; there was only one group name for her to remember. 'First up, if you're not successful, don't be discouraged. Rejection is part of the writer's lot, so take it as a life lesson and move on.' She glanced down at her paper, increasing suspense.

Jaz gave me a quick eyeroll.

I returned a tense smile.

'The group attending the winter retreat is . . . The Core Wounds.'

Ethan's face loosened with relief, and he unclenched his hand from my leg.

Jaz squealed.

Theo bumped fists with Ethan.

I gave Jaz a thumbs-up, but the joy wouldn't come. I was an imposter, dragged along on Jaz and Ethan's coattails.

'Well done. We have some hard work ahead of us. This is where the real journey starts.' Lula nodded at us, turned, and strode out the door.

I sensed the other students' eyes on us. Low murmurs filled the room, and I heard Ethan's name. Everyone knew Lula and his father were friends. Sebastian Hill had written a glowing cover quote for Lula's latest book. Had Lula now returned the favour?

Ethan's face pinkened.

I squeezed his hand. I knew how hard he was trying to get out from under his father's shadow.

'Stuff 'em,' said Jaz in a low voice. 'We won that fair and square. It's going to be amazing. Go us.' She put up her hand and we all slapped it.

I forced my mouth into a smile. So, we'd got into the retreat. The stakes were higher now. With Lula, no sooner did you clear one obstacle than another arose. We'd reached the next level, and this time we'd be pitted against each other. Who would be The Chosen One?

*

The winter retreat took place in the week before Christmas. The mornings were foggy now, and the path slippery with ice. The trees at the meadow's end had lost their leaves, laying bare the ruined tower's grey stone. I had to pile on layers of clothes to walk from my accommodation block to the main building.

Ethan complained about it when he slept over. 'Why don't we stay in my room while it's cold?'

Ethan had a room in the main building. It was spacious, with its own fireplace and a separate study area with a desk. Compared to my room in the newer accommodation block, it was luxurious.

'I like being in my own space,' I said. 'And the walk past the pond in the cold gets my brain started.'

Ravensthorpe felt spooky with only the five of us there. The other students had gone home for the two-week holiday. As my footsteps echoed in the empty corridor, stories about the Ravensthorpe ghost whispered in my head.

I felt a cold blast, like an icy wind blowing, but it was the middle of summer.

I heard a scream in the corridor but there was no one there.

I saw a man in the meadow dressed in white robes with a red cross on the front. He walked straight through the wall of the ruin.

I'd poo-pooed these stories. Now though, in the deserted corridor, I quickened my pace. I didn't want to run into a ghostly Templar knight.

When we gathered around the common room fire, Theo, Jaz and Ethan were as nervous as me. We had no idea what to expect.

We'd cornered two members of last year's winter retreat group, but they'd been tight-lipped about what happened there. Their eyes had flickered between each other uneasily when we'd asked them how it went. It took them a long time to reply.

'It's . . . intense,' Elise, a small, dark-haired girl had murmured.

'It's probably better to go in blind?' said her friend, Toby, a thin boy with a shock of red hair.

'Just try to, um, keep your head together.' Elise paused. 'Felix was The Chosen One if you're wondering.'

Toby snorted. 'He's too *special* to hang out with the likes of us now.'

'Who else was in your group?' asked Jaz. 'There were four of you, right?'

Elise swallowed. 'Rafi, but . . . he left after the retreat.'

'Why?' I asked.

She bit her lip. 'We can't talk about it. It's personal. He . . . he won't be coming back.' Naturally, this conversation did nothing to improve our confidence.

The door to the common room opened, and Lula wheeled in a whiteboard. Without acknowledging us, she picked up a black marker and wrote on it, her squeaking pen making me wince. *What do you fear?*

A chill ran up my spine.

'This is going to be our focus for the week.' Lula met our eyes, one by one. 'The best writing comes from a deep, deep place.'

'The core wound,' Jaz said.

My eyes flicked to her. She was always so eager to impress Lula. I suppose we all were though.

Lula nodded. 'Correct. When people read, they're not looking for the shallow banalities of everyday interactions. They are looking for the real, unvarnished story. The truth. So, we are going to delve deep to find the splinter that will feed your writing.' Lula tapped at the whiteboard. 'What do you fear?'

I tucked my sweaty hands beneath my legs.

Lula pointed at Theo. 'Theo, what do you fear? Start by saying, *I fear*.'

Theo swallowed, his Adam's apple bobbing in his throat. 'I fear people will realise I'm, uh, not as clever as them.'

Lula's eyebrows twitched, but she didn't comment, just pointed at Ethan.

Ethan hesitated. 'I fear people will discover I'm not a patch on my father.' His voice was croaky.

'Tess?'

A lump filled my throat. 'I fear I'm going to be exposed as someone with no original ideas.' This was true, but it wasn't what I feared most. I feared letting Mum down, crushing her dreams. Was everyone keeping their worst fear in reserve?

'Jaz?'

'I fear . . .' Jaz stopped and took a deep breath. Her face was frozen. 'I fear I'm broken, and I'll never be whole.'

The room went quiet.

Lula nodded. 'Excellent. Put it into the work.' If this was a competition, Jaz had won that round.

I gazed at Jaz. *Broken*. What did she mean? I'd come into her room one morning and seen her swallowing a white pill. Her cheeks had pinkened and she'd grimaced. 'Happy pills. They keep me on the level. Let's go.' It was clear she didn't want to talk about it. I guess we all had our means of coping.

Lula picked up her notebook – an old Moleskine with a faded brown cover. Opening at a dog-leafed page, she read. '*The sadness will last forever*.' Closing the book, she looked up. 'Any idea who said that?'

'Weren't they the last words of Vincent Van Gogh?' asked Jaz.

'Correct. Van Gogh knew how to explore the wound. Great art requires sacrifice.' Lula tapped the board. 'Whenever you're short of inspiration, ask yourself this. What do you fear?'

*

As the week went on, we alternated between discussion and sharing our writing.

Ethan read out a short story about a boy who found a dog with a litter of puppies under his house:

'*He gave her food and covertly shifted boxes to obscure her litter from his father. However, one day when he returned from school, the mother dog was pacing back and forth outside the house, emitting anguished cries. Her litter had vanished.*'

Suspecting his father, the boy took revenge, masterminding a series of spooky events. The last of these, a puppy haunting, drove his father from the house. When Ethan finished reading, he took a deep breath and shut his laptop.

'Very Cormac McCarthy,' said Theo.

Ethan's cheeks coloured, and he reached down to pat Zebra who lay at his feet. The puppy was four months old now and growing into himself. At Ethan's touch, he thumped his tail.

'There's a lot going on under the surface in that story.' Lula smiled. 'Good job exploring the wound, Ethan.'

Ethan's mouth twitched, and he looked away.

I shared part of my feminist dystopian story.

'*The scent of fear mingled with the stench of decay in the dimly lit corridor of the Warden's Tower. Mara traced her fingers along the cold, stone walls. With each meeting of the Resistance her resolve had—*'

'Stop,' Lula snapped. 'Enough.'

My stomach twisted as I looked up. Ethan squeezed my hand. We all knew what it was like to be the object of Lula's disdain.

'What makes you think this is interesting to others?' Lula's voice was cold. 'If you can't do better than that, you may as well drop out now, Tess. I've told you what you should be writing about. You're tiptoeing around it. Find the truth in your work. Dig deeper.'

I pressed my fingernails into my palms, thinking of what she'd said at my birthday party. *There's something you're not saying. And until you do, your writing will be boring and weak.*

Lula walked to the white board and wrote on it. *I am out with lanterns, looking for myself.* 'Who said that?'

'Emily Dickinson.' Jaz got in first again.

'And what does it mean?'

There was a moment of silence, then I took a breath. 'You need to shine a light into dark places to find your truth?'

Lula nodded, then clapped her hands together. 'Okay, begone. All of you, go and hold a lantern to your darkest places.'

*

Up in the library, I opened my birthday party story and read through it. Lula's words rung in my head. *If you can't do better than that, you may as well drop out now.* My chest tightened, and I took a deep breath. *I am out with lanterns . . .*

I wrote and wrote, through the night. Dropping the pretence that this was fiction, I wrote it as memoir. *Delve deep to find the splinter that will feed your writing . . .* It was painful, this writing, like peeling off layers of skin. But the lure of being The Chosen One kept me there, kept me digging deeper. If I shared my deepest scars, would Lula notice me? Is that what she was looking for? Someone with wounds?

I fell asleep on the library couch, and woke in the morning curled in foetal position, my neck muscles tight. As I got to my feet and stretched, feet pattered on the stairs outside. Opening the library door, I peered out.

Jaz was running down the spiral staircase to the ground floor. Her short hair was fluffed up around her head, as if she'd just got out of bed. Where had she been? Her bedroom was in the outside accommodation block, like mine. Theo and Ethan had rooms in this building though. I lifted my gaze to the spiral staircase. *And Lula.* My scalp prickled, unease running through me.

I felt like we were all in a pressure cooker, and it was bound to explode.

Chapter 22

Unreliable Narrator

Now

Two wizened old men examine me as I limp past. I know what they're thinking. *There's no way she's going to make it.* My first *meseta* town has a down-at-heel vibe. Apart from the men perched on chairs in the sun, the stone-walled main street is empty.

Ethan and Jaz are in the *albergue's* red-dirt courtyard, drinking red wine. It's the first time I've seen Jaz drinking on this trip. The *meseta* must be getting to her. I remove Dapple's panniers. As usual, this is the signal for her to fling herself down and roll on the lone patch of grass at the edge of the dusty courtyard.

'She loves doing that.' Jaz looks like a Botticelli angel, her lips stained from the wine, as if she's eaten red lollipops.

'So, first day on the *meseta*.' Ethan seems to have

forgotten our terse lunchtime exchange about drugs and alcohol. 'Anyone cracking up? Any epiphanies?'

The honk of geese. The smell of damp earth. Jaz. You can run, but you can't hide. My newly started Ravensthorpe memoir. I don't want to share any of this though.

Jaz gets a faraway look. 'It's very spiritual.'

Ethan eyes her intently. 'In what way?'

'The wilderness. The space.' Jaz waves her wine glass. 'It goes on forever. I looked out, and I felt . . . so alone.'

Wilderness. Space. The *meseta* isn't exactly the Kalahari Desert. It's just a gruelling slog through flat, shadeless fields. I suppose there is something meditative about the monotony though.

Jaz doesn't notice my quizzical gaze. 'It's like Lula says, this is the true Camino now. It's austere. It teaches humility.'

Theo appears, sunburnt and weary-looking, his black hair dusty. He strides over to our table, his eyebrows drawn. 'Have you seen her?' His voice is low and urgent.

'Who?' says Jaz.

My hand tightens around my wine glass.

Theo drops into a seat. 'The bloody policewoman.'

Jaz's face pales. 'What policewoman?'

'The policewoman who questioned us at Ravensthorpe. She's here on the Camino. She walked right past me.' Theo's eyes dart around the courtyard. 'You haven't seen her?'

Ethan and Jaz shake their heads.

Theo's gaze falls on me. 'You've seen her.' It's not a question.

I open and shut my mouth, my pulse thumping in my neck.

'Why didn't you tell us?' Theo's brown eyes are cold.

Because I don't trust you. 'I . . . don't know.'

Ethan's eyes narrow. 'Have you been talking to her?'

'Yes. We've talked.' A prickle of hostility rises off the group. They think I'm a rat fleeing the sinking ship of our secret. 'Not about Lula,' I blurt. 'We just chat.' *And possibly she sends me threatening poems.*

'Chat?' Jaz's brow wrinkles. 'About what?'

'The weather, the trail . . .'

They clearly don't believe me.

'What's she doing here?' says Theo.

'She's not in the police anymore. She told me she's walking the Camino because she's got PTSD.'

Theo frowns. 'From what?'

'She wouldn't say. I've tried Googling her name, but nothing comes up, which is weird.'

'What the hell, Tess.' Ethan's face colours. 'You knew she was following us, and you didn't say anything?'

I bite my lip. I can't explain my strange, tenuous bond with Nola. How she's never told anyone what I did to his car. Just because she's kept that secret, doesn't mean she's not investigating us though. 'I wanted to get to know her better. To find out why she's here. I didn't want to freak you out.'

Their eyes tell me they're unconvinced.

'You're not trying to do a deal, are you?' says Ethan. 'Turn us in.'

'What?' I swallow. 'No. Of course not.'

'We're all guilty,' says Ethan. 'We were all there.'

'Do you think I don't know that?' Sweat trickles from my armpits. 'I told you. We haven't spoken about that.'

176

They're all staring at me. Even Jaz. It's them against me. The way it was at Ravensthorpe. 'She's got a notebook. She writes in it all the time. I'll try to get a look at it.'

'Okay, good. Find out what she's up to,' says Ethan.

I get to my feet; I can't sit here trying to pretend we're all friends. 'I'm going to have a shower.'

'Don't think you can pull one over on us,' says Theo. 'We're watching you.'

My legs are weak as I walk away.

As I come into the *albergue* boot room, my eyes fall on a pair of boots in the corner. My breath hitches. They're dark green wellies. Like Lula's. Picking them up, I examine the tread. It has studs, like the footprint outside the castle. A faint scent reaches me. *Apples*. Lula's shampoo. My heart beats a startled rhythm as I stare around the boot room.

The meseta will make you or break you, says Lula's voice in my head.

*

I don't linger over dinner; the atmosphere is still tense. When I check my phone in the bunkroom, there's a message from Camryn Li.

How's the feature going? Send a draft ASAP so I can provide comments.

My stomach squirms. *Send a draft ASAP?* I'm supposed to have a draft already? Camryn and I are on different planets. There's no aspect of her reality which overlaps with mine. The only writing I've been doing is my Ravensthorpe memoir, and I only started that today. Still, clearly that's not what an editor wants to hear.

Going well, I type. *Will get draft to you soon.* Pressing send, I drag my fingers through my hair. I've got nothing to say yet, I don't have any dirt. I'll read Ethan's book again, it might give me some ideas.

Curling up in my bunk, I take up where I left off. The physicist is discussing a student's essay with her.

'*"Extraordinary. The way you've intertwined the path Einstein walked to unravel the universe's mysteries. The compass, the clocks, the falling man." She paused. "But I must be frank. This is not science; it's creative writing."*

'*Anita's face flushed. "But I'm exposing patterns. Isn't that what science is about?"*'

I stop reading, my spine tingling.

I'm exposing patterns. Isn't that what science is about?

I've seen those words before. Where? *Think, Tess.* In a flash, it comes to me. *Lula's laptop.* The morning after she died.

I sit bolt upright, banging my head on the bunk above me, but I hardly notice. My heart is a thumping bass drum. Ethan stole Lula's story. I should have known when I recognised the characters. Basing characters on her students is Lula's signature style.

Yes. I suppress an urge to pump my fist. What a scoop. This is exactly the dirt I need for my *Artemis* article.

Who doesn't love a celebrity author plagiarism scandal?

*

In the morning, it's sprinkling with rain, so I put on Dapple's raincoat as well as my own. Despite her quirks, I'm becoming fond of her. The idea of Theo reclaiming her is disconcerting; Dapple is my support team.

There's a spring in my step as we hit the trail. I have a red-hot plagiarism exposé to write, and only twenty kilometres to walk today. A mere trifle.

As it turns out, twenty kilometres is a long way on an old Roman road in the rain. The dust has turned to clay and every step's a struggle. Dapple negotiates the mud more daintily than me.

After a couple of hours, I pass a woman whose pink trainers are coated in mire. Mascara is streaked down her cheeks, but she smiles as Dapple and I tromp past. My first overtake on the Camino! A surge of satisfaction fills me. I'm nailing this.

At that moment, a bicycle pilgrim tears past with a hearty *Buen Camino*, splattering mud everywhere. Dapple snorts, shies and turns, pulling me back towards Hornillos. 'Idiot,' I yell, as I chase after Dapple back past the startled woman. By the time I pull Dapple up, I'm, once more, the slowest pilgrim on the Camino.

It's a tough day. The plastic-shopping-bag man strides past, bags swinging from his hands. Today he's wearing a garbage bag as a raincoat. Did he just decide to step out one day on a whim? Wheat fields turn to pasture. I greet a shepherd who's tending sheep, but he ignores me. With so many pilgrims, I expect he's jaded.

The rain eases as Castrojeriz comes into sight. Rust-coloured buildings ring a green hill topped by a ruined castle. I hope Ethan doesn't want to climb up to that one too. Dapple and I ascend steep, cobbled streets to the *albergue*. The sun's peeking out now and wet clothes drape the *albergue's* stone walls.

Ethan and Jaz are sitting on a wooden bench outside. Tethering Dapple, I join them, avoiding Ethan's eyes. *Plagiarist.* I feel like it's written all over my face. Why would he pass off Lula's work as his own? The fear of exposure must be hideous.

Jaz eyes my mud-coated legs. 'Keep those legs away from me.'

I head inside for a wash. The bunkhouse is empty, and I spot Ethan's backpack propped up beside a bunk. I step closer, thinking of his notebook. Maybe there's something in it I can use. Has he been reflecting on his plagiarism sins?

My eyes dart around the room. All is quiet. Lifting the top of his backpack, I peer in, pushing his clothes aside. I can't see his notebook, but on top of his sleeping bag is a brown glass bottle filled with a dark liquid. The label is in Spanish. I lean closer. *Jarabe de—*

'What are you doing?'

My heart leaps and, dropping the backpack lid, I turn. It's Theo. *Of course it would be.* I swallow. 'I, uh, thought this was my bag.'

'Your bag's over there.' He points.

'Oh.' Blood floods my face. 'They look so similar.' This is somewhat true. Both our bags are blue.

Theo's brown eyes lock on mine. 'Come on. We both know you were having a snoop. What are you after? Intel for your friend, the cop?'

'Don't be stupid. It was a mistake.' I push past him, feeling his eyes boring into my back as I head for the shower. Sweat trickles down my neck. Will he tell Ethan?

When I come back out, Ethan is pointing towards a church steeple. Theo isn't around, and he shows no sign of knowing about my snooping. 'According to Lula, there was a miracle at that church.'

Jaz eyes him. 'What kind of miracle?'

'While the church was being built, a cave-in killed some people, but the Virgin Mary brought them back to life.'

Ethan's voice is laconic, but Jaz's eyes light up.

I'm not sure if Ethan should encourage her religious fervour. My stomach rumbles. 'Food time?'

In the village, we find a small restaurant with a blackboard outside – *pilgrim dinner, three courses plus wine, ten Euros*. It's hard to go past, so we troop in.

Theo is there, so we join him. He gives me a hard stare, but he can't have told Ethan about my snooping yet. Is he waiting for the perfect moment to bring me down?

The waitress has bouffant black hair and Cleopatra eyes, like Amy Winehouse. She tells us, in her thick Spanish accent, the main course is *something* stew.

After she leaves, we discuss among ourselves what she said.

'Was it pork belly?' asks Theo.

'Or pork stomach?' says Ethan.

When the main course arrives, we examine it. Glutinous lumps of grey meat with a honeycomb texture swim in an oily sauce.

I wrinkle my nose. *Pork stomach*. I've never been a fan of offal. I poke at it with my fork. The sauce is rich and tasty, but the meat is chewy and slithery, like squid only worse. I'm hungry though, so I eat it all.

We talk about the people we've met on the Camino. The American girl who talks about nothing but drugs. The Japanese guy who's having an existential crisis at the thought of working non-stop for the rest of his life. And the elderly English man with dementia, accompanied by his go-getting wife.

'How about the plastic-shopping-bag man?' I chuckle, avoiding Theo's eyes.

Everyone looks at me blankly. How have they not seen him?

'Everyone on the Camino has issues.' Theo's gaze meets mine.

My stomach quivers. Is he going to tell Ethan about my snooping?

'Present company excepted,' says Ethan.

I suspect we're all thinking the same thing though. You guys have issues. But me? I'm fine.

Slabs of carrot cake slathered in cream arrive. Ethan declines it and heads for the loo. We're lying back in our chairs with the languid air of overfed pythons when Jaz speaks.

'According to Lula, we're going to meet the Devil soon.'

Ethan lowers himself back into his chair. 'How will we know him?'

'He has a black-feathered staff,' she says.

Ethan laughs. 'And what happens when we meet?'

'He'll test you in the way that is hardest for you,' says Jaz.

The hairs lift on my arms. She sounds so serious.

Theo's eyes fall on Ethan. 'Maybe he'll put you back on top of the *New York Times* bestseller list if you sacrifice your first-born son.'

Ethan's jaw clenches. 'Or he'll teach you to write, in exchange for your immortal soul.'

Tension crackles between them. Clearly Ethan and Theo are not the pals they used to be. Is that why Theo hasn't told him about my snooping?

'Don't mock,' says Jaz. 'The Devil might visit you out of spite.'

Back in the bunkroom, as I'm working on my Ravensthorpe memoir again, my phone buzzes with a message from Camryn. *Waiting for your draft. Hope you're getting some good material.*

My fingers tingle, thinking of the unexploded bomb of Ethan's plagiarism. But, no, I won't tell Camryn yet. I need more details. I have to talk to Ethan about Lula. Also, what was that bottle in his bag? *Jarabe*. I Google it. *Syrup*. Not helpful. But then it occurs to me; is Ethan using cough syrup to get high? I know that's a thing. And it would make sense, given his drug-taking history. Maybe that's all he can find here in Spain. That would be a good little snippet for my story if so.

You are going to love this story! Draft coming soon, I reply, then return to my memoir.

183

Chapter 23

The Chosen One

Then

In the dark days of winter, we wrote, we wrote, we wrote. At midnight we were still by the fire reading from our work.

Well, the other three read. I hadn't found the courage to read again since Lula had slammed my feminist dystopia. I'd been working on my new memoir version of the birthday party story, but the thought of sharing it made my pulse pound. I didn't know if I could. Sharing this story would feel like placing my soul under the microscope, not just my words.

Every time my turn to read came around, I shook my head. 'I'm not ready.' The others looked at me sympathetically. Secretly though, I sensed they were glad I'd removed myself from competition. *One down, three to go.*

Theo came into his own. His work wasn't to my taste but now, I saw what it might become. How he could claim his own style.

Lula nodded after he read out a piece about shooting a deer in Scotland with his father when he was ten. It hadn't been a clean shot, and he'd had to cut the deer's throat.

Kill it like a man, his father had said.

Theo had dispatched the deer, but he'd cried, fat tears falling onto its lifeless body.

Don't be a pussy, his father had growled.

'Hemingway-esque,' Lula said. 'I like the raw masculinity. There's a place for that.'

Theo's cheeks flushed pink with pleasure.

Mostly though, Lula's critiques were cutting and personal, even with Ethan and Jaz, her apparent favourites. 'You're not digging deep enough. Put everything into the writing. Every splinter, every harsh word, every time you were cruel, or someone was cruel to you. Remember, what do you fear?'

Around the fire, late at night, we talked about the kids we'd hated at school. Ethan admitted to being bullied. I told them how I'd never known my father. 'I used to imagine he was a great writer. But Mum would have told me if he was. He could be a murderer for all I know.'

We cried, and the more tears there were, the more pleased Lula was.

Jaz wrote about sleeping with an older man, a friend of her father's, when she was at secondary school.

I remembered her story about the girl who was obsessed with her teacher. Was this the real version now, the splinter that had fed her writing?

'I'm not sure if it was abuse or not,' she said when she

185

finished her reading. 'He was handsome, and charming. And I was sixteen, so it wasn't illegal.'

'That was abuse, Jaz,' I said. 'There was a power imbalance.'

She gazed at me, chewing her bottom lip. 'Yes, you're right, there was.' Her eyes dropped back to her laptop.

Lula's jaw twitched. 'Channel it into the work. Your vulnerability is your strength.' Her eyes fell on me as she said this.

My stomach squirmed. We only had two more nights on the retreat. My mind flashed to the first day I met her. *What are you willing to sacrifice for writing success?*

My life, I had answered. It was time to make good on that. Lula had made it clear what she wanted from me. I needed to give it to her or drop out now.

After we wound up, and the others went to their rooms, I climbed the stairs to Lula's office. Bending down, I took a deep breath, closed my eyes, and pushed my story under her door.

As I straightened, a high-pitched giggle came from inside. *Jaz.* I stood there for a moment, wishing I could pull my story back, then turned and walked away.

*

The next night, we finished our workshop earlier than usual and sat around the fire with a drink. Ethan was beside me on the couch, his shoulder warm against mine. He seemed relaxed; his writing was going well. He was almost certainly the frontrunner to be The Chosen One.

Lula had given no indication that she'd read my story. I felt sick with shame. She must have hated it, and decided it was best ignored. At least she hadn't torn me to shreds in front of the group.

'So, the day after tomorrow I'm going to announce "The Chosen One".' Lula made air quotes with her fingers. 'If any of you have been holding back on something that will help me decide, now is the time to bring it out.'

I swallowed. I had nothing left. I'd given my story everything, and it wasn't enough.

She took a sip of her wine. 'This opportunity to work with my agent is a special one. One that won't come around again. I'd be nothing without Ellery. We've been together since my first book, and we're like this.' Lula held up two fingers twined together. 'Every book I write, Ellery's right there with me. It's a marriage.' She met our eyes. 'Writing can be lonely. You need someone on your side to fight for you. A warrior who has your back. And when that warrior is Ellery, you're in good hands.'

She got to her feet. 'I'll be working in my office. Feel free to interrupt if you have something to tell me.' Her eyes met mine. 'Tess, can you come up in a few minutes?'

My story. My hands turned sweaty. This couldn't be good.

After Lula left, the others all turned to me.

'Why does she want to talk to you?' asked Theo.

I wiped my hands on my jeans. 'Probably wants to tell me I'm wasting her time, and I need to dig deeper.'

Jaz gave me a sympathetic smile. 'Why would she tell you that? Go on. Let us know what happens.'

I remembered her laughter in Lula's room last night.

Had she been lobbying on her own behalf? Is that what I needed to do too?

Ethan nudged my shoulder. 'Good luck. I'm sure you'll be fine.'

They thought I was a lost cause, and they were probably right.

*

'Come in,' Lula called when I knocked.

My stomach churned.

You're so close, said Mum's voice in my head. *Do whatever you need to do.*

Lula's office was a cosy space. A red sofa filled one corner, and books crammed a ceiling-high bookcase. Lula was behind her desk, tapping on a computer. Looking up, she waved me towards the sofa. She stood up and came around the table, perching on it, to face me.

I sat on the edge of the couch, tucking my hands under my legs. It took an immense effort to stop my legs twitching.

'That story of yours,' she said. 'The one you pushed under the door.'

I swallowed.

'I liked it.'

A tidal wave of warmth rushed through me. *I liked it.* I wanted to jump up and punch the air. It was pathetic, the power she had over me.

'A friend of mine, Robert Pettigrew . . .'

I'd heard of him. He ran a small but well-regarded publishing house, *Persuasion Press*.

188

'He's looking for a piece for an anthology. Best Young Brits, or something to that effect. It's a last-minute thing. Some issue with a story he'd commissioned. So, it's a rush job. They're going to press in a couple of days. I'll ping you his contact details and tell him your story's on the way, shall I?'

I gaped, repeating her words in my head. Had I misunderstood? 'You're recommending my story to him?'

'Correct.'

My heart thumped wildly. She was recommending my story to *Persuasion Press*? For an anthology of best young Brits? I was having trouble processing it.

Lula picked up her phone and tapped at it. My phone buzzed with a message. 'I'm sure he'll like it.' Lula gazed at her screen. 'Deadline's midday the day after tomorrow.'

'Oh.' My mind went in circles. I was going to be published. It was an introduction. I'd get myself noticed. It would lead to other things.

Lula looked up. 'All right?'

'Yes. Thank you. Amazing. Wow.'

'Give it a brush-up first. There's plenty of time.'

'Yes. I will.' *A brush-up?* I had no idea what she meant, but I couldn't ask. I'd slaved over that story; I'd put everything I had into it already. And the deadline was the day after tomorrow.

Lula got to her feet.

I did the same.

'This will be good for you,' she said. 'They usually get that anthology reviewed in *The Times*.'

The Times. Adrenaline raced through me. 'Thanks, Lula. Thanks so much. I'll – I'll get to work on it right now.'

Lula winked and walked back around behind her desk. Our interview was over.

'Oh, and Tess,' she said as I reached the door.

I turned back.

'Come and see me when you're ready to send the story. If I like what you've done with it . . .' Holding my gaze, she pointed at me. 'You're The Chosen One.'

Outside in the corridor, I slumped against the wall, my legs turned to jelly. My ears were ringing, and her last words repeated over and over in my head. *You're The Chosen One.*

Exultation fired through my blood. Stroking my fingers over the books outside Lula's door, I imagined mine beside them, my name in gold letters. *Tess Brody.* Excitement fizzed inside me. Lula was right; there was no other high like success.

I wanted more.

Chapter 24

Battle between Good and Evil

Now

The sun bathes the *meseta's* wheat fields in a golden glow and the path stretches out like a river. For a moment, I'm glad I'm here. Then last night's offal stew reasserts its greasy presence in my stomach, and I remember that, according to Lula, I'm about to meet the Devil.

Stopping for a rest, I gaze out at the fields. Dapple and I are all alone. It's hot and there's not a skerrick of shade, just wheat, wheat, wheat. Beyond the wheat field, rises a round, fortress-like medieval Templar church.

'I've got five Camino apps, but this one's the best.' Theo drops onto the bench beside me.

I jump. I'd been so dazed, I hadn't seen him coming.

He holds his phone out. 'See, it tells me where we are, and also . . .' He taps the screen. 'It gives rankings to all the restaurants.'

My stomach rumbles. *The Devil will test you in the way that is hardest for you.* 'How far to the next restaurant?'

Theo taps his screen. 'Another ten K.'

Ten K. And I'm already hungry. 'Is it a good one?'

He inspects his screen. 'No. Two stars.'

Theo is definitely the Devil. My eyes focus on his phone and my breath stills. 'I thought you all left your phones behind.'

Theo rolls his eyes. 'Yeah, that was Ethan's idea obviously. I bought one in Burgos. Don't tell the others.'

My mouth goes dry. *The texts at the wine fountain and in Burgos. . .* His phone doesn't look new. He could have had it the whole time. 'You've scratched the screen already.'

Theo meets my eyes. 'It was second-hand.' He gestures towards the Templar church. 'I've heard there's a Templar who runs an *albergue* further down the trail. He wears the clothes and carries the sword and all. He protects pilgrims on the trail.'

'From what?'

Theo looks stumped.

'Overpriced *bocadillos*?' I suggest. 'Grumpy baristas?'

Theo flushes. 'The Templars are all about defending values. That's important these days, right? The way the world's going.'

I have no reply to that, so an awkward silence falls. Dapple munches on the grass.

Theo looks at me over the top of his aviator sunglasses. 'So, why were you searching Ethan's bag?'

I swallow. 'I told you. It was a mistake.'

Theo stares at me as he gulps some water. 'I haven't told him. Yet.' He taps his eyes and points at me. 'But I'm watching you.'

I roll my eyes, but my bravado is only skin deep.

'This is another great app.' He scrolls. 'It reminds you that you're going to die. It's a Buddhist thing – he who thinks of death five times a day is happy. There, I've sent you the link.' Pulling my phone from my hands, he taps at the link then hands it back. 'Well, *Buen Camino*.' He strides off, leaving me disconcerted.

I'm not ready to move on, so I pull out my e-reader and finish Ethan's book. It's fantastic. I can see why he stole it. Does he think he's safe from discovery now? My chest tightens. *Plagiarism*. He must have been so desperate to impress his father. The ironic part is, he didn't need to do that. He's talented, I'm sure he would have got his own work published if he'd persisted.

Many hard kilometres later, my phone buzzes, and I pull it out. *Don't forget you're going to die.* A shiver runs up my spine, *then* I realise. It's the app Theo sent me. Did he intend it to sound so threatening? I bet he did.

In the afternoon, I run into Theo again. He's sitting on a trackside marker looking tired and miserable. He gazes at me from under his cap. 'I have four weeks' holiday. And I do this? I must be frigging crazy.'

I sense an opportunity. I've had enough of his attempts to spook me. And he could blab to Ethan about my snooping

193

at any moment. 'I heard the Costa Brava's nice. Beautiful swimming, good food. It's not far, you can catch the train from the next town.'

'Tempting.' He nods slowly. 'That's, uh, not a bad idea. Better than slogging it out here. I might check it out. Guess you can hang on to the donkey for now.'

I feel instantly more cheerful. 'Have a cocktail for me.' Raising my hand, I trudge on.

'Congratulations,' calls Jaz as I stagger up the pathway to the *albergue*. The Templar flag – a red cross on white background – flutters above. 'You've made it half-way.'

Half-way. I feel twenty years older already. If I keep ageing at this rate, I might die on this trip.

Jaz is sitting at a table, drinking red wine. Judging by the cheeriness of her call, and her flushed cheeks, she's half-pissed. The *meseta's* messing with us all.

I look around. 'Where's Ethan? He always gets to the *albergue* first, doesn't he?'

She shrugs. 'Haven't seen him all day.'

My gut clenches. He's taken off, I'm sure of it. He lulled me into a false sense of security, then, *bam*, vanished. Does he know I'm on to his plagiarism? Did Theo tell him about my snooping?

'You know how it is; people come and go.'

But what if he's given up? Or . . . is it because of Nola? Is he trying to give her the slip? And now Theo's gone too. That leaves me and Jaz to take the fall.

'Hey, I'm still here,' Jaz says.

I give her a tense smile. She must wonder why I care so much about Ethan disappearing.

Jaz has dark rings under her eyes. 'I hardly slept at all last night. I wake in the night and it's like electricity is running through my body.'

The *meseta's* getting to her; she's always been tightly wound. I'd better keep an eye on her. 'You need to sleep, Jaz.'

'Sleep is a waste when life is so exciting.' She smiles. 'So, how's your story going?'

For a moment I think she's on to me. 'Huh?'

'Your transformation article?'

'Oh.' I'd forgotten about that. I gaze at Jaz. Are we friends again? Maybe it's time for me to come clean. Or partly clean. 'I haven't been entirely truthful about my article.'

'Oow. Spill.' Jaz raises her eyebrows.

'So . . . I'm writing a story about Ethan searching for a miracle on the Camino. Seeking inspiration for his second book. I've got a contract with *Artemis*.' I don't mention the real focus of my article. The dirt. I'm not completely sure I trust her.

She grins. 'Wow. Go you. I love *Artemis*.'

'You can't tell him.'

Jaz snorts. 'As if I would. After what he did to you at Ravensthorpe. He totally has it coming.'

I stare at her. 'So, you believe me now?'

'Of course I do. I'm sorry I acted like I didn't at Ravensthorpe.' Jaz touches my arm. 'I'm glad you're here, Tess. I thought you'd hate me.'

'No, I'm glad you're here too.' I am but doubt flutters in my chest. Can I trust her?

My phone buzzes. *Don't forget you're going to die.* I

have got to delete that app; it's such a downer. I've seen the memorials on the wayside. Pilgrims are dropping like flies. Many people I started with I've never seen again. Are they dead?

A black and white puppy flops onto the paving stones nearby. 'Is Zebra still around?' I ask, reaching down to stroke its soft hair.

Jaz shakes her head. 'No, it's so sad. He died of cancer. He was only young, too. Ethan was devastated.'

'Oh.' The breath puffs out of me. Another link to my past broken.

I sip my wine. *That moment outside the gig with Ethan and the puppy.* . . If not for Zebra, Ethan would have ended up with Tabitha. We'd never have formed our critique group. I probably wouldn't have made it on to the winter retreat. So many things would have been different. Would Lula be alive? My stomach contracts. Would Mum?

I swallow. I haven't told Jaz about Mum. I haven't told any of them. The wound is too raw to expose in front of people I don't fully trust.

As I wipe my sweaty palms on my trousers, I tip over my wine glass. The puppy lifts its head, as a red tide spills from the table. Where the hell has Ethan gone?

*

Ree, the American, approaches as I'm resting in a tiny patch of shade beside the path. Everyone on the trail seems off-beam today – the *meseta* is weaving its spell – but she looks fresh and well-groomed. Her large camera dangles from her neck. That must be heavy. Either she is way fitter than she looks, or she's catching the bus.

'I'm glad to see you are a true pilgrim,' she says.

'How can you tell?' I'm keen to know what special pilgrim characteristics I'm displaying.

'You have a donkey.'

'Ah, yes.'

'Some pilgrims have their bags transported.' Her face curls. 'They may as well be in Saint Moritz or Ibiza. Pff.'

Saint Moritz. Ibiza. I wish. And why didn't I consider pack transportation before I took up with a surly donkey?

'Pff. Some even stay in hotels instead of *albergues*.'

I sigh with longing.

'They have clean sheets and fluffy towels. Pff. It is not the pilgrim way.'

Clean sheets, fluffy towels. I swoon. Unfortunately, I must stick to *albergues*, where hopefully I will run into Ethan. Besides, I can't afford it.

She gives a final 'Pff' and departs with a waggle of her red-painted fingernails.

Soon after, I walk through a long, shadowy underpass. *Don't quit before the miracle,* someone's scrawled on the wall. As I read it, my phone buzzes and a message flashes up on my screen. *Iris.* She's replied to my email at last.

Dear Tess,

Returned from a solitary writing sojourn, sans internet, to your missive, which is now a relic of a bygone era. It appears my email identity has been breached. The intrigue

deepens! If you're seeking me along the sacred Camino, I'm afraid I must disappoint, ha ha! Ever yours,
    Iris

The hairs lift on the back of my neck. Iris was hacked. She didn't send the invitation. So who did? Someone wanted us here, brought us here. *Why?*

I freeze, listening. A footfall sounds in the shadows behind me. A cold chill slips down my spine. There it is again – the tap of a footstep echoing off the stone walls.

Dapple's head comes up, and she bares her teeth.

Jaz's words fill my head. *Donkeys are good at sensing danger.*

The dark underpass feels suddenly alive, coiled with threat. Heart thumping, Dapple trotting beside me, I run.

Footsteps clatter behind us as we sprint for the distant circle of light.

Chapter 25

Anonymous

So, our little team has reached their journey's midpoint, the deepest part of the dark, dark wood. As mountaineers know, when you reach the summit, the most dangerous section lies ahead.

The middle reached, a sinister core,
Where secrets lie, forevermore.
The night's embrace, a chilling kiss,
As they navigate this dark abyss.

Would you agree that my poetic skills are blossoming like a spring rose?

Xx Anonymous

Chapter 26

Makeover

As I hobble, exhausted, into the courtyard in Mansilla, my pulse skips a beat. There, sitting in the sun eating an orange and peacefully reading his book, is Ethan. His shirt and socks hang, dripping, on the line beside him.

I eye him as I approach. I'm still jumpy after my scare in the tunnel. It was just the shopping-bag man behind me as it turned out, but still. Iris didn't organise this walk. And Jaz said Ethan encouraged her and Theo to come . . .

Was it him? Did he send me the invitation? But why? My chest tightens. This must all be about Lula. If I could only remember what happened that night.

Ethan is unsurprised to see me. 'We meet again.'

Taking off Dapple's panniers, I slump beside him. 'Where have you been?'

He shrugs. 'Needed some solitude. Thinking things through. Why, have you missed me?'

'I thought we were walking together.'

'Didn't realise we'd signed a contract.'

I'm the one with the contract, but I can't tell him that.

'Jaz has gone to check out the town,' he says.

'Theo's gone to the Costa Brava.'

Ethan snorts. 'Good.'

'Aren't you two mates?'

'We used to be.' Ethan's mouth twitches. 'So, León tomorrow.'

'Tomorrow?' I've lost track of time. León is a major city. And the *meseta's* endpoint. Has it been ten days already?

'I'm thinking of catching the bus.'

My mouth drops open. 'The bus? To León?'

'I've heard it's not such a nice walk.'

'But . . . That's beside the point.' If anyone was to raise the spectre of alternative transport, I'd have thought it would be me.

Dapple snorts, throws herself onto the grass, and does her usual roll and bray.

Although, now I have Dapple, catching a bus isn't an option. I swallow. What if he's about to give up? 'If you catch the bus once, what's to stop you catching it again?'

'Nothing at all.'

'Exactly.'

'Well, I salute your resolve, but I think I can be flexible.'

I frown at him. 'What's brought this on? Are you tired?' His face looks drawn. He's lost some weight too. Ethan had appeared so indestructible, but now he's fraying around the edges.

'I'm fine.' Ethan rolls his eyes. 'It's not a big deal. Get over it.'

'It's the *meseta*, isn't it? It's broken you.'

Ethan glares at me. 'The *meseta* has not broken me.'

'I think it has. That's why you went off by yourself, isn't it? You were hoping for some magic out there on the plains, but it hasn't happened. No miracle. I'm right, aren't I?'

'No. I wanted a break from you all. Is that so hard to understand?'

I shrug. 'If you say so.'

Ethan shares his orange with me, but there's a tense silence between us. I get Dapple settled in a paddock next to the *albergue* and go to bed early.

Jaz is still out. It's unlikely too much can go wrong though; it's a small town. I doze restlessly until her bunk rustles – she's back – then drift off into a deep sleep.

*

I wake to the usual empty dormitory. As I pick up my backpack, a scrap of paper falls to the floor. My fingers tingle as I pick it up. I hope it's not another threatening poem. But no, there's a name scrawled at the bottom. *Jaz*.

Hi Tess,

I've caught the bus to León and am taking another route to Santiago from there, a wilder route.

I realised on the meseta that I need to get away from the crowds. There's a special church I want to visit too. Don't worry about me. All going well, I'll see you in Santiago,

Jaz.

202

I sink onto my bunk, my chest heavy. I should have kept a closer eye on her. She's religiously crazed and hasn't been sleeping. And now she's off in the wilderness by herself. Anything could happen out there. And we were just getting to know each other again.

I thought our team had made it through the *meseta* unscathed, but no. Jaz has vanished, Ethan's catching the bus, and Theo's absconded to the Costa Brava.

It's true what they say, in the end the *meseta* messes with you all. Except for me. Apart from the threatening poems, and not knowing who invited me here, or why, I'm fine.

I scratch an itch on my chest. Then one on my leg. Several on my stomach. What's happening? My whole body explodes in a frenzy of itching. I pull up my shirt. Raised lumps cover my chest. I touch my face. They're all over my cheeks too. *Bedbugs.*

The warden is sweeping nearby. If she sees me, she'll make me do a full bedbug eradication. The other pilgrims said you need to hot wash all your clothes. But I don't have time for that, I have to find Jaz.

My eyes fall on Jaz's bunk. Her cross is still there. Why did she leave it behind? She was so attached to it. It must have been a mistake. This proves it, she is not okay. Picking the cross up, I tuck it under my arm.

'*Chinche*.' The warden is right in front of me. She points to my face.

I'm trapped. I consider ducking around her and making a break for it, but by the time I get Dapple ready, she'll catch up to me anyway. And I suppose I should try to do the right thing.

'Wait.' She turns and walks away down the corridor.

I find myself unable to disobey. Hopefully it won't take too long.

Returning, she points at the toilet and hands me a white kaftan-like smock. She passes me a large plastic bag, waves her finger at my clothes and points at the bag. 'These too.' She points at the backpack containing my spare clothes. I shuffle, shamefaced, into the toilet.

Propping the cross in the corner, I remove my clothes and place them, as well as all my spare ones from my pack, in the plastic bag. I put on the smock she's given me, which must be the decontamination outfit. Dragging the bag and the cross behind me, I exit.

Gingerly, the warden takes the plastic bag from me and holds up two fingers. 'Two hours.'

Two hours. I can't wait for two hours. I need to find Jaz.

She glances at Jaz's cross. 'Your Camino is *muy religioso?*'

'*Si.*' As soon as she leaves the room, I hoist the cross over one shoulder, gather up the floor-length smock, and waddle outside. I'll have to abandon my clothes.

Dapple's out in the paddock, munching on grass. I tie the cross to the panniers and shamble down the street. People give me extra space, like I'm an over religious leper.

A cluster of pilgrims huddle at the bus stop. Ethan isn't among them; perhaps he caught an earlier bus. They all look guilty. This is handy, as they don't inspect me closely. As I walk out of town a few drops of rain fall, which suits my glum mood.

Realisation hits. If I can't find Jaz, I'll be all alone with Ethan. And, for all I know, he's the threatening poet. I swallow. I have to find Jaz. It's nineteen kilometres to León, a short day. I lengthen my stride. After tripping on my smock a few times, I pull out a belt and strap it at the waist to keep it off my ankles. Dapple picks up on my urgency and ambles along at the speedier end of her usual pace.

Her cooperation doesn't extend to skipping lunch break though. I wait for the mandated two hours of grazing, gnashing my teeth. 'Jaz will be gone before we get to León.'

She ignores me.

My phone buzzes. *Don't forget, you're going to die.* Right now, this is the least of my worries.

As Dapple and I plod on, we pass a scarecrow draped in ribbons. Beneath it, are funeral notices mixed with photos. The Camino, it seems, is partly about death. Or possibly the desire to live on afterwards?

My eye snags on a funeral notice held down by a rock. My heart explodes. *Lula.* It's the Order of Service from her funeral. I pick it up, my hand shaking, and her photo hits me like a punch. There she is, leaning against the door at Ravensthorpe, laughing. *Alive.*

The typed text jumps out at me and it's like I'm back there. In the pew with the singing policewoman. *Amazing Grace . . . Address by Ethan Hill . . .*

And then at the bottom, something new. Something wrong. Written in black pen, in sharp, neat capitals is a poem.

AN EYE FOR AN EYE
AND A LIFE FOR A LIFE
LET THE GUILTY SHAKE WITH FRIGHT,
THEIR DARK DEED WILL COME TO LIGHT.

xx Anonymous

The words blur as sweat trickles down my spine. *An eye for an eye. A life for a life.*

Someone left this for me. I'm the only one of our group walking this section of trail today. Skin tingling, I scan the path, but I'm alone. It's a threat. And it's personal.

Who brought me here to the Camino? It feels like a trap. The smartest move would be to abandon ship and head home. But that would mean giving up on revenge. On the article. On the chance to turn my life around.

Gritting my teeth, I stuff the funeral notice in my pocket. 'Come on, Dapple.' I pick up her lead. If this melodramatic poet thinks they can scare me into giving up, they don't know who they're dealing with.

Chapter 27

Gothic Horror

Then

'So? What did Lula say?' asked Jaz when I came back to the Ravensthorpe common room after my meeting in Lula's office.

They'd fallen silent as I'd entered. I swallowed. They'd been talking about me. Probably discussing how I was about to be booted off the retreat. My head was spinning after Lula's bombshell. *The Chosen One*. I didn't know I was in the running. I was sure it would be Ethan or Jaz. I tried to tamp down my excitement.

They stared at me as I gave them an edited version. The *Best Young Brits* anthology, not Lula's parting words. *You're The Chosen One*. I couldn't tell them that. The words tumbled out of me. My thoughts were so scattered, their frozen faces barely registered.

'Congrats.' Theo's voice was flat.

'Yeah. Amazing.' Jaz forced a smile.

Silence fell, and I turned to Ethan.

He gave me a smile that was more of a grimace. 'Good one, Tess.'

'Um, yeah.' My throat tightened as my eyes flickered from face to face. Had I expected them to be glad for me? They'd thought I was out of the running, but now I'd sprung this on them – a story they hadn't even seen. Did they think I'd deliberately kept my story secret, then pulled it out at the last minute? Sweat trickled from my armpits. Just as well I didn't tell them about me being The Chosen One. 'I'd better go work on it. The deadline's the day after tomorrow.' I walked out, leaving a silence behind me.

Later that night, as I worked on my story in the library, angry voices filled the corridor. Was that Ethan and Lula? Getting up, I opened the door. I couldn't make out what they were saying, but I heard my name. A door slammed, and it went quiet.

I didn't go to Ethan's room that night, and he didn't come to mine. I was the successful one now and he didn't like it.

I worked on my story until late in the night, and, after a short nap, all the next day. I wasn't happy with it. I had until midday tomorrow though. I'd get it right. I had to; this opportunity would never come around again. It didn't matter that this story made my stomach churn. As Lula said, what mattered was finding the truth deep inside me. As dusk fell, in an effort to relax, I channelled Ernest Hemingway with a scotch and soda. I was still on edge, so I poured another before I joined the group.

Ethan and I usually shared a beanbag, but tonight he

was in an armchair. As I sat in the chair next to his, he smiled, but it didn't reach his eyes.

My chest tightened. Why couldn't he be glad for me? I would have been if it was him. In honour of our last night on the retreat, I was wearing the velvet dress I'd got for my birthday party. I smoothed it down with my hands. The softness was comforting.

'We're doing something different tonight.' Lula dropped into an armchair. 'We need a change of pace. It's time for an artist date.' She ignored the puzzled looks on our faces. 'Many writers went to extraordinary lengths to gain inspiration. Graham Greene trekked across Africa for a month to investigate slavery. Screenwriter Bill Broyle lived alone on a desert island to research his movie *Castaway*. I, myself, went half-mad while hiking the Camino pilgrimage. The best work comes when we're close to the edge.' She paused. 'Or, preferably, over it. Have you heard of Chris Burden and his performance artwork *Shoot*?'

We shook our heads.

'He made a movie of himself being shot by a gun as a work of art.' She met our eyes. 'So inspiring, don't you think?'

I tried to murmur admiration like the others, but unease gnawed at my gut. Is that what she expected from us? To put our lives on the line in the pursuit of art?

Leaning down, she dug around in her leather satchel.

My pulse skittered; I half expected her to pull out a gun.

But when she sat up, she held a small plastic bag. 'Did you know it's the winter solstice tonight?'

None of us did. We'd all been too focused on the writing.

Lula shook her head. 'Writers should be sponges.

Everything feeds into the work. Tonight is the longest night of the year. Darkness has reached its peak. How will this affect our psyche?' This was a rhetorical question, as she continued. 'In the pagan tradition, the shortest day is a time of power. It marks the start of the sun's return. A cause for celebration.' She fingered the plastic bag.

I eyed the bag. Where was she going with this?

'In mid-winter in the Arctic, shamans would arrive with gifts of red and white psychedelic mushrooms. They'd climb down through the top of snow-covered yurts and hang them above the fire. When people ate the mushrooms, they had visions of dancing elves and flying reindeer with red mushroom-shaped noses.' She paused. 'Remind you of anything?'

'Rudolph the red-nosed reindeer,' said Jaz.

'Spot on.' Lula held up the plastic bag, which was filled with a greyish powder. 'What do Jack Kerouac, John-Paul Sartre and Elizabeth Barrett Browning have in common?' Her eyes scanned the room. 'They all did some of their best work while high.' She paused. 'Who's up for a creative adventure?'

The others nodded with enthusiasm. Avoiding their gaze, I sank lower in my beanbag. I didn't want to take mushrooms. I didn't even want to be around people who were tripping.

Ethan was always popping one thing or another. Uppers, downers, party pills. 'They're just a mood stabiliser,' he said.

I'd got used to it, but psychedelics were different. The idea of losing control scared me, and I knew addiction could run in families. Besides, I'd been drinking. Alcohol and mushrooms weren't a good combination. If I didn't join in though, would Lula change her mind about me? Decide I wasn't worthy?

Lula didn't notice my apprehension. She vanished into the kitchen, returning with a glass teapot filled with an inky indigo brew and five mugs. Pouring the tea into the mugs, she passed them around. 'I've added liquorice tea and honey to make it taste better.'

Picking up her mug, she sipped at it, and the others followed suit. Wrapping my hands around my mug, I raised it to my nose. It smelt earthy, with a liquorice overtone. Would anyone notice if I didn't drink it? Could I tip it out somewhere?

Lula pointed to the corner, where a bauble-covered Christmas tree rose from a pot, its fresh piney scent filling the room. 'The pagans used to bring a pine tree inside for the Yule festival. It was a home for the wood spirits, to keep them warm during winter.' She took another sip of her tea. 'So, tomorrow I'm going to announce The Chosen One.'

The breath caught in my throat.

'Thought I should give you a heads-up. The person who is top of my list knows who they are. Things could change though. Let's see how we go tonight.'

The room went silent, and Ethan's body stiffened. I stared straight ahead, my cheeks burning. I sensed the others' side-eye glances. They knew.

'A toast.' Lula raised her mug and flashed her teeth. 'To Beira, the goddess of winter. She who is fierce and cruel and rules the harshest season from her throne on Ben Nevis. She who controls the storms with her giant hammer and transforms into a bird.'

We all raised our mugs to her, but unlike the others, I only pretended to drink.

Jaz wrinkled her nose as she swallowed. 'It's bitter.'

A trickle of sweat ran down my chest. Why had Lula said that about The Chosen One? What was she playing at? And what did she mean, *let's see how we go tonight*?

Around me, they all sipped their mushroom tea. I felt their eyes on me. I'd never expected to be The Chosen One. But now I wanted it. I wanted it so much it made my chest ache. I'd tasted the first rush of success, and I wanted more.

'Let's light the candles.' Lula pointed at the scented candles, which sat in a row on the bookcase.

Sensing an opportunity, I rose to my feet. 'I'll get matches.' Ducking into the kitchen, I emptied my mug down the sink. Refilling it with hot water, I dropped in a liquorice tea bag and added a slosh of whiskey for courage. I'd stick with the devil I knew. 'Couldn't find any,' I said as I came out.

'Sorted.' Ethan held up his lighter. Half the candles were already lit.

I dropped back into the seat next to Ethan and sipped at my liquorice tea.

Theo turned the sound system up and a choral chant filled the room. High, clear voices. Something you'd hear in church. An unusual choice.

We all stared at him, and he shrugged. 'Thought it might fit the mood.'

Surprisingly, it did. The music created a spooky, gothic vibe that spoke of winter rites and hooded monks.

Placing my mug on the arm of my chair, I got up to go to the toilet. I swayed as I headed for the door. Was I too heavy handed on the whiskey? I wouldn't drink any more after this, I had to work on my story tonight.

Coming back, I settled into the chair.

'Careful, almost knocked it over.' Ethan handed me my tea.

Taking the mug, I swigged it down. Whiskey and liquorice tea wasn't a good combination. It had a bitter aftertaste. Could I excuse myself to do some work now?

Lula held up a large black key. 'Want to go up to the ruins? It's a good place for a winter ritual.' She got to her feet.

'Yeah, wow.' 'Amazing.' 'Totally.' The other three jumped up, their voices excited.

Lula tilted her head at me, the key dangling from her finger.

I needed to finish my story. But I wanted to see the ruins. And I had to keep Lula onside, show her I was up for creative adventure. *Let's see how we go tonight.* 'Sounds incredible.' I pushed myself up from my chair. I'd have a quick look at the tower, then get back to work.

'Take the candles,' said Lula. 'There's no light out there.'

We pulled on our coats, hats and gloves, grasped the candles, and streamed outside. Lula, Ethan and Theo set off towards the ruins, but I stopped as the freezing air hit my face. Mist poured from my mouth. It hovered, a sparkling cloud. A faint tinkling noise reached my ears. As I turned my head, it grew louder and softer. Was the mist from my mouth tinkling? What was happening?

Jaz grasped my arm. 'Come on, Tess.'

As we ran across the meadow to the tower, a strange lightness filled my head. The others were waiting at the bottom. Lula pulled open the heavy door, revealing a dark chamber inside. Holding up the candles, we climbed in single file up the narrow spiral staircase. A damp cold emanated from the stone walls. As we emerged onto the platform at the top a frigid breeze hit us, ruffling our hair, and blowing out a few candles.

I didn't feel cold. My head was now so light, it had left my body. I floated above, looking down at the group huddled on the tower. It was hard to tell them apart in their woolly hats and coats. A couple of snowflakes floated past my face.

Lula held up her candle and shadows flickered on her face. 'Beira, Queen of Winter, now rules the land.' Her voice was smooth honey.

I stared at her, hair prickling on my neck. Lula's face was changing. It wrinkled and sagged, as if she'd aged thirty years in a minute. The light of her candle stretched, beaming laser-like up into the sky. To the stars. In the light of her candle, her wrinkled face gleamed periwinkle blue. What was going on? I hadn't taken the mushrooms, but . . . *periwinkle blue?*

'Blow out the candles,' said Lula. 'Let's meditate on the sun's return.'

I blew, a stream of sparkle, and an inky blackness swallowed us. I stared at Lula and my breath quickened.

My lips parted but I couldn't speak; I was frozen. Crooked red teeth shone in her mouth as her words floated from the darkness. Above them a single eye glowed in the middle of her forehead. Her tatty jumper was now a black robe covered in skulls and a hammer hung from her hand.

Beira.

'Picture what you desire.' Lula's voice echoed around me.

A book floated in my mind. A book with my name on it. In large, gold writing.

'Do you see obstacles to your desire?' She was talking directly to me.

An image emerged. Lula announcing The Chosen One. It wasn't me. I clenched my hands as a lump filled my throat.

'How can you remove these obstacles?'

After this, I couldn't separate what was real and what I imagined. The skulls. Her red teeth. The glowing book. Lula's echoing voice. *What do you desire? What is in your way?* A truncated *oof* of surprise. Then a giant bird with the face of an owl flew over the tower and a cold, nameless dread filled me. I ran.

I fled down the dark spiral staircase, feeling my way through the darkness, my hand brushing the cold stone wall. Footsteps clattered behind me. I ran faster. I was being chased by a towering one-eyed hag with a hammer. The stairway went on and on. The footsteps behind me came closer. Hot breath burned my neck.

And then I was out, the cold air a slap to the face. I tried to run, but the ground lurched, and the trees clawed at me. I stumbled on, my thoughts spiralling. *What happened? Where am I?* A sour taste flooded my mouth, and my legs barely held me. Voices called in the distance, but I couldn't understand what they were saying.

'Tess.'

This voice came from nearby. It sounded threatening.

I ran.

Chapter 28

Forced Proximity

Now

'Hi, Tess, we meet at last.'

My phone rang as I sighted the spires of León cathedral. I only accepted the video call because I thought it might be Jaz. By the time I remembered she didn't have a phone, it was too late. Now, I'm staring at a young woman whose wispy black hair is bright pink at the ends. She's wearing a baggy cardigan over a checked shirt which is buttoned to the neck. My pulse ratchets up a notch. We've never met, but I know her from my online stalking.

It's Camryn Li from *Artemis*.

I raise my hand. 'Hi, Camryn. Great to see you.' I'm tempted to hang up. It wouldn't be hard to simulate a bad connection and drop out. I thought I'd be on top of things when I first spoke to Camryn – a super-fit, high-achieving journalist with a sizzling feature. Instead, I'm a poxy, bedraggled, smock-wearing pilgrim who has spent every spare minute she has working on a stupid memoir instead of the article she's contracted to write.

Somewhere in another space-time dimension, as Ethan's physicist would say, my feature is already gracing the *Artemis* front page. But unfortunately, Camryn, not being a physicist, won't realise that.

'What's wrong with you?' Camryn frowns. 'You look terrible. Or, sorry, is that how you usually look?'

'No, I usually look much better.' I touch my bumps. They're tender and itchy. 'I've got bedbugs.'

She gasps. 'What are you going to do about it?'

I spot a green neon cross ahead – an opportunity to buy time. 'There's a chemist over there. I'd better get some stuff.'

Camryn frowns. 'Is that a donkey next to you?'

I glance at Dapple, as if I'd just noticed her. 'Yes. It is.'

'Is it yours?'

'She's on loan.'

'Is that a thing on the Camino? Donkey borrowing?'

'Ah, yes, it is.'

'What's that on its back?'

'It's a cross.'

'So, you've gained a donkey with a cross on its back! Excellent. That's so biblical, it should play well in your article.' Camryn slips into journalist mode. 'I see you have a cross around your neck as well.'

I'd forgotten about the cross I got at mass. 'Oh.' I finger it. 'It was a giveaway.'

'A giveaway.' Her voice is dry. 'Where from?'

'Mass.'

'You're going to mass?'

218

'No. Well, just once so far.'

'Interesting.' Camryn's brow wrinkles. 'Why are you wearing a white kaftan? This isn't some kind of cult, is it? I'm not sure *Artemis* readers would go for that.'

My phone buzzes. *Don't forget you're going to die,* pops up on the screen over her face. I tap it and it goes away.

'What are you doing?'

'Nothing.' *Bloody Theo.* 'It's this app I can't get rid of.' I lead Dapple towards the pharmacy. 'There's nothing to worry about. It's kind of intense here, but in the Camino context, it's all perfectly normal.' I wave my hand to imply a donkey with a cross is a must-have accessory, and white robes the favoured daywear. 'Okay, off to get bedbug stuff now.'

'Hang on, let me take a screen shot for our socials.'

Wait, what? 'Gotta go. Bye.' As I hang up, there's the click of a screenshot. *Damn.* This is not the look I was hoping to rock on the *Artemis* socials.

The pharmacy assistant recoils when she sees me and speaks rapidly in Spanish. Grasping a plastic bottle from behind the counter, she thrusts it at me. 'Fifteen Euros.'

I pay and depart, unsure what I've purchased. Is it to put on me, or my things?

Leading Dapple through the narrow streets, I find the place Ethan's booked. This was supposed to be a treat for us, a reward for crossing the *meseta.* It looks pretty upmarket and considering my unsavoury state, I'm unsure of my reception.

The poem on Lula's funeral notice keeps repeating in my head. *Let the guilty shake with fright.* So creepy. Considering the weird app Theo forced on me, everything points to him. But hasn't he left the trail? So, who wrote it? Ethan?

Opening the door, I peer in, but the receptionist shrieks. '*Chinche*.' She makes shooing gestures with her hands.

Backing outside, I wait in the street. Am I permanently banned? But the receptionist emerges, eyeing me suspiciously.

'My clothes are clean.'

She narrows her eyes.

'No bedbugs.' I gesture at my robe. 'All clean.'

Giving an abrupt nod, she leads me – keeping her distance – around the back to a courtyard. Once Dapple's taken care of, she beckons for me to come inside.

Upstairs in the room, Ethan's reclined on a bed, reading his track notes, and looking much fresher than the last time I saw him. He definitely caught the bus. 'Nice outfit.' He scans my face. 'You seem to have a bedbug issue.' He eyes the cross. 'And a religious issue.'

'It's all in hand.' I eye the spare beds. This will be awkward. We haven't shared a room since we were together at Ravensthorpe. 'Jaz has gone off on some other trail. I have to find her. She's been really hyped up lately; I'm worried about her.'

'The *Camino Primitivo*? That would be it. It takes off from León and joins up later.'

'I thought I'd try to catch her, take a bus. If you could look after Dapple?'

'Why? She's a bit wound up, but she'll be okay. Anyway, there's no way I'm taking that crazy donkey. Theo pulled a swiftie palming her off on you.'

'But . . .' I clench my hands. I'll have no chance of catching Jaz if I don't get the bus.

'She's saddled you with the cross, huh?' Ethan grins.

My cheeks burn. First the donkey, now the cross. Am I just the heir to Jaz and Theo's discarded brands? 'No. I don't think she meant to leave it behind.'

Ethan lifts his shoulders. 'It's a thing, you know, carrying someone's cross.'

'It is?'

'Mm, starting with the guy who carried Jesus's cross. I'd love to help out, but . . . We used to do crucifixion re-enactments at church when I was a kid.' He shudders. 'To be honest, it's triggering.'

'I get it.' I eye the extra bed. So now, it's Ethan and me.

*

'This wine is hideous.' Ethan passes me the cheap plastic bottle we bought at the supermarket.

We are perched on a bench beside the cathedral eating cold empanadas as a bitter wind slices straight through my robe. As I take a swig, two figures dressed in Roman outfits, right down to the helmets and swords, walk past. Red hair flashes inside a helmet. *Nola?* No, it's a man. Where has she gone?

Slowly, the sun sinks behind the cathedral, and despite the wine's sourness, we both drink way too much. Is Ethan finding our forced proximity as awkward as me? The wine loosens my tongue. 'Do you ever wonder how things would have turned out if Lula hadn't died?'

221

Ethan's blue eyes meet mine. 'All the time.'

'Everything would have been different. Everything.'

'It would.' Standing, he puts out his hand to pull me up. The familiarity of his skin makes my body tingle.

'We were good together, weren't we?' His voice is low.

I look away. He felt it too. Our shoulders bump as we stumble into the laneway near our hotel. My stomach flutters, but I clench my teeth. I haven't forgotten what he did.

But then he stops in front of me, puts his hands on my shoulders and turns down his face.

And, just like that, I'm back in the street with the puppy. I'm the Tess who has just met Ethan. The Tess who has her whole life before her. And I want so much to be that Tess.

In this moment, with Ethan's hands warm on my shoulders, it feels like everything that came after that never happened.

Chapter 29

Western

Ethan and I press up against each other in the narrow laneway, his lips against mine. It feels right, him and me. We fit. Just the way we always did. His hands are hot on my back, drawing me in. Body to body. Breath to breath.

And I forget. Why I'm here. Why I hate him. Why I'm going to destroy him with my article.

But as we kiss, something turns. Sharp and sour, like a warning. My gut churns. I reach for the wall to steady myself as the ground shifts beneath my feet.

'Are you okay?' Ethan pulls back enough to see my face.

His voice sounds far away, muffled by the roar in my ears.

I stagger back, and his hands fall from my shoulders. Black spots dance in front of my eyes. The stone wall behind him undulates and swirls like melting ice.

And I'm no longer in the laneway. I'm back. The tower.

The night. Snow falling like ash. This time there's something new. A voice.

Kill.

Ice fills my body. I gasp and the vision fractures. But the nausea lingers.

I lock eyes with Ethan, and my voice emerges, low and trembling. 'What happened to Lula that night?'

Ethan's brow furrows. 'Why do you always want to talk about that? Don't you think we need to move on?'

'It's always there. Hanging over us. But we never talk about it.'

His eyes narrow. 'Which part do you want to talk about?'

'Was it an accident? Her fall?'

Ethan clenches his fists. 'Of course it was. No one killed her.'

'But . . .' My heart thumps in my chest, the word echoing in my head. *Kill.* 'We did. Didn't we?'

Ethan stares at me, the pulse beating in his neck. 'For fuck's sake, Tess.' He throws his hands in the air. 'I can't deal with this.' Turning, he strides back down the laneway towards the cathedral.

As he vanishes around the corner, my phone buzzes. I clench my jaw at the sender's name. *Anonymous*

Looking cosy there.

The hairs lift on my arms as I scan the dark alleyway. It's empty. But of course – *the León Cathedral webcam.* Heat flushes over me. I am so over this. I'm going to have it out with them. I tap on the number.

It rings, then someone picks up.

Soft breathing fills my ear. 'Who are you? What do you want?' The line goes dead. My phone buzzes.

I want revenge, oh yes I do,
For what you did to Lula, true.
I'll haunt your dreams, I'll stalk your days,
Until you pay the debt you've made.

xx Anonymous

I swallow. For what *I* did to Lula? What, exactly, did I do? My hands feel clammy as the shadows press in, but I'm not going to let this poet intimidate me. I tap out a Haiku.

Your poetry falls,
Flat as a leaf in autumn,
No beauty to find.

There's no response. My mouth twitches. *Take that, bad poet.* Putting my phone away, I walk back to the hotel.

In the room, I lie awake, my thoughts spiralling. *Anonymous. Ethan. Lula.* Why is Anonymous targeting me? Yes, I was there. But is one of us more guilty than the others? The flashback returns to me. *Kill.* Was that Ethan's voice?

*

Rustling plastic bags wake me in the morning. 'I've got such a headache,' Ethan mutters. 'That wine was terrible.'

225

I keep my eyes closed, my cheeks burning at the memory of the kiss. How could I? It must have been the Spanish wine; I felt like I was under a spell. For once, the flashback saved me. Who knows what would have happened otherwise? I clench my fists. It was so stupid. I'm here to get revenge, not rekindle our relationship.

I crack my eyes open. He's looking right at me. My mouth goes dry. 'I don't feel great either.' It's not just the hangover, my bedbug bites are itching, my knee is sore, and a scratchy throat signals an incoming cold. 'That was a mistake. Last night.'

Ethan holds my gaze. 'Yes. It was.' He shoulders his backpack.

I let out a breath as he disappears out the door. That can never, ever happen again.

Packing up, I hit the road, although it's the last thing I feel like. Dapple is in a bad mood too and goes slower than usual. On the positive side, my new robe makes for comfortable walking. There's none of the inner thigh chafing I was getting with my leggings. I can see why Mum was into kaftans. My chest aches. I'm here for Mum. I can't get distracted.

Leaving the rambling industrial outskirts of León behind, I set out along a dirt road which winds through the rubble of wheat fields. My cold sets in. Before long, I have a hacking cough and a running nose.

Remembering the screenshot Camryn took yesterday, I stop to check the *Artemis* socials. *Oh no.* There I am – baggy white robe, red lumps on my face. The top of the cross, and Dapple's nose, are just in screen.

Artemis freelancer Tess Brody is gonzo journalist extraordinaire, reads the caption. *Guess which famous author is on the Camino right now? Read next month's edition for Tess's celebrity exposé!*

I pull at my hair. It's lucky Ethan doesn't have a phone. My eyes flick through the comments. *What's that on her face? What's with the outfit? Why is she carrying a cross? Celebrity exposé, huh? Wonder who?* I gnaw at my lip. I so need to write this article. If only I could get Ethan to talk about Lula.

Around midday, I spot a group having a catered picnic in a field. A waiter is dispensing wine and succulent-looking dishes. Classical music drifts towards me from a violinist, dressed in a white shirt and black trousers.

They all look up as I stumble past, coughing, my robe trailing in the dirt, my bedbug bites itching. One of the picknickers has dark hair and red lipstick. Is that Ree? Ree, who was so scornful of luxury pilgrims? She shows no sign of recognition as she raises a morsel of tapas to her lips. I march on and am soon convinced it was a mirage. It's too unlikely to be true.

My destination, Villar de Mazarife, could be a setting for a Wild West movie. Plonked in the middle of a flat plain, its buildings match its red-dirt streets. All it needs is a rolling tumbleweed or a slumbering Mexican in a sombrero. Instead, a cowboy on a horse herds a flock of sheep past me as I stop to get my bearings.

Nearby, the skull of a horned animal, possibly a goat, peers over a yellow-painted wall. It's macabre, but the sign says *albergue* so I head for it. The goat's skull turns out to be attached to the prow of a Viking ship, which adds a surreal touch to the town's already off-kilter air.

Tables dot the grass courtyard, and I spot Ethan at one. And opposite him . . . my jaw clenches. *Theo*. What happened to the Costa Brava? Didn't I make it sound enticing enough? Ethan and Theo have a carafe of wine in front of them and are deep in discussion. My stomach sinks as I touch Dapple's furry neck. Is he here to reclaim his donkey?

Ethan doesn't pause his conversation as I join them. My throat tightens. It's like last night's kiss never happened. Which, obviously, is fine by me. But still.

Theo looks annoyed to see me. The feeling is more than mutual.

'. . . so I'm still looking for a miracle,' Ethan says.

I remove Dapple's panniers, prop the cross on the table, and help myself to wine. Dapple wanders off to roll on the succulent grass. Slumping in my chair, I blow my nose and give a pathetic cough. They ignore me. My head spins as I drain my wine, and the sunlight is overbright. Am I feverish?

Dapple waves her legs in the air and hee-haws. I'm overwhelmed with affection for her eccentric ways. Is it really time for us to part? I decide not to draw out the agony. 'What happened to the Costa Brava?' I say, as soon as there's a break in conversation.

Theo blinks. 'Felt guilty. Decided to keep walking.'

'So, I suppose you want Dapple back?'

'I guess. If you don't want her.'

Dapple stands and trots over. She blows down my neck and I pat her velvet nose. 'Good donkey, good girl.' I'm blinking back tears when Theo's words register. 'Are you saying you don't want her back?'

He nods. 'It's, like, way easier without a donkey.' His eyes slide to Dapple. 'I'll take her back if I have to.'

Dapple snorts a fine spray of mucus over my neck. I take it as a sign of affection. 'No.' I smile with sudden joy. 'I want her.'

'You do?' Theo's eyes widen. 'She's yours.'

I stroke Dapple's nose and sip my wine, trying not to show my delight. He might take her back if I'm too enthusiastic.

Donkey issue resolved, Theo turns back to Ethan. 'What sort of miracle would you accept as proof?'

'The usual. A weeping statue. Walking on water. Rising from the dead.' Ethan sips his wine.

I feed Dapple a handful of muesli. I'm so glad we're sticking together. We're not the A team, but we're *amigas*. What will I do with her once I reach Santiago though? A donkey is a big responsibility, especially a superior donkey like Dapple.

'What about surviving a bad car crash?' Theo asks.

As I reach for my wine glass, I notice a wine stain on the table. It has several parts – a long thin bit, a couple of blobby bits nearby. If I squint . . . And if I add a little more. I dip my finger in the wine glass.

Ethan shakes his head. 'Miracles have to violate natural laws.'

'How's it going so far?' I squint against the sun streaming around Ethan's head. 'Your miracle hunt?'

'Badly.'

I hope he's not thinking of giving up.

Theo's eyes flicker to me, and back to Ethan. His lips part.

The hairs lift on the back of my neck. Somehow, I know what he's about to say. Now that he and Ethan are on good terms again, he's going to tell him how I snooped in his bag. I have to stop him.

Chapter 30

Paranormal

'It's a miracle!' My robes billow around my legs as I stand. I point down at the wine stain. 'Look, it's like the Shroud of Turin.'

Ethan and Theo squint at the tablecloth.

'Oh, yeah,' says Theo. 'Not a bad likeness.'

Ethan tilts his head, and points to the long bit. 'That's the beard, right?'

Soon we're surrounded by an excited crowd. Many snap a picture – me in my robes with Dapple and the wine stain. The cross is propped on the table next to us. Talk about an Instagram moment.

One woman looks overcome. 'I almost gave up on the *meseta*, but I saw that sign *Don't Quit Before the Miracle*, so I kept going. And here it is.'

'Miracle or no miracle?' Theo asks Ethan.

Ethan laughs. 'God's going to have to do better than that.'

It's all getting too hectic, so I push my way out through the crowd. Inside, the rooms are empty; everyone's outside viewing the miracle. It's an odd *albergue*. Drawings and writing cover the walls. Graffiti is clearly encouraged. In my worn-out, feverish state, the visual chatter is overwhelming.

A four-bunk room has Ethan and Theo's packs in it, so, propping the cross next to the window, I lie on a bottom bunk. There's no escaping the graffiti though, it's everywhere.

What do they have to say? These pilgrims who have walked for three weeks to get here? *You are perfect. Do it with passion. Be true, be you.* I came into the room for a rest, but now it's like I'm at a personal improvement rally. Platitudes assault me from every direction. There's one outlier. *If you don't have a place to sit, you've always got my face.* This pilgrim hasn't read the Camino manual yet.

My phone buzzes. *Don't forget, you're going to die.* I don't have the energy to figure out how to get rid of this app. My bedbug bites itch, my lungs burn when I cough and my knee aches. I glance out the window. The crowd around the table is growing. A couple of women are kneeling. This makes me feel bad, a silly stunt that was just meant to distract Ethan has got out of hand. I should go out and explain my role in the wine stain.

As I turn my head, my heart leaps at a flash of red hair in the corridor. No doubt it's another Nola mirage. I focus. No, this time, it's her.

Nola leans against the door, wearing a black T-shirt with

black hiking leggings. Her pale skin glows in the light from the window. 'Buen Camino, Tess.'

My chest tightens. 'Buen Camino.' Why, apart from that one sighting by Theo, does she only appear to me? Yes, we had the car-scratching thing but that's hardly the basis for an ongoing relationship. It isn't unusual to bump into pilgrims, but there is definitely something strange about Nola's appearances. Is she stalking me?

'Everything that will happen, has already happened,' she says.

My mind spins – *what the?* – then I recognise the quote. 'Have you been reading *Darker Matters*?'

'Sure. It was a bestseller and all.' She points at the wall.

I follow her gaze to the graffiti. *Everything that will happen, has already happened: Ethan Hill.* Well, that's fame for you.

'You look worried,' she says. 'What's up?'

I feel the urge to unburden myself. Why does she have this effect on me? Nola and I are far from friends, and yet . . . 'Things are strange here. I may have given the impression a miracle took place.'

'A miracle?' Stepping inside the room, Nola leans against my bunk. 'Tell me more.'

I tell her about the Jesus made of wine. Heaving myself out of bed, I look out the window. 'Someone's leading a prayer service around the table now. What if it gets out of hand?'

Coming to the window, she laughs. 'You could go down and explain your role in it?'

I sigh. 'I thought you might say that.'

'I'm just giving advice. It's not a police directive.'

My stomach tightens at her mention of police. I point at the bunk opposite. 'There's room here if you're staying?' It might give me a chance to sneak a look at her notebook.

'Thanks, but I just called in for a drink. See you down the track.' She raises her hand.

I can't let her go; this is so frustrating. 'Wait. Why are you following us?'

She silently meets my gaze.

My spine prickles.

'What makes you think I'm following you?' Her green eyes study mine. 'Is it your guilty conscience talking, Tess?'

I stare at her. The poem Anonymous texted me in León darts into my head. *I want revenge, oh yes I do, For what you did to Lula, true.* She must be the threatening poet. She's already admitted to writing poetry, after all.

'*Buen Camino*, fellow pilgrim.' Nola gives a small smile and departs.

I let out a breath. What does she want? For me to confess? But I can't confess to something I don't even remember. Pulling out the Spanish brandy I bought to replace my gin, I take a gulp. It eases the itching. The sound of praying drifts in the window. Standing up, I lean out. A breeze has sprung up and my robes billow around me. 'It's not a miracle,' I yell. 'It's a wine stain.'

Dapple raises her head from the grass and brays at me. I wave at her, and she flicks her ears.

The group around the table gazes up at me. I repeat myself, but they stare back in awed silence. I can't yell anymore, it's too hard on my throat. I sit back on my bunk.

Someone's squashed an insect on the wall next to me. A spider. 'Look,' I say, as Ethan comes in. 'This squashed spider looks like Jesus too.'

'Hallelujah.' He gazes down at me.

I clench my jaw. *Damn.* Last night's kiss was such a bad idea. What's worse is I'd like to do it again.

'You've created a bit of a stir out there.'

'Don't blame me, I tried to set them straight.'

'That may have had the opposite effect.'

I prop my head up. 'Huh?'

'Here, I took a photo.' He hands me his camera.

On his screen, I'm leaning out the window, my white robes billowing, the cross beside me. The afternoon sun glows, halo-like, in my tangled hair. Even the bedbug bites add to the illusion – I look exactly like an old-time prophetess.

'There's another photo too.' Reaching over, he scrolls back. 'What are you up to, Tess?' His voice is cool.

I gaze at the screen. Nola and I are framed in the window. We're both smiling, like we're the best of friends. Or conspirators. I swallow. 'It's not how it looks.'

'So, how is it?'

I want revenge, oh yes I do . . . 'She appears. She talks to me. She says she isn't following us. I have no idea what she's doing.'

'Why does she talk to you, and not the rest of us?'

My mind lurches to the laneway. His car. But I can't mention that. And besides, that can't be the reason she's targeting me. Unless there's something I've forgotten about that day? 'I don't know.'

'What did you talk about this time?'

'My tablecloth miracle. The nature of time.' I point to the graffiti. 'She's read your book.'

Ethan looks nervous.

Why? Because we're discussing his plagiarised book? *Or . . .* 'Do you think Nola's a crazy stalker fan?'

'It's happened before.' Lying on his bunk, he closes his eyes. 'Theo thinks you're selling us out. Doing a deal.'

I swallow. Has Theo told him I was looking in his backpack? 'I'm not.'

'You'd better not be. You're in this as deep as we are.'

My stomach twists. 'I know that.'

Ethan's eyes open, and he meets my gaze. 'You need to find out what she's up to.'

My pulse thumps. 'I'm trying.'

'Well, try harder. If it's about Lula . . .'

I stare at him. *It is definitely about Lula, what else could it be?* 'If it's about Lula, then what?'

'You know what we need to do.' His voice is flat, but his blue eyes bore into mine. 'Unless you're happy with the idea of going to prison?'

The breath catches in my throat. Does he mean what I think he means? But we wouldn't do that. We're not murderers. Are we?

As I roll over, away from his gaze, my eyes catch on a flash of red. A lollipop, still in its wrapper, is tucked down the side of my mattress, against the wall. My body jerks away from it, as if it's a coiled snake. *Nola.* Who else could have put it there? I pull it out, carefully, so Ethan can't see. My stomach flip flops as I read the neat black writing on the wrapper.

ALL MURDERERS ARE PUNISHED, UNLESS THEY KILL IN LARGE NUMBERS (VOLTAIRE).

Chapter 31

Conspiracy Theory

Then

I woke, clammy and cold, in a quiet, darkened room. My head was throbbing, and it took a while to get my bearings. A dim light came through the window. I was in the Ravensthorpe common room.

My velvet dress was tangled up around my knees. Pulling it down, I sat up. There was a rip in the bottom and mud stains around the hem. As I moved my arm, I winced. My mouth was parched, and a wave of nausea swept over me.

What happened last night? I hadn't drunk much, and I didn't usually get a hangover. Under the sickness and aching muscles, burned an emotion I couldn't name. Embarrassment? Shame? Horror? My chest tightened. There was something I couldn't remember.

Crawling to my feet, I pulled the heavy curtain back, squinting against the glare. It had snowed last night, and the garden was dazzling. A layer of ice coated the pond. The door creaked behind me, and I turned.

Jaz raised her hand. 'Hi.' She looked pale and sick too.

'What happened last night?' I gestured at my torn dress. 'Did I get tangled up in some bushes?'

Jaz's face wrinkled. 'You were pretty out of it. We all were.'

'But . . . I didn't have any mushrooms. And I didn't drink much.'

She raised one eyebrow.

A memory assaulted me. *Red teeth. One eye.* My stomach roiled. Did someone give me mushrooms? 'I think . . .' I lowered my voice. 'I tipped out the mushrooms in the kitchen, I didn't want them, but I think my drink was spiked.'

'What?' Jaz's eyes widened. 'Who by?'

I tried to replay the night's events. It was all so blurry. I'd tipped out the mushrooms and come back with liquorice tea. So, what happened after that? I'd gone to the toilet. Ethan had handed me my mug when I came back. 'Ethan. He was right next to me. He did something to my tea. You know what he's like; he's always trying to get me to take drugs with him.'

Jaz's face was bleached of colour. 'Ethan? Would he do that?'

I let out a puff of breath. 'You don't believe me?'

'Um, yes, of course, but . . .' Jaz put her hand on my arm.

'Hi,' said a voice from the door. It was Ethan. He avoided my eyes.

Why wouldn't he look at me? My gut churned. 'What

time is it? Where's Lula?' I looked around the room. 'Have you seen my phone?'

'I haven't seen her,' said Ethan. 'Maybe she's hungover too.' He pulled out his phone. 'It's one-thirty.'

'One-thirty?' My mind raced. *The story.* It was due at midday. Pushing past Ethan and Jaz, I ran from the common room, and upstairs to the library. Was it too late to send the story? Lula had said midday, but surely it wasn't too late. They had to allow some leeway.

Opening my laptop, I willed it to fire up quickly. I'd have to send them the version I already had. Tapping on my emails, I opened a new message. As I clicked to add an attachment, my eyes moved to my inbox. There was a message. From Persuasion Press.

My pulse raced as I clicked on it. Were they chasing up my story? I scanned the words. They didn't make sense.

I'm sorry but this story is not suitable for our collection.
Regards,
Robert Pettigrew, Editor

What story? I hadn't sent them my story. Had I? A flash of memory hit me. *Last night.* My hands on the keyboard. My stomach twisted. What had I done?

The message was in my sent emails. *My story*, said the subject heading. Nausea welled up as I clicked on the attachment. I dug my fingernails into my hands as I read. It was complete and utter garbage. A random slurry of ideas. There were spelling mistakes and gaps in the text. My protagonist ate dry toast continuously. '*Why? Was it symbolic?'* An elephant was asleep in the corner of her lounge room. *Why?* What planet was I on when I wrote this?

Shutting the laptop, I rested my head on top of it. I wanted to crawl into bed, pull the covers over my head and never come out. After a few minutes, I lifted my head. Lula would help me. She could explain. She was the one who gave us the mushrooms, so it was her fault. The editor was a friend of hers. She would sort it out. Getting to my feet, I jogged down the corridor.

Lula wasn't in her room, but her door was open. Hesitating, I stepped inside. A light glowed on her computer. It was on standby. My heart thumped as I stepped closer. Maybe there was an email there from the editor. But if she found me here . . .

I touched the mouse, and her screen came to life. A page of writing appeared. Either she didn't use a password, or she'd just walked out. Glancing over my shoulder to check I was alone, I looked back at the screen.

It was engrossing, I kept scrolling down. Was it a new novel? After a few pages, I pulled myself away. Lula could turn up any moment.

Back in the common room, Ethan, Jaz and Theo were sitting around the fire, which they must have just lit. They all turned to me as I came in. I had the sense I'd interrupted a discussion.

'Has anyone seen Lula yet?' I asked. 'She's not in her room.'
They shook their heads.

'I don't think she's here.' Jaz's voice was thin. 'We've had a look around.'

As I gazed at them, a memory clawed its way into my

mind. *The tower. The darkness. An oof of surprise.* 'What happened at the tower last night?'

Their eyes flickered to each other, then Ethan got to his feet. 'We need to check the tower.'

*

Ethan led the way, creating a path through the ankle-deep snow. It dampened the bottom of my velvet dress and soaked through my lightweight shoes. I shivered. None of us were dressed for this.

In the distance, the tower looked like an oil painting with its fresh white coating. The door was open. As I glimpsed the shadowy staircase, my chest tightened. Another memory surfaced. *Running down the stairs. Cold stone against my hand.*

'Should we walk around the tower?' said Jaz.

'You go one way, we'll go the other,' said Ethan.

'I'll check up on top,' I said. I'd only climbed a few steps when a muffled scream reached me. *Jaz.* Running outside, I followed her footsteps through the snow.

They were gathered around a snow-covered lump. Still. Silent. I stepped closer, ice spreading through my veins, a scream caught in my throat.

Lula lay on her back. Her face white and frozen. Eyes staring upwards, eyelashes coated in snow.

Ethan knelt, checked for a pulse at her throat. He shook his head, his face grim.

I swayed as it hit me – a blow to the heart. *Lula was dead.*

We huddled in stunned silence next to her body. Not looking at each other. A cold rock filled my belly as the frigid air sliced through my dress. I wanted to stop time. To rewind. To hold back whatever had to happen next.

Jaz said it first, her voice strange and small. Hands thrust into the pockets of her jeans, nose pink with cold. 'No one can know we were up in the tower with Lula.'

I tore my eyes from Lula's body. 'Why? It was an accident.' I swallowed. 'Wasn't it?'

'They'll ask why we didn't get help,' said Ethan. 'Why we left her here all night.'

'They'll find out about the mushrooms.' Theo's eyes darted towards the main building, checking we were alone. 'They're a class A drug.'

'We'll all get expelled from Ravensthorpe,' said Jaz.

'Or sent to jail.' Theo's voice was almost a whisper.

'We might be suspected,' said Ethan.

I stared at Lula's body. At her ice-coated face. Nausea swirled inside me. 'Suspected of what?' My voice was a dry rasp. I craned my head towards the tower. The wall was broken on this side. 'It was an accident,' I repeated, more to myself than to them.

'Still. It's best if no one knows we were here.' Jaz's face was white, her mouth pinched. 'It looks bad. It's too late. She's so grey, she's probably been dead for hours.'

'Drugs, suspicious death of a famous author, students gone wild.' Ethan's breath turned to fog as he spoke. 'The tabloids will have a field day. It will follow us forever.'

Despite the cold, sweat slid down my spine. Were we really going to do this? Lie to the police?

They all stared at me.

My brain screamed *no*, but they were all so sure it had to be this way.

It started to snow. Thick, soft flakes.

Their eyes drilled into me.

I closed my eyes for a moment, and when I opened them, I nodded. 'Okay.'

Standing there next to Lula's cold body, as snow coated our hair, we fleshed out a plan.

And I knew – deep inside – that nothing would ever be the same.

Chapter 32

Cursed Protagonist

Now

Dapple comes to a standstill at a cobblestone bridge and noses the cross on her back.

'Is the cross too heavy for you?'

She snorts in agreement.

'You've been carrying it for two days without complaint.' I don't have the energy to deal with a donkey strike. I slept badly, due to my itching bites and the brooding atmosphere in the bunkroom. *You know what we need to do.* Surely Ethan didn't mean. . . *that*?

The words on the lollipop slide into my head. *All murderers are punished, unless they kill in large numbers . . .*

Dapple stares at me implacably. Our power dynamic has shifted. She knows Theo's palmed her off on me for good, and now she's doing as she pleases.

I have no bargaining power, so I sigh and take the cross off the pannier. Dapple watches as I experiment with different carrying positions. The traditional over-the-shoulder mode works best. We plod on.

I hope, when we meet again, Jaz appreciates the effort I've made to carry the can for her sins. There are my sins to consider too of course. It's ridiculous, but carrying the cross makes me feel I'm atoning.

A couple of kilometres later, I spot graffiti on a roadside sign. *True pilgrims walk in silence*. This seems rather judgemental.

Ree appears beside me, as immaculate as ever. Lifting her fancy camera, she takes a photo of the sign.

I snort. 'Isn't everyone who does this a true pilgrim?' Considering her strident complaints about fake pilgrims though. . . she probably agrees with the graffiti.

But she nods. 'That is true. Thank you, Tess.'

'You're welcome.'

She strides off ahead, her gait jaunty and her glossy hair swinging.

Camryn video calls as I trudge along. Today, her hair sprouts from a ponytail and she's wearing a pink jumpsuit. She gasps when she sees me. 'Your face. It's getting worse.' I touch my face. My bedbug bites are bigger and puffier. 'Are you okay?'

As well as the bites, my nose is running and my knee throbs with each step. But no one, especially not a potential employer, wants to hear about minor ailments. 'I'm fine.'

Camryn's brow wrinkles. 'I notice you have the cross on your shoulder now. And you're still wearing the robes.'

'Yes. It's a Camino thing.'

She frowns. 'Are other people doing this, or just you?'

Could I invent a troupe of cross-carrying donkey pilgrims? *No, too far-fetched.* 'Just me.'

'Why?'

I explain about Jaz and her quest for redemption, without being specific about her sins.

'That makes no sense. This isn't the Middle Ages.'

I plod on. 'Yes, but here on the Camino some things haven't changed.'

'Well, I suppose that's a compassionate thing for you to do, if the cross does need to be carried.'

'It does. You'll have to trust me on that.'

'Can't the donkey carry it?'

Dapple swivels her ears.

'The donkey has enough on her plate.'

'I see. And the robes?'

'My clothes were confiscated because of bedbugs.'

'Wow. Bizarre.' Camryn tilts her head. 'You're off in your own strange little bubble over there, aren't you? I hope you're working on the feature.'

Aargh. The feature. I can't deal with this right now. Simulating a *crackle, crackle* sound, I hang up.

*

'*Buenos Dias.*' The young Spanish man points towards his wares – fruit, cake and drinks. We are on a tree-lined plateau far from civilisation.

I stop for a drink of water, and he gives Dapple an apple.

247

He gestures at my robe and cross. 'You are *traditionale*.' He clenches his fist. 'A strong pilgrim.'

'Oh, not really,' I murmur.

'I heard you were coming. The wise woman with a donkey, they said.' He flashes his white teeth.

'What? Me?'

'Yes. Everyone is talking about the miracle of the tablecloth.' He points at his chalkboard. *Everyone who does this is a true pilgrim: Tess.*

My cheeks burn. Ree must have told him that.

'Do you have any more words of wisdom for me?'

My phone buzzes. 'Don't forget you're going to die?'

He nods. '*Gracias*. That is so simple but profound. We are all going to die.'

I depart to a warm '*Buen Camino*.'

As I descend into another valley, my destination, Astorga, appears on a hill in the distance. Two cathedral spires rise above the houses. But the town appears to recede as I advance. As I force my weary legs up a steep hill, my phone rings with another video call. *Camryn*. Not again!

Camryn is sipping green liquid from a glass and wearing workout gear now. Her pink singlet reveals an intricate vine tattooed on one shoulder. 'Tess, what happened? We got cut off. So, how's the feature going? It's due in less than two weeks.'

Less than two weeks? 'That won't be a problem.' I decide to distract her. 'I like your tattoo. I've got a tattoo of—'

'Cool. Cool. Send me what you've—'

A woman in a white robe with a red cross on the chest strides past me. She's holding a staff with a water-carrying gourd at the top, in historical pilgrim style. Giving the old *Buen Camino*, she vanishes, robes floating behind her, red hair flashing in the sun.

Was that Nola? Or did I imagine her? On the Camino, it's not unusual to have visions. The actress Shirley MacLaine had revelations of her exotic past life as a harem girl. Lula met the Devil. The Camino is not the real world – anything goes.

'Who was that?' pipes Camryn from my phone.

So, she *was* real. 'It might have been a Templar?'

'Huh. Is that normal?'

I hesitate. 'More or less?'

Camryn frowns. 'Just wanted to let you know. A vacancy has come up for an intern. I'm telling all the freelancers. Do a good job of this feature and you might be in with a chance. If you're interested?'

A ripple of possibility fills me. *Tess Brody, Artemis intern.* 'Yes. I'm interested. Definitely.'

'Cool. So, give it your best shot.' A hand taps Camryn's arm, and she has a muttered conversation off camera. 'Got to go. Send me a draft ASAP. Delve deep to find the splinter that will feed your writing, Tess.' She hangs up.

I walk on. *Imagine.* Me, an Artemis intern. 'I so need to make a start on this feature.'

Dapple flicks her ears. *Just get on with it.*

'Easy for you to say, but . . .' A flash of clarity hits. 'I need to finish this Ravensthorpe memoir first. To remember what happened. Once I've done that, the article will be easy.'

Dapple snorts her endorsement.

And it's only then that Camryn's words repeat in my head. *Delve deep to find the splinter that will feed your writing.* Adrenaline rushes through my body. That's what Lula used to say. My mind spins. Did Camryn know Lula? Sweat trickles down my spine. Is it possible that Camryn is *Anonymous*?

No. She can't be. What about the notes and the lollipops? It must be someone on the trail. Unless she has an accomplice?

*

Dapple and I are plodding past a wire fence threaded with crosses made from sticks, when two boys appear beside us.

'You are Tess.' The speaker is dark-haired, tattooed and wearing only short shorts. His voice is deeply accented.

I nod.

'We are from Romania,' says the other one, who is blond, and also bare-chested. 'Do you have some words of wisdom?'

'Don't forget you're going to die?'

'We heard this already,' says the dark-haired one. 'From the guy with the food stall on the hill. It is written on his chalkboard.'

'We want to know your other secret,' says the blond one.

My other secret? I don't have one, but these boys are so eager and, to be honest, so cute, I'd like to oblige. It comes to me – Ethan's book. 'Time is an illusion.' I wave my hand towards the hills. 'We're not walking to Santiago. We are already there.'

The boys give me a sidelong look. The blond one says something, and they laugh. 'Thank you, Tess,' they chorus, and skip up the hill out of sight.

Wow. My pilgrimage persona is really levelling up. Not only have I acquired a donkey, white robes, and a wooden cross, I am now a woman of wisdom. What next? Will I graduate to reincarnated Egyptian princess? This is going to make a great article, once I eventually write it.

*

Rabanal is a hillside village, bisected by a steep street. The stone buildings and sweeping views remind me of pictures I've seen of Nepal. Fluttering Tibetan prayer flags on a shop maintain the illusion. A lump fills my throat. Mum and I planned to go trekking in Nepal one day.

Dapple and I walk past a wall adorned with a scrawl of white chalk. *We are not walking to Santiago, we are already there: Tess.* I snort. How long can I keep this guru act up for?

The English volunteer at the *albergue* coos over Dapple. 'Leave her here. I'll take her out to the garden.' She eyes the cross on my shoulder. 'You mustn't miss the mass. It's a Gregorian chant. Very special.'

My cold has subsided to a lingering cough, but I'm still shattered. Dumping my things on a bunk, I shower, then head out to the balcony, which overlooks distant mountains. Swallows dart out from their nests in the terracotta roof. In the garden, Theo and Ethan are drinking wine, with Dapple munching nearby. Things are weird between us, and they think I'm conspiring with Nola, but it looks so peaceful that I head on down.

Theo and Ethan are both a little cool, but they don't raise the topic of Nola. When we've emptied the bottle, Ethan stands. 'Time for the Gregorian chanting.'

As we slide into a pew near the front of the crowded church, I ask, 'What is a Gregorian chant anyway?'.

'Medieval Christian music,' says Theo. 'Sung in Latin, acapella style, no accompaniment. Remember that music I played at the winter retreat?'

My hands go clammy. *The common room at Ravensthorpe. Choral music filling the room . . .*

The monks begin to sing, their eery melody filling the church. It presses in on me, crawls under my skin. My vision blurs as the memory rushes back. *The candles. The inky tea. Lula.*

As the monks' voices soar, my throat clenches and I cough. The music swells, but heads turn as I cough and splutter uncontrollably – eyes streaming, chest burning. I can't stop. I need to get out.

Theo and Ethan frown as I squeeze past them. Lungs hacking, I scuttle past the worshippers, trying to exude an air of humble apology. I cough and cough, each breath harder to catch.

My robe catches on the side of a pew, yanking me sideways. The two Romanian boys eye me warily as I wrench the fabric free, my coughs echoing off the stone walls. Their eyes follow me to the door, the chanting trailing behind me.

The wooden door groans shut, blocking the sound, and my coughing stops instantly. I slump against the door, panting, my heart pounding. As I dig around in my pocket for a tissue, my fingers touch something else. *Paper.* I pull it out.

Nausea churns inside me. Block letters. Black. Familiar.

THE SADNESS WILL LAST FOREVER – VINCENT VAN GOGH.

Images tear through my mind. *The ruin. The scream. The bird. Running. Running. Running.* Bile rises in a hot bitter wave, and, leaning over, I vomit onto the cobblestones.

Chapter 33

Christmas Story

Then

'The snow will have covered any signs we were there last night.' Ethan leant back on his chair in the common room, his tone flat, almost casual.

He still wouldn't meet my eyes. Maybe it didn't mean anything. Or maybe it meant everything. The whole situation felt warped, as if the world had spun off its axis. It seemed unreal to me, how quickly we'd agreed to bury the truth. But we'd made our pact, and it was too late to turn back now.

'We were all wearing gloves, so we won't have left any prints,' said Jaz.

Theo gazed at his phone. 'The mushrooms won't show up on the toxicology reports. So, they shouldn't ask about that. If they do, we know nothing.' He tapped. 'The penalty's up to seven years for possession.'

The blood left my face. I'd had no idea.

We washed all the cups from last night and burned the small plastic bag that had held the mushroom powder in the fireplace.

'They'll ask us why Lula was on the tower,' said Ethan.

We all stared at each other.

'Suicide,' said Theo. 'Everyone knew she was up and down. She'd had those bad reviews.'

'If we leave a note, they won't question it,' said Jaz.

'But we can't write in her handwriting,' said Ethan.

I stared at them, a lump filling my throat. Were we really talking about this?

'I've got it.' Ethan pulled thin thermal gloves from his coat pocket and drew them on. Walking over to the table, he picked up Lula's faded brown notebook. Opening it at a dog-eared page, he read the line Lula had read us a few days before. '*The sadness will last forever*.' He looked up. 'Sounds like a suicide note to me. She's even underlined it. We can bookmark it and leave it on her desk. It's got her prints on it.'

Theo and Jaz nodded.

'Good thinking,' said Theo.

'Tess?' Ethan said.

'Okay.' We were so far in; we may as well go all the way.

'So, now we call the police?' asked Jaz.

'Wait.' Doubt niggled at my mind. 'I need to be clear before we talk to the police. Why didn't any of you check on her last night?'

'We didn't know she fell,' said Jaz. 'Same as you. It was all pretty wild up there. I was hallucinating some weird stuff. Demons, witches, trolls. That was strong gear. We figured she'd come in.'

It made sense, but I wasn't sure I believed her.

After we called the police and reported Lula's death, things happened quickly.

'Just act natural,' said Jaz. 'Distressed, I mean.'

That part wasn't hard. I felt fuzzy and disorientated. Beneath the shock of Lula's death was a dull, sad ache which was only partly for Lula. My story wouldn't appear in *Best Young Brits*. I wouldn't be The Chosen One. After that night in Lula's office, I'd texted Mum to tell her about it. I'd made it sound a sure thing.

I'm so proud of you, she'd replied. *I knew you were special.*

I couldn't bear to imagine her face when I told her it wouldn't happen.

Two uniformed coppers arrived, a man and a woman. We told them where Lula's body was, and soon after that a police van appeared and drove over to the tower. We were all interviewed separately in the common room. The older cop did all the talking, while the younger one, the red-haired woman, took notes. She was so quiet, I hardly noticed her.

I stuck to the story. We'd had an evening tutorial with Lula, then she'd gone upstairs to do some work. It wasn't until she didn't show up for the next day's tutorial that we went looking for her. First around the building, then in the grounds. We'd found her body in the snow, and the door to the tower was open.

After they'd interviewed us all, the police told us we

were free to go home for Christmas. If they needed more information, they'd follow up.

It was only after the police had gone, when I was in my room packing, another memory lurched into my mind. *Hands*. Hands on Lula's chest. My heart jolted. Was it a real memory, or another hallucination? Last night's events were a kaleidoscope. Fragmented and strange.

Jaz and Theo had already driven off when I emerged, but Ethan was waiting outside the front door, hands thrust deep in his overcoat pockets.

I hadn't confronted him about the drink spiking yet. Even so, things were awkward.

'Do you want a lift back to London?' he said. It was clear he was hoping I'd say no.

I didn't want to sit in a car with him for two hours, wondering if he'd drugged me.

'No, it's easier to catch the train. We're on opposite sides of the city.'

Relief swept over his face. After a silent car ride, we pulled up at the station in Bishopsgate.

'See you in the New Year.' He gave me a cursory goodbye kiss. His family were heading off to ski in the Italian alps after Christmas, so we didn't need to pretend we'd catch up in London.

He started the car, and was about to leave, when I put my hand on the window. He wound it down. I swallowed, my pulse rising as I lowered my head to his level, meeting his eyes. I had to ask. 'Ethan . . .'

He raised his eyebrows.

'Did you spike my drink?'

His face went white, then red. He shook his head. 'Jesus, Tess, no.' There was a desperate note in his voice. He didn't sound surprised though. I noticed that.

I bit my lip as I straightened. 'I think you did.'

His red sports car had roared from the car park before I reached the station.

*

'Her story's going to be reviewed in *The Times*.' Mum's cheeks flushed pink with pride.

We were having a dreary Christmas lunch with my grandparents at an Indian restaurant in Manchester. I hadn't told Mum what had happened at Ravensthorpe. Lula's death hadn't hit the news yet, maybe the police were holding off until after Christmas.

'And she's got a hot-shot agent already . . .' she continued.

I smiled through gritted teeth. Mum would have loved to make it an achievement trifecta with the addition of Ethan, but I wasn't going to give her that.

After Christmas, I spent a lot of time in my room drinking. It was the only thing that dampened the guilt over our cover-up. My anger about the drink spiking. And my anguish about the *Best Young Brits* story and The Chosen One. I needed to break it to Mum that my accomplishments had come to nothing, but I couldn't bring myself to talk about it.

I didn't try to write. It was pointless. I'd had my chance and I'd blown it. As I sat on my bed drinking gin, I tried to imagine Ethan schussing down the slopes. I'd never been skiing. I was half-expecting a message from him, but it didn't come. Had we broken up? I didn't feel as shattered by the idea as I might have expected. That night on the tower had changed everything.

Had Ethan deliberately sabotaged me so I couldn't finish my story? He knew I was front runner to be The Chosen One. I'd heard him arguing with Lula. Was he trying to convince her to pick him instead? It made sense he'd spiked my drink. He'd wanted me to take drugs with him. And he was the one who handed me my tea.

On New Year's Eve, I went out with some girls from school who I'd run into on the street. I got trashed and was bad company. My mind was on Ravensthorpe. The night of Lula's death was still a blur, but sickening fragments spooled through my head. The running. The hammer. *The hands.* Had someone pushed Lula?

If someone had, I was implicated too. I'd lied to the police. I'd let them think it was suicide. I'd helped to bury the truth.

On New Year's Day, I headed back to Ravensthorpe. Classes didn't start until the next day. Somehow though, I knew they'd be there.

*

'Happy New Year,' said Jaz, when I walked in, but her tone didn't match the words. They were sitting around the common room fire.

Ethan gave me a half-smile, then returned his gaze to the fire. He didn't try to kiss me. His face was tanned, with white rings around his eyes from his sunglasses.

'How was Courmayeur?' I asked with forced lightness as I sat down.

'Crowded.'

My chest tightened. He hadn't even looked at me when he replied.

It was only eleven a.m., but they'd opened a bottle of wine. I found a glass and joined them. We made desultory conversation about our Christmases. Jaz had been at her family's country house in the Cotswolds and Theo's family had jetted off to Tenerife. He'd caught the sun too. My lunch in Manchester sounded even more drab in the retelling than it had felt at the time.

No one mentioned Lula's name. Her presence hung in the air though. It hung in the shadows under our eyes and the false note in our voices. Who would be the first to mention her? It was almost a relief when it came – a sharp rap on the door.

Our eyes snapped to the window. Outside stood the two police officers, caps pulled low against the wind. We met each other's eyes – a silent acknowledgement of our pact.

My pulse fluttered as I showed them into the common room. 'Tea? Coffee?' My voice sounded too bright.

They shook their heads, taking in the now-empty wine bottle as they sat.

'The post-mortem results have come in,' said the older police officer. 'Ms Thornton didn't die from the fall.'

He paused, his dark eyes fixing on each of us in turn.

I held my breath, stared straight ahead.

'She had fractures, but they weren't fatal.' His voice was

steady. 'She died later. From hypothermia. Probably took a while.'

The blood drained from my face. *Lula.* Lying there alive. Alone. Unable to move. Snow falling on her face. My throat closed. If I hadn't run, I could have saved her. 'Any of us could have.'

'Shame no one noticed she was missing,' said the policeman, almost to himself. 'Would have made all the difference.'

We avoided each other's eyes. The young policewoman scribbled in her notebook. Sweat trickled down my spine. Did we look guilty?

'Anything to add to your statements?' the policeman asked.

I shook my head, fingernails digging into my palms, biting down an urge to scream, to confess. This was so much worse. How could we have done that? Left her there?

'Well.' He dropped his card on the table and stood, replacing his cap. 'There's my number. If you think of something.'

And then they were gone.

The silence was unbearable.

'Fuck.' Ethan stood abruptly and left the room.

Theo put his head in his hands, his shoulders rigid.

Jaz was frozen, pale. She closed her eyes, just for a second. Then she got up and left without a word.

I stayed there, staring at the card on the table.

I couldn't sleep that night. I kept turning it all over in my head. If I hadn't been tripping, it all would have turned out differently. I wouldn't have run. I would have saved Lula. I would have got my story in on time and been in *Best Young Brits*. I would have been The Chosen One.

By spiking my drink, Ethan set things on a different course. I'd become an accomplice to manslaughter. Or . . . My body turned cold. *Murder*.

I must have slept eventually, as I woke in the night covered in sweat. My heart was pounding, and my sheets were tangled around my legs. A vivid dream replayed in my head.

Lula stood over me, a hammer dangling from her hand. Her teeth were red and her face blue with cold. *I am Beira*, she said in a voice cold as ice. *I cause thunder and storms. I cause trees to wither. You were never The Chosen One, Tess.*

As I lay there awake, I thought about what Ethan had done. A resolve solidified inside me. I couldn't let him get away with it.

Chapter 34

Atonement

Now

'Today is the highest point, Dapple. The Iron Cross.'

Pilgrims bring something to the Iron Cross in memory of someone who couldn't walk with them. Or as a symbol of something they want to give away, Lula says in her book.

Dapple meets my eyes with a glum expression, then turns back to gaze out at the rain and the grey fog which blankets the hills.

'Yes, you're right, it's not going to be fun in the rain. But it has to be done.' Fastening on her yellow raincoat, I hoist my cross and set out. The streets are quiet. All the pilgrims are ahead.

I'd slept badly, my mind replaying the writing on the note. *The sadness will last forever.* It was the Van Gogh quote we'd chosen for Lula's suicide note. Who put it in my pocket? Ethan and Theo were beside me in the church . . .

But anyone could have slipped it in there while I was in the shower, I'd left my robe outside the cubicle. Nola? I haven't seen her here, but that doesn't mean she hasn't seen me.

Before long, we pass a village sign – Foncebadon. 'Shirley MacLaine said this village was inhabited by a witch and a gang of demon dogs,' I tell Dapple. 'She barely escaped with her life. But that was years ago so hopefully they've moved on.'

We pass a man fixing stonework. A terrier yaps at us from behind a fence. 'So far, so undemonic,' I mutter. As we carry on though, I see smoke curling out of a chimney. *The witch's chimney?* The quiet streets seem eerie and, despite myself, I'm slightly spooked. On the outskirts of town, I startle at a flash of grey in a field. A large animal lopes through the mist and is gone. I stare at the swirling fog. 'Was that a wolf?'

Dapple's ears are flat against her head and her teeth are bared. *Sensing danger.* Wasn't there a hiker killed by wolves in Greece? Does that happen in Spain too? I pick up the pace. Dapple is keen to move on as well and we climb higher and higher into the mist.

As the rain increases, my poncho's limitations become obvious. Soon, I'm wet through, the bottom of my robe clinging to my legs. I suppose Ethan and Theo are already ensconced in a cosy café on the other side.

Dapple gives me a reproachful look.

'I know, you hate the rain. I do too.' I trudge up the hill, cursing the weather. What am I doing here? I bend over as a coughing fit strikes. As I straighten, my eyes focus on a dark shape emerging from the mist above. As I plod towards it, it reveals itself as an enormous metal cross protruding from a pile of rocks.

In my disgruntled state, this oversized cross in the middle of nowhere strikes me as morbid. Why would you worship the symbol of a cruel execution? As I think this, my toe strikes a rock. I stumble and the heavy cross on my shoulder pulls me forward. The air puffs out of me as I hit the ground.

I lie in the mud with the cross pressing into my shoulder, gasping for air. Dapple lowers her head and snorts a spray of mucus onto the back of my neck. The ludicrousness of my situation strikes me. How have I become a robe-wearing, donkey-leading, cross-carrying pilgrim, stuck in the mud in front of a giant cross? If anyone saw me now, they'd have a good laugh, as so they should. My life is a joke.

I lift my head. The Iron Cross looms dark against the swirling mist. A sob wells from inside me, and another. I'm wet, cold, sick, tired, and just plain sad. How did I get to a point where my only way forward is to stalk an author who's pursuing faith?

There seems to be no point in moving. In fact, with the cross on top of me, I don't think I can, so I lower my head and lie there in the dirt, rain pattering on my back. Dapple nudges me with her nose.

I gaze up at the Iron Cross again; it now appears to be floating in the mist. An urge to pray blooms inside me. It's illogical but irresistible. I give in to it. *Please God, forgive me for not making Mum proud.*

As I lie there in the mud, Jaz's cross heavy on my back,

Mum's voice whispers in my ear. *Sobriety, and kickboxing. That's the key, Tess.*

Sobriety and kickboxing . . .

Ethan's words return. *Alcohol is a drug too.*

Do I have a drinking problem? It's true that after a night out, there can be blank sections in my memory. I feel vaguely guilty, and it takes me a while to recall what I've done. Did I get into an argument at a party? Or trip over the stairs on the way home? But everyone does that, don't they? My drinking is a choice, not a need.

If that's true, Mum murmurs, *why don't you prove it?*

Dapple nudges me with her nose again.

I resist, but the appropriate penance is clear. 'Jeez, okay, I'll give up drinking. For a while. To show I can. And I'll . . .' I hesitate.

Dapple nudges me again.

I breathe heavily, the rain drenching me. 'All right, all right, I'll take up kickboxing.' As if in answer to my prayer, my phone rings. I lever it out of my pocket, holding it in the shelter of my body, so it doesn't get wet.

Camryn's face fills the screen. 'Tess?'

'Hi, Camryn.' I bet none of her other freelancers are making this bad an impression.

She frowns. 'What's going on there? Are you lying down? Is that the donkey behind you?' Her voice fades out, but her face remains.

As I lie there staring at her, her words return. *Delve deep to find the splinter that will feed your writing.* Something twists inside me. 'Camryn? Did you know Lula?'

Her voice echoes, as if coming from the end of a tunnel.

'Lula? Why are you asking about Lula?' The connection crackles.

'You said that thing. About the splinter.' A sob escapes me. I don't understand anything. I wish at least one person in my life would be exactly what they seem to be.

Camryn's voice emerges with a crackle. '. . . mad bitch.'

The connection dies. My phone is flat. *Mad bitch*. Does she mean me? I lower my head into the mud, close my eyes and cry.

*

'Sad?' asks a soft voice.

I blink. Was I asleep? A figure is standing over me, backlit against the sky. My heart skips a beat.

Nola. She's wearing a white rain poncho with a hood and holding the staff with the water gourd on the end. Strands of red hair plaster her pale face.

A shiver runs through me. Did she put the note in my pocket?

Lifting the cross off me, she holds out her hand. I take it and she pulls me up. She gestures at the cross on the hill. 'It's a sad place.'

'Yes.' The Iron Cross in the rain is making me sad, and the cross on my shoulder even sadder. And now Nola's here and she seems sympathetic, but she's probably been writing me threatening poems and wants me jailed for what we did to Lula.

Unless that's Camryn?

Beckoning me, Nola walks away, up the pile of rocks to the cross. Letting go of Dapple's rope at the bottom, I follow. Flags, ribbons and trinkets decorate the rockpile. At the top, beneath the cross, mementos are strewn across the rocks. Children's shoes. Flowers. Shells.

Pilgrims bring something here in memory of someone who couldn't walk with them. Or as a symbol of something they want to give away, says Lula in my head.

Nola stands next to the cross, looking at me. She's waiting for me to deposit my special object.

'I don't have anything.'

She blinks into the rain, her gaze fixed on mine.

I feel judged. She's not only Nola the ex-policewoman, she's Nola the Templar now. Protector of holy sites and pilgrims. She knows who I am, what I'm doing here, how pathetic I am. She knows the promise I made, there in the mud. She knows everything.

Below the rocks, Dapple, draped in her yellow raincoat, looks at me. Her brown eyes urge me on.

I want to produce something. To placate them, so we can move on. I shiver. I'm so cold and wet and sad. I have to get off this hill. But what? *Not kickboxing. I can't do that here.*

Dapple and Nola wait.

Of course. I take off my day pack, forage around and pull out my little bottle of brandy.

Nola nods and Dapple snorts in agreement.

Resisting the urge for one last swig, I place it under the cross. It looks so jolly there with its bright red label and glistening amber fluid. I imagine its warmth burning my throat. *One sip. It would do me good.*

'Come on.' Nola climbs down from the cross.

As I follow, an orange flash catches my eye. I lean closer. It's a photo, inside a plastic bag, with a rock on top. As I pick it up, my pulse jumps. It's us. But I've never seen this photo before.

It was taken at my birthday party. Ethan's in his orange party jacket. Lula stares into the camera, her brown hair falling over her eyes. Theo's head emerges from between Lula and Ethan's shoulders. Jaz leans against Lula, and me . . . The hairs lift on my arms. My hair is messy and my eyes unfocused. I'm leaning against Ethan; his arm is around me. I look completely out of it. That's not what chills me though. It's the red circle scrawled around our faces.

I shiver. Who took this photo? Who placed it here? Is it a symbol of someone they wish was with them, or of something to leave behind? I turn the photo over.

On the back is some writing in the familiar neat capitals. My throat tightens as I read it.

THEIR INK SPILLS LIES, THEIR PENS DECEIT, EACH CRAFTED WORD A SOUR DEFEAT.
BUT THEIR SINS WILL COME TO LIGHT, THEIR CRIMES EXPOSED IN BROAD DAYLIGHT.

xx Anonymous

Chapter 35

Detective Story

Nola waits below the rock pile, a white outline in the mist. Rain washes over my face as I gaze at her, my pulse thumping in my neck. What does she want? Why does she keep writing these poems? I have to get it out of her.

Tucking the photo into my pocket, I pick my way towards her. On the way I pass sprouting dandelions, golden against the mist. I pluck a few, tucking them under a rock. 'For you, Mum.' I'd like to say more, but words fail me, and Nola is waiting.

We walk in silence down the hill, Dapple clopping behind. Soon, we arrive at a ramshackle stone building. Nola goes in, disappearing into the shadows. After a moment's hesitation, I follow. I'm like one of those oblivious girls in horror movies who stumble into the villain's lair, but I'm so cold and wet, I can't go on.

It's dark inside, but a fire's burning and I perch next to it.

Templar flags hang on the walls. Despite the rusticity, there's a power point, so I put my phone on to charge. There's no reception here though, so I can forget about calling for help if Nola turns on me.

Nola lights a gas stove and makes a cup of coffee, which I gratefully drink. She gives Dapple, who is under the eaves, some hay. For a vengeful nemesis, she's strangely benevolent. Through the open door of an out-building, I spot several mattresses. This appears to be a rundown *albergue*. Should I stay here? I don't suppose anyone will miss me. Nola and I can have it out. A fight to the death. It will be a relief to get it over with.

Nola sits on a stool, contemplating the mist outside, and probably plotting my destruction.

I clear my throat. 'So, you're a Templar now?'

Nola's green eyes meet mine. 'I'm giving it a go. I met a Templar, back a way. He was sick, so he asked me to fill in for a bit.' She gestures around the shack. 'You can be a Templar too; I could do with the help.'

The idea is strangely tempting. Could this be my penance? 'Are female Templars a thing?'

Nola nods. 'Ermengarda of Oluja commanded an entire Templar monastery.'

'Huh. She sounds quite a gal.'

Nola gives a small smile. 'So, you left your brandy behind at the cross. Do you have a drinking problem?'

I gaze out at the mist. 'No. Maybe. Sometimes I drink too much. A break won't hurt.' I meet her eyes. Enough about me. 'Why are you here, Nola?'

Nola gestures around. 'Looking after the Templar *albergue*.'

I snort. 'No. On the Camino.' My voice rises. 'What do you want?'

Nola pauses. 'I grew up in that village. Bishopsgate. The one near Ravensthorpe.'

Nola's like a politician; she only answers the questions she likes. 'But aren't you . . .?'

'Irish? Yes. My family moved over from Cork when I was ten. Haven't lost the accent. I went up to London after school. Joined the police force. They wanted someone who knew the area, so they sent me back there. I used to see all the Ravensthorpe students in the village. You were all so colourful. So different to everyone in the village.' She turns to meet my eyes. 'I was at your birthday party.'

'You were?' My heart skips a beat as I touch the photo in my pocket. Did Nola take it? I swallow. 'I was so drunk that night. It's a bit of a blur.'

'You don't remember me, but I remember you.' Nola's mouth twitches. 'I'm sorry. Did that sound a bit creepy? I'm not stalking you.'

My nails dig into my palms, it sounds an awful lot like she is. *Nola was at my birthday party.* She knew who I was when she interviewed me after Lula's death.

Nola looks out the window where the mist swirls. 'I've got jobs to do. Got to earn my keep.' She gets up and steps outside.

I'm about to follow when my eyes land on her notebook, which she's left sitting on the bench. I check the door. There's no sign of her. Holding my breath, I stretch my hand out, pick it up, and flick it open. Her name is on the inside cover, in neat black handwriting. Fionnuala Kelly.

Fionnuala. Nola is an abbreviation. No wonder I haven't been able to Google her.

A footfall sounds outside, and I drop her notebook to the table, my stomach fluttering.

Nola's head appears, backlit in the doorway. 'Coming?' Her eyes flicker towards the notebook. Did she see?

I head outside. *Fionnuala*. It's a distinctive name. I should be able to track her down now. The rain has eased, but a wet mist lingers. My robe's gone from sodden to damp, and I shiver in the breeze. A wooden cross stands beside a flagpole. Grasping a rope, Nola raises the Templar flag. It flutters languidly, the red cross on white background.

I salute. It seems to be called for.

Two pilgrims come down the track and pause, eyeing us. It's the two Romanian boys, now wearing matching yellow ponchos. To them, I must appear to belong here. A vision of an alternative universe flashes before me. I'll stay here with Nola and learn the ancient rites. We'll roam the Camino, helping distressed pilgrims like the knights of old. She'll forgive me for what I did to Lula. *Or exact her revenge.*

I raise my hand to the boys, but they exchange a glance and vanish into the mist. My currency as the wise woman has diminished. *Wise* may have morphed into *crazy*.

Mad bitch. Camryn's words echo in my head again.

My stomach rumbles and the wind flattens my robe against my ankles. An urge to return to the humdrum world of *boccadillos*, hot showers, and *café con leche* strikes me. Comfort is not a priority here on the hill. I'm not ready to follow Ermengarda's example yet. 'Well, I guess I'll be off now.' I'm aiming for casual, but my voice sounds high and uncertain.

Nola gazes at me inscrutably as the mist swirls around us.

My throat tightens. Is she going to try to stop me?

But she inclines her head. 'Okay. I'll be seeing you.'

'Thanks for the coffee.'

She meets my eyes. 'Be careful, Tess.'

My pulse judders. It's not a throwaway line. I stare at her, my mind on the photo and the latest poem. *Their sins will come to light*. 'I will.' Retrieving Dapple, and my phone, I leave Nola to her medieval rites.

As I descend, my eyes catch on yet another trailside memorial to a dead pilgrim. I suppose, with so many people on the trail, it's natural some die. It does seem unusually common though. Is being a pilgrim perilous?

The rain stops as I get to Molinaseca at the bottom of the hill. Fields glisten in the afternoon sun. The town is spick and span, with cobbled streets, flower boxes, and an arched bridge over the river. I glance back at the hill. It's covered in mist. Nola, the cross, the wolf, Camryn's call, it's like they happened in another world.

My phone beeps to show it has a signal. Pulling it out, I Google *Fionnuala Kelly* plus *police* and *private investigator* but draw a blank. What else? She said she grew up in Bishopsgate, so I try that. *Fionnuala Kelly Bishopsgate*. A picture appears. *Bingo*. It's from *The Bishopsgate News*. My heart skips a beat.

Famous author mentors young Bishopsgate writers, reads the caption. I enlarge the picture. There's Lula, a bit younger than when I first met her. She's standing with a group of teenagers in school uniform. One has red hair down to her shoulders and a broad grin on her face. It's unmistakeably Nola.

I swallow, staring at the photo, my eyes flicking between Nola and Lula. They are next to each other, their shoulders brushing. Lula knew Nola when she was a teenager. She mentored her. They were close. I touch the photo in my pocket and certainty hits me. I suspected before, but now I am sure. Nola is stalking me, and she's here for revenge.

You know what we need to do. My stomach clenches. Is Ethan saying the same thing about me?

Chapter 36

Secrets and Lies

Then

My gut churned as I sank onto a beanbag in the Ravensthorpe meeting room. It was the day after the visit from the police, and the rest of the students had returned.

Ethan was on the far side of the room. Our eyes met, but his slid away before mine. A wave of heat swept down my body.

Jaz crouched against the wall, her knees to her chest. Her face was pale, and she avoided my gaze too.

A hush filled the room as Iris walked in and stood at the front. 'I'm sure you've all heard about Lula Thornton's tragic death.'

A couple of girls started crying.

'Lula will be a massive loss to Ravensthorpe, and to the wider world. I know many of you will be deeply affected. Counselling shall be offered to those who need it. Her funeral will be in London the week after next. There won't be any classes on that day, and you are all invited to attend.

'I understand the collective grief enveloping us all. Lula possessed an extraordinary and boundless talent. Nevertheless, she would have wanted the work here to go on as usual.' Iris glanced at the sobbing girls. 'You know what Lula would say? Channel it into the work. That shall be all for now. Continue, Matthew.'

After a short pause, Matthew, a third-year student, stood up and went through the business carried over from before Christmas. One boy had thrown a plate at a wall in a creative rage. Someone suggested he be banned from classes for two days. The motion passed unanimously. A girl complained someone had taken her knitting, a scarf, from the common room. The red-faced culprit confessed, offering to make amends by adding some rows to the scarf before returning it. This was acceptable.

'Anything else?' asked Matthew.

My hands turned clammy. I didn't want to raise this in the meeting, but I was out of options. I didn't know what else to do.

*

I'd tried to talk to Ethan about the drink spiking several times, but he was avoiding me. In the cafeteria this morning, he'd left as soon as I headed towards him. Why would he do that if he didn't spike my drink? I couldn't just let it slide; he needed to be held to account. Before the meeting, I'd decided to speak to Iris.

Climbing the stairs to Iris's room, I'd knocked on her open door.

Annoyance flashed across her face as she looked up from her computer. 'Yes?' Her fingers didn't leave the keyboard.

'Can I talk to you?'

'About?' Iris had dark circles under her eyes. It was the first day of classes after Christmas, so no doubt she was busy. Especially with Lula gone.

'I have a . . . complaint. About another student.'

Iris breathed out sharply, not hiding her impatience. 'Our meeting is in an hour. That is the correct venue for voicing disputes. You know the procedure?'

I nodded. *Nobody needs to feel embarrassed about raising any issue, no matter how big or small,* Lula had said.

Iris gave a tight smile. 'If there's nothing else?'

I shook my head and backed away.

*

Anything else? Matthew's words hung in the air as I got to my feet.

All eyes were on me.

'I think . . .' My eyes flickered to Ethan's and away. 'I think I was . . .' My mind fluttered around. How to say this? In the end, I just said it. 'My drink was spiked. Before Christmas.'

The room went still. I felt their eyes on me – Theo, Ethan and Jaz. Willing me not to mention the mushrooms.

278

Matthew gulped, his Adam's apple bobbing in his long neck. He cast his eyes around the room, looking for help. 'Are you . . . are you accusing anyone in particular?'

My eyes found Ethan's. I swallowed.

Ethan's face paled.

'Ethan,' I said.

Iris got to her feet, her voice cutting through the murmurs. 'That's a serious accusation, Tess. Are you certain?'

I pressed my nails into my palms and tore my eyes from Ethan's. 'N-no. I can't remember what happened. That's how I know my drink was spiked. I hadn't drunk much.'

Iris's blue eyes bored into mine, then she turned to Ethan. 'Did you spike Tess's drink?'

'Of course not,' said Ethan.

'What do you think your drink was spiked with?' asked Iris.

My mind went blank. If I mentioned the mushrooms, our whole story would fall apart. 'I don't know,' I mumbled.

'Do you have anyone to corroborate your story?' Iris asked.

I shook my head. 'I can't remember. I think he put something in my tea.'

'Ethan?' said Iris.

Ethan flushed. 'I didn't. I'd never do that.'

'Does anyone have something to add?' asked Iris.

The moments after this were all jumbled up in my memory. Voices battered my ears.

'Tess was drunk,' said Ethan.

'Ethan wouldn't do that, I was with him all night,' said Theo.

279

'She drank practically a whole bottle of gin at her birthday party. So, you know . . .' said Tabitha.

It went on. I was in the stocks, accusations being flung like ripe tomatoes. My legs wobbled and I touched the wall to steady myself.

'Was anyone else there?' asked Iris.

My eyes sought out Jaz's. Surely, she at least would say she believed me? But, face pinched, she looked away. 'I was, but I didn't see anything.'

No one was on my side. Ethan was Sebastian Hill's son. He was popular, gifted, an asset to Ravensthorpe. Without him by my side, I was nobody.

After an eternity of angry noise, I fled the room.

*

Iris called me into her office for 'a chat' after the meeting. 'You do realise these sorts of accusations put Ravensthorpe at risk,' she said.

My cheeks flushed. If she'd spoken to me before the meeting, I wouldn't have had to do it.

'There are plenty of people out there who would seize on this. If the media got hold of it . . . I mean, Ethan, because of his father, there'd be considerable interest.'

I understood. If it came to a showdown between me and Ethan, I was no one. My body felt frozen. 'Can I go now?'

'Naturally. You are free to do whatever you want here at Ravensthorpe.'

Whispers followed me everywhere that day. *Bitch. Lying cow.*

Jaz was the only one who talked to me, and she was stilted. 'Maybe you got it wrong about Ethan?' she said as we drank tea in the common room.

'But someone . . . Someone gave me mushrooms. And it was Ethan who handed me the tea.'

That night when I climbed into bed, I screamed as my legs touched something icy. My mind went straight to Lula's frozen face in my dream. Pulling off my covers, I found a pile of snow between my sheets. Suppressed sniggers emerged from the other rooms as I carried it outside in my wastepaper basket.

When I came back to my room, a piece of paper lay on my pillow. Sweat trickled down my neck as I picked it up. Words in black marker pen were scrawled across the page.

I know you killed Lula.

Locking my door, I lay on the edge of the bed to avoid the damp patch. All night I curled there, awake, trying to put together the events of that night. Was it possible? Did I kill Lula? Surely, I'd remember.

Next day, I called a taxi to take me to the train station. My last vision of Ravensthorpe was a face pressed to the upstairs window as I drove away. It was Jaz.

Heathcliff's words filled my head. *I have not broken your heart – you have broken it; and in breaking it, you have broken mine.*

*

On the train, my mind turned to Mum. She'd be at work now, going through her day, blissfully imagining me at

281

Ravensthorpe. She had no idea I was about to break her heart. Although . . . the story I wrote for *Best Young Brits* would have broken her heart in a different way if it had been published. *Write it like you hate her*, Lula had said.

I brought the story up on my phone . . .

The Birthday Party

'Can Laura come home with me tomorrow?' I swung off Mum's hand. It was my first week at primary school, and I was ecstatic to have made a friend.

Mum wrinkled her nose, surveying the passing children on the street. 'I don't think so. You're a special girl, Tess. These other girls . . . they don't have your intelligence, or sensitivity. Anyway . . .' She squeezed my hand. 'You don't need friends, you have me. We have fun together, don't we?'

I nodded.

Leaning down, she wrapped me in a warm hug, and I melted.

Mum wasn't like the other mothers who gathered at the school gate. She was younger, and prettier. She didn't join their gossiping cluster but stood apart. Her colourful clothes and luxuriant hair put their drabness to shame. I felt proud of her. She was right, with a mother like her, who needed friends?

As the years went on, my budding friendships faltered on the rocks of Mum's decree. I wasn't allowed to go to other girls' places or to bring them home. Even when I was invited to a birthday party, Mum wouldn't let me go.

'We're not like them, Tess. Can you imagine the food they'll be eating?'

I could. And I wanted it. I'd seen kids eating crisps and sausage rolls from the canteen while I gnawed on my hearty salad sandwich.

By fourth grade, I was sick of being special. An idea blossomed. I would – somehow – persuade Mum to let me have an eighth birthday party. It would be a success. Then the other girls would see me as one of them.

I started my party campaign well ahead of time, using the most direct path to Mum's heart. Literature. I combed our library in search of inspiration.

'Bilbo has a birthday party in Lord of the Rings,' I said casually over dinner one night.

Mum smiled. 'Yes, that's right, an eleventy-first birthday.'

'Winnie the Pooh has a post-flood party,' I said a few days later. 'And there's a tea party in Alice in Wonderland.' It was a terrible party, but still.

Mum nodded, meeting my eyes, but didn't comment.

'Look, practically every book in our library has a party in it.' I gestured towards a bookmarked pile – The Great Gatsby, Harry Potter and A Christmas Carol. 'I can show you.'

Mum sighed. 'What are you after, Tess?'

'I want to have a party. For my eighth birthday.'

'Here?' Mum frowned. 'You want to bring those girls from your school here?'

I nodded, eager.

'No. That is not going to happen.'

'Please.' I brought out more examples. Pride and

Prejudice, Anna Karenina *and* Rebecca. *'They all have parties.'*

Mum rolled her eyes.

'Dick has a birthday party in Cold Comfort Farm *too.'* Cold Comfort Farm *was one of Mum's favourite novels, she read it every year.*

Mum held up her hand. 'Enough. Stop it, Tess.'

I put my hands together in prayer position. 'Please.'

Her eyes narrowed. 'All right, fine, you can have a party.'

I was too busy jumping for joy to take any notice of her final words.

'And don't blame me if you don't like it.'

In the lead up to the party, I discussed the menu with Mum. 'Sausage rolls and crisps first. Then hotdogs for main course. Cake for dessert. And lolly bags to take home.'

She raised her eyebrows but agreed.

I was surprised it was so easy . . .

As the train pulled into Deptford Station, my finger hovered over the delete button. I didn't want to read on. The party in this story was different to the one I first wrote. It did share some features. *The cheese ball. The carrot slices. The curry. The baked bananas for dessert . . .* But it told the truth.

I hated baked bananas and curry, and Mum must have known how bizarre my school friends would find them. The lolly-free lolly bags that I'd spent so much joyful time decorating were a deliberate sting in the tail. She had sabotaged my party.

When I was suspended from school afterwards for

kicking my classmates, I expected Mum to be angry, but she smiled gently as she walked me home from school.

'Those weren't nice girls, Tess. They aren't good enough for you. Don't lower yourself to their level. Wait until you go to Ravensthorpe. You will meet some people as special as you there.'

It hadn't been Mum I was defending at school; it was myself. *Baked banana girl.* After the party, the sniggers trailed me everywhere. And the nickname stuck right through primary school.

I never tried to bring a friend home again, and I never went to anyone else's house. I waited for Ravensthorpe, for that future me who would have friends. And look how that had turned out.

Deptford. Mind the gap, blared the loudspeaker.

I pressed *delete*. The story vanished. Standing, I pushed my way towards the platform, sweat trickling down my back as the guilt hit again. I had loved writing that story. Unlike all my attempts at fiction, it had gushed out of me like blood from an artery.

But what would Mum say when she discovered the girl she'd poured her life into wasn't special at all?

Chapter 37

Superpowered Team-up

Now

Heat radiates off the pavement in Villafranca. While we started the Camino in patchy snow, it's been getting hotter and hotter.

'Check that out,' says Ethan.

Propped in a corner next to a bar is a walking pole. I've seen lots of decorated staffs on the Camino, but this one is next level. It has ribbons, strips of leather, medallions, shells and fake flowers. At the top is a bunch of black feathers.

The Devil has black feathers on his staff, whispers Lula in my head.

I'm taking a photo, when a woman steps from the bar, beer in hand. My heart skips a beat. *Nola*. She's ditched the Templar outfit and is back in her black hiking leggings, matched with a black vest and a broad-brimmed black hat. She's clearly the staff's owner.

Sweat trickles down my back as my mind leaps to the photo of her and Lula together.

'*Hola*,' Nola says. 'You like my staff? I decorated it myself.'

'I do.' My voice comes out croaky. I gesture towards Ethan. 'You remember Ethan?'

Ethan's eyes narrow as he realises who she is.

Nola nods. There's a tense silence. 'Want to have a beer with me?' she asks.

Ethan and I exchange a glance.

'Okay,' he says. Clearly, he wants to find out what she's up to.

The waiter comes to take our orders. 'Two beers?' he asks.

Nola shoots me a sharp glance. She hasn't forgotten the brandy I abandoned at the Iron Cross.

I sigh. 'Mineral water for me. With bubbles,' I add in an attempt at jollity.

I hope Nola doesn't let on that we met at the Iron Cross. Ethan will wonder why I didn't tell him. I haven't shown him the photo of Nola with Lula. It might set something unnerving in motion. *You know what we need to do . . .*

'You're heading to O Cebreiro tomorrow?' asks Nola.

'That's right.' Ethan's voice is wary.

Theo appears, his eyes widening as he spots Nola.

'Want to join us?' asks Ethan.

Theo shakes his head, his hands clenched around his shoulder straps. 'Got to drop my stuff in the *albergue*. I'll catch you later.' He continues up the road.

Nola turns back to us. 'What route will you take?'

Ethan sips his beer. 'Is there an option?'

Nola lowers her voice, as if imparting a secret. 'I'm taking the dragon tea route.'

Dragon tea? 'That's a strange name,' I say.

Nola shrugs. 'You should come with me. I could do with some company.'

I stare at her. Nola's been so secretive, and now she wants to walk with us?

'You haven't heard of it?'

We shake our heads.

'It's not widely known. It's the high route.'

'High route?' I'm not keen to make things any harder for myself. Or to take an unknown route with Nola.

'I've heard it's beautiful. Not many pilgrims walk it these days. Those who choose it . . .' She puts down her glass with a bang. 'Experience a spiritual awakening.'

Ethan leans forward.

I shudder. She knows exactly how to reel him in.

'It's not for everyone. Only for those who want to go deeper.' Nola gets to her feet and shrugs. 'Perhaps it's not for you.' Picking up her staff, she walks away, bells tinkling with each step.

Ethan narrows his eyes. 'Why does she want us to go up there with her?'

'I have no idea.' Although . . . maybe I do. Should I tell him about Nola and Lula?

'It could be an opportunity to find out what she's up to. You know what they say. Keep your friends close, and your enemies closer.'

'I prefer to keep my enemies as distant as possible.' I am not at all keen on the idea of the dragon tea route. Finishing our drinks, we pull ourselves up and head for a restaurant. I order the pilgrim three course special, while Ethan has bean soup. 'Can't face any more pork,' he mutters.

'Have you heard of the dragon tea route?' Ethan asks the waiter. 'Over the hill to O Cebreiro.'

The man looks uneasy. 'I have heard there is an old high route. No one does it these days. You follow the valley. It is safer.'

Ethan nods, and I'm glad the dragon tea route threat is fading.

But as we head back to the *albergue*, there is Nola. Seated at a different bar with a gleaming bottle of beer in front of her. She waves us over, calling to the waiter. 'A beer and an *agua con gas* for my friends.'

The waiter plonks down a beer and a sparkling water.

Ethan sips his beer. 'The dragon tea route. Tell me about it.'

Satisfaction flickers over Nola's face. 'The normal route between Villafranca and O Cebreiro is boring, along a road, next to traffic. The dragon tea route is for people who've had enough of following the arrows.' She meets Ethan's eyes. 'It's for those who don't want to stick with the herd.' She points to the blue-tinted hills next to the town. 'Up there. It will be beautiful. No other pilgrims. It is the true Camino. The way it used to be.'

Ethan's mouth flickers. 'Okay, I'm in. Tess?'

I clench my jaw. Damn.

Nola tilts her head. 'You're afraid?'

My pulse flutters as I meet her eyes. I need this dragon tea route like a hole in the head and I'd much rather avoid Nola if possible. But if Ethan's going to have an epiphany up there, I can't miss it. I drain my mineral water and slam my glass on the table. 'Hell, no. Bring on the dragon tea route.' My stomach clenches.

'Tess.' The voice is faint. 'Ethan.' A girl with a backpack is walking towards us. Her fair hair is tied back with a red bandanna. Her once-pale face is brown.

Jaz! I jump to my feet and run towards her. Jaz looks dirty and tired. I'm so happy to see her. We hug, like it's the natural thing to do. As if we haven't been ignoring each other for years.

'What the hell are you wearing?' she says.

I look down at my robe. It has come to feel normal. Every couple of days I've rinsed it out and walked around in my rain poncho until it dries. 'It's practical.'

'You look weird.'

'Maybe I should get new clothes?'

'Maybe?' She laughs. 'Definitely.' Jaz looks over at the bar and her forehead wrinkles. 'You're drinking with the policewoman?'

I lift my shoulders. 'Ethan reckons we should keep our friends close and our enemies closer.'

'But which is which?' Jaz grimaces. 'You wouldn't believe how tough it was out there on the *Primitivo*. There were such long distances, and it was so steep. So, I decided to come back on the main trail.' She pauses. 'I saw Theo down the road. He said you carried my cross here?'

'Yes. Dapple and I did. Mainly me, Dapple wasn't too

keen on it. I hope you want it, because, honestly, it's been a nightmare.'

Her mouth opens and shuts. 'Wow. You carried it all the way here? You did that for me?'

'Yep.'

'Why?'

It's a good question. 'Because . . . I thought you'd want it?' I want to add *and because we're friends*, but I'm not sure if it's true.

Jaz's face goes soft. 'Thank you.' She swallows. 'I didn't mean to leave it behind. I was a little . . .' She waves her hand. 'Woo woo.'

Jaz joins us and orders a red wine. She and Nola nod at each other cautiously. Theo reappears and lowers himself into a seat. Nola beams at him and he returns a smile that is more of a grimace.

'Have you heard of the dragon tea route?' Ethan repeats Nola's spiel. 'What do you reckon?'

'God, I'm a bit worn out from the *Primitivo*,' says Jaz.

'It's only one day.' Ethan points up at the hills. 'Don't you want to get away from the crowds?'

Jaz sighs. 'I guess if you guys are doing it.'

'Theo?' asks Ethan.

Theo's eyes flick from Nola to Ethan, and something flashes between them.

My mouth turns dry. *You know what we need to do.*

'Sure. Why not?' Theo says. 'It'll be a long day, though, all the way to O Cebreiro. Maybe we should break it up?'

'Sleep out?' Ethan asks.

'The weather's good,' says Theo. 'Wouldn't be hard.'

291

My adrenaline spikes as an idea hits. 'It's May Day tomorrow, Beltane. If we sleep out on the dragon tea route, why don't we do a ritual? A pagan celebration for the spring equinox?' The dark energy of the Yule ritual on the Ravensthorpe tower has followed me for years. It's time to cast it off. Mum and I always used to celebrate Beltane. And it will make fantastic copy for my article.

'Could be good inspiration,' says Ethan.

After a moment's hesitation, Jaz, Nola and Theo agree.

'Do you remember that old horror movie *The Wicker Man*?' Jaz asks. 'The one we all watched together at Ravensthorpe?'

Nola raises her eyebrows. 'Is that the one about the policeman who gets sacrificed by a sinister Beltane cult? Should I be worried?'

We all laugh, but it sounds a little forced.

Chapter 38

Survival in the Wilderness

We are out on the street early, waiting for Nola. The sun is yet to rise over the hills, but it's already warm.

'Is this a good idea?' asks Jaz. 'Going up there with her. What if she's, like, planning something?'

'Like what?' asks Ethan.

'Attack us? Force us to confess?' says Jaz.

My mouth goes dry, and I dart my eyes up the street. There's no sign of Nola. What if Jaz is right? I need to tell them what I know. 'I found something out,' I blurt. 'Nola knew Lula. She mentored her when she was at school.'

Ethan's face flushes red. 'What?'

Pulling out my phone, I show them the screenshot of a teenage Nola with Lula. They stare at me.

'Why are you only showing us this now?' Theo's voice is low and angry.

My cheeks burn. 'It's hard to explain. I . . .' Anything I say will sound weird. 'It's complicated.'

Ethan and Theo meet each other's eyes, a silent understanding passing between them.

A shiver runs down my spine.

'You think she's out for revenge?' Jaz asks.

'She's . . . hard to read,' I say. 'It's possible she's playing some sort of long—'

Ethan holds up his hand and jerks his head towards the top of the street.

Nola is standing on the rise, backlit by the sun. She looks ominous there in her black clothes, a gunslinger with a grudge. 'Let's go,' she says as she reaches us.

By unspoken agreement, we follow her. If it comes to a showdown, there's four of us and only one of her. What am I thinking? That's not going to happen. But the words on the lollipop repeat in my head.

All murderers are punished, unless they kill in large numbers.

The early-starting pilgrims are following the arrows, but we go against the tide. On the edge of town, we turn right up a steep hill. There's no one around. As the birds sing tunefully, a flash of inspiration about my article hits.

Yes, I've got it. The rituals will be bookends. The Yule ritual to begin, though I'll leave out the tower. The pilgrimage and the plagiarism in the middle. The Beltane ritual to end. *Genius.* I don't need to finish my memoir first after all.

My mind returns to Camryn's words at the Iron Cross.

Mad bitch. I cast them from my brain. I have enough to think about, it will all be fine.

Suddenly, everything seems manageable. So what if Nola is the threatening poet? If she knew anything, she'd have used it by now, wouldn't she? And we're nearing the end of the Camino. Yes, it will all work out.

After a tiring climb, we come to a small road sign which says Dragonte. *Ah, Dragonte, not dragon tea*. The others act as if they knew this all along. Maybe they did. We climb further, coming to a deserted village, where we stop next to a fountain. Dapple appears invigorated by this break from the main path. She's been keeping pace with everyone.

'Pretty steep.' I wipe the sweat from my face. The sun's well and truly up now.

Nola leans against the stone wall. 'The Templars designed this route to wear out their enemies. They would lead them on a chase over the hills. After hours of riding when they couldn't fight anymore—' She claps her hands. 'The ambush would appear and strike them down.'

I stare at her. 'So, we're doing a route specifically designed to exhaust people? You didn't say that yesterday.'

'As I said, it's only for the brave.' She grins. 'It goes like this.' She moves her hand up and down to indicate three hills, then looks at the map on her phone. 'We're going off the road now, into the wilderness. The only way to do this is to keep moving fast. Imagine we're the Templars, and our enemy is chasing.' She turns to Dapple. 'Okay, donkey?'

Dapple snorts.

She looks at the rest of us. 'Okay?'

Ethan, Theo and Jaz get to their feet.

Nola looks at me.

I'm slumped beside the fountain, panting. Reluctantly, I stand.

'Okay.' Nola points towards a hill in the distance. 'That way.'

She takes off at a walk so fast it's practically a jog and vanishes into the forest. Ethan and Theo follow, while Jaz, Dapple and I trail behind. Jaz appears to have qualms about abandoning Dapple and me in a Spanish wilderness. I'm touched.

We follow the overgrown track into a shady chestnut forest. Descend to a stream. Wade across. Scramble up a steep, muddy slope. Fight our way through brambles. Push through high grass and emerge onto a ridge. The view is stunning, but the others have vanished. There are no trail markers, and in fact there doesn't appear to be a trail.

Jaz and I glance at each other.

'Do you feel like we're the enemy and Nola's trying to wear us out?' I say.

Jaz nods. 'Look, there's a village in the distance.'

We head towards it. Descend to another stream. Wade across. Scramble up another steep, muddy slope. Fight our way through more brambles. Push through higher grass and emerge onto another ridge. It's midday now, and the sun is intense overhead. We survey our surroundings. Dapple looks at us accusingly.

'Is that the village over there?' I point at buildings in the distance.

'Looks like it.'

Descending to yet another stream, we do it all again. Muddy slope. Brambles. Chest-high grass. We emerge onto another ridge. My legs are jelly. I'm shattered. There's no village in sight, just endless hills stretching into the distance.

'Where did the village go?' asks Jaz.

I lift my shoulders. 'Behind the next hill?'

Jaz frowns. 'Or not?'

'Bring on the ambush. I don't care.' I collapse to the ground. 'Can you see a trail anywhere?'

'No.' Jaz lowers herself beside me. Even she looks tired. Admittedly, she's carrying the cross.

We meet each other's eyes. We're in the middle of nowhere with no trail and no village in sight. 'Now what?' I ask.

'Let's rest for a moment.' She lies on the grass.

I do the same.

It's quiet here. No birds, no buzzing insects, only the sound of Dapple pulling up grass. It's like we're the only living creatures left on Earth. I close my eyes, feeling as if I've gone back in time. Back to the grass at Ravensthorpe. Jaz is silent for so long; I think she's gone to sleep. Dapple snorts and tears at the grass next to us.

When I open my eyes Jaz is gazing at me intently. My heart skips a beat.

'I hear you and Theo ran into each other at one of Ethan's book talks,' she says.

Chapter 39

Celebrity Lifestyle

Then

Book discussion. Ethan Hill. Darker Matters.

The email was from a writing site I subscribed to. My breath caught as it popped up in my inbox and a hook slipped down my throat, pulling me back towards Ravensthorpe.

It had been several months since Ethan's book came out. Since Mum and I had formed our revenge plan. I'd been stalking Ethan, looking for material for my take-down article, but found nothing. I hadn't gone to any of his events so far though. I couldn't bear it.

You should go to this one, Mum said in my head. *This might be your chance for a scoop.*

Ethan's talk was to be held on a canal boat, which was set up as a bookstore on Regent's Canal. It had a performance stage on top, with armchairs and a microphone. Mum and I tossed around a few ideas for sabotaging the event.

'Cut the line to the microphone?' I swished the yellow kaftan around my legs. I always felt closer to her when I wore it.

A bucket of old prawns on the boat?

'Spray water at the books?'

Release a herd of pigs?

In the end we decided I'd just go along and gather information. Although if an opportunity for disruption arose, naturally I would take it.

The evening of Ethan's talk was warm and still. Crowds jostled on the canal path, and in the bar above. His publishers clearly had no idea how popular it was going to be, or they would have chosen a larger venue. I blended with the crowd on the upper level, not pushing to the front. I didn't want to be seen. I just wanted to see, to witness what he had become.

As I peered through the shoulders in front of me, my gut twisted. Ethan was on top of the boat. I'd seen him going about his daily life, but this was different. He'd metamorphosed into a celebrity author.

Another well-known author gave a speech, then Ethan read from his book. He'd always had presence, but now he had more. He'd nailed the Bret Easton Ellis bad boy vibe, and he was taking off in the same way. Burning jealousy filled my chest. I couldn't listen. I pushed my way to the bar for a drink, only returning when the reading was over.

After the event, Ethan sat in a red-striped deckchair beside the boat and worked the signing queue like a pro. He flicked back his hair and beamed at each person who presented their book for signing. As usual at literary events, it was mainly women. They turned away with bright eyes, their books clutched to their chests. Let's face it, authors with sex appeal were few and far between.

I headed for the bar again. I wouldn't be lining up for a copy of *Darker Matters*. I shouldn't have come. Seeing Ethan's success had ignited dormant embers inside me, stoked the fires of my addiction. I wanted what he had. What I would have had if it wasn't for him. I clenched my jaw as I waited for my drink.

I'd just been knocked back for another journalism internship, so I was more than a little raw. It didn't take me long to get half-tanked. I was leaning on the bar when I noticed a guy with floppy black hair across the room. The realisation followed a heartbeat later – it was Theo. His brown eyes met mine.

He looked so pleased to see me that, somehow, I was pleased too. He pushed his way towards me and gave me a hug. Gesturing with his chin towards the boat, he grimaced. 'Have you read it?'

I shook my head.

'I have. It's not, like, all that.'

I laughed. 'There's no jealousy like writer jealousy, hey?'

His cheeks coloured.

We slipped straight back into our easy banter. It was as if I'd forgotten how we parted. It was only as the night wore on, I saw how he'd changed. His laugh was brittle, and his drinking had a different purpose. He knocked back tequila shots like he was being paid by the glass.

I asked him how the writing was going, and he rolled his eyes. 'Tell me, honestly, Tess. Do you think I can write?'

I hesitated. I'd never liked his writing, but . . . 'Lula compared you to Hemingway, didn't she?'

Theo snorted. 'Lula was a crazy, manipulative she-devil. She'd say stuff like that to unbalance you. Then the next thing, *bang*, she'd dig in the knife. She knew how insecure I was about my writing, and she exploited it. In the end . . . I had absolutely no idea whether I was any good or not. But I would have practically killed my own mother to hear Lula say I could write.'

He paused to down his drink. 'Writing is all I ever wanted to do. Now though, it's a bloody curse. Look at Fatty. Here he is, the only one of us published, and he's so wound up about his next book, he can't enjoy it.'

'Fatty?'

'We used to call him that at school.'

I frowned. 'But he isn't.'

'He used to be, but he lost all the chub during secondary school.'

I thought of what Ethan had said. *I was an outcast.* 'That was mean.'

'Kids are like that.' Theo lifted his shoulders. 'So, you're not planning to read *Darker Matters*?'

'Nope.'

He laughed. 'Bearing a grudge?'

'A grudge? For getting my drink spiked? Yes.'

Theo looked away from me and his eyes narrowed.

I followed his gaze. Outside the bar, Ethan was being interviewed for TV, a microphone held to his mouth. A group of fans surrounded him, hanging on his words.

Dropping his empty shot glass on the table, Theo ran

his hands through his hair. 'Let's get out of here and go to another bar. He's having an after party at his place, but . . .' He shrugged. 'Meh.'

'Good idea.' We left through the door furthest from Ethan.

After the second bar closed, we weaved our way along the canal path. It was empty now. Everyone had moved on to the after party or gone home.

'Should have been you and me, Tess,' Theo said. 'We got along well, didn't we?'

'Go the clowns,' I giggled. 'Boo the sages.' I stumbled, grazing my arm on the canal wall, and Theo pulled me up. I was well and truly pissed. I leant against the wall to hold myself upright.

Theo put his arms around me and pressed his lips to mine.

I was startled, but I kissed him back. What did it matter? I'd never see him again.

The kiss went on for a while, then Theo's hands reached under my skirt.

I yelped and pulled away. 'I don't—'

'Oh, come on.' He pressed against me. 'You know you want to. We should have done this ages ago.'

I tried to push him away, but he grabbed my hands with one of his, still kissing me. His grip was so strong it felt useless to struggle. My head swam. Did I consent to this? This was Theo. We were friends. Did he think I wanted it? My heart skittered. 'No.' I said, as he pushed against me. 'Stop it.'

But he didn't.

I saw red. It was instinctive, my kickboxing training

coming into its own. I raised my knee and drove it into his groin.

The effect was immediate, he stumbled backwards, gasping.

But I couldn't stop now, the anger was a bonfire inside me. In my head, it wasn't just Theo in front of me, but Ethan too. It was all those students in the meeting at Ravensthorpe. It was the person who put snow in my bed and whoever left that note on my pillow. I kicked his knee. Hard. I was wearing my Doc Martens, and the blow sent him tumbling to the ground.

'What the fuck, Tess. I was just mucking around,' he mumbled, clutching his knee.

'I said no.' I stared at him, my body stiff and cold, my mind numb. I wanted to kick him again, but I clenched my teeth and pulled myself away, climbing up the stone stairs from the canal to the street.

Unsurprisingly, I hadn't heard from him again.

Chapter 40

Monster Hunt

Now

'So, Theo said you two hooked up.' Jaz's voice is casual, but her eyes are intent.

Heat pulses through my body. 'Is that what he said?'

'Is that not what happened?'

I pull up grass and shred it into pieces. 'I wouldn't call it that.'

'What would you call it?'

I grit my teeth, anger rising inside me. 'I was drunk. He knew I wasn't into it, but it didn't stop him.'

Jaz's eyes widen. 'What are you saying? He . . . raped you?'

I meet her gaze. 'I'm saying I was drunk, and he tried it on. He wouldn't stop, so I kneed him in the balls. Then kicked him in the knee.'

Her mouth twitches and she puffs out a breath of air. 'Sounds like he deserved it.'

'So, he's going around saying we hooked up?'

'Yeah, he's such a jerk.'

My nails bite into the palms of my hands. 'When did he tell you that?'

'On the way to Spain. He was trying to needle Ethan. Theo can't handle that Ethan is this big shot author and he's a gardener.'

'A gardener? He told me he was working in communications.'

Jaz snorts. 'In his dreams. He operates a leaf blower at Greenwich Park. I saw him there.'

'It's weird he would lie. There's nothing wrong with being a gardener.' I think of how he blushed, back in Pamplona, when I said he knew a lot about plants.

Jaz lifts her shoulders. 'Guess it's not what he had in mind as a career plan. Though, neither of us have exactly followed our career plan either, have we?'

Silence falls. Jaz chews on a piece of grass. I gaze out at the hills; where have the others gone?

'Speaking of career plan,' Jaz says. 'What happened to that story you wrote about your eighth birthday party? You should enter it in a competition or something.'

I swallow. Jaz doesn't know about the new version of the story, the one I wrote for Lula. It was all true, but it felt like a betrayal. I'd rather remember Mum the way I first wrote her. 'Thanks,' I mutter. 'But I don't like it anymore.'

'Your mum sounded so cool in that story.'

I take a breath. 'She was.' My voice is a whisper, and I blink back tears.

Jaz turns to me, her brow furrowed.

'She died.' Tears roll down my face.

'What?' Jaz takes my hand, her eyes wide. 'Oh, Tess, I'm so sorry, I didn't know.'

The air fills with the history between us, and a lump chokes my throat. If we'd still been friends, if Ethan hadn't blocked my calls, I would have had someone to share my pain with.

Jaz squeezes my hand. 'What happened?'

So, I tell her, tears trickling down my face. About our argument over me leaving Ravensthorpe, how I ran out, how she died. 'I think she was coming to look for me.'

Jaz puts her arms around me, pressing her warm body to mine. 'I know you loved her,' she whispers into my hair.

'I did, I really did.' Pain stabs in my chest. 'But . . .' Straightening, I meet Jaz's eyes. 'She wasn't quite the way I depicted her in that story. I wrote another version for Lula. A more honest version. Mum was . . . controlling.' I tell Jaz how she'd isolated me, stopped me from having friends. 'When I went back home after Ravensthorpe, it felt like I was going back to that time. Just her and me. I felt trapped.'

'That sounds so tough, Tess.' Jaz's eyes are wide. 'I'm sorry you didn't feel like you could talk about her before this.'

The moment extends, filled only with the sound of Dapple munching.

'She would hate it so much that I'm still a waitress.'

Jaz smiles. 'But you're not. You're amazing. Look at you, walking the Camino, an article in *Artemis*. You're killing it.'

I give her a shaky half-smile. 'I haven't written it yet.'

As I gaze out at the hills, something catches my eye. I point at some figures, way in the distance. They're on top of a low, green hill next to a ruined stone building. We get to our feet.

*

'Almost there,' yells Theo as we get closer.

My pulse thuds in my neck. Talking to Jaz about that night with Theo has brought it back. I'd pretended to myself it was just one of those things. *Bad almost-sex. Somewhat rapey.* Happens to us all. Put it behind you.

Jaz glances at me. 'You okay?'

I tamp down the anger, attempt a smile that doesn't quite get off the ground.

As we reach him, Theo points to the ruins. 'We're going to spend the night there.'

I shiver. In the twilight, the ruins look dark and forbidding. Staggering up to them, we throw down our packs.

Nola gestures, palm-up, towards the building, as if welcoming us into a display home. 'Guess this was quite the hacienda back in the day.' The stone-walled mansion has vines growing over the doorway and gaping black holes in its red tiled roof.

Ethan emerges from inside. 'Cool place, huh?'

I nod, though it's not exactly welcoming.

Nola holds up some cracked pottery cups. 'Look what I found.' Her voice is bright, and she has a hectic, wound-up air.

My chest tightens. Why has she brought us all here?

'Great.' Jaz takes the cups from her. 'I'll rinse them in the creek, and we can drink our wine from them.'

'Time to get organised.' Ethan opens his pack and pulls out a packet of paper plates, coloured pens, and a pair of scissors.

Nola snorts. 'Is this a kids' birthday party?'

*

Back in Villamayor, we had divided up the tasks for our ritual.

'I'll make animal masks,' Ethan said.

Tapping at my phone, I held up a picture from *The Wicker Man* – a group wearing creepy rabbit, goat and deer masks. 'Like this?'

Ethan peered at it. 'I'll try. Depends what they've got in the supermarket.'

'I'll research Beltane songs and chants,' said Jaz.

I tapped at my phone again. 'I'll bake bannock.'

'What's that?' asked Jaz.

'It's a traditional bread the Celts used in rituals like Beltane. It sounds easy, just flour, milk and butter. I can sort out the offerings for the altar too.'

'Great.' Jaz turned to Theo. 'You can make mulled wine.'

Theo sighed. 'I hate mulled wine, but okay, whatever.'

Nola knocked back her beer. 'Sounds like you guys have got it covered.'

*

Now, Ethan sets to work with his scissors and pens, Theo mixes mulled wine, Jaz gathers wood for the bonfire, and I ponder how to cook my bannock. Nola appears to have vanished.

Making bannock is not as easy as it sounds. The bonfire isn't ready yet, but I gather a few sticks and build a small cooking fire. Dapple grazes beside me as I mix my ingredients, and wrap the dough in foil.

While it's cooking, I brush Dapple's coat. Raised voices reach me. *Nola and Theo.* They are over at the forest's edge. Theo gesticulates, and Nola takes a step backwards. I gnaw on my lip. What have those two got to talk about? *Lula?* They stare at each other, then Nola turns and walks back towards the ruin. Theo stares after her.

A burning smell wafts from the fire. *Damn.* Picking up a stick, I poke my tin foil bundle from the fire.

'Need a hand with that bannock?'

I jump. It's Nola.

She squats beside me, sipping from a plastic bottle of red wine. 'We Irish are experts.' Her notebook presses against the pocket of her black hiking trousers.

'That would be great.' I eye the notebook. I'm sure everything would be explained if I could look in there. Maybe later tonight, after she's asleep . . .?

Nola mixes up another batch of dough, and places it on the fire. Sinking to the ground, she gulps at her wine and strokes Dapple's soft nose. Her mouth twists.

'You okay?' Nola still has an erratic vibe about her. Was it the argument with Theo?

'To be honest . . . I'm feeling a little odd.'

'Why's that?'

She exhales. 'It's an anniversary today.'

I eye her. 'Anniversary of what?' It doesn't sound like she's celebrating.

She tips the wine to her mouth. 'I told you why I left the police?'

'PTSD?'

'Yeah.'

I gnaw my lip. Is this something to do with Lula? 'Do you want to talk about it?'

'No. I shouldn't have mentioned it.' She upends the bottle in her mouth. 'You don't want to hear that story.'

'I do.' I swallow. If this is about Lula, I need to know. 'I'd like to hear it.'

Nola places her wine bottle on the ground. She glances around. No one else is in sight. 'Okay, I'll tell you. You're right. I need to talk about it. I apologise in advance though. It's a shitty story.'

My heart flutters. 'Okay. Go on.'

Nola gazes at the fire. 'It happened six years ago today.'

Six years. But Lula died three years ago . . .

'It was a beautiful spring day. You know, the kind that lifts your spirits?'

I nod. Where she's going with this?

'In the village, the girls had got out their summer dresses, but they had to wear cardigans on top.'

I can see it. The Bishopsgate high street. Pale legs in floral skirts.

'I was out in the car, following up a graffiti complaint,

when the call came through. It was a domestic. At a local farm. The wife had taken out a restraining order on her husband, but he'd shown up. Demanding to see the kids. They'd argued. He'd hit her and driven off with the kids. She was frantic.'

My chest constricts. This isn't about Lula. I should feel relieved, but I don't. I might know this story. I hope it's not that story.

Nola puts her hands to the side of her head, pulling at her short hair. 'Oh, Jesus, I don't know if I can talk about it.'

I touch her hand. 'Go on.'

Nola clenches and unclenches her jaw. 'I drove out there straight away. The mother . . . She was standing outside the cottage. She had a red mark on her cheek where he'd hit her. As soon as she saw me, she burst into tears. "They're only babies. Two and four", she said.'

I want to put my hands over my ears, but I don't.

Nola gazes up at the darkening sky. 'I found the car in a pond. I'd followed the tyre marks.' Her sea-green eyes meet mine. 'I couldn't swim, it wasn't a requirement for my police force. I'd never learnt. The nearest pool was miles away.' She puts her face in her hands and her shoulders shudder. 'I couldn't help them.'

I touch her hand. 'I'm so sorry, Nola. I knew what happened. But I didn't know it was you who was there.'

Nola's shudders continue. As they subside, she looks up at me, her eyes red. 'So . . . that's why I'm here.'

'On the Camino?'

Nola sniffs. 'Jesus. Is the bannock burning?'

311

'Oh, no.' I pull it from the fire. 'It's only a bit burnt. Go on.'

'I'm here for redemption, I suppose.' She pauses. 'Among other things. You know that day in the laneway? When you keyed Ethan's car?'

I stiffen.

'I was having an episode. A panic attack. My heart was thumping so hard, I thought I was dying. I'd come up for the funeral. Lula's funeral. I was curious. I wanted to see who would come. How you'd all be. I had questions. About what happened that night.'

I swallow as I stare at her. She's not a policewoman anymore, but she could still turn us in.

'But on the bus, I saw a woman with two little kids and . . . My mind shut down. That's what was happening in the laneway that day.'

I see her there. Curled up on the ground. Sweat beading her forehead.

'It kept happening. The episodes. I couldn't stand it anymore. It was breaking me. There in the laneway, I'd decided there was no point in going on. I'd have to top myself. But you marched in there.' She gives a brief smile. 'You were so full of life. It was obvious you were furious.' Nola meets my eyes. 'You were dressed in black like a dark angel. This is going to sound weird, but . . . it lifted my spirits. The cheek of you.'

I snort.

Nola's mouth twitches. 'The sheer bloody cheek of you.'

The release of tension feels like a champagne bottle

blowing its top. Mirth bubbles up in me and my snort turns into a laugh.

Nola laughs too. 'That red, shiny car. I didn't know what he'd done to deserve it. But, Jesus, you gave him what he had coming.'

We laugh and laugh, tears running down our faces, the pain metamorphosing into a strange kind of joy.

I sense, rather than see, Theo appearing around the building. He gazes at us, his expression blank.

Nola wipes the tears from her eyes. 'I decided right then. When I saw you key that car. I needed to pull myself together. And I did. I enrolled in swimming lessons. So, that's why I never reported you. You're my dark angel, Tess. And . . . that's why I wanted you up here with me tonight. On the anniversary. To take the edge off things.'

Is that why she's been following me? If so, I'm not sure how I feel about it.

Theo walks towards us, his shoulders stiff. 'What are you two up to?'

My mind flashes to Ethan and Theo, their eyes meeting on the street. *If it's about Lula . . . You know what we need to do.*

'Nola,' I whisper as Theo approaches. 'I don't think you should stay here with us tonight.'

Chapter 41

Sacrifice

'Who's for mulled wine?' Theo holds up the pottery cups

I put out my hand before I remember I'm not drinking. I imagine the fruity taste on my tongue. Warmth spreading through me. The way it will soften the hard angry edges of what Theo did after Ethan's book talk. The horror of what happened to Nola at the pond. Draining the cup, I hold it up for a refill, ignoring Nola's pointed gaze. It's quite annoying, to be honest. I know what I promised on the Iron Cross, but a couple of drinks won't hurt.

'Sooner you than me.' Theo gulps from a plastic bottle of red wine as he tops me up. 'Mulled wine is revolting.'

I haven't had the chance to talk to Nola alone again. I was probably overreacting anyway. Surely, she isn't in danger? As I sip at my wine, I add the final touches to my altar, placing meat and cheese on a boulder beside the fire. Authentic Beltane fare. Combined with my bannock, it's a feast. Someone's picked flowers, and I sprinkle petals around the food for a festive touch.

Dapple eyes the altar with greedy interest, so I feed her a handful of muesli and tether her to a tree where she can't reach it. She munches contentedly.

As darkness falls, we all gather at the fire. Jaz adds more wood, and it blazes up, sending sparks into the night. Behind us, the stone ruin flickers in the orange glow, its broken roof a jagged silhouette. Up here in the hills, the night air is cold, and the surging flames a welcome warmth on my legs.

'Time to get dressed.' Ethan shakes out some brown plastic, revealing a poncho, which he pulls over his head. 'I've got one for everyone. They were only three Euros, and they'll give a good *Wicker Man* vibe.' He passes around the ponchos, which morph into brown, monkish robes in the firelight.

'Close your eyes, and I'll give out the masks. Grass rustles under Ethan's feet as he walks around the circle. 'Pull your hoods up and I'll switch you around, so no one knows who's who.'

Ethan places a mask over my face, and his hands press on my shoulders as he moves me to the other side of the fire. Flames crackle as he walks away.

Eyes still closed, I breathe in the piney scent of burning cypress.

A cough comes from beside me. *Theo*. His shoulder nudges mine.

My stomach tightens, images shooting into my mind. *The canal path. His hand on my wrists.*

'Can we swap masks?' he murmurs.

I don't ask why, I don't care. Suppressing an urge to kick him, I thrust my mask at him, take his, and, eyes still closed, shuffle further away.

Grass rustles and Ethan's hands touch my shoulders as he moves me again. 'Now, open your eyes,' he says.

And there we are, transformed into wild creatures. My eyes roam around. Black and white Badger. Round-eyed Owl. Brown Bear. Pointy-eared Wolf. I must be orange-nosed Lion. It's not quite *The Wicker Man*, but in the dim light, with our hoods up, it's hard to know who's who.

'And now we dance,' says Badger.

Placing my mulled wine beside the altar, I follow the others as we skip clockwise around the roaring fire.

'It is Beltane, a celebration of oncoming summer. A time when the Celts built bonfires and made sacrifices to their deities,' intones Badger. 'The fire symbolises the sun's growing power, as it drives away the winter darkness.'

My dance brings me back to the altar again, and I pause for a gulp of wine. It's fruity and warming.

'At Beltane, the veil between worlds is thin,' says Badger. 'The spirits arise. The dead mingle with the living.'

Ice runs up my spine. *Lula*. Her body covered in snow.

'And now, to invoke the sun's return, it is time for the sacrifice,' Badger continues.

I hand Badger a paper plate, heavy with chunks of bannock. On the back of one chunk, I've marked a cross, using charcoal from the fire. In pagan tradition, the one who picks the marked bannock is the evening's sacrifice.

Badger passes around the bannock and, as the fire spits

out a flying ember, Wolf holds up a chunk marked with a rough black cross.

'The sacrifice.' Badger points at Wolf.

'The sacrifice,' we repeat.

'To ensure a fruitful year ahead, Wolf must jump over the fire,' says Badger.

Taking a running jump, Wolf clears the flames.

We all cheer, and Wolf does a jig.

We gnaw on our bannock, washing it down with more mulled wine. I feel dreamy and lightheaded as I drain my cup.

'Now we will sing "Sumer is Icumen in",' says Badger.

We know this one from *The Wicker Man*. In the movie they sing it in Olde English, but that's too hard. We follow Badger's lead.

Summer has arrived,
Loudly sing, Cuckoo!
Seeds grow and meadows bloom
And the forest springs anew,
Sing, Cuckoo!

As we sing, I'm transported to another time. A time when you would be happy just to survive the winter and know – if the correct sacrifices were made – better days were ahead.

Happy Beltane, darling. Mum's voice fills my head. I see her dancing around the house in her yellow kaftan, flowers in her hair. Tears prick my eyes. She would have loved this.

Merrily sing, Cuckoo!
Cuckoo, cuckoo, well you sing, cuckoo . . .

As we finish the song, Badger throws her cup into the fire. We follow suit. Badger sings a song about bonfires and dancing and fairies and spirits. It's a repetitive chant, and we sing along as we dance around the fire, our ponchos floating around us.

Between verses, we live up to our animal spirits, yipping and howling, growling and hooting. It's wild and exhilarating. I forget how tired I am as energy races through me. It's good to cut loose. And my article will write itself after this.

Wolf drops down next to the fire. This is the signal for the next phase – the leaping. Jaz told us in traditional Beltane ceremonies, people often lie close to the fire, while others leap over them. It's a fertility ritual. Smoke swirls in our faces as we jump over the prostrate Wolf. We whoop as we jump, spurring each other on to higher and more dramatic leaping. It's like a child's playground game.

'Wolf, I release you from your sacrifice,' calls Badger. 'It's Bear's turn.'

But Wolf doesn't move.

Bear taps Wolf on the shoulder.

Wolf lies motionless beside the fire, flames playing over his black nose and whiskers. We stop our leaping and come to a standstill.

Bear pushes at Wolf's shoulder. 'Hey, get up, it's my turn.'

Wolf flops over onto his back, his poncho hood falling off.

'You okay?' Bear kneels to pull up Wolf's mask.

It's Theo. In the flickering flames, his eyes are open, but

his face is still. Floppy black hair spills out from the sides of his mask.

A gust of wind swirls smoke over his lifeless body as I drop to my knees. Pulse pounding, I touch his forehead. It's clammy. Cold. Lula's face bursts into my mind, icy and pale. Lips blue. Eyes glassy.

We all freeze. Then my gaze jerks up – *Bear. Badger.* Where the hell is Owl?

My head spins. The firelight pulses, its crackling growing louder, like it's inside my skull. The flames stretch, clawing at the sky. Orange lasers. Badger and Bear stare back at me. Their shapes are warped – part human, part beast. Their whiskers twitch and their fur ruffles in the breeze.

I touch my own face. *Fur.* Lion fur.

Then I'm not here anymore. It's another place. Another night. The tower. The bitter wind. *Kill.* The word crashes through me. I see hands. Hands on Lula's chest.

The flashback passes as fast as it hit, and I return to this night, the cardboard masks, the flickering fire, and my hammering heart.

Theo is still motionless. I choke back panic. My school first aid course rushes back. 'Help me roll him,' I yell.

Ethan and I roll Theo onto his side. Pulling his chin down, I thrust my fingers in his mouth. There's nothing stuck in there. I poke my fingers further down, into his throat. Theo shudders.

I pull my fingers out as he coughs. With a convulsion, he disgorges a stream of hideous green vomit. Groaning, he clutches his stomach and vomits again.

Theo's eyes open. 'I feel like shit,' he whispers. He vomits again. Over and over, until he's dry retching. Moaning, he closes his eyes. His breathing becomes heavier. He twitches.

'Was it something he ate?' asks Jaz.

'We all ate the same stuff,' I say.

'Should we call for help?' Jaz sounds panicked.

I check my phone. 'No reception.'

Ethan looks around. 'Where's Nola?'

We peer into the darkness, but there's no sign of her. Owl has gone. We meet each other's eyes. Are we thinking the same thing?

I told Nola she wasn't safe, but did I get it wrong? Was it us who weren't safe with her? Fragments of memory slot together. Nola and Theo arguing in the forest. Theo drinking from a plastic wine bottle. Was that Nola's bottle? Did she put something in it? Or in the marked bannock?

Darkness presses in around us. The forest rustles, as if someone is walking through it. Is she still here? Circling us? Ethan builds up the fire, and we huddle around it.

Theo moans and dry retches.

It's getting cold. None of us are keen to go inside the ruins. It's damp in there and even colder. An hour or so passes in silence. Theo twitches and moans.

'He'll be okay, won't he?' says Ethan.

His words fall into a long, drawn-out silence as we gaze at Theo.

'Hope so,' I say at last.

The fire crackles in front of us and we fall silent again.

Jaz's words emerge, half-whispered. 'Do you think about what happened to Lula much?'

My shoulders tighten. Are we going to talk about this? Now? I've been wanting to talk about Lula, but now. . . I'm scared of what might come out.

'All the time,' says Ethan. 'She inhabits me. There's never a time when she's not there.'

'Same.' I press my fingernails into my palms. 'We ran away and left her to die. Then we let her family think she killed herself. I didn't know they were Catholics. They probably think she's gone to hell.'

'We didn't know it would turn out like that.' Jaz's voice trembles. 'But I wish . . . I wish we'd just confessed. It's so hard keeping a secret.'

Our eyes flicker to each other, then out towards the darkness. Where did Nola go?

'Too late now,' says Ethan.

I swallow. *The hands in my flashback*. Whose were they? Sweat beads my forehead. I remember so little. How do I know they weren't mine?

I need to distract myself. Turning on my phone torch, I stand and collect more sticks for the fire. My beam falls on Theo's vomit. The green bile is speckled with tiny flecks.

'Is that bits of leaf?' asks Jaz.

We all peer at the specks of green.

'It's not oleander, is it?' says Ethan.

My pulse jumps. *Oleander?* I remember what Theo said. *It's deadly.*

'Did you put oleander on the altar?' asks Ethan.

'No, of course not,' I say.

Ethan stands and walks over to the altar. He picks up a pink flower with leaves attached. 'Is this oleander?'

My mouth goes dry and my voice emerges in a croak. 'It looks like it.'

Jaz and Ethan cast unreadable looks my way.

I swallow. 'I didn't put that there.' I sound unconvincing. If I didn't, who did? 'Why would I poison Theo?'

Jaz stares at me and I know she's thinking about the night of Ethan's book launch.

My heart flutters as my gaze returns to Theo. His eyes are closed, his body still. A chill runs over me. 'He hasn't moved for a while. Is he okay?'

Picking up his hand, Jaz feels for a pulse. The colour drains from her face.

Chapter 42

Anonymous

I've toyed with these puppets enough. My patience has almost expired. As they enter the final, fateful stretch of their odyssey, let me leave you with one last poem.

There once were four with wounds so sore,
Their secrets festering to the core.
For their evil deeds they'll pay the price,
No pleading will make it nice.

I am no judge of the elusive realm of verse, but you cannot doubt the sincerity of my words. If we do not speak again, know I am, always,

Your friend,
Anonymous

Chapter 43

Fairy-tale Retelling

Flames flicker over Theo's rumpled poncho. He could be sleeping, but he's not. There's something too still about him, too final.

Jaz lowers her cheek to Theo's mouth to feel for breath. Her face is grey when she looks up, hollowed out.

'He's not . . .?' The breath rasps in my throat.

She nods, her lips pressed tight.

I rock on my heels, a sour taste in my mouth. I didn't like him, I *really* didn't, but I didn't want this. I look out at the night, my stomach roiling. Is Nola out there? Did she do this?

Ethan's face is pale and drawn. 'God, things weren't great between us, but I can't believe he's dead.'

'Same.' Jaz's voice is low.

We are silent as the fire crackles. My eyes keep coming back to Theo's dull, lifeless face. It feels like the world's gone out of focus and it won't snap back.

Ethan is still holding the sprig of oleander. His eyes meet mine and he clenches his fists. 'Did you do this?'

Nausea rushes through me. 'No. Of course not.'

'You're the one who prepared the altar. And you know what oleander looks like.'

My eyes dart to Jaz, looking for support.

'It must have been Nola.' She doesn't sound as certain as I'd hoped.

My gaze returns to Theo's lifeless face. 'Should we, I don't know, say a prayer?' My voice comes out in a croak.

Jaz and Ethan gaze at me wordlessly.

Looks like it's up to me. But I don't know any prayers. Then something comes to me; I clear my throat. '*All conquering Lord, whom sinners adore . . .*' I sing a few lines, my voice quavering.

Jaz and Ethan look at me quizzically as I stop.

'It's a hymn. I heard the Australians singing it.'

Ethan nods. 'RIP, mate. I'll—' His voice breaks. 'Miss you. Sorry things have been so weird between us lately.'

Silence falls, the fire crackles.

'RIP yourself.' The voice is hoarse and weak.

I stare at Theo. Did I imagine that?

'Don't bury me yet,' Theo whispers. His eyes open. He gags and moans. 'Fuck me. What did you put in that bloody bannock?'

A wave of giddiness sweeps through me, and I laugh as the tension bubbles out of me.

Ethan's face is white, but he laughs too.

We all drop to the ground next to Theo and help him sit up. I hardly know how it happens, but now we have our arms around each other, crying and laughing. It feels like there's something cracking open inside me.

Ethan locks eyes with Theo. 'Who did this to you?'

Theo shakes his head. 'No idea. It was horrific though, I felt like I was dying.'

'You know Nola best, Tess,' says Jaz. 'Would she do that?'

Would she? Ice fills my veins. *You're my dark angel, Tess.* 'Maybe.'

'She and Lula,' says Jaz. 'They looked close in that photo.'

'You think she's been biding her time for the last three years and now she's going to knock us all off to avenge Lula?' Ethan sounds dubious.

'It could have been her who invited us here.' I swallow; there's something else I should tell them. 'Iris emailed me to say she'd been hacked. It wasn't her who sent the invitation.'

They all stare at me.

'Why are you just telling us this now?' asks Ethan. 'What else are you hiding?'

Heat rises in my cheeks. 'Why would I tell you anything? You all ganged up on me at Ravensthorpe. You didn't invite me on the pilgrimage. You keep having these little tête-à-têtes without me. I could ask you the same question. What are you hiding from me?'

Ethan clenches his jaw, but doesn't say anything.

'Whoever invited us, it worked, didn't it?' I continue. 'We're all here. And Theo's been poisoned.'

'So, what now? Are we going to keep walking?' asks Jaz. 'With this . . . stalker after us?'

Ethan pulls at his hair. 'If Nola, or whoever, is out to get us, they'll find us as easily in England as here.'

'We should keep going,' says Theo. 'We can't let them intimidate us.'

We huddle together as the horizon lightens. The others look dirty and tired in the morning light. As I knead my stiff neck, my chest tightens. 'Any idea how to get back to the track?'

They shake their heads.

'Nola was the only one who had a map,' says Ethan.

My mind churns. We have no reception, and no idea how to get out of here. And there may be a killer on the trail. My eyes fall on the pink oleander flowers scattered on the ground. Who picked them? I know it wasn't me.

We pull off our ponchos as the sun hits. Ethan gets up. 'Let's try to find the trail.'

He and Jaz wander off.

'Tess,' Theo says as I'm about to follow. His face is drawn and pale. 'I'm so sorry about what happened between us. That night of Ethan's event. I don't know what was wrong with me. I'm not going to try to make excuses. I was an idiot.'

I gaze at him. 'Yeah, you were.' I turn away. I'm glad he's not dead, but I don't know if I'm ready to forgive him.

While Theo rests, we scout around the ruins. Spiky bushes cover the ground, making it hard to go far.

'Over here,' Ethan calls. 'Looks like an arrow.'

Jaz and I push our way through the undergrowth towards him. There, beneath the long grass is a stone marker with a faded arrow. An indistinct trail runs past it.

'What's that?' Jaz points. A scrap of paper lies at the foot of the trail marker with a pebble on top. Bending over, she picks it up and unfolds it.

I lean over her shoulder, a prickle running down my spine. The writing is in capital letters, like the other notes. It's a poem. *There once were four with wounds so sore . . .*

'What the hell?' Jaz's face crinkles. 'Who uses *nice* in a poem? Can you imagine what Iris would say?'

Ethan snatches the paper off her. 'Is Nola threatening us? In bad rhyming poetry? What's that, a limerick?' He shakes his head. 'Unbelievable,' he mutters, but his face is pale.

Should I tell them about the other notes? I open my mouth, then shut it again. Either of them could have written this note and left it there. They could have written the other notes too. I have no way of knowing it was Nola.

Jaz turns to me. 'You don't seem surprised. Did you write this?'

Her mind is running on the same tracks as mine. 'No, don't be crazy.' I can't tell them about the other poems now, it will make them suspect me more. 'I couldn't write a poem to save myself.'

'It's so creepy,' says Jaz.

Back at the fire, we collect Theo and Dapple, and walk through long grass, along the narrow trail. Ethan carries Theo's backpack while Theo follows along behind, slower than usual.

The trail takes us through another deserted village, and down a steep, rocky hill. The sun is overhead as we reach the valley and the main Camino track. It's a highway compared to where we've been.

I freeze. 'What's that on top of the trail marker?' As I walk closer, it reveals itself to be a single black feather.

Jaz stops beside me. 'Is that from Nola's staff?'

'Has to be.' I twirl the feather in my fingers, then stick it through my belt. *You're my dark angel, Tess.*

*

The sun is touching the horizon when I spot O Cebreiro church on the hilltop. As usual, the others are ahead. Dapple and I pass a marker which tells me we're in Galicia now, a part of Spain with Celtic roots. It's like Ireland – emerald green and hilly. Thatched, circular barns and grey-rock cottages spread out along the ridge. It smells medieval, of cows and wood smoke, and looks magical in the evening half-light. Walking up to the church, I tether Dapple and go in.

Inside, it's quiet and so dark it takes my eyes a while to adjust. At the front, a candle-rimmed shrine holds a chalice and silver tray which featured in a miracle Ethan told me about. A priest who'd lost faith recovered it when his wine and wafers changed into the body and blood of Christ. 'Sounds like a fairy tale,' I said. 'Or Brothers Grimm,' he'd replied.

High on the wall, a placid-faced Madonna holds a baby Jesus on her lap. Fresh flowers lie beneath her. My pulse leaps at a muffled noise behind me. There's someone in the pews. *Ethan.* His head is bent, and his eyes closed. *Is he praying?* I quietly leave.

As I head for the *albergue*, an owl hoots above. *To whit*

329

to woo. My mind turns to our animal masks. Nola was the owl, the only animal missing at the end.

It was confusing at first, up there in the dark. Hard to work out exactly who was who. Those flickering animal faces framed by hoods. If you wanted to poison someone, it could have been tricky to pick the right one. Only Ethan knew for sure which animal was which.

Except. . . My stomach flips. He didn't.

After the shock of Theo's poisoning, it completely slipped my mind. Theo and I had swapped masks.

And, before we swapped. . . *I* was the wolf.

＊

Next day, when I'm alone on the trail with Jaz, I tell her about the mask swap.

'You know how Theo is about wolves; he's got the tattoo. He asked to swap, and I wanted to get rid of him, so I did. Ethan was the only one who knew which animal was which. And he gave me the wolf mask. Do you think . . . he could have meant to poison me?'

'Why would Ethan want to poison you? He's more likely to want to poison Theo, the way they've been at each other's throats.'

'Maybe he knows I'm writing about him.'

'You and Theo are hard to mix up.'

'We're about the same height. It was dark, and the ponchos covered our heads, he might not have looked beyond the mask.' My mind returns to the bottle in Ethan's backpack. What was it?

Jaz gives me a side-eye look that makes my gut twist. Does she think it was me who poisoned Theo?

*

On the way to Melide, I run into Ethan in a café. He offers me wine, but I shake my head. After my lapse on the *dragonte*, I've resisted.

'I can't believe we're almost there,' I say.

'I just want to get it over with now.' Ethan's eyes are red, and his movements slow. He looks tired; I guess I do too.

'I told you I was here to find a miracle.' Ethan swigs his wine. 'So I can write about it. And for, you know, redemption.'

My ears prick up, and I nod encouragingly. 'Mm?' I still haven't started my feature. After what happened on the *dragonte*, I feel less ready than when I started. But if I don't write it, all this will have been for nothing.

'It's more complicated. And also, more ridiculous. Lula's priest . . . He told me Lula is in purgatory. Because she died by suicide.'

I frown. 'But she didn't.'

'No.' Ethan pauses. 'But after he said that I looked into it. Lula was a lapsed Catholic. That's just as bad apparently.' He expels a breath. 'It's so hard to believe in this, isn't it? But I was brought up with it. They used to tell us we'd be stuck in purgatory for two thousand years if we weren't a practising Catholic when we died.'

'Yikes.'

'If she is stuck in purgatory, it's our fault. Imagine. An

331

eternity of waiting at the bus stop. You know how impatient she was. So, I decided to do this stupid pilgrimage to absolve Lula's sins. It's a thing – like you and Jaz's cross.'

'But didn't Lula get her own get-out-of-purgatory-free pass when she finished the Camino?'

Ethan shakes his head. 'She had that breakdown and went on a bender in Santiago, remember? Only got out of jail in time to catch her flight.'

'Oh yeah, I forgot.'

Ethan shifts in his chair. 'The catch is the priest tells me it won't work unless I'm a believer. It's driving me batshit crazy, but I owe it to Lula to give it a go.'

'I guess someone has to do it.'

Ethan straightens, peering towards the window.

I follow his gaze, my pulse quickening. *Nola?*

He shakes his head. 'I thought it was her.'

'I keep thinking I see her too.'

Ethan drains his wine. 'Should have taken care of it when we had the chance.'

I stare at him, and I can't tell if he means it or not.

Chapter 44

Redemption

'Bloody late joiners,' huffs a weary-looking pilgrim.

An exuberant group in matching T-shirts is ahead of us in the reception queue. Many pilgrims, it turns out, only walk the last hundred kilometres to Santiago. According to the church, this is enough for the certificate. Those who start further back get nothing extra. Except for a sense of superiority.

I gnaw my lip as I lay my sleeping bag on the bunk. I thought I'd figure things out on this pilgrimage, but the opposite has happened. The ripples from our past keep spreading, muddying the water as they go.

Tomorrow, we get to Santiago. I haven't finished my memoir – how can I when I don't know the ending? But I need to make a start on this feature. It's all I've got left to hang on to. I need to do it for Mum. And the thought of going back to waitressing is unbearable. I can't put it off any longer.

This article will kick-start my career. Besides, returning the advance will add to my dire financial straits. And, despite what feels like a delicate truce, Ethan still has it coming.

Sitting on a bench in front of the *albergue*, I open my laptop and type. *Ethan Hill, an avowed atheist, is trying to find a miracle* . . .

'What are you up to?'

My heart jolts.

Ethan stands over me, gazing at my screen.

I click on my email, and the typing disappears. 'Just catching up on my emails.'

He eyes the new T-shirt and hiking trousers I bought in Arzua to replace my robe. 'I kind of liked the robe, do you miss it?'

'Yes, but I haven't thrown it away.' My voice quavers. Did he see? Surely, he'd have said if he had?

I'm still on edge when we gather at the table for dinner. Despite the tasty chicken paella, it's a sombre affair. We fork up our food in silence.

'This is like the Last Supper,' I say, when I can't stand the quiet any longer.

Ethan fixes his gaze on me. 'And which of us is Judas?'

My gut contracts, but I laugh it off. He would have said something by now if he knew. Wouldn't he?

*

Narrow bar-lined streets lead towards Santiago Cathedral. We pass rows of souvenir shops selling Camino paraphernalia.

Backpacks with scallop shells. Water bottles with yellow arrows. Head wraps with *albergue* stamp patterns.

I scream and jump backwards as a man leaps out at me from a shopfront. He's wearing medieval clothing – leggings and pantaloons. 'What is your name?' he demands.

As soon as I tell him, I regret it. He walks ahead of us down the narrow bar-lined street, strumming his lute and singing a song with only one recognisable word. *Tess*.

As we near Santiago Cathedral, excited groups in matching outfits jostle in the street. We follow our pied piper past rows of Camino paraphernalia. Backpacks with scallop shells. Water bottles with yellow arrows. Head wraps with *albergue* stamp patterns.

The streets open into a plaza, and we're there, at the place we've been walking towards for thirty days. Removing his felt hat, the singer holds it in front of me. I root around in my pocket and, finding nothing smaller than a ten Euro note, give him that.

'Expensive song,' mutters Ethan.

The man saunters off, whistling. In the plaza outside the cathedral, pilgrims mill around, crying, embracing, or looking lost. My breath catches as I spot a young woman with red hair, but it's not Nola. Scaffolding covers the cathedral; repairs are in progress. The main door is closed. We walk around to the side, but a security guard stops us.

'No packs.' He points at Jaz. 'No cross.' His eyes move on. 'And no donkey.'

Jaz's face pales. 'But I've carried this so far. I have to take it into the cathedral.'

The security guard is firm. 'No large objects.'

I suppose we'd all imagined arriving at Santiago in triumph. Being treated as heroes and ushered into the cathedral. But here we are. Is arrival an anti-climax for everyone?

'Fuck it,' says Ethan. 'Let's go get a drink. We can see the cathedral tomorrow once we've dumped our packs.'

Jaz stands frozen to the spot.

I put my hand on her shoulder. 'It doesn't matter, Jaz. You've done all you can.' I gaze at the cathedral spires. 'Can you believe it? We're here.' My voice sounds flat.

'I'm going to get my completion certificate,' she says. 'Who's coming?'

'I will,' says Theo.

'Can't be bothered,' I say. 'Even if it will save me from two thousand years of purgatory, some time in the future.'

'Me neither,' says Ethan.

'Okay, see you guys back in the plaza.' Jaz raises her hand, and she and Theo walk down the stairs near a bagpipe player and disappear.

Only now, do I realise the significance of Ethan's decision. I stare at him. 'But don't you need the certificate? For the get-out-of-purgatory-free pass? For Lula? Isn't that the whole reason you're here?'

He rolls his eyes. 'I'm so over it. I refuse to believe that getting a certificate will make any difference to Lula's afterlife experience.'

Ethan buys a bottle of red wine, and we perch on a wall with a cathedral view. A mouldy Saint James sits on top of the blackened spires, staff in one hand, the other raised in prayer.

Taking Dapple's panniers off, I place them beside us. The

sun is low, but heat leaches from the cobblestones. A low rumble of thunder crawls across the sky.

I am Beira. I cause thunder and storms.

'Well, I chased religion across Spain for thirty days but didn't nail it.' Ethan drinks from the bottle.

I eye him, my article's tone now clear. *Gut-wrenching. Definitely.* 'Me neither. The closest I came to a spiritual experience was when I fell over in front of the Iron Cross. And that was just one of those weird Camino things.'

Ethan holds the bottle towards me.

Don't do it, says a voice in my head.

'Come on, you're in Santiago, it's time to celebrate.'

'Weren't you the one who thought I had a problem?'

Ethan lifts his shoulders. 'We all have problems.'

He's right. Why did I give up drinking anyway? I take the bottle.

Sobriety and kickboxing. Mum's words ring in my head.

I let out a breath. I mightn't have done any kickboxing, but at least I've stayed sober. *Mostly.* Lowering the bottle, I pass it back to Ethan.

Something flickers across his face. Disappointment?

I tuck my feral hair behind my ears. 'It doesn't seem real, the last month, does it?'

'Nope.' Ethan salutes the cathedral with his bottle. 'It's been a hostage situation. I've had Stockholm Syndrome.'

'Is this the end of the line? In your search for faith?'

He meets my eyes. 'The priest suggested coffee mornings.'

I snort. 'Can't see you doing that.'

'No. I'm more of a Road to Damascus guy. The sudden epiphany.'

'There's still the pilgrim service tomorrow.'

'Last chance for deliverance. Not holding my breath.'

We sit in silence for a while, looking out at the cathedral. Ethan offers me the bottle again. I waver, but refuse.

'I wasn't in my right mind when I set out on this walk,' he says. 'Don't know if I am now.'

I eye him. Is he more guilty than the rest of us? Did he push Lula? Is that why he's here? I raise my water bottle. 'To Lula.'

Ethan lifts his wine bottle. 'To Lula.'

A drop of rain plops onto the plaza in front of us.

Dapple snuffles and I stroke her nose. I have a flight booked in a few days and a donkey to re-home before then. Not to mention an article to write. All the problems which the Camino held at bay are about to crash down on me.

Ethan's mouth twitches. He turns to me and narrows his eyes as thunder reverberates through the air. 'Are you writing a story about me?'

A bolt of panic hits my gut. He must have been biding his time. Thunder rumbles while I scramble for an answer. I'm tempted to deny it, but under a cathedral in a gathering storm . . . Even an unbeliever has qualms. I decide on a half-truth. 'I've been commissioned to write a story. For *Artemis*. About your search for a miracle. The second book.'

Ethan stares at me. Lightning flashes, a streak of white light. 'You scheming witch.'

I blink. 'That's harsh. I–'

Ethan's face reddens. 'I'll sue you.'

The air turns still and cold. The birds stop singing. A

338

trickle of sweat runs down my spine. Can he do that? I'd like to recover the situation, but – *what the?* I point.

Ethan turns and stares.

The scaffolding glows with a pale blue light. Saint James shimmers in the glow pulsing beneath him. He looks eerily holy.

The hairs lift on my arms and my fingers tingle. The metallic taste of electricity is bitter on my tongue. There's a crack and a bang as lightning strikes the cathedral. I jump up, my heart racing. Is this it? The reckoning for Lula's death? Is the Almighty about to smite us down?

'The scaffold's attracting lighting. You'll get zapped if you don't move. Not that I care.' Swinging his backpack over his shoulder, Ethan runs from the plaza.

'Wait.' I throw the panniers back over Dapple, and chase after him. But when I round the corner, he's gone. Fat raindrops explode on the cobbles around me.

*

My hotel room costs as much as a week on the Camino. It has pink shampoo arranged in a scallop shell, fluffy towels and soft sheets. It's excessive, but the receptionist did find a paddock nearby for Dapple at only five Euros a night.

Opening the glass doors, I walk out onto the balcony and spot a yellow arrow on the opposite wall. In the morning, pilgrims will go past. I let out a breath. I'm not a pilgrim anymore, just a tourist in a room with fluffy towels. I'm tempted to head out and find a bedbug-infested bunk in an *albergue*, but that would be silly, I've already paid.

339

I message Theo to let him and Jaz know I've got two beds for them here. Clearly, I won't be sharing with Ethan. Sitting up in bed, I open the laptop. For the first time in a month, I'm truly alone. I gaze at my screen. I need to tell Ethan why I'm writing this. Get him to admit what he did. I have no way of contacting him though. And I need to make a start.

Looking up from the laptop, I focus on the mini bar. I've been trying not to think about it, but I've lost the battle. Walking over, I pick up a miniature whiskey and crack the lid. The action reminds me of Larrasoaña, of our shared meal, made out of nothing but oat bars, cheese bread and my gin.

I raise the bottle. 'Here's tae ye.' But, as I put the bottle to my lips, I hear Mum's voice again. *Sobriety and kickboxing.* I sigh, toss the bottle in the bin, open my document, and write.

*

Sun hits my face and I open my eyes. Pilgrims are streaming past the window. I almost reach for Dapple's panniers. But, no, it's over. Dapple is enjoying a well-earned rest in a grassy paddock down the road. I gnaw at my lip. What am I going to do with her?

Theo and Jaz are in the other beds, fast asleep. Ethan is missing in action. There is no sign of Jaz's cross. This settles it, everything has changed.

Getting dressed, I pick up my laptop and let myself out. Over coffee and tortilla, I read through my work. It has drama, intrigue and interest. It's well written. And, most importantly, it has dirt. Lots of excellent dirt. Camryn is going to love it. Draining my coffee, I shut my laptop. So, why do I have this growing sense of unease? I need him to confess to spiking my drink, and to the plagiarism. It's not only the prospect of being sued that worries me. I need to know he deserves this.

Jaz and Theo are still asleep when I get back. 'Better get a move on if we're going to make this pilgrim mass,' I say, and they groan. My eyes fall on a crumpled heap of white on the floor. My robe. Yes, that's the right outfit for a pilgrim mass. I pull off my T-shirt and trousers and put it on.

'Where's your cross?' I ask Jaz when she gets out of bed.

'I ditched it. I got it here; that's the main thing.' She wrinkles her nose. 'Why the robe?'

'Thought it was appropriate for the occasion.'

She rolls her eyes.

The cathedral's almost full when we get there, but it's fifteen minutes until the mass starts.

'Let's check out Saint James.' Jaz points to stone stairs leading into an alcove.

Walking up the stairs, we enter a chamber with a statue of Saint James. The saint has his back towards us, facing out to the church. A woman is hugging the statue's back and murmuring a prayer in Spanish. Jaz follows, embracing the statue. Theo goes next. As he stands, his eyes are bright.

Are those tears? I wrap my arms around Saint James too, peering over the statue's shoulder, to the packed cathedral below. A guy with dirty-blond hair is sitting in the front row. *Ethan.* He won't be going anywhere until after the service. As I scan the congregation, my eyes catch a flash of red. My breath stills.

Nola raises her head, and the hairs lift on the back of my neck. I'm hidden behind the statue, and high in the eaves, but I could swear she's looking right at me.

Chapter 45

Family Drama

When we emerge from the chamber, Nola has vanished. There are so many people, she could be anywhere. Ethan's still in the front row, but I can't get to him.

We stand on the side, behind two middle-aged American women.

'Did you see the tattoo shop up the street?' drawls the one who I now realise is Ree. 'I want to get a scallop shell on my ankle.'

'Yeah. I'm going to get a yellow arrow,' says the other. 'On my wrist.'

I flash my eyebrows at Jaz. 'I'm getting a donkey,' I murmur. 'On my butt.'

'Me too.' Jaz giggles and it feels almost like old times.

The service starts, but it's in Spanish, so I tune out. Then things get interesting. A troupe of men in white robes and red scarves come out. Lighting a burner on the end of a long chain, they pull on a rope to swing it. A nun sings while the burner flies higher and higher, soaring into the cathedral naves, trailed by a frankincense cloud. It's a mysterious ritual but somehow moving.

As soon as the service ends, I dart forward, pushing my way through the crowd towards Ethan. I call his name as he stands. I need to have it out with him.

He glances towards me, glares, and heads in the other direction. I jostle and push, yelling his name. Despite my efforts, by the time I make it to the side entrance, he's gone.

I scan the church. There's no sign of Nola and I've lost Jaz and Theo now too. Emerging into the plaza, I gaze up at the cathedral. People are moving around on top. Back in Burgos, Ethan said he wanted to go up on the roof. Is he there now?

Going back into the cathedral, I find an archway leading to stairs. A group emerges, but Ethan isn't among them. I check the sign giving the tour times, but there isn't one for a while, so I duck inside.

Climbing up a narrow flight of stone stairs, I emerge into a shadowy room filled with spooky life-size puppets. I don't linger. As I climb on, holding up the bottom of my robe so I don't trip, I pass a carving of a lion's head, high on the wall. My breath hitches. *My mask* – Theo gave me the lion in place of the wolf.

I clench my jaw as I climb. *Theo. The wolf mask.* If someone poisoned the wolf, did they think it was me? Was it Ethan? Did he know about my article even then?

Light appears ahead and I emerge onto the cathedral

roof. The spires tower above me. There's no one around. I turn full circle, gazing at the view over the red roofs to the blue hills beyond, and my stomach clenches. It reminds me of the tower at Ravensthorpe. A footfall sounds behind me, and my pulse jumps as I turn.

'Hi, Tess.' Ethan's brown poncho flutters like a monk's robe in the breeze.

I swallow. It's just the two of us here.

'Great view, isn't it?'

My chest tightens and I take a step backwards.

He steps closer. 'What's up? Are you scared of heights?'

I step further backwards. 'Was . . .' My voice comes out in a croak. 'Was it you who poisoned Theo?'

Two swallows dart over Ethan's head, disappearing into their nest on a ledge. He stares at me, his face frozen.

I take a deep breath. 'It was you, wasn't it? You gave oleander to Theo.'

His face comes to life in an angry flush. 'Don't be ridiculous, of course I didn't.'

'Because we swapped masks, and you thought he was me.'

Ethan's brow wrinkles.

I take another step backwards. 'Were you trying to kill me?'

'Why would I do that?'

'Or maybe it wasn't oleander . . . I saw something in your bag. A bottle with Spanish writing. Was that it? Is that what you used on Theo?'

Ethan's cheeks redden. 'Were you looking through my things?'

345

I clench my fists, my pulse pounding. 'What was it?'

His flush deepens. 'It's none of your business.'

'If you don't tell me . . .' My mind races. 'I'm calling the police.'

Ethan stares at me. 'You're calling the police?' He shakes his head. 'Good luck with that. You're in it as deep as me.'

I exhale. He's right.

Ethan glares at me. 'It's nothing. It's not connected with Theo. I don't . . . It's hard to talk about.'

I frown. 'What? It can't be that bad. Not if you didn't poison Theo.'

He gazes over my shoulder, then grimaces. 'I've – God, this is so embarrassing. I've got an eating disorder.'

My thoughts scramble. Not what I expected. 'An eating disorder?' But it makes sense. *I was a chubby kid. We used to call him fatty.* Ethan disappearing after meals. The way he played with his food. How tired he's been looking. 'When did that start?'

'In primary school. My father called me fatty in front of my friends and it caught on.'

'He sounds awful.'

'He's a sadist. He's not who people think he is. When I was a kid, I used to fantasise about killing him. They were detailed fantasies . . .' He trails off.

I stare at him.

'I was forever trying to please him, but nothing I did was ever good enough.' Ethan's mouth twitches. 'He was livid when *Darker Matters* outsold all his books. So, there's that.'

I'm about to mention the plagiarism when he goes on.

'I binge. And then I use ipecac to vomit. I tried to stop on this trip, but I cracked. That's why I got locked out in Burgos. I scoured the whole city until I found some.'

His pale, sick face under the *albergue* overhang – he hadn't been high; he'd been throwing up. 'But Ethan, you can't do that. It's dangerous.'

He shrugs. 'I figured something out on this walk. So, it wasn't a dead loss. Being a celebrity isn't good for me. It was cool at first, but it messes with my head. It's like I'm two people. Real me and celebrity me. I've got to figure out a different way of doing this. I don't want to end up like Lula.'

'Like Lula? How?'

Ethan sinks to the ground, wrapping his arms around his legs. 'You know how she was. Up and down. Good reviews, bad reviews. Selling well, selling badly. The writer's life. I don't know if I'm cut out for it.' Ethan looks away. 'She was jealous of us. Because we had it all ahead of us, and she was on the way down. That's why she acted the way she did. Setting us against each other.'

I gaze down at him, the rooftop shimmering in the sun. 'Ethan, I know you plagiarised her book.'

Ethan's face pales. 'What?'

'I saw the novel on her laptop. The night she died.'

Ethan's body is still, but his eyes narrow. 'I didn't.'

Heat rises inside me. 'It's the same. The physicist. The theory of relativity. The characters. They're us, aren't they?'

Ethan shakes his head. 'You can't write about that. You can't. It will ruin me.'

'So why did you do it?'

'It wasn't plagiarism. Lula and I discussed it, that's all. After she died, I figured I may as well use the idea. I hadn't read her novel. I wrote that book.'

'It was exactly the same, Ethan. Exactly.'

A pulse pounds on Ethan's temple. 'How can you remember that? After three years? How much did you read anyway? You didn't read it all, did you?'

A twinge of doubt fills me. Ethan stole Lula's idea. Some of her words. But was it mostly his writing? It's possible.

Ethan sighs. 'Okay. Yes, I used some of her words.'

'Some?'

'Quite a few. I needed to publish. To show my father I could do it.' He gives a small smile. 'It's almost a relief. To be found out. It's been hanging over me ever since it came out.' He pauses. 'Are you going to write the article?'

'I have to. I'm committed. I've spent the advance. And it's a big opportunity.'

Ethan's face flushes. 'I'll probably be disinherited.'

I can't let myself feel sorry for him. I'm just getting started. 'What about the drink spiking? That was you, wasn't it?'

Ethan hesitates.

I clench my fists. 'I knew it. I knew it had to be you.'

He opens and shuts his mouth, then speaks in a low voice. 'I thought it was harmless.'

'Harmless?' Heat floods through me.

'I just wanted you to join in. For us to share that.'

My body quivers with rage. 'If I hadn't been tripping, I could have saved Lula. None of that would have happened. It was the exact opposite of harmless, it ruined everything.'

'I'm sorry.' His voice is soft.

I take a breath. 'You blocked my calls to Jaz too, didn't you? So we couldn't work it out. The spiking. She saw you pick up her phone.'

Ethan frowns. 'No. I don't know what you're talking about.'

He doesn't sound convincing. I've had enough of him; I turn away towards the stairs.

Ethan gets to his feet and steps after me. 'Why didn't you ever reply to my message?'

I turn back. 'What message?' I snap.

'I texted you. About a month after you left Ravensthorpe, to apologise. For the drink spiking. I felt terrible about it. And I wanted to talk to you. About Lula.'

My mind whirs. 'I never got a text from you.' *About a month after I left Ravensthorpe.* That was when Mum died. 'What did your text say?'

'Just, sorry. And I asked you if you wanted to talk some time. About what we did.'

Nausea churns through me. 'You mentioned what we did?'

'Nothing specific, but yeah.'

My nails bite into the palms of my hands. 'What did you say?'

'God, I don't know. That I was feeling awful about what we did to Lula, and I wanted to talk.'

The breath rushes out of me. That was why Mum dashed out that night. She'd put two and two together. She mightn't have guessed the whole thing, but enough to make her delete the text so the police wouldn't find it if they checked my phone. Rush from the flat. Enough to make her so frantic to find me she didn't see the car.

'Are you all right?' Ethan asks. 'I wondered why you never replied. I thought you must be so angry you'd blocked my number.' He hesitates. 'You're right, I did pick up Jaz's phone. But not to tamper with it. I wanted to see if you'd changed your number, but Jaz sprung me before—'

'Just stop.' I put up my hand. 'I can't listen to you. You spiked my drink. You sent a text that ruined everything.'

He steps towards me. 'I missed you, Tess.' He reaches out to touch my shoulder.

Rage flares inside me and I push him away.

He stumbles backwards.

'We're done. Don't ever contact me again. You're dead to me.' The words drop from my mouth like pebbles. I stride away, my legs shaking. As I climb down the shadowy staircase, I freeze. Was that a footfall behind me? I turn, but there's no one there. If it's Ethan, I've nothing to say to him. I keep going.

As I stride across the plaza away from the cathedral, my phone buzzes.

Look up. It's frigging Anonymous again.

Craning my neck, I look up at the cathedral roof. Something is falling. A silent scream catches in my throat. It tumbles and turns. It's a person. A brown poncho drifts like a broken parachute. *Ethan.*

The cathedral blurs in front of me. I scream. I want to run, but my head swims. My vision narrows. The light glows and dims. And I'm back there. On the tower at Ravensthorpe.

Leaving my body, I float above, looking down. At the dark figures huddled against the cold. One, two, three, four, five students. No. Four students. And Lula.

I come around to the buzz of my phone, the cathedral a brown haze in front of me. My heart explodes. Ignoring the phone, I race towards the cathedral. To where he fell. On the cobblestones ahead, I see it.

A crumpled brown poncho.

Chapter 46

Misunderstood Villain

Tears blur my sight as I stare at the crumpled poncho. Clenching my fists to still the trembling, I step closer. *Ethan.*

A figure emerges from the cathedral door – a dark outline in the shadows, a blur in my peripheral vision. I can't tear my eyes from the brown, wrinkled heap. A stone fills my chest. *You're dead to me.*

'Tess?'

I drag my eyes from the crumpled shape.

The figure raises his hand. He is tall, with dirty-blond hair. He looks like Ethan. It can't be him though. I don't trust my senses.

He waves again.

'Ethan?' My voice emerges in a whisper as I turn back to the poncho. A wave of relief washes over me. It's just a poncho, a crumpled plastic poncho.

Ethan strides over and grasps my arms. 'Are you okay? You look like you've seen a ghost.'

I point at the poncho. 'I thought . . .' I clear my throat. 'I thought it was you.'

'I left it behind up there. It must have blown off.' Ethan searches my face. 'But aren't I dead to you anyway?'

I half laugh, half sob. 'It was a metaphor. I didn't mean it literally. I thought someone had pushed you over.'

As if summoned by my words, my phone buzzes. I tap at the screen. A poem appears. A Haiku.

> *At world's end we'll meet,*
> *In the quest for the truth,*
> *To reveal your lies.*

Sucking in a breath, I show Ethan.

His eyes widen. 'What does that mean?'

I meet his gaze. 'There are some things I need to tell you all.'

*

The four of us perch on our hotel room beds and I tell them everything. The poems. The lollipops. The wellies in the boot room. The photo of my birthday party. For the first time since Lula died, there are no secrets. Not on my part, anyway.

When I finish, they stare at me in silence and it's hard to read their expressions. Are they going to accuse me of holding out on them again?

353

But Jaz touches my hand. 'I wish you'd told us sooner. You've been carrying this all by yourself.'

'I understand why you didn't,' says Ethan. 'We didn't give you much reason to trust us.'

'What happened to us?' Theo pulls his hands through his hair. 'We used to be such good friends.'

'It was Lula,' I say. 'She drove a wedge between us.' It feels so good to talk to them freely. Like we've gone back in time and we're The Core Wounds again.

'It has to be Nola who's doing this,' says Theo.

'What's her endgame?' asks Ethan.

'To get revenge for Lula?' I say. 'To send us to jail?'

'To kill us?' Jaz mutters. 'There wasn't much room for error with the oleander poisoning.'

Theo reads the Haiku again. "At world's end we'll meet." What the hell does that mean?'

'World's end,' says Jaz. 'Sounds familiar.'

I Google *World's end* and *Spain* together. 'Here it is. It's Finisterre, a headland on the coast near here. The pagans called it World's End because it's the most westerly point of Europe. It's where the sun vanishes into the sea.'

'But that's three days' walk, isn't it?' says Jaz. 'I met some pilgrims who were going there.'

'We can catch the bus,' I say.

'You want to face her down?' Jaz sounds dubious.

'If we don't, this will hang over us forever,' I say. 'We'll never know when she might expose us. We need to find out what she wants. What she knows.'

'You're right,' says Ethan. 'Whatever she has planned, we need to see it through to the end.'

Theo taps at his phone. 'There's a bus in half an hour.'

*

Jaz and I sit together on the bus. We look out the window in companionable silence.

'Look.' I point. 'Pilgrims.' Two pilgrims with backpacks stride into the forest.

'Feel guilty for not walking?' Jaz asks.

'No.' I twist my hair between my fingers. 'But I. . . miss walking with Dapple.'

Jaz smiles. 'Yeah, she's a character, all right.'

I'd ducked over to the paddock before catching the bus. Dapple looked very content, grazing with another donkey, but she trotted over to say hello. My chest tightens. What will I do? I can't leave Spain until I find her a home.

Jaz meets my eyes. 'Thanks for carrying my cross, Tess.'

'Someone had to do it.'

'You know how it goes; you carry mine, I carry yours. I owe you a favour.'

'I look forward to it.' I pause. 'So, do you feel like you've repented now?'

Jaz grimaces. 'God, I don't know. *Lula*. She and I . . .' She trails off. 'It was complicated.'

Complicated. . . Images spool through my mind. Jaz running down the spiral staircase at Ravensthorpe in the morning. Her messy hair. The way her cheeks had pinkened when I teased her about dancing with Lula at Ethan's party. 'Oh.' I meet her gaze. I suppose at some deep level I already knew this. *Lula*. She twisted us all around her little finger. 'That can't have been good.'

Jaz closes her eyes for a moment, then opens them again. 'No. Once we started, I couldn't . . . I didn't know how to stop.'

'She shouldn't have done that.'

Jaz blinks. 'Yeah. I know. It was wrong on so many levels. I feel like she chose me because . . . Because somehow, she knew that was my weakness, my *core wound*.' Jaz gives a bitter smile. 'Sex is how I seek approval. There was that older man, when I was at school . . . She saw that in me. And she used it.'

I reach out and squeeze her hand.

'She made me feel special. She told me I was brilliant and beautiful. She told me . . . that I was going to be The Chosen One.'

My eyes widen. 'She told you that?'

Jaz nods.

Theo looks back at us from his seat a few rows ahead. 'We're here.'

*

Seagulls squawk as we walk up Finisterre's guano-stained street. We pass a shop selling Indian clothing, find an *albergue*, and check in.

'Why don't we split up and look for Nola?' says Ethan. 'Check out the town, the beach, the headland, then meet back here.'

'Okay. I'll head up to the lighthouse.' My fingers tingle.

It's three kilometres to the lighthouse, the official journey's end. *The end of the world.* Will she be there?

'I'll check the beach,' says Jaz.

I tie a jacket around my waist as we both head for the door.

'*I cannot live without my life!*' says Jaz as she waves goodbye. It's our traditional *Wuthering Heights* farewell.

Warmth fills my chest. She hasn't said that to me since Ravensthorpe. I give the standard response. '*I cannot live without my soul!*'

As I set off, a prickle in my neck makes me stop and turn back.

Jaz is looking after me, her face solemn. She meets my eyes, forces a smile, then turns away.

I feel an urge to follow her, but I need to find Nola. My walk is along the side of a road, with beautiful views to the sea. Along the way I pass a statue of a pilgrim in traditional dress, leaning forward, as if into a raging headwind.

Two pilgrims dressed only in short shorts overtake me, jogging. '*Buen Camino*,' they shout, punching their hands in the air. 'Made it.' It's the two Romanian boys.

I wave back. 'We're not walking to the lighthouse, we are already there,' I call, and their laughter drifts back to me.

In front of the lighthouse, a Camino marker shows the distance to go – 0.00 km. I stop. *Here I am.*

Even at the end of the world, there are souvenirs. Passing a rack of *Camino* T-shirts, I follow a path towards the headland. On a rock nearby is a solitary boot, rendered in bronze. It looks lifelike – wrinkled and worn, as if it's walked for thirty days to get here.

I scramble further down the hill, following a trail of discarded boots. Many are almost unused, I guess their owners just did the last hundred K. The coastal heath bursts with yellow flowers and the sea sparkles. It reminds me of Devon, the way the rocks drop straight into deep blue water. I hadn't expected it to be so beautiful here.

I come to a standstill, my pulse thumping.

On the headland, Nola is perched on a rock admiring the view. Her red hair waves in the breeze from the cliff as she raises her hand. 'Welcome to the end of the world.'

The hairs lift on my arms. Was it her? Is she seeking revenge for Lula's death? Walking towards her, I sit, keeping my distance. If I keep her talking, I can figure out what to do.

'This is quite the spot, isn't it?' She points at a rocky outcrop. 'That's the site of the Celtic sun temple, Ara Solis. They were all about cycles, the pagans. Time going around and around. No beginning, no end.' She moves her finger in a circle. 'You can feel the power, can't you?'

Ethan would scoff, but as I listen to the sea crashing on the rocks beneath us, I do sense an echo of the aeons of worship. Or is that my racing heart? 'So, you're into paganism?'

'Possibly.' Nola gestures at the sea. 'They call this *Costa da Morte*. Coast of Death.'

A chill runs down my spine. 'Because of shipwrecks?'

Nola's gaze is quizzical. 'That, and because it was the place where ferries departed to the island of the dead. For the pagans.'

'How do you know all this stuff?'

'I listen to podcasts.'

Like all my conversations with Nola, I'm skating across the surface. Deep water lies beneath. 'So, how was your Camino?'

'Challenging.' Nola's sea-green eyes meet mine. 'You spend so much time in your head. Everything goes through the mincer and spits out in a different form.'

I take a breath. 'Why did you disappear, up there on the *dragonte*?'

Nola is silent for some time. 'I didn't feel comfortable. And after you said I should leave . . . It seemed like a good idea. It was a difficult day for me, I didn't need the extra aggravation. But Tess.' Her gaze meets mine. 'What exactly were you warning me about up there?'

'Oh.' I swallow. I can't tell her I thought they were going to kill her. 'The others were . . . uncomfortable with you being there.'

'Understandable. We do have history.' Nola gets to her feet. 'So, I'm going for a wee walk now.'

Is that it? She's toying with me. 'Will I see you again?'

'Are you staying in the *albergue*?'

'Yes.'

'Well, I'll see you there.' She turns away.

I wipe my sweaty hands on my pants. It must be her. I turn up at the end of the world, and here she is. I can't bear to drag this out any longer. 'Nola. I know you poisoned Theo and sent all those poems.'

She swings back to me. 'What?'

'Theo. You poisoned him. You told me to meet you here.'

359

'No.' She shakes her head, her face pale. 'I didn't. Honestly. Is he okay?'

I let out a breath. She is an exceptional actor.

'What happened?'

'Theo, as you well know, was poisoned. Most likely by oleander. It was touch and go, but he survived.'

Nola gasps. 'I didn't know. I swear.'

'You've been sending me threatening poems.'

'I have no idea what you're talking about.'

'So why are you here? I had a text telling me to come here. And here you are. Bit of a coincidence, no?'

Nola lowers herself back onto a rock. Drops of sweat bead on her forehead. 'I got a text telling me to come here too. When I saw you here, I thought it must have been from you.'

'What? No.'

'I do know something, but it's not what you think. I didn't poison Theo, or any of that other stuff.' She rubs at her face. 'I suppose I may as well tell you now. I'm a private investigator.'

My heart skips a beat.

'Someone hired me. An anonymous client. To follow you on the Camino and report on your whereabouts. It seemed harmless. And an opportunity to work things out in my head. Like I said on the *dragonte* route. Redemption. That's all I've been doing, I swear.'

My mind skitters, trying to catch up. 'You've been following us, and telling your unknown client where we are?'

She nods.

'And you have no idea who this client is?' I'm not sure if I believe her.

'No. It's not all that unusual in my profession.'

I narrow my eyes. 'But you're not just a random private investigator, are you?'

'What do you mean?'

'You knew Lula. She was your mentor.'

Nola's eyes widen.

'Did you love her?'

Nola laughs hysterically, the sound bouncing off the rocks like a seagull's cry. 'I can't believe you think that.' She wipes tears of laughter from her face. 'I hated her. Honestly, I could not have detested her more. Can I tell you a story?'

I nod.

'Well.' Nola gazes out to sea. 'When I was a kid, growing up in Bishopsgate, I dreamt of being a writer. I planned to study literature at university. In my last year of school, something exciting happened. An author came to my class. Lula Thornton. I'd had one of her novels assigned at school and I'd loved it.'

I stare at Nola. Where's she going with this?

She looks out at the crashing waves. 'Lula was captivating. Assured. Worldly. The college where she lectured seemed a place out of a fairy tale. The students who went there were enchanted beings. Beautiful. Colourful. Rich.

'Lula said she had a programme. An outreach programme. Some English A-level students could come to the college and do creative writing with her.' Nola smiles. 'Oh, you can imagine. It was like getting the keys to a magic kingdom.

'There were five from the village who were chosen. We rode our bikes up to Ravensthorpe on Friday afternoons.

Our sessions were held in The Blue Room. It was so beautiful in there, looking out through the bay windows to the pond. It made me feel special.

'I began to dream I'd go to Ravensthorpe one day. I knew it was expensive. My parents could never afford it. I was the keenest in the group though. I never missed a session. The others had commitments, netball and football. Suchlike. But I had nothing. All I ever wanted to do was write.

'One day, the others weren't there. There was a flu going around, and a football match. So, it was just me.

'"I'm glad it's just you, today," Lula said. "I've been wanting to speak to you alone. You're talented, Nola. You should come to Ravensthorpe next year."

'I blushed. "We can't afford it," I said.

'"There's a scholarship," she said. "For talented students of limited means. If I recommend you, I'm sure you'd get it."

'"You'd do that?" I asked.

'"For the right person. Someone who fits. Someone who's not afraid to make sacrifices."'

Nola meets my eyes. 'Can you guess how that turned out?'

Of course. Lula's novel *Lil*. A red-haired teenager dreams of being an artist but is ruined by her obsession with a well-known painter. 'Lula stole your soul and sold it to the highest bidder?'

'In a manner of speaking. She treated me like her special protégé. Encouraged me to write all sorts of weird things. Things I regretted later. I skipped school to go up to

London with her and meet her publisher. She implied that he would be my publisher too, one day. I worshipped her. As a mentor, I mean. Someone to look up to. I thought she cared for me too.'

Nola grimaces. 'But as it turned out, I was just a character study. A wind-up doll she could write about. She never mentioned the scholarship again. And after she'd got what she needed for her novel, she blocked me completely. Just like that.' Nola snaps her fingers. 'One day I was her precious friend, the next she had me sent away when I knocked on the Ravensthorpe door. She rang the school and told them I was harassing her. She gaslit me into thinking I'd imagined our whole relationship. It was only when her book came out that I knew I hadn't.

'It half-killed me. You know what you're like at that age. Everything hurts so much, I guess I went a bit crazy. I bombed my A-levels, so I couldn't go to university. I was lucky to get into the police force.' Nola meets my eyes. 'Lula Thornton destroyed the life I should have had.

'I should have let it go, but I had this fascination. For how it might have been. I'd go to student parties at Ravensthorpe. Imagine myself there. It was like prodding myself with hot needles, but I couldn't stop.

'That night Lula died, I was walking around Ravensthorpe. I did that when you were all on holidays. Especially after . . . after the kids drowned. It was beautiful there, it calmed me. I didn't know about the winter retreat, so I wasn't expecting you there.

'When I saw the lights on, I looked in the window. Like a picture you were. Gathered around the fire, with her in the centre.' Nola's mouth twists. 'When you all rushed outside, I hid around the corner.'

Nola looks up at the sky. 'And this . . . This blackness came down on me. It was the PTSD I suppose. It was all mixed up in my head. Lula. That man with the kids. After you went up the tower, I followed. Quietly.'

My flashback outside Santiago Cathedral lurches into my mind. I'd floated above, looking down. *One, two, three, four, five. And Lula.* I'd been right, there were six of us there.

'It was so dark when you blew the candles out. I knew you wouldn't see me. Lula was right next to me when I came out from the stairs. She was carrying on, the way she did. About the winter goddess. I was so fucking sick of it.

'She said that thing about removing obstacles. And . . .' Nola meets my gaze. 'I decided to push her. I was about to do it. I had my hands out . . .' She shakes her head. 'I was touching her, but someone else pushed her first.'

Chapter 47

Survival Story

Someone else pushed her first.

Nola's words hang in the air and her green eyes bore into mine. My body feels too light. Like I might float away.

Nola swallows. 'My client, whoever they are, must know I was there. I think they plan to expose us all.' She hesitates. 'Or worse.'

My stomach lurches and I jump to my feet. 'We need to find the others. They're in danger.'

*

'Jaz? Theo? Ethan?' My words echo through the *albergue*, but there's no reply. Inside the empty bunkroom, on a bottom bunk, my laptop is open. I frown. I didn't leave it that way. Stepping forward, I touch the mouse and a document appears on the screen.

Sweat trickles from my armpits. It's my Ravensthorpe memoir. But I don't recognise the words. I find my glasses in my jacket and put them on. Who wrote this?

Nola steps next to me and we read it together.

Hello dear reader,

I know it's poor form introducing a new point of view character at this late stage. Lula wouldn't have approved. But Lula is dead.

And about that . . .

It's been three years since that night on the ruin and it's time to come clean.

It was me. I pushed Lula.

Lula and I were lovers. It was a strategic move on my part. It's true Lula was attractive, and interesting. But I did have some expectation of special consideration.

As soon as Tess told us about the anthology, I knew. I'd talked to other students about how she operated. She'll give her favourite a test, they said. Like a story to finish in a short space of time. I was furious, but I kept my powder dry. If I could get Tess out of the way, I'd be the obvious choice.

I knew Tess. She'd wait until the last moment to send her story. She'd work on it and work on it. I needed to nobble her, so she didn't finish.

Tess was my friend. But when it came down to it, I cut her adrift easily enough. She wasn't like the rest of us. She was smart in all the wrong ways. I planned to keep her up all night, then slip her some of my Valium so she'd sleep through the deadline.

But when Lula pulled out the mushrooms, my plan changed on the fly.

And the pushing?

Up there on the tower, I sidled up to Lula. 'So, who's going to be the chosen one if Tess hasn't got the goods?'

'Theo,' Lula said.

It was instinctive. I didn't realise there was no wall where she was standing. It was only later it occurred to me. She was probably joking. She had a pretty good sense of humour, Lula.

So, having made my confession, I shall now do a Vincent Van Gogh. Farewell!

xx Jaz.

*

Do a Vincent Van Gogh? Bile rises in my throat as I read the words again. The room swims in front of me. *Jaz.* I see her looking back at me outside the *albergue.* Her solemn face. She was planning this then. Grief stabs through me.

A few phrases lodge in my brain. *Get Tess out of the way. Cut her adrift. Smart in all the wrong ways.* My eyes sting. Was Jaz ever my friend?

My eyes catch on the last line again. *Do a Vincent Van Gogh.* Unease prickles inside me. The words are a signal. A message only I would understand. We used Van Gogh's words to fake Lula's suicide. A rush of relief makes me giddy as it hits me. 'The confession's fake.'

Nola turns to me. 'How do you know?'

367

'I can't explain, but it is.'

'Why would she do that?'

I stare at Nola. 'Maybe someone forced her to write it. Or she's protecting someone.' My pulse patters. 'We need to find her. I think she was heading for the beach. Or the headland.'

'I'll search the headland, and you check the beach.'

Running outside, I follow the track towards the beach, racing across grass-covered dunes, my lungs burning. On the dune top I stop, panting, and scan the beach. It's empty.

Then my breath catches. Someone is in the sea. They're a long way away, along the cliff base. I can't tell who it is, but they're floating, motionless, not swimming. Is it Jaz? Fear flutters in my chest.

I'm driven by instinct. Running down the beach, I pull off my boots and trousers and launch myself off the rocks. The cold makes me gasp. I duck under a wave, swimming front crawl, heading for the last place I saw her. I keep swimming, but when I stop to catch my breath, the sea is empty. I turn in a circle, scanning. She's vanished.

The sky's a deeper orange now, and the sun touches the water. Has Jaz gone back to shore? As the sun dips below the horizon, I turn back towards the beach. I'm a long way out, further than I realised. That doesn't bother me at first. I swim front crawl, pausing to check progress.

I'm not getting any closer. If anything, the shore is further away. The waves are getting bigger. Realisation sweeps over me. I'm caught in a rip.

My belly clenches, but I know the drill. *Don't try to fight it. Swim in at an angle, until you're out of the current.*

It's hard work though – the churning sea, the cold. I'm not a strong swimmer and I'm tiring. I stroke on, aiming diagonally for the shoreline.

It's dark now, no one's going to see me. I try to ignore the shadows beneath. Do they have sharks in Spain? I keep swimming until my arms turn to jelly. I can't go on. I'm no longer sure I'm going to come out of this alive.

As I float on my back, images drift into my head. *Green grass. A honking goose.* The sky swirls and pulses. The waves whisper in Jaz's voice. *You're so oblivious, Tess.*

Not a flashback. Not now. But it comes.

I'm back there. The tower. The hands. But this time there's more. Jaz takes my arm. Her voice whispers in my ear.

You can't believe Lula. She offered me the anthology too. And told me I'd be The Chosen One. She said the same to Ethan and Theo. She's playing us all. We're just a piece of performance art to her. She wants to see how far she can push us. The more drama there is, the better for her writing.

I keep floating as the stars come out. Pulsing purple and violet waves of light. Jaz's voice is all around me. In the waves. In the sky.

She's playing us all.

I'd thought the sun long gone, but one last ray shoots from the horizon. It lights the clouds triumphantly, like a message straight from God. Warmth fills my chest. Is this the miracle I've been waiting for? *Why not?* How can it hurt? I pray.

I offer Him a deal, the only deal I've got.

Chapter 48

Psychological Thriller

'Are you all right?' The voice is familiar.

I roll onto my back. Ree, the annoying American, is standing over me, her large camera dangling from her hand. I'm on the beach, covered in sand, and I have no idea how I got here. Did my prayer work?

'It's Tess, isn't it?' Ree bats her mascara-clad eyelashes.

She's not as put together as usual. Her hair is ruffled, and she has a smear of dirt on the knee of her pants.

'Didn't recognise you at first,' she says. 'I was told it was dangerous to swim here. Several pilgrims have drowned. You're lucky you didn't get caught in a rip.'

I sigh. Of all the people I'd rather not have to deal with right now. 'I'm okay,' I mumble. 'But—' I jolt into a sitting position as it comes back to me. 'My friend might be out in the sea.' I point. 'I need to find her.'

'Oh, dear.' Ree looks out at the sea. 'I'm sure she's okay.

Maybe she's come in somewhere else. Let's get back to the *albergue*. If she doesn't show up soon, we can call for help.'

Crawling upright, I walk on jellied legs back to my clothes. I hug myself, rubbing my upper arms for warmth. Uncontrollable shivers rack my body. Retrieving my clothes, I put them on, zipping up my jacket.

I peer out at the dark sea. Is Jaz out there? Fear grips my belly. She's a strong swimmer, I soothe myself. And it might not even have been her. As Ree and I walk up the beach, I spot a scallop shell. Picking it up, I show it to Ree. 'Proof I made it to the end.'

She turns it over in my hand. 'Someone lost their souvenir.'

The shell has a red cross painted on it, like the ones for sale in Santiago. It's not a wild scallop at all. I suppose it doesn't matter.

As we walk over the grasslands back to town, my mind replays Jaz's words from the flashback, over and over. *She's playing us all. You're so oblivious, Tess.* I can't make sense of it. I think of the swim, my exhaustion, the praying. The gentle wave that carried me shoreward. My chest aches. Is Jaz out there?

She isn't in the *albergue*. And neither is Nola. She must be still searching.

'Let's give it a minute before we call for help,' says Ree, soothingly. 'She might be on her way back. Are you sure she was out there?'

I shake my head. 'I thought I saw someone, but they were a long way away.'

371

'I'll make you a cup of tea. You English folk are always drinking tea, am I right?'

I nod, gnawing at my lip.

'Did you have a good Camino?' Ree chirps as she puts on the kettle.

I sigh. 'Parts of it were good. Other parts not so good.'

Her brow wrinkles. 'You get out what you put in. You need to focus on the positive.'

Something snaps inside me. 'I'm sick of focusing on the positive. I don't want to keep being my best self, being grateful, embracing change. I want . . .'

She leans back from me.

'Sorry. I don't know where that came from.' What do I want? I came here to get things sorted out, but now they're more jumbled up than before.

Ree hands me the tea and I gulp it down. I'm still cold from the swim. 'I'm going to have a shower.'

When I come out of the shower, Ree has her back to me, fiddling around on the kitchen bench. I'd love another cup of tea, but I'd rather not talk to Ree. Her endless chirpiness gets me down.

Her phone rings and she picks it up. 'Ellery here. No, I'm sorry but that won't do it. We have a lot of interest.' She sounds completely different on the phone. Gone is the saccharine sweetness, replaced by a crisp, businesslike tone.

'Okay, talk to your team and get back to me.' Her posture looks different too, her shoulders are pulled back and she's standing up straighter. Ending the call, she reaches into her pocket, pulls out her red lipstick and reapplies it.

It takes a moment to hit. *Ellery*. Ree is an abbreviation, her full name is Ellery. Lula's agent's name is Ellery. For some reason, I'd assumed Lula's agent was a man. But Ellery is a woman's name too. Her phone conversation – it sounded like a discussion an agent would have. My spine prickles as Lula's voice fills my head. *It's basically a marriage. You need a warrior who has your back.* If she is Ellery Eppis . . . Is she the stalker? Has she been right in front of me the whole time?

Heart racing, I scan the room. Is there anything I can use as a weapon? Or am I overreacting, and she's just a particularly annoying pilgrim? My walking poles are against the wall. It can't hurt to be prepared. Edging towards them, I grasp one. I yawn. I'm so sleepy.

Ree turns. 'Ah, there you are.' A smile spreads across her round face. She's back to sweet, syrupy Ree.

She doesn't look like a crazed stalker, not now. But the woman on the phone, she sounded like she could rise to the occasion. Where are the others? I listen for footsteps, but they don't come. I slide my phone out of my pocket.

'I bought a cake in the village to celebrate finishing the pilgrimage. It's a *Tarta de Santiago*, one of those special ones made of almond meal? It's gluten-free, if that's an issue for you.'

There's a flattish cake on the table with a cross of Saint James marked on the top in icing sugar.

'Do you want a big slice or a small one?' Ree lifts her hand to reveal a knife much too large for cutting cake.

I clutch my pole tighter. 'Small.' My voice is slurred. That swim tired me out.

'What are you doing with that pole?' She cocks her head.

I swallow. 'Are you Ellery Eppis?'

There's a brief hesitation before she smiles. 'Why, yes I am. Well deduced. The very same.'

My stomach lurches, but I try to keep my voice calm. 'Lula's agent?'

'Lula's *former* agent.' The warm drawl is gone.

I swallow. 'It's you, isn't it?'

She raises one eyebrow.

'You poisoned Theo.'

She gazes at me wordlessly.

'How did you do it?' My voice is a croaky whisper. I clutch my phone tightly. I'm having trouble concentrating. I yawn and blink.

'It was straightforward.' Her voice is flat. 'Nola told me where you were heading, so I followed you up there. I pre-prepared a brew of oleander leaves and poured it into Nola's wine bottle when she left it unattended. I didn't expect Theo to pick it up, but whatever.' She shrugs. 'You're all as guilty as each other.'

I look past her, towards the door, but there's no sign of the others. 'What do you want?'

Ree's eyes narrow. 'I was always suspicious of you all; I didn't believe Lula would die by suicide. And she would never have used Vincent Van Gogh's last words as a suicide note. So tacky. It was obviously a cover-up. You let her die in the snow. Of hypothermia. After all she did for you. I stewed on it, but I didn't know how to make it right.

'But when I read Ethan's book, I had to act.' She clenches her jaw. 'Did he think I wouldn't notice? Lula and I worked together closely. I recognised her words at once. What a bunch of deceitful ingrates you were. And you thought you'd got away with it.

'You had to pay. All of you. You were all there that night. I knew Ethan was stuck on his so-called second book and wouldn't be able to resist my invitation. And once he was in, you all would follow. Nola becoming a private investigator was a bonus. Lula had her pegged. "If I ever die in suspicious circumstances, look at Nola, she's obsessed with me," she said.'

I take a step backwards, clutching my pole. 'You're crazy.'

'No. I'm perfectly sane. Holding a grudge is only human. You, of all people, should know that. Lula was my first client. I was a bookseller until I met her. She used to come into my bookshop when she lived in New York, and we hit it off. When she wrote her first book, she asked me to represent her, and both our careers took off from there. We weren't just client and agent; we were best friends. Creative partners. Lula was a genius, and you . . .' Her face twists. 'You and your writing group will only ever be wannabes.' She snorts. 'The only way Ethan could get published was to steal Lula's work.'

I stare at her, mesmerised, and yawn again. 'Was it you? The poems, the texts? The lollipops?'

Ree beams. 'Yes, did you enjoy them? That was all rather fun. I'm no poet but I had a good time writing them.'

'But why? Why did you send them to me? Why not the others?'

'I knew it would make you suspect them. And vice versa. Divide and conquer. I didn't want you getting too cosy and

375

working things out.' She pauses. 'Also, Lula told me you were The Chosen One, so it seemed appropriate.'

'Me?' Jaz's words echo in my head. *You can't believe Lula. She offered me the anthology too. And told me I'd be The Chosen One. She said the same to Ethan and Theo.* 'But she told all of us that. Didn't she?'

'Oh, possibly, and I'm sure she had her own fabulously creative reasons for that.' Ree bares her white teeth. 'But you were the real one. She showed me your writing, and I agreed.'

I'm so tired, but heat rises inside me. 'What do you expect to get from this?'

The knife flashes in the fluorescent lights as Ree turns it in her hand. 'One of you has to step up and take the blame. Someone must go to prison for this. So, was it you? Did you push Lula? And, yes, I read Jaz's confession, but she's a cunning little minx, I'm not sure I believe it.'

Nausea washes over me, and I touch the bench to keep myself upright.

'Was it you?' Ree steps closer, the knife gleaming in her hand.

Chapter 49

Alternate Reality

The fluorescent lights pulse like a warning. The walls ripple, snakelike, sinuous. Ree steps towards me, the knife in her hand blazing like a flame.

My balance tilts. The air tightens. And then I'm back. Ravensthorpe. Before everything went wrong.

*

'We should go to the ruins,' Lula says. 'I've got a key.'

Jaz's eyes widen and my blood races with excitement. The ruined tower. At last.

Outside, mist pours from my mouth as freezing air hits me. The mist sparkles and tinkles as it floats away.

Lula, Ethan, and Theo vanish into the darkness.

Jaz grasps my arm. A golden glow surrounds her head.

'I need to tell you something.' Her voice is low. 'You can't believe Lula.' Jaz glows red now. 'She's playing us.'

We run across the meadow to the tower, shielding our candles with gloved hands. The heavy door is open, and voices echo down the spiral staircase. Ethan and Lula.

'My father . . . kill . . .' It's Ethan's voice.

Theo appears from the darkness. 'Just taking a piss.'

We hold up the candles as we climb, their flames flickering against stone. As we emerge at the top, a frigid breeze blows my candle out.

'Beira, Queen of Winter, now rules the earth.' A blue tint seeps over Lula's face and deep wrinkles gouge her cheeks. 'Blow out the candles. We'll meditate in the darkness.'

Candles are puffed out and Lula's face glows brighter. I shiver. Crooked red teeth gleam in her mouth as her words float from the darkness.

'Picture what you desire.'

A book appears. A book with my name on it.

It's what you were born for, says Mum.

'Do you see obstacles to your desire?' Lula's voice booms.

You can't believe Lula.

'How can you remove these obstacles?'

Do whatever you need to do, says Mum.

Lula swims before me. Her hag-like face. Her snarled red teeth.

You can't believe Lula. She's playing us.

My hands meet Lula's chest. It's too easy. A soft gasp. A startled oof. And she's gone.

In the dark space where she'd stood, a giant bird with

the face of an owl spreads its wings and soars into the sky.

*

Guilt tears at my stomach like barbed wire. My mind flashes to that note on the pillow at Ravensthorpe. *I know you killed Lula.* No name. No signature. But they were right.

'I killed Lula.' My words emerge in a slurred croak.

Ree's mouth twists into a feral snarl, her knuckles whitening on the knife as her grip tightens. She takes a step forward.

My leg muscles tense – instinct screams at me to run – but my body won't move. I can barely stand. I sway like prey in the spotlight.

A door bangs. Nola appears, followed by Ethan and Theo.

My chest clenches. *Where's Jaz?*

'Don't listen to Tess.' Nola's cheeks are flushed, and her hair ruffled from the wind. 'She can't remember what happened. It was me. I pushed Lula. She ruined my life.'

Why is she saying that? It's not what she said at the lighthouse.

Ethan's eyes flicker between us. 'But . . . It was me. I pushed her. After she said that thing. About removing obstacles. I had to be The Chosen One. Imagine how it would have looked, Sebastian Hill's son, not being chosen.'

I don't understand what's happening.

After a brief silence, Theo throws his hands in the air. 'Okay, jeez, what is this? *I am Spartacus?* It was me. I know you all think I can't write to save myself, but I wanted to be The Chosen One too. Lula told me I was, she said I was the next Hemingway. But then she pulled it out from under me.' He takes a breath. 'She laughed at me. Said she was just joking. I pushed Lula.' His eyes flicker to me. 'Also . . . I changed your number in Jaz's phone and blocked your real number.'

I stare at him. 'What? Why?'

'If you got together, I thought you'd figure out it was me who pushed Lula.' He swallows. 'I'm sorry. There's something else too, I—'

The door bangs and Jaz runs in, dripping wet, her T-shirt clinging to her.

Relief makes my legs weak.

Jaz is panting, her eyes wild. 'Oh, thank God, you're okay, Tess.'

'I'm fine.' I blink, struggling to clear my head. 'What happened to you?'

'I came back to the *albergue* to get a jacket and I saw her' – Jaz points at Ree – 'Reading your laptop. She didn't see me, but it made me suspicious. After she went out to the kitchen to make a drink, I sneaked in and saw your Ravensthorpe memoir. And I had this idea, to throw her off your scent, so I added my note for her to read when she came back. You carried my frigging cross, after all, so . . . You didn't believe all that stupid stuff I wrote, did you?'

I shake my head.

'So, I left the confession there, and ran out along the headland, looking for you. But, when I stopped on the cliff, she just appeared and pushed me over. Lucky it was a clean drop into the water. But it took me ages to swim all the way back to the beach.'

Ree narrows her eyes. 'So, your confession wasn't true?'

'Well, one part was true.' Jaz's eyes meet mine. 'I did push Lula.'

Ree glares at us, her nostrils flaring. 'You can't *all* have pushed Lula.'

'You have *no* idea what it was like up there.' Jaz's eyes dart around at us all. 'Don't you remember? She kept circling, saying that thing, over and over. Pushing us.'

As Jaz says this, the memory claws its way forward. The last piece of the puzzle.

What do you desire? What is in your way?

Lula's voice. Lula's hands, pushing Jaz in the chest. Jaz stumbling backwards, heels skidding near the broken edge of the tower. Lula advancing again, eyes wild, yelling. *Come on, tell me. What's in your way?*

And then it happened. In an instant. A confusing, drug-addled, pitch-black instant. Lula raised her hands to push Jaz again and we'd moved as one. To protect Jaz. To stop Lula. To make it end. No wonder the memory fractured in all of us. No wonder we all thought *we* were the one who killed her.

'She *staged* it,' I say. 'She wanted a moment. A climax. A drama she could write about. She told us about that artist who was shot as performance art. That's what she was chasing. Something violent. Something extreme.'

'She was baiting us,' says Jaz. 'When she said that thing about obstacles, she was hoping we'd implode. She'd set it up so we'd turn on each other. But instead . . .'

'We turned on her,' says Ethan.

'Lula was a *monster*,' says Nola. 'I was a kid, and she *used* me. Told everyone I was obsessed with her. I trusted her, and she took all the secret parts of me and turned them into fiction. It destroyed me. Crushed my ability to write.'

'Lula wrote about me too,' I say. 'She didn't even try to disguise my identity. Everyone knew it was me; she used details from a story I'd written for class. She turned me into a joke.'

'Lula gave us hallucinogens,' says Ethan. 'She made it clear we had to take them if we wanted to be The Chosen One.'

'Lula manipulated us all,' says Theo. 'She exploited our weaknesses and turned us against each other. Her fans have *no idea* what she was like. Not yet.'

'Lula seduced me,' says Jaz. 'She let me think I'd be The Chosen One if I slept with her. All I had to do was give her everything.'

Ree turns the knife in her hand, her nails scarlet against the handle. 'Listen to yourselves. *Wah, wah, wah*. Lula was mean to us.' Clenching her fist, she raises the knife.

I jump, my heart pounding, as she plunges the knife into the cake. It quivers there, catching the light, held upright by the chopping board.

Ree's eyes rake us all. 'Lula was an artistic genius. Did anyone complain when Picasso treated women like doormats? When Gaugin took Tahitian child brides? Male artists have been doing this shit for centuries. Life isn't fair, get over it.' She rolls her eyes. 'So, you all killed Lula? Is that the story?'

After a brief pause, we all nod.

'Fine. You're all going to jail.'

'If we go to jail . . .' I speak slowly; I can hardly keep my eyes open. 'You're coming too.' I hold up my phone and press *play*.

Ree's drawl emerges. *I pre-prepared a brew of oleander leaves and poured it into Nola's wine bottle . . .*

Ree pales.

'I'll tell the police you pushed me over the cliff,' says Jaz.

'I have all your threats on my phone,' I say. 'They'll be able to trace them to you.'

Ree puts her hands on her hips. 'So, what do you all want? A deal? Is that it?' Her crimson mouth twists, and a mirthless laugh escapes. 'You want to be The Chosen Ones?'

Chapter 50

Deal with the Devil

'I've decided to walk back to France,' Theo says casually as he swallows his cake.

We are sitting around the table in the *albergue*, demolishing Ree's cake. Our mood is weirdly calm, though my guilt about Lula's death sits like a rock in my stomach. We are bound together now, not by our lies, but by the truth. By unspoken agreement, we've decided to sleep on Ree's offer.

The sedative Ree gave me is wearing off, but I'm still befuddled, so Theo's words take a moment to register. My mouth drops open. 'You're kidding. It was bad enough to walk here. Why would you turn around and walk all the way back?'

'I'm, uh, not ready to finish. If you want, I can take Dapple back to the farm where I got her.'

I straighten, suddenly alert. 'You want to take Dapple?' I should feel grateful, but I don't.

384

'If that's okay?' He eyes me warily. 'I'll take good care of her, I promise.'

I suck in a breath. 'Of course. Amazing.' It's the perfect solution. But I don't want to say goodbye to Dapple.

'It's weird how we all pushed Lula, huh?' Theo finally acknowledges the elephant in the room. 'This whole time, I thought it was just me.'

We all stare at him for several long seconds.

'Understatement of the year,' says Jaz at last.

'I used to think Ravensthorpe was a utopia.' Ethan snorts. 'It was more of a dystopia, though, wasn't it?'

Nola gives a sad smile. 'It was its own world. Beautiful and terrible, and somehow enchanted.'

'And Lula was the witch in the tower,' I say.

'Yeah.' Ethan gets a faraway look. 'It felt like when you went through that front gate with the mosaic, you changed. Became this . . .'

'Needy, hungry, success-craving writer,' I say.

'She was like a cult leader,' says Jaz. 'You know, the love bombing, then the withdrawal of affection. It makes you crazy, you'll do anything for approval.'

'Divide and conquer,' says Theo. 'That's what The Chosen One was all about. Classic cult control technique.'

We fall silent. My throat feels thick. *Lula.* Yes, she was all of that. We were young and impressionable, and she messed with our minds. But did she really deserve to die?

*

Before I go to bed, I check my emails. My muscles tense as I see her name. *Camryn.* I've been trying not to think about her.

I've been calling and calling. Your feature is due in three days. Why haven't I seen anything? Send me what you've got. We can rework if needed.

Does she still think I'm a mad bitch? I pull at my hair. *Sorry,* I type. *I have a draft. Can we talk tomorrow?*
All right. Ten-thirty.

I stare at the bunk above me. *My article. Ree's deal. Lula . . .* I thought this Camino would present me with solutions, but it hasn't. Or not yet.

You're so close, Mum whispers in my ear. *Do whatever you need to do.*

*

'She's a good donkey. A very good donkey,' I say to Theo as Dapple mouths muesli from my hand. We have caught a taxi out to her paddock in Santiago.

Jaz, Ethan and Nola lean against the taxi while I say my farewells.

'I'll send photographs,' he says. 'And you can check in on the webcams.'

'She needs long lunch breaks.'

'I know.'

'I've given you her raincoat, haven't I? And the brush and hoof pick?'

He nods.

'Meter is on,' calls the taxi driver.

'Just a moment.' I duck under the fence. Dapple snorts. 'Come on, Dapple.' I run, and Dapple trots beside me. I run faster, and she brays and breaks into a gallop.

I run and run until I'm gasping for breath. *I killed Lula*. I'm trying to run the feeling out of me. I didn't mean to kill her, but I did. We all did. As I run, images race through my head.

Lula with her arms outstretched on that first day at Ravensthorpe. 'Welcome to this special place.'

Lula's golden eyes on mine. 'What are you willing to sacrifice for writing success?'

Lula outside the barn, mist drifting from her mouth. 'There's something you're not saying. And until you do, your writing will be boring and weak.'

Lula. In a way, I suppose I was in love with her. We all were. We loved her, and we hated her too.

I slow to a walk and stop. Dapple stops too. I stroke her forehead, press my nose to hers. 'Are you ready to go home to France?'

Dapple's ears go back and forth, which I decide is her way of saying yes.

'I've always wanted to run with a donkey,' I pant as I come back to the fence.

Theo smiles and, after an awkward pause, he speaks. 'You know why I'm doing this, don't you?' he says in a low voice.

'No.'

'To repent. I don't mean Lula; I mean for what I did to

387

you. Jaz's phone. And . . . that night on the canal. Maybe, in time, you can forgive me.'

I hesitate. 'Maybe.'

'And Tess, I tried to tell you before. That note on your pillow at Ravensthorpe . . .'

I stare at him. 'You did that?'

He nods.

'Why?'

'I was panicking. I wanted to muddy the water, to share the blame if the police suspected me. It was such a crazy night, I figured . . .'

'You figured I might believe it.' A laugh bursts from my mouth. 'Wow. That's ironic.'

Theo grimaces. 'I guess it is.' He lets out a breath and holds up his hands. 'Anyway, that's all. My slate is clean. You know everything now.'

As we drive away in the taxi, I crane my head backwards. Theo is stroking Dapple's face, the velvet warmth of her nose. My fingers tingle with longing.

Santiago Airport is bright and modern. Light floods through the windows. The departure area is full of pilgrims with scallop shells on their packs. We check in. My pack is lighter than it was; I've lost my spare clothes and the walking poles. We don't go through security yet, there's plenty of time.

'I'll see you guys in a minute. Got to make a call.' I head for the plastic seats near the window.

Camryn appears on my laptop wearing a grey beanie and a tartan shirt over a white T-shirt. Her wispy hair is blue on the ends. 'So, what's with the secrecy? How controversial can it be?'

Very.

'Send it over. We can talk about it after that.'

'Okay.' I take a deep breath. I can't bring myself to ask about the mad bitch thing. 'Sending it now.' But as I hover the cursor over *send*, Ethan's voice is in my head. *You can't write about that. Please.*

My mind turns to the deal I made, out there in the water, when I thought I was drowning. Is a promise still a promise if it's made to a being you don't believe in? I've Googled it. My survival wasn't a miracle. Ninety per cent of people caught in a rip will, in due course, be deposited back on the beach. If they can keep their heads above water, they'll be fine. Yes, I'd prayed. But I was just hedging my bets.

Outside the airport, buses come and go. If God exists, He's out there on the street. He's here in the airport. He's everywhere, watching everything. *The tedium.*

'Haven't got it yet,' says Camryn.

I'd almost forgotten she was there. 'Oh, sorry. Must be a bad connection.' I make a *crackle crackle* noise and end the call.

My heart pounds as I run my hands through my hair. *Damn you, Ethan Hill.* It's no good, I can't do it. Maybe he deserves to be exposed as a plagiarist and a drink-spiker, but I'm not the one to do it. Because that was the deal I made in the sea, to give up on revenge. To – *gulp* – forgive.

'Sorry, Mum,' I whisper. 'Even The Count of Monte Cristo forgave his tormentors in the end.' I wait for her voice. For her to argue, to urge me on, but she is silent. Heaviness fills my chest, and I blink back tears. For the first time since she died, she's really gone. Was that all my revenge plan was? A way to keep her alive for a bit longer? The core wound working its way to the surface?

Taking a deep breath, I let it out. It's time for me to be my own person, not the one Mum wanted me to be. I'll write this article, but I'll write it my way. I press Camryn's number on my phone.

'Tess?' Her voice is sharp. 'You're testing the friendship.'

I swallow. 'Camryn? Did you call me a mad bitch that last time we talked, when I was lying on the ground with the cross on top of me?'

Camryn snorts. 'No. But maybe I should have?' She pauses. 'I was talking about Lula.'

'You knew Lula?'

'Yeah. I'm a survivor. I flunked out of Ravensthorpe after first year. Took me years of therapy to get over that place.' She pauses. 'So, what have you got?'

'I'm sorry, but that article about Ethan . . . didn't work out.' I press on before she can stop me. 'I've got an idea for a different article though. I can write it quickly, and I think it's going to blow you out of the water.'

'I'm listening . . .'

After Camryn hangs up, a notification appears on my laptop screen. My photos are uploading from my phone.

I gaze at them. The images appear mythical already. As if they happened in another world or lifetime. There's the mist at Roncesvalles Pass. Jaz striding ahead of me through an olive grove with her cross on her back, a scallop shell dangling from her backpack.

My eyes drop to my backpack. I've tied the scallop shell

I found on the beach in Finisterre beside the one from Saint Jean. I gaze at the shell. What are those scratches? Tiny letters? I peer closer. There's a J, a heart, and a T. *J heart T.*

Jaz. Was it her shell? My mind returns to the cold, dark water. *Green grass . . . a honking goose.* The memory floods back. That morning, all those years ago, when Jaz and I woke up on the grass beside the river, she'd reached over and squeezed my hand.

A vibration had run through my body at her touch. I'd turned to look at her.

Her face was lit up in the sun and grass clippings decorated her short, blonde hair. 'You and me,' she said, 'are soul mates.'

'That is irrefutable.' I'd squeezed her hand back.

'*Be with me always – take any form – drive me mad!*' she said.

We'd gazed into each other's eyes, and for a moment I thought we might kiss. I wanted to. But the goose honked at us, and the spell was broken.

'You're so oblivious, Tess,' she said as we walked back to Ravensthorpe.

'What do you mean?' I asked, but she shook her head. And, soon after, I met Ethan. I barely considered how that felt to Jaz. She covered up her hurt so well.

J heart T. My breath stops in my throat as it hits me, a punch to the heart. She loves me. Everything Jaz did makes sense now. She tried to take the blame for Lula's death to protect me. In her own crazy way, she loves me. And I love her too.

The glass door to the airport slides open and a woman strides through, pushing her sunglasses on top of her head. She looks like she's stepped out of a New York board room. Her black pantsuit is teamed with pink high heels and her glossy hair gleams.

Ree is right on time.

The Devil will tempt you in the way that is hardest for you.

As I walk over to the others, Lula's voice whispers in my mind. *What are you willing to sacrifice for writing success?*

Ree waggles her pink nails at us. 'Hi, guys.'

You and I are the same, Lula said at my birthday party. *You want success so much it hurts.* We have everything to gain by accepting Ree's offer, except . . .

My offer of representation comes with a non-disclosure agreement, she'd said. *You can never talk about what Lula did at Ravensthorpe.*

Ree lowers herself into the seat opposite us. The light from the window streams around her face.

We haven't decided what we're going to say to her. We've tried to discuss it, but it's like each of us is waiting for someone else to make the call. We all know what this means. A fast-track to success. And it's a one-in, all-in, deal. Even for Ethan, who already has an agent. But Ethan's agent isn't Ellery Eppis, the kingmaker.

You guys decide, Theo had said.

'So, do we have a deal?' Ree asks.

Our eyes flicker to each other.

'Yes,' I say.

Jaz, Nola and Ethan stare at me.

Ree beams.

'But it's not your deal, it's our deal,' I say.

Ree raises one eyebrow. 'Oh?'

Jaz meets my eyes and I blink twice. It's our secret signal, I'm trusting she'll know what I mean.

'The answer is no,' says Jaz.

'We don't want to be The Chosen Ones,' says Nola.

Ree blanches. 'You'll regret this.'

'I don't think so,' I say.

'So, our deal is . . .?' Ethan glances towards us.

'You keep quiet about what happened to Lula on the tower,' says Nola.

'And we keep quiet about how you tried to kill us on the Camino,' says Jaz.

'And we can say whatever we want about Lula,' I say.

'It's a take it or leave it deal,' Ethan adds.

Ree's mouth twists, and it takes a few seconds for her to respond. 'Okay, whatever. Your loss.' She stands, straightening her pantsuit and looks at each of us in turn. 'Now, you'll never know what you might have been. And I hope it haunts you till the day you die.' She walks away, heels clicking on the floor.

Silence falls as the sliding doors swallow her.

I expect to feel a sense of loss, but I don't. I've always been desperate for literary success. Would do anything for it. But now, I'm okay with the idea that it might not happen. And if it does, I'll try not to clutch at it like an addict. *Like Lula.*

*

As we stride towards the boarding gate, I catch sight of myself in the window, my hair floating around me.

You look like Kate Bush.

Putting one ear pod in my ear, I give the other to Jaz, find *Wuthering Heights* on Spotify, and press play.

It's a funny old thing, life. Who knows if it goes in a line or a circle or, as Ethan said in his book – which was actually Lula's book – everything happens all at once? But if you're lucky, maybe, just maybe, you'll get the chance to do things right the second time around.

Jaz and I will rewind our history and start again. We're going to get up to all sorts of mischief together. I just know it.

As the music soars, an image fills my head. Jaz and me in the Ravensthorpe common room twirling like Kate Bush.

We twirl like Kate Bush.

We twirl.

Epilogue

Svengali

Eighteen months later

Ree turns the volume up on the television as *The Book Show* comes on.

The male host, a handsome man with a weathered face, kicks off. 'Well, coming up tonight, we have a treat in store when we interview five of our newest literary sensations. Tell us a bit about them, Mary.'

His partner, a coiffed blonde with bright red lipstick, beams. 'I'm so excited to meet these five, Terry. It's quite a story.' Her face falls into a more sombre expression. 'Most of us would have read Tess Brody's Press Award-winning *Artemis* feature about Lula Thornton.'

'Yes, what a story. She was a master manipulator by all accounts.'

'Absolutely, a nasty piece of work, though a talented writer.'

'Love the art, hate the artist?' says Terry.

'Exactly, and of course Tess Brody is one of our guests tonight.'

'Let's bring them in, shall we?' Terry beams towards the side of the set.

Three young women and two men appear to audience applause and take their seats.

Ree examines them. Someone's doing a good job of building their brand. They're the intellectual version of a K-pop band, each character artfully created. Jaz – *Sporty Spice* – wears no makeup and a striped T-shirt with an oversized cardigan over black jeans and Doc Martens. Nola – *Ginger Spice* – wears a tailored white blouse with a white blazer, and Tess – *Scary Spice* – wears a black turtleneck with flared black trousers. Her dark hair is wild and untamed. Ethan has his usual Brett Easton Ellis vibe – cap, T-shirt and jacket – while Theo is more of a Jack Kerouac with his tight T-shirt and ruffled hair. Five good-looking young writers, a publicist's dream.

'Welcome, Jasmine, Nola, Ethan, Theo and Tess,' says Mary. 'Your time on the Camino was incredibly productive.' She gives a mischievous smile. 'Seems there was a bit of magic in the air because you've all had an astonishing burst of creativity, haven't you?'

'Lula Thornton used to say a writer will do anything for inspiration,' says Tess. 'For all her faults, she was right about that.'

'It sounds like a harrowing trip though.' Terry's voice is sympathetic. 'Theo, you got severe food poisoning. And Tess, you almost drowned, didn't you?'

'Yes, Jaz went out swimming and I thought she was in trouble, but it turned out I was the one in trouble.' Tess laughs.

Jaz reaches out and takes her hand and the two gaze at each other adoringly.

Ree eyes their intertwined fingers. *How sweet.*

'Why don't you all pull out your books and give us a quick introduction?' says Terry. 'Let's start with you, Tess.'

Tess holds up her book. 'My book is called *Leaving Lula*. It's a follow-up to my *Artemis* article which cracks open the poisonous underbelly of Ravensthorpe. I always used to think I'd write fiction, but it turns out non-fiction is more my forte.'

'And do you have any plans for another book?' asks Terry.

Tess smiles. 'My job at *Artemis* is keeping me busy for now, and I'm loving it. Never say never though.'

'What about you, Theo?' asks Mary.

Theo flicks back his hair. 'The Camino was incredibly transformative for me. So much so, I did it twice.' He holds up his book. '*Rebooted by a Donkey: Letting go of Toxic Masculinity on the Camino* is, uh, the story of my journey.'

'Oh, yes, the donkey,' coos Mary. 'Where is she now?'

'I, uh, got attached, so I brought her back to England. She's living with me in Dorset. There are lots of other donkeys, so she's happy there. Tess visits her all the time too.'

'Lovely. And Ethan, you have another hit on your hands. Your novel has been top of *The Times* fiction bestseller list for three weeks in a row now.' Mary claps her hands. 'Can you give our audience a quick summary?'

'Yes, love to. My new novel is called *Fatty*. It's a dark psychological thriller about a toxic father and son relationship. And, can I just add, all royalties are going towards anti-bullying charity *Bully Bust*.'

'Fabulous,' says Mary. 'And we're very privileged to have you here, because this is the first appearance you've done since your novel came out. Why is that?'

'The celebrity aspect of being an author doesn't agree with me.' Ethan smiles briefly. 'I've become a bit of a recluse, and I'm happy to let my work speak for itself. But the others persuaded me to turn up for this interview, so here I am.'

'Well, we're honoured. And now to you, Jasmine and Nola. I believe your novel has sold in twenty-six territories, is that right?'

Nola smiles. 'Twenty-seven as of today. We just signed with Poland.'

'Congratulations,' says Terry. 'How does that feel?'

Nola and Jaz glance at each other. 'Amazing, incredible, surreal,' they murmur over the top of each other.

'You conceived this story while doing the Camino pilgrimage, didn't you?' asks Terry.

'Yes,' says Nola. 'Lula used to talk about the concept of the core wound, a secret hurt that works its way to the surface. And, well, to some extent Lula is our core wound.'

'So, writing this book was a way of healing that wound,' says Jaz.

'I think of it as an exorcism.' Nola smiles.

Jaz holds up the novel. 'It's called *Smashing Svengali* and it's a feminist retelling of the Svengali story. We're thrilled it's resonating so widely.'

Ree snorts. She's always admired Svengali, the so-called villain of George Du Maurier's novel, *Trilby*. Svengali had his issues but, let's face it, Trilby would have been nothing without him.

'It's unusual to write a collaborative novel,' says Terry. 'What made you decide to do that?'

'We realised we had this shared experience of Lula,' says Jaz.

'And we have complementary skills,' says Nola. 'I'm a good plotter, Jaz is good at character . . .'

'And we're both mad fantasists.' Jaz laughs.

'Our agent, Christie King, thought it sounded great, so we went for it,' says Nola.

'It's been so much fun,' Jaz adds.

Ree turns the television off and takes a swig of wine. Let them enjoy their moment in the sun. Literary fame is a butterfly – beautiful but fleeting. Picking up her phone, she scrolls through her latest queries from prospective clients. There's one here who sounds like she might be suitable.

It was Ree who taught Lula everything she knew about manipulation. Every year Lula would send her The Chosen One, ripe and ready for Ree to spin straw into gold. They weren't chosen for their writing ability, or not only for that. Lula knew what Ree wanted. The Chosen One had an undefinable quality. Something mouldable and needy. They had to want success more than anything. Lula had told Ree about Tess and she sounded perfect. Pity that didn't work out.

Still, plenty of fish in the sea. *Cliché, delete*, she thinks automatically. Tapping on her email, she reads the submission again. Yes, this one will do nicely. *Authors.* They'll sacrifice anything for success.

A Letter from Lisa Walker

Thank you so much for choosing to read *The Pact*. I hope you enjoyed it! If you did and would like to be the first to know about my new releases, sign up to my mailing list below.

Sign up here! https://lisawalkerwriter.wordpress.com/

The idea for this novel sparked ten years ago, when I was walking the Camino, and writing it has been the longest of long games. I've taken many twists and turns, many wrong paths, but here we are – the journey ended, or just beginning. I'm so excited to share this story with you and see the ripples of that thirty-day walk still spreading.

I hope you loved *The Pact* and if you did, I would be so grateful if you would leave a review. I always love to hear what readers thought, and it helps new readers discover my books too.

Thank you,
Lisa

https://www.lisawalker.com.au/
https://www.facebook.com/lisawalkerhome
https://www.instagram.com/lisawalkerwriter/

Acknowledgements

I owe an enormous thank you to many people.

To the talented team at HQ who worked so hard and made this book so much better. Special thanks to my editor Sophia Allistone and Georgina Green. To Teresa Palmiero, for a sharp-eyed copy edit.

To my agent, Jane Novak, for her wisdom and patience with my idiosyncratic writing process. To my writing group and hive mind, who have lived with this story for so many years: Kayte Nunn, Jessie Cole, Siboney Saavedra, Michelle Granieri Taylor, and Helen Burns. To Joanna Barnard for a perceptive reading.

I completed an earlier version of this story as part of a PhD in creative writing at The University of Queensland. Thanks to my always encouraging supervisor, Venero Armanno. I am also grateful for the research scholarship which supported me during this time.

John Brierley's *A Pilgrim's Guide to the Camino de Santiago* was my constant companion on the Camino.

Thanks too to *WebExhibits* and Michael Douma for curating and exhibiting Vincent van Gogh and Theo van Gogh's letters, from which I used the quote 'The sadness will last forever'.

To my family, John, Simon and Tim, who humoured me by walking the Camino. You made the journey so entertaining. Not all our misadventures on the trail have made it into this book, but several have!

Dear Reader,

We hope you enjoyed reading this book. If you did, we'd be so appreciative if you left a review. It really helps us and the author to bring more books like this to you.

Here at HQ Digital we are dedicated to publishing fiction that will keep you turning the pages into the early hours. Don't want to miss a thing? To find out more about our books, promotions, discover exclusive content and enter competitions you can keep in touch in the following ways:

JOIN OUR COMMUNITY:

Sign up to our new email newsletter: http://smarturl.it/SignUpHQ

Read our new blog www.hqstories.co.uk

𝕏 https://twitter.com/HQStories

f www.facebook.com/HQStories

BUDDING WRITER?

We're also looking for authors to join the HQ Digital family!

Find out more here:

https://www.hqstories.co.uk/want-to-write-for-us/

Thanks for reading, from the HQ Digital team

ONE PLACE. MANY STORIES

Bold, innovative and
empowering publishing.

FOLLOW US ON:

@HQStories

Inheriting
the
Cottage
by the
Loch

BOOKS BY KENNEDY KERR

LOCH CAMERON

The Cottage by the Loch

A Secret at the Cottage by the Loch

The Diary from the Cottage by the Loch

A Gift from the Cottage by the Loch

An Invitation to the Cottage by the Loch

Keepsakes from the Cottage by the Loch

Lost Memories of the Cottage by the Loch

MAGPIE COVE

The House at Magpie Cove

Secrets of Magpie Cove

Daughters of Magpie Cove

Dreams of Magpie Cove

A Spell of Murder

Kennedy Kerr

Inheriting
the
Cottage
by the
Loch

bookouture

Published by Bookouture in 2025

An imprint of Storyfire Ltd.
Carmelite House
50 Victoria Embankment
London EC4Y 0DZ

www.bookouture.com

The authorised representative in the EEA is Hachette Ireland
8 Castlecourt Centre
Dublin 15 D15 XTP3
Ireland
(email: info@hbgi.ie)

ISBN: 978-1-83618-960-2
eBook ISBN: 978-1-83618-959-6